BEYOND THE
FARTHEST SUNS

BEYOND THE
FARTHEST SUNS

THE COMPLETE SHORT FICTION OF
GREG BEAR
VOLUME THREE

OPEN ROAD
INTEGRATED MEDIA
NEW YORK

Cover art by Greg Bear

"The Venging" first appeared in *Galaxy,* 1975
"Perihesperon" first appeared in *Tomorrow,* 1975
"The Fall of the House of Escher" first appeared in *Beyond Imagination,* 1996
"The Way of All Ghosts" first appeared in *Far Horizons,* 1999
"MDIO Ecosystems" first appeared in *Nature,* 2001
"Hardfought" first appeared in *Isaac Asimov's Science Fiction Magazine,* 1983
"Judgment Engine" first appeared in *Artificial Life (Insects),* 1993

Cover design by Mauricio Díaz

978-1-5040-2149-4

Published in 2016 by Open Road Integrated Media, Inc.
345 Hudson Street
New York, NY 10014
www.openroadmedia.com

CONTENTS

THE VENGING

*I wrote "The Venging" in 1973, while I was working at the Reuben
H. Fleet Space Theater in San Diego, California. With this story, I
created my first major female character, Anna Sigrid Nestor, and
the first episode in a future history that would come to include two
novels—Beyond Heaven's River and Strength of Stones—and three
shorter pieces, the second being Perihesperon. "Hardfought" men-
tions a world also found in "The Venging," Myriadne, but it much
farther advanced in time.*

*In the late 1960s and early '70s, black holes—collapsed stars so dense
that their gravitational field traps all light—were hot. Literally. (Well,
warmer than the background of deep space, at any rate—but very popular, no doubt about that.) Stephen Hawking had just shown how black
holes could radiate heat from their event horizons. The truly hip debated
whether or not black holes had "hair," whether there could be naked
singularities—black holes without event horizons—and other weighty
matters. Kip Thorne was speculating on time travel and wormholes,
and lots of us were writing stories about this fascinating topic in physics.*

I bought and read a copy of the monumental textbook Gravitation *by Misner, Thorne, and Wheeler, and managed to understand
about a third of it. I read all the popular articles and books I could
find on the subject. Somehow I absorbed much of the theory and proceeded to both paint portraits of black holes and write about them.*

*Here's a black hole story such as Jean Paul Sartre might have
written, with no exit. I fancy there's also a touch of Jack Vance. The
language is enthusiastically and unabashedly science fictional, and I
was quite proud of it at the time.*

And wrapped around it all is the tale of my first brush with Jim Baen, Galaxy Magazine, published hard science fiction, my opinions about living forever, and the Walt Disney Studios.

First the story, and then the aftermath.

Waltz the night away, woman, Kamon thought, exuding a base undersmell of fury. *Your husband will be dead soon, and all your property scattered like seeds to hungry birds.* He coiled near the parapet, watching the dancers below execute their moves to strains of Ravel's *La Valse.* He focused on one dancer in particular, dressed in a simple, sheer blue gown, brown hair cut close to her head, thin arms graceful, delicate face lost in the ecstasy of the waltz: Lady Edith Fairchild.

Three small moons hung above the etched glass lamps surrounding the dance floor, one at the horizon above labyrinths of hedgerows, another to the west topping the Centrum Minara, and a third at zenith, the largest. The moonlight gleamed from the polished dance floor, shaded by swirling gowns and white breeches.

"Enjoying the view, I hope," an old woman said. She had moved up quietly behind him. Kamon swiveled his head and regarded her through multi-faceted eyes, then turned back to look down from the parapet. The old woman wore a plain black robe, revealing by dress if not manner that she was an Abstainer. He recognized her, but he did not wish to release his fury yet.

"It is a bit limited," he said, his words clipped by a non-human vocal apparatus.

"You can see the entire floor from here," the woman said. Despite the ominous black in his skin, she would not leave him be.

"The *subject* is limited," he clarified. "Their pleasures are mindless, don't you think?"

"When I was young I enjoyed such pleasures, and I wasn't mindless. Foolish, to be sure; very foolish."

"I find it difficult to believe Anna Sigrid Nestor was ever foolish."

"Kamon, you're getting old, too. You must be twice as old as I am. You know how foolish the young are. No awareness of death."

"I have been aware of death since I was a few brief days old, Baroness. Do you forget that my kind have no way of reversing age—no *juvenates*, as you call them?" He turned one jewel-like green eye on her but kept the other on the dance floor.

"You'll probably still outlive me." Nestor stepped up to the parapet and put her hands on the railing. "Keeping an eye on Edith Fairchild, or just dreaming of assassinations and seizures?"

"Your exalted status gives you no right to show me human sarcasm," Kamon said. "You are not so strong you can feel secure against my kind."

Nestor's face tightened and her wrinkles deepened. "You're a *wretch*, Kamon." She turned to stare into his leathery face, dominated by the triangular mouth that articulated so many languages, human and otherwise, so well. Teeth like a lamprey, mind to match: vicious by design.

I am not a bigot, but dear God, I despise his class of Aighors, Anna thought. "Our pact compels my silence, but I weary of the support of your kind," she said. "I'm here to rescind our agreement."

"That will be of advantage no one," Kamon said, skin assuming a dismal shade of gray-brown.

She took some satisfaction from his discomfiture. "Be quiet until I've finished. I'm disgusted that I've let self-interest blind me to your plans for so long. Disjohn Fairchild is my friend. He is a good man, perhaps a better human than I. I have a duty to such a man, Kamon. Among all of us, his kind is rare, You and I are proof of that."

Kamon bowed elegantly, long upraised torso supple as a snake. "I will convey your message to the Administers. I am sure they will wish to alter the performance of the next auspices, knowing you are no longer a partner."

Administers performed auspices—rituals of forward-seeing and propitiation—for dozens of species associated with the mercantile consolidations. Like the Romans of ancient Earth, they sought signs in the deeply imbedded patterns of nature. But none were as fanatically devoted to the practice as the Aighor members of Hafkan Bestmerit.

Anna abhorred judging other species by human standards. If the Aighors wished to sacrifice the most perfect of their young and seek signs in their bowels, so be it. Human considerations meant nothing to them. But she had once attended such a ceremony, and the memory still sickened her.

"Hear me," she said, drawing herself up. She was pitifully small compared to the Aighor. "I deny the support of Hafkan Bestmerit, and rescind the oath of non-interference. I will do everything I can to prevent your kind from stripping Fairchild of his life and holdings. I will defend him with all my power. That's no small force, Kamon."

"The Baroness is influential," the Aighor acknowledged, resorting to third person now that the honorable relationship had been formally ended. He bowed and swung the anterior half of his body into a coil. "But she is not omnipotent. Her weapons are registered. She must answer to the Combine, as all of us do. This makes an interesting challenge."

Anna fumed at the reminder. "Hafkan Bestmerit wishes to establish stronger ties with United Stars, my allies. Strike against me, and you offend them. You're perched on the horizon of a very dark singularity, Kamon. Beware falling in."

She walked off, leaving the Aighor to resume his scrutiny of the dance as it came to a close. His three lips pressed tight over forty-eight needle-sharp teeth, an expression of thoughtful concern.

After the final dance, Lady Fairchild made her way through the throngs with a nod here and a word there, smiling to all, face flushed, deporting herself as if in a Jane Austen novel or a scene from Imperial Russia. As soon as she was off the dance floor, however, her demeanor changed. She looked around like a bird, head moving nervously, jerk, jerk, jerk. Her hands trembled. Tiny rivulets glistened on her neck and cheek as she entered the gilded elevator. Her shoulders slumped.

In the upper reaches of the hotel, she climbed a flight of stairs edged with malachite, and at the top, found the door to the Fairchild suite and spoke her name. The door opened.

Inside, she reached to pull up the hem of her gown and sat on the padded bar ringing the sleep field while she undid her shoes. One finger prodded the sleep field button. The bed hummed and she fell back, hair fanning.

Disjohn Fairchild stood over her, his entrance quieter than the sleep field. "What's wrong?" he asked.

"I saw the Aighor," she answered. "He watched me from the balcony above the dance floor." Her voice quavered with anger. "They could at least have the decency to hide themselves while they scheme!"

"They're too honest and aboveboard for that," Disjohn said, sitting beside her. He frowned at the ceramic wall mural, then at his shelves of old books—all as familiar as his own hands. He had no official connections with the Centrum, but his value to them was such that he had used this suite and his billet on the Centrum world for twenty years. It was more than home; it was the repository for his life's work. *Christ,* he thought. *It's my world and all I am, and it can't save me.*

But what was there to be afraid of in the short term? The Aighors would not do anything drastic now. They would wait for weeks, months, even years, for a time when he was offworld and away from all his protections. Likely enough they would strike when he went to Shireport to deliver his personal lectures.

They would declare a cultural insult, announce the terms of the vendetta, commandeer his ship if they could, and do away with him cleanly—in deep space. There wasn't a thing Dallat or United Stars could do about that. Complex diplomacy was involved, and

Fairchild was not so important that his friends and allies would risk the anger of the Centrum to defend him.

Of course, if he could reach Shireport safely, there were Crocerians who might consent to go with him—paid, say, in data trade preferences for two years. The Aighors wouldn't touch his ship from Shireport to Ansinger with the Crocerians aboard.

When he delivered his lectures at Shireport, he would apply for United Stars zone protection to Ansinger. Ansinger was the largest USC stellar province, ten systems. He could transfer his funds and data banks—those parts he could mobilize and take with him—convert his lands and holdings to transferrable commodities, perhaps yet more data, and establish himself on a terraformed world in undeveloped Ansinger. Buy a continent on Kresham Elak. Set up a school for diplomats' offspring. "Get the hell *away!*" he shouted.

Edith flinched.

He apologized and stroked her long, silky hair. "Thinking about alternatives." But going to Ansinger meant the loss of most of what he had accomplished here, the subtle nets of interpersonal relations; he would not be able to return to the Centrum world, ever. His wife's life would change, as well.

"Why are they so vindictive?" Edith asked. "You did such a simple thing, so . . . *innocuous.* You meant no harm or insult. Why go after you, personally? Why not just ask you to remove the station?"

He shook his head. "Not so simple from their point of view." That had to be their reason; that he had pioneered and promoted the construction of the Precipice Five station. He could think of no other.

The station studied black hole emissions from the Pafloshwa Rift. The Aighors called such emissions *thrina*, and had constructed extensive religious rituals around them. In some way the station had violated tabu—who could know what human words applied, if any?—and the Aighors held Disjohn Fairchild accountable.

"They can't destroy the station," he said. "It's under United Stars jurisdiction now, thanks to Anna Nestor. If they attack USC personnel, the Centrum has to intervene. That would result in severe restrictions. But I'm under Dallat protection, and Dallat hasn't yet signed a full agreement with the Centrum. . ... Still a renegade consolidation. Until an agreement is signed, the Aighors can resort to pre-human law and call a cultural vendetta."

With their early half-understanding of human tongues, the Aighors had called it a "venging."

"Their laws are so damned complicated," Edith said, staring at the night-sky ceiling.

"Not really, once you've been around them for a while."

"You almost make it sound just."

"Their laws kept interspecies conflict to a minimum for a thousand years before we arrived," Disjohn said quietly. "Roger Bacon was messing around with crude lenses when the original pacts were established."

Edith stood up from the sleepfield and unhitched her gown in the back, letting the folds pile themselves automatically into a tight, square pile. At fifty she wasn't doing at all badly, he thought, and without yet relying on juvenates.

As if she were reading his mind in part, she said, "They don't have any way of staying young."

"So?"

"They don't have any way to prevent death. Maybe that's why they cling to old religions and rituals. It means personal survival after death, or whatever their equivalent is."

"You mean, what I've done blocks their chances of immortality?"

"They bury their dead in black holes, don't they?"

"Yes, but *before* they die. Pilgrim ships of old and sick."

"Maybe studying the thing takes it out of religion and puts it into science. Science still says nobody survives after death. Maybe the intellect can't accept what the subconscious—"

"That's archaic," he said. "And they aren't human, besides. Their psychology is nothing like ours."

Edith shrugged and lay back on the bed. He crawled in beside her and the lights automatically went out.

What if his actions *had* condemned the Aighors to eternal darkness? He shuddered and closed his eyes tight, trying not to think; above all, not to empathize with his enemies.

Kamon looked across the message spheres on the floor before him and crossed his eyes in irritation. This gave him a double view of the opposite sides of the octagonal room—*gepter* knives hung ceremonially on one wall, over the receiver-altar which periodically reproduced the radio noise of the Thrina as sound; wooden tub next to another wall, filled with mineral water smelling of sulfur and iodine salts.

He picked up a sphere and put it in the depression in his tape-pad, then instructed the little machine to record all the successive layers of information and display them linearly. The method tasted too much of human thought-patterns for his liking, but it had been adopted by Hafkan Bestmerit as a common method of using interculture information. It was disgusting that a single cultural method should control information techniques stretching halfway across the galaxy.

But such was the dominance pattern of the young humans.

The pad's read-out began immediately. The first message was from the council at Frain, the Aighor birth-world. The council had examined the theological and ethical problem of Fairchild and his sacrilege, and supported the judgment of the district priests.

Fairchild's alien origins and upbringing did not exempt him from the Venging. He had condemned millions of Aighors to oblivion after death. He had profaned the major region of Thrina pilgrimage by treating it not with deep reverence, but as an area for rational investigation.

The death-ships could no longer drop the assembled dying pilgrims below the event horizons of their chosen black holes. They would no longer experience the redemption of Zero, or bathe themselves in the source of the Thrina song.

Kamon seethed. He was one of those potential pilgrims.

He had wanted so much to live forever.

Kiril Kondrashef stared at Anna Sigrid-Nestor with large, woeful eyes. "Fairchild has bitten off more than he can chew," he said, "but I see no way USC can interfere. We're conducting high-level talks with Hafkan Bestmerit, very delicate. If I were to start an incident I would forego my employment quick as that." He snapped his fingers in demonstration, jowly face gleaming pale in the white light of his reading bureau.

"So I can expect no support from USC?" Anna said, anger coloring her cheeks.

"At the moment, no."

"Then what do you suggest?"

"Fairchild could make his way to some immunity zone like Ansinger. He can seek USC support, but only by renouncing his associations with Dallat. As I understand it, that would mean giving up most of his wealth."

"What can I do to help him now?"

"Give him the advice I've given you. But keep your nose out of it. Stay clear unless you want USC to renounce its connections with you."

"Kiril, I've known you for over a century now. We're about as friendly as two old wolves can be. You bailed me out of my doldrums after the death of my first husband. More even, we're both Abstainers. For us, immortality is no desirable thing. Yet now you tell me you won't do anything to help a man who has done more good for colonists and the consolidations than anyone, Dallat associations or no. You're being incredibly two-faced, I think."

Kiril chuckled ruefully. "I don't like your tactics much and I never have. You tend to stamp when you should tread softly. A good many fragile and important deals hang on this matter. Do you have any idea—you must have, you're no idiot—how difficult it is for species to coexist when all they have in common is the fact that they're alive? Whole civilizations walking on tiptoes through trip-wires, all the time. Anna, you could start a collapse you can hardly imagine."

She sat in front of his desk, hands gripping the edge as if to push it aside. Her forearms were rigid but her expression hadn't changed the mild, grandmotherly smile she'd put on when she came in.

"Besides," he continued, "your weapons are registered whenever fired, in defense or otherwise, and the situation is recorded in stasis memory. You can't get around that. We'll have you on the carpet if you do anything that can't be strictly considered defensive."

"I've never been able to figure out a bureaucrat," Anna said. She sighed and picked up her silk duffel bag to leave. "I've never used my weapons. Ever."

"Garden tools, once," Kiril reminded her.

She stared at him, shocked that he would mention that.

"I'm frightened, Anna," he said. "Very frightened. The fates of individuals mean nothing in this kind of dispute."

She took a transit tube beneath the modular city as any pedestrian might have, nothing more than an old woman. In her bag she carried several pictures of young men, one of whom attracted her very much. She glanced at them several times as she rode, trying to lose herself in reverie and allow her limbic mind to feel its way through to an action. Gut-level thought had carried her through crises before.

She picked out one photograph and tapped it against her cheek as she left the tube at an underground terminal. She walked below the Myriadne starport, largest on Tau Ceti II. Shuttles landed and departed dozens by the hour overhead, smooth bronze and silver bullets homing for their mother ships.

One such bullet, small and utilitarian, waited for her. She rode a wheeled maneuvering tug out to it.

In ten minutes, she was off-planet, riding in her spare personal quarters, surrounded by a detailed projection of the journey.

Disjohn Fairchild was an intelligent man. He would already be implementing some of the suggestions Kiril had made. They were the only outs he had for the moment, with or without her help. She calmly analyzed her own reaction to the suggestions, watching sun, planets and stars form a glittering bow around her ship. Then she smiled grimly and went to sleep as the stars winked out.

When she came awake three hours later, dark still surrounded her. It grew muddied and started to take on form. There was a queasy moment, a tiny shiver, and the outer universe returned. Occasional wisps of color appeared and vanished streamer-like along the forty-five degree rotated starbow.

She began to wonder what Kamon had meant by the reminder that his kind had no juvenates. She went to the ship's library to do research. On her way, she lifted the photograph to a ship's eye and told it, "Him."

They would pick up the young man at Shireport.

Edith Fairchild grew tired of the viewscreen's translation of what was happening outside the ship. She frowned and closed her eyes, trying to wipe her mind clear for a moment. The books in front of her ghosted and darkened, and she swam in a small red sea of interior designs.

After a moment, she no longer thought in words, and pictures came to her clearly.

Three large, very fast starships all moved across hyperspatial geodesics toward a common goal. They left tracks—she could see them in an allegorical fashion—in amorphous higher geometries. They were aware of each other's presence and direction.

One belonged to Anna Sigrid Nestor. Edith wondered what this woman's purpose might be, beyond friendship. Nestor and Disjohn had communicated briefly a few hours before, and Disjohn had told her to leave well enough alone.

But Edith was sure she wouldn't.

One ship carried a being not classifiable in terms of terrestrial biology, having aspects of many phyla. Kamon was called "he" by default—a cultural tendency to view the convex sexual form as male. But Kamon was neither male nor female in the reproductive process of his kind. He gestated young. His children, by human standards, were not his children.

His neurological make-up differed radically from a human's. The arrangement of his nervous system was central, not dorsal. He had three brains spaced around his esophagus. One of his brains was an evolutionary vestige, in charge of autonomic and emotive functions. Very powerful in influence despite its size, it connected with the two other portions by fibers substantially larger than any human nervous connection—networks of medullae, each marvelously complex.

He could contemplate at least four different things at once while involved in a routine action. While driven by what humans might consider a mania, the Aighor could think as rationally as any calm human. He was a dangerous enemy, highly motivated. In this match, Kamon had the upper hand. He would know everything they had planned—with benefit of manic certainty and calm intellection—and he'd act without hesitation.

But Kamon was not supernatural. They could elude him. They could survive him.

Perhaps Sigrid-Nestor could help by distracting him. There was at least hope, and perhaps even a good chance. So why did she feel so dark inside, and cold?

She closed her books, stood up slowly from the table, and went to join her husband on the bridge.

"A ship riding protogeometry has three options in case of attack," Graetikin, the captain, was telling Disjohn as she entered. Graetikin nodded at her and continued. "It can drop into half-phase, that is, fluctuate between two geometries . . ." His finger lightly sketched an equation on the tapas pad. "Or drop into status geometry, our normal continuum. Or it can dispatch part of its mass and create pseudo-ships like squid's ink. This happens to some extent during any transfer of geometries, to satisfy the Dirac corollaries, but the mass loss is extremely low, on the order of fifty or sixty trillion atomic units, randomly scattered."

"What about protection from shields?"

"Shields only operate in status geometry. They're electromagnetic and that implies charge-holes in hyperspatial manifolds."

"It would have been easier if we'd had a few Crocerians," Fairchild said wistfully. When the ship had put in at Shireport, all the Crocerians he'd asked had politely refused, not wishing to gamble, or, if gambling, betting on the Aighors. The Crocerians were a pragmatic species.

"I'd never fight Aighors if I could avoid it," Graetikin said. "I would avoid it by not having them challenge me."

"We're forced to take that risk."

"It's up to you. Once committed to a protogeometry vector we can't back down."

"How far ahead of us is he?"

"About four light-hours, following a parallel course."

"How much of a jump can we get if we take one of these protogeometries?"

"He'll learn about our jump about a tenth of a second status time after we make it. That gives us a good hour or two at the other end of the pierce."

"They might take that as an affront," Disjohn said, looking at Edith.

"Why, for God's sake?" Graetikin said. "We'd have to jump into some manifold or another anyway."

"Protogeometry jumps are a waste of energy, unless one wants to gain a certain advantage." Fairchild pushed away from the anchored chair and drifted across the cabin. "Cat and mouse. If I give any clue that I think they're after me, they'll interpret it as a cultural insult. Kamon won't miss a trick."

Graetikin shrugged. While talking about things that could mean life or death, he had doodled an equation among the others on the tapas. He had been working on this problem in his head for months, unaware he was so close to a solution. His eyes widened.

He had just described what the Thrina were in terms of deep proto-geometries.

He quickly branched off with another equation, and saw that in any geometry outside of status—any universe beyond their continuum—the Thrina would be ubiquitous. That, he thought, did qualify them for godhood somewhat.

He would transmit the equations and solutions to Precipice 5 when he had a chance, and see what they made of it. But for the moment, it wasn't relevant. He folded the tapas and put it into his shirt pocket.

"We're four light-days out from Shireport, and sixty parsecs from the Ansinger systems. We made it to Shireport without harassment, and that makes me suspicious. So far we've only been tailed." Graetikin turned to look at Fairchild floating on his back in mid-air. "They're usually more punctual."

The Aighor captain lay against the wall with his throat and three brains smashed flat. He managed a final gasp of query before Kamon pressed the slammer button again and laid his head out. The thorax and tail twitched and the arms slowly writhed, then all motion stopped. Kamon's mate-of-ship huddled against the back of the cabin and croaked tightly, regularly, her face black as blood with fear. Kamon put the slammer down and sent his message to the Council at Frain.

"The diplomatic team has caused damage to the Venging," he said.

The hazy, distorted image of the Auspiseer chided him for his vehemence. "They have called the meeting at Precipice 5 partly for your advantage," the Auspiseer said. "The human Fairchild's ship has been notified en route to Ansinger, and he cannot refuse."

"But I have already missed several chances to attack."

"The captain's reluctance to destroy the Fairchild ship was part of his training. You should have been more gentle with him."

"He is of the governing breed. They've become almost human in the past centuries."

"The Council allowed the meeting at Precipice 5 to be called for a number of reasons. For one, it temporarily eases our relations with the humans. And for another, it puts you in a better position should the discussions be unsuccessful.

"The Council cannot discount your premature release of Captain Liiank, without benefit of pilgrimage. You will execute yourself upon completion of your mission."

"The release of Fairchild will sanctify the Rift Thrina, and I will take my end there."

"Wise and good."

"But I have lost the Fairchild ship now because of the Captain's reluctance. It will take time to recapture the advantage."

"What else has offended besides Fairchild?"

"His station."

"Kamon, you are officially declared rogue. We are not answerable for your actions. We will broadcast suitable warnings to that effect."

"That is how I've planned it, Auspiseer." He ended the communication and turned to speak to his mate. She had regained her composure and was adjusting her belts of prefertilized egg capsules. "We will gestate no more young," he said.

The tip of her tail indicated she understood.

"So far, three things have gone wrong with the predictions," the Heuritex said. "I've calculated based on all known constants and variables, all options open, but the trend is against the predicted results. I must remind you that there are large areas of the problem of which I am totally ignorant, making the model inadequate."

"In short, you're useless," Anna told the machine.

"That is as it may be."

"I should replace you with my gigolo."

"He's a handsome bastard, I'll say that for him."

"What if we assume that Kamon is going to behave erratically, say, deranged by being denied an afterlife?"

"We have more options."

"Then that's our operating hypothesis. No, wait. Use this—Kamon will behave *as if* he is deranged, by human standards. I never underestimate opponents."

"Do you wish that to be an hypothesis, or an assumption? There is a difference, you know."

"Whichever way it works. You know what you're doing better than I do, dearie."

"Incorporated. The resulting future model, still highly inadequate, indicates that the meeting at Precipice 5—course corrected for that destination, by the by—will not take place. The station will be destroyed. Kamon will probably be the destroyer, and the Aighors will claim Kamon has gone rogue to deny responsibility."

She paced in front of the panel, then asked for gravitation to be reduced and then shut off, and floated at ease. "Warn Precipice 5 to be on full alert when Disjohn arrives."

"Done."

"And contact USC, division of Martial Support, at Shireport. Tell them there is going to be a confrontation in the Pafloshwa Rift, coordinates unknown."

"Such an action will mark you as a rogue agent as well," the machine said, a speculative tone in its voice.

"Whatever for?"

"It indicates a willingness to engage in battle, since you are heading toward the Rift of your own free will."

"Not exactly my free will. USC doesn't know I'm aboard this vessel, so they'll assume—will have to assume, and believe me are smart enough to assume—that whoever advises the Captain is not playing with a full deck of cards."

"I advise the Captain."

"I will have you overhauled when we get back to Ansinger."

"That will be a good time to install the new Parakem function modules. Where are you, since you're not here?"

"On Tau Ceti II. I made an appointment with Jessamyn Negras for a business talk, and she hates me enough to keep me waiting for at least a month. She will refuse to believe anyone would miss out on the blessed chance to talk to her. And appropriately deluded recorders are going at all times in my apartments. I'm there, that's certain."

"I see," said the Heuritex.

Kamon regretted killing the captain before learning all there was to know about ship operation. The Aighors who crewed the vessel were all competent in their special tasks, and the computers were helpful, but an overall cohesion was, if not lacking, at least shaky.

Kamon absorbed the captain's library rapidly. He was gratified to know an Aighor pilgrimage fleet was forming on the borders of the Rift. His kind cheered him on, and the government—diplomats and rulers alike—had not yet sent a ship to stop him. It would be useless if they did.

Coldly, precisely, he figured where difficulties would arise. First would be the protection of Precipice 5—negligible defenses, all things considered. Second would be the presence of Anna Sigrid Nestor, whom of all the humans he had met he most admired. Third—the final battleground would not be Precipice 5. He would have to chase Fairchild across the Rift.

The station would be destroyed before the human ships arrived.

Fairchild's ship saw the dead ruin of Precipice 5, issued a distress signal on the station's behalf, and headed at full power for deep space. The ship was away from the major gravitational effects of the small system in hours and shamelessly relied on protogeometry jumps to take it deep into the Rift. It then shut down all activities not connected with life-support, went into halfphase, and laid ghost images across a wide range of continua.

Graetikin silently cursed the Dallat conventions which made all private ships carry nothing more offensive than meteoroid deflection shields. He had spent his first thirty years in space as an apprentice commander in the Centrum Astry, helping to command ships armed to the teeth with all conceivable weapons, from rocket projectiles to stasis-shielded neutronium blocks which, when warped into the center of another vessel, quickly gravitated everything into super-dense spheres. Now he was facing a violent confrontation with nothing more offensive than flare rockets and half-phase warps.

It was like the final charge of an old lion against warriors wielding assegais. Fairchild's motives and the Aighor's motives didn't concern him. Both in their own ways were altruistic and noble, concerned with good tasks. But he was concerned with surviving to captain another ship, or at least continue captaining this one.

He didn't mind Fairchild's employ. The man was reasonably sharp and knew how to provide for the upkeep of his ships. If he had the tact of a young bull in dealing with alien cultures, that was usually not Graetikin's concern.

Between and around these thoughts, he re-worked his equations describing the Thrina. There was a cool, young hypothesis on the horizons of his mind, and it tantalized him. In reworking the expressions on his notepad, he found four connections with Parakem functions that he hadn't noticed earlier. These implied that the Thrina, though ineffectual in a cause-effect relation in most geometries, had interesting properties in coincidence-controlled geometries. They could influence certain aspects of status geometry, where cause-effect and synchronicity operated in struggling balance.

He raised his eyebrows.

And that implied something extraordinary. . .

"There is a good possibility we can contact Fairchild if he chooses to coast free within the next thirty-five hours," the Heuritex said.

Anna grumbled out of a light doze. "What was that?"

"We can join forces with him at points I have calculated along geodesics meeting in higher geometries."

"Translate for us mortals, please." She straightened in her command chair and rubbed her face with her hands.

"I think we can join with Fairchild's ship before Kamon reaches it. Here is our condition: fifth standard day of flight; all three ships are deep into the Rift. Fairchild is inert, following a least-energy geodesic in half-phase. Kamon is matching the most likely direction of that geodesic, though I'm certain he has no clear picture of the ship's present position along such a path. We follow Kamon closely. And we are constantly correcting our charts with observations of the Rift pulsars and singularities."

"Yes, but what's this about joining Fairchild?"

"His vessel alone is not sufficient to propel itself away from Kamon. He has little or no chance of escape in the long run. But with our two ships linked, we can create a broader affect-beam in protogeometry—"

"You can arrange this in more than just theory?"

"I think so, madame. I can contact Disjohn Fairchild's ship in a code only it can understand, and arrange for the rendezvous without the Aighor knowing."

"You're a maker of wonders, and you draw my curiosity like a magnet . . . into areas I'm sure will baffle me. I'll think on it," she said.

Why hesitate? she asked herself. Because now, faced with the possibility of doing what she had started out to do—save Disjohn Fairchild at any cost—a miserable, cold sensibility started to creep in. She needed to think about it long and hard. There were too many considerations to weigh for a hasty decision.

She made her way to the ship's observation chamber. Far out on the needle-like boom which extended from the crew ball, an isolated, multi-sense chamber seemed to hang in dark space. But its walls were transparent only by illusion. Trillions of luminous cells provided adjustable images of anything within range of ship's sensors, down to the finest detail a human eye could perceive. Images could be magnified, starbows undistorted into normal starfields for quick reference, or high-frequency energy shifted into visual regions. If need demanded, such subtle effects as light distortion in higher geometries could be brought within human interpretation. The sphere could also synthesize programmed journeys and sound effects, or any combination of fictions and synaesthesias.

Anna requested a tour of the nearby singularities. "Will there be a specific sequence, madame?" the media computer asked.

"Only an introductory tour. Explain what I'm seeing."

"Some singularities are made obvious by surrounding nebulae," the voice-over began, along with the visual journey. "These are veils of supernova dust and gas that have been expanding for hundreds of millions of years." Fading in, wisps like mare's-tail clouds in a sunset, backed by velvet space. Hidden within, a tiny spinning and glowing cloud, a pinprick, not worth noticing . . . geometric jaws gaping wide, tides deadly as any ravening star furnace.

"Others are companions to dim red stars, and thus are heavy X-ray sources. They suck in matter from their neighbors, accelerate and heat it through friction, and absorb it in bottomless wells.

"There is no comprehensive explanation why the majority of the Rift stars supernovaed within ten million years of each other, half an eon ago, but the result is a treacherous graveyard of black holes, white dwarfs, and a few dim giants. They all affect each other across the close-packed Rift in complex patterns.

"Some can be seen through distortion of the stellar background. The rings of stars around a black hole show the effects of gravitational lensing. Light is captured and orbited above the event horizons, producing two primary images and a succession of weaker images caused by anomalies in the spinning singularity. Gas falling into the holes produces hot points of high energy radiation, red-shifted into the visual spectrum by enormous gravitational fields. These are surrounded by rings of stars, images of stars from every angle—every visible object, including those behind the observer. There are gaps of darkness and then succeeding rings like the bands on an interferometer plate, finally blending into star-images undeviated by the singularity."

She was reminded of electronic Christmas ornaments from her childhood. Anna knew what she saw lay only a few million miles away, so close her ship could reach out to touch it in mere minutes.

"Dear God," she murmured. To fall into one of those things would be to transcend any past experience of death. They were miracles, jesters of spacetime. Her eyes filled with tears which nearly broke their tension bonds to drift away in free-fall.

"Where no such diffractions and reflections are visible, perhaps absorbed in dark nebulosities, and where no X-ray or Thrina sources give clues, naked singularities stripped of their event horizons lurk like invisible teeth. These have been charted by evidence obtained in protogeometry warps. There is no other way to know they exist."

The Thrina song of a nearby singularity was played to her. It sounded like the wailing of lost children, sweetly mixed with a potent bass *boum,* an echoing cave-sound, ghost-sound, preternatural mind-sound. "No reason is known for the existence of the Thrina song. It is connected with singularities as an unpredictable phenomenon of radiating and patterned energy, perhaps in some way directed by intelligence."

Nestor left the sphere and drifted quickly back through the extension to the crew-ball.

Her hands shook.

Kamon followed and waited. A ship could remain in half phase only so long before its unintentional mass loss (how easily he had spotted and avoided the ghosts!) reached a critical level.

His shipmate meditated and fasted alone in her cabin. Kamon was left with the silent computers—it was blasphemous for an Aighor machine to have a voice—and a few aides to see to his food and wastes. He preferred it that way.

At one point he even ordered them to clear away the captain's smashed body so he might be more alone.

The Venging was close. He had had no further contact with the Council at Frain or any other Aighor agencies. He had spotted and charted the course of Anna Sigrid Nestor's ship, and felt his own sort of appreciation at the intuition she was following him personally. She was on her own Venging.

Such was the dominance pattern of humans.

"Four minutes thirty seconds before critical point," Graetikin said. Lady Fairchild gripped her husband's arm tighter. For a society woman she was holding up remarkably well, Graetikin thought.

The worst was yet to come. Kamon would inevitably chase them down, and there was only one chance left. Graetikin's recent equations implied they would survive if they took that chance, but *how* they would survive—in what condition, other than whole and alive—was unknown. It was a terrifying prospect.

"We have to leave half-phase," Fairchild said. "And we have to outrun him. There's no other way." Edith nodded and turned away from the bridge consoles.

"Have you ever wondered why he called a Venging?" she asked.

"What?" Fairchild asked. He was focusing on the blank viewers, as if to strain some impossible clue from them. It was useless to look at half-phase exteriors, however. The eye interpreted them as if they weren't there, and indeed half the time they weren't.

"Kamon has to have a reason," Edith said, louder.

"I'm sure he does," Graetikin said.

"I've been trying to find out what that reason is. I might have a clue."

"That doesn't concern us now," Fairchild said, irritated. "Reason or no, we have to get away from him."

"But doesn't it help to know what we're going to die for?" Edith cried. "You know damn well we can't outrun him! Graetikin knows it, too. Don't you?"

Graetikin nodded. "But I wouldn't say we're going to die. There might be another way."

"You know that?" Fairchild asked.

Graetikin nodded. "First, I'd like to hear what Lady Fairchild has to say about Kamon's motive."

Disjohn took a deep breath and held up his arms. "Okay," he said to his wife, "Lady Ethnographer, tell us."

"It's all in the library, for whoever cares to look it up. Some of it is even in the old books. We've known about it for a century at least—the basic form of the Aighor pilgrimage. They have three brains, that's well-known—but we've ignored the way they use those brains. One is for rational purposes, and it can do everything a computer can do, but it isn't the strongest. Another is for emotive and autonomic purposes, and that's where the seat of their religion is. We don't know exactly what the third brain does. But I have an idea it's used for preparing the other two brains for a proper death. It has to balance them out, mediate. If the rational brain has an edge, the pilgrim won't be prepared for death. I think the research conducted by the station gave the Aighors a dilemma they couldn't face—the rational treatment of subjects hitherto purely religious to them. It gave their rational minds an edge and caused an imbalance. So the pilgrims couldn't be delivered to the black holes without wholesale failure in the proper rituals of dying."

"And?" Graetikin asked, fingering his stylus. It seemed there was another foot to drop in the matter, and she wasn't dropping it.

"That's it. I can't speculate any further. I'm not really an ethnographer. But sometimes I wish to hell *you* had been, dear husband!" There was no bitterness in her voice, only a loving rebuke.

Fairchild stared stonily at the empty screens.

"You have another way?" he asked Graetikin.

"It's possible," Graetikin said. He outlined his alternative. From the ninth word on Fairchild went pale, convinced his Captain had broken under the strain.

Anna lay in the half-dark and watched the young man dress. For the first time in years she felt guilt that her emotional needs should draw her away from constant alertness. But this was the first time she'd been with the handsome lad for anything more than companionship. He had proven serviceable enough and charming.

Her aging frame didn't bother him. He was a professional and perhaps more than that, a sympathetic human being.

"I don't understand all you've told me," he said. His brown skin shined in the golden lamps of the sanitoire. "But I think what you're asking me is, do you have a right to put your whole crew in danger. You're the captain, and I signed on—"

"Not as a crew-member," she reminded him.

"No, but I signed on with the understanding there might be hazards involved."

"These aren't the normal hazards."

"But if it serves your purpose to link up with the other ship, how can I or anyone else persuade you not to?"

"I have responsibilities to the people who work for me." She was reminded of what Kondrashef had said to her. Even if they could link up with the Fairchild ship, what guarantee did she have that the Heuritex's predictions were completely accurate? They didn't know precisely what Kamon's ship was capable of. Already they'd been surprised several times. And her first lieutenant, Nilsbaum, had worked the problem out on an alternate computer, a human-manufacture Datapak. It had given them an eighty percent chance of hitting a singularity if they linked and performed a protogeometry jump. The Heuritex had disagreed. But still, the danger existed.

"I can't blast the bastard," Anna said, "because every potshot is registered by the tattling machines I had to hook up to pass USC regulations. I can't tamper with them—they retreat into stasis whenever they're not registering."

She looked sharply at the Polynesian. He looked back at her, his face blank and expectant. "Go take a shower," she said. Then, softer, "Please. You've helped me—very much." She turned over and relaxed to the sounds of the door closing and water running.

She was staring at the drifting colors on the nacreous ceiling when the intership chimed. She reached over to depress the switch and listened half-drowsily. The voice of the Heuritex brought her fully awake.

"Madame, we've contacted Fairchild's ship. First Lieutenant Nilsbaum requests your presence on the bridge."

"I'll be there. Any answer from Disjohn?"

"He refuses to allow a link-up. He says he has two reasons—first, that he will not jeopardize your life; and second, that his computers predict failure if such a plan is carried out. I don't understand these machines of human construction."

"Did he say anything else?"

"He warned you to leave."

She rolled over in bed and cupped her chin in her hands. The shower was still running. "Another question," she said.

"Yes, madame."

"What happens if we hit a black hole?"

"Depending on the angle of impact, we have several varieties of doom. If we go straight in, perpendicular to a tangent, we pass through two or more event horizons, depending on the theoretical geometry you subscribe to."

"What are event horizons?"

"Simply the horizons beyond which no further events can be seen. The gravitational field at that point has accelerated any particle close to the speed of light. From an outside point of view, the particle's time has slowed to almost zero, no motion at all, so it will take an infinite time to hit the singularity below the event horizon.

"But from our point of view—if we are the hypothetical particle—we will hit it. Not that it will matter to us, though. Long before we pass through the inner event horizon, tidal forces will strip us down to subatomic particles."

"Not too pleasant."

"No, but there are other options. At a lesser angle, we might pass through an outer event horizon at a speed sufficient to propel us into another geometry, and out again someplace else—a different place and time in our own universe, perhaps, or in another universe. We might survive that, if certain theoretical conditions prove true—though it would be a rough trip and the ship might not emerge in one piece."

"How can there be more than one event horizon?"

"Because black holes rotate. May I draw you a comparison of two Kruskal-Szekeres diagrams?"

"By all means," Anna said, activating the display screen on the intership.

But the mosaic-like charts did little to help her comprehension. She had forgotten most of her physics decades before.

"Out of half-phase," Kamon said to himself, "now!"

The image reappeared. He had misjudged the geodesic slightly. The ship was a light-hour farther away than he had predicted, which meant the ship's appearance was an hour off from actual emergence. He felt a brief confusion. But the ruse—if ruse it was—had gained them a very small advantage.

He immediately switched to subspace sensors.

Fairchild's ship was over four light-hours away. More disturbing, it was heading toward a nebulosity which charts said contained three collapsars, two of them black holes. Kamon deftly probed the nebula with his protogeometry sensors.

None of these singularities had ever been used for pilgrimages, thus they did not radiate Thrina songs. The area had not been thoroughly charted except on visual and radio levels from thousands of light-years away, where the patterns of the roiling gas-clouds had given away the presence of hidden collapsars.

His scan revealed another member in the family, elusive and sacred: a naked singularity. The very presence of humans in such a region was sacrilege—and if they were choosing suicide over destruction at his hands, the danger was unthinkable. A shudder racked his entire body. He had heard of humans going insane under stress, but if they fell into a singularity here, the Venging was a failure and the Rift would never be sacred again.

He forced himself to be calm. They wouldn't know how to prepare themselves for the Fall. They knew nothing about the mental ritual involved. It would be, in effect, nothing more than a suicide.

Or it might be something much worse, for them.

But Kamon would take no chances. He must destroy them before they ever reached the cloud. For the first time he felt anxiety that he might fail, even fear.

"It can't be done!" Lady Fairchild shouted. "Disjohn, I'm not ignorant! I know what those things are. Graetikin has to be insane to think we can survive that!"

"I've heard him explain it. The computers back him up."

"Yes, on his assumptions!"

"He's on to something new. He knows what he's talking about—and he's right. We don't have any other choice. The Aighor has every advantage over us, including religious zeal—as you pointed out. We've tested our course on the computers again and again. We have one chance in a thousand of coming out alive. With Graetikin's plan, our chances are at least a hundred times greater."

"We're going to die, is what you're saying, either way."

"Probably. But there's something grand about this way of going. It robs Kamon of his goal. We hold the upper hand now."

"You know what will happen if we suicide in one of the singularities?" Edith asked.

"We don't plan on suiciding."

"Just going down one, we make this entire region useless to them for their pilgrimages. Mixing souls is an abomination to them, just as mixing meat and milk is to an orthodox Jew."

"There was a hygienic reason not to mix meat and milk."

Such bloody-minded rationalism. "Are we so materialistic that we can't see a reason for this kind of tabu?"

Fairchild swung out his hands and turned away from her, talking loudly to the wall. "Damn it, Edith, we have to use Occam's razor! We can't multiply our hypotheses until we avoid stepping on cracks for fear of killing our mothers. We're rational beings! Kamon has that advantage over us—he is not acting rationally. He's on a Venging, like a goddamned berserker, and he's got a faster, better armed ship. We're doomed! What should we do, bare our breast to him and shout 'mea culpa?'"

Edith shook her head. "I don't know. I just feel so lost."

Fairchild shivered. His teeth clicked together and he wrapped his arms around himself. "You're not alone. I'm petrified. We're about to do something no one else has ever done."

"Except Aighors," Edith reminded him. "And they've always been prepared for it."

"He won't let us dock with him, he's turning toward the singularities—there's nothing more I can do," Anna said. "He's choosing suicide rather than death at Kamon's hands. Or is he up to something else?"

"I can offer no explanation, madame. Either something has malfunctioned or they have gone insane."

"I *hate* Kondrashef," Anna said quietly. "He has always been right, has always given advice I could never follow—and he's always been so damned, irrefutably correct. But I've got to follow my own wyrd." She sighed and leaned back in her chair. "Can they receive any messages now?"

"They are in the cloud. There's too much interference."

"Veer off. Circle to the opposite side of the nebula and see if anything emerges on that end. I've met Fairchild's captain—he's a brilliant man. He may have more up his sleeve than we can know."

Dumbfounded, Anna watched the final act on her sensors and tapped her fingers on the Heuritex.

Probability fell apart at the ergosphere interface of a singularity. Whether the same conditions applied to a naked singularity or not, Graetikin didn't know—he guessed they would.

But they wouldn't have to face the danger of the tidal forces—there would be no event horizons, no overt indication of in-rushing space-time. The singularity ahead had collapsed from a star oblated by the presence of other stars, and the result was a hole in space-time stretched out into a line. If conditions still applied here, he'd have to figure their chances of survival on a near-intuitive hunch.

It was clear to Graetikin now. Inter-universe connections of necessity were devoid of probabilities. They were truce zones between regions of differing qualities, differing constants. Hence, somewhere above the singularity, reshaping of in-falling material had to take place.

Perhaps the Aighors weren't far wrong after all.

He worked all his findings into a single tight-packed signal on several media, and broadcast it to space in general. When he was finished he turned to Disjohn and Edith and said, "Feels good to toss out a bottle, anyway. If someone picks it up, well and good. If not, we've lost a few terawatts."

Kamon could either back off, let them escape and hope for an encounter later, or he could pursue to the very end. But he was becoming fatalistic. It seemed the Fairchild ship was behaving not with human insanity, but with divine irrationality—a shield to his Venging. That could imply they were operating in the Grace of the Thrina, not against it. He wished he could consult the Council about this new insight, but there was no time. Whether correct or not, it made him reluctant to interfere. That small reluctance made him hesitate.

"No!" he shouted, pounding his thorax in disgust. "They are only insane! There is no Grace upon them!"

But it was too late. He had followed the Fairchild ship into the nebulosity on a matching course. They could only construe that as an intention to continue the chase.

Since they were insane, they would destroy themselves.

In his self-rage, he considered destroying the Nestor ship for personal satisfaction. But he had other things to do. He had to prepare himself mentally for the Fall. He told the others to begin their rituals.

They would follow all the way in.

"Course plotted," the computer told Graetikin. "There will be a proper configuration at these points on the chart. We can meet the singularity's affect-field here, or here—that is, at these points in our future-line. If we fail within any width of time measurably in quantum jump intervals, we will come in at a closer angle, and the warp-wave of our approach will create a temporary event horizon which will destroy us. These are our options."

"Initiate the action and test it on a closed loop. Then choose the best approach and put us there. Kamon hasn't left our tail?"

"No, he still follows. And still jams."

"Then my message didn't get through." Somehow it didn't matter much.

Fairchild gave the final order. Edith watched from his side with a small, knowing smile. She was trying to remember her childhood. There had been so many pleasant things then. She'd married Disjohn, in fact, because he reminded her of the strength of her father.

She needed that strength now.

She wished she had the strength of a father near.

The ship was otherwise empty. Her corridors echoed as the impact of the nebula's clouds bucked her and made her groan.

The tiny neutron star pulsated regularly, surrounded by a halo of accelerated particles, a natural generator of radio energy. The two normal singularities orbited each other, light-days apart. The violet influx of gases outlined them clearly. Like two whirlpools whose surfaces have been smeared with oil, they glowed in disparate, shimmering mazes of light. Starlight ran in rings around them. Ghost images of each other flickered in the rings, and the ghosts carried rings of stars, and images of other ghosts.

The universe was being twisted into ridiculous failures and inconceivable alterations.

Here time and space rushed into multi-dimensional holes so rapidly that an object had to move at the speed of light to stay in one place. It was a Red Queen's race on a cosmic scale.

In drawing diagrams of what happens in the singularity below the event horizons, space and time axes cross and replace each other. The word "singularity" itself is a phrase of no more significance than "boojum." It implies points in any mathematical fabric where results start coming out in infinities.

Thus, Graetikin knew, they would soon step off the pages of one book which had told their lives until now, leave that book behind and everything associated with it, and risk a plunge into null.

The naked singularity invisibly approached.

Kamon's thoughts grew fuzzy and uncoordinated. He bristled with rage as one portion of his mind came unbalanced in the ritual, and kicked out with his tail at the bulkhead before him. He dented the inch-thick steel. Then he regained his balance.

The holy display of the black holes dominated everything.

He was ready. A tiny reserved part of him set his weapons for a last-ditch attempt, then vanished into the calm pool of his prepared being.

Disjohn Fairchild felt a giddiness he'd never known before, as if he were being spun on a carnival toy, but every part of him felt it differently.

"I'm expanding," Lady Fairchild said. "I'm getting bigger. Alice down the rabbit hole—"

Still the ship fell.

And fell.

Edith gasped. The bridge darkened for the blink of an eye, then was suddenly aglow with scattered bits of ghost lightning. She held her hands in front of her eyes and saw a blue halo around them like Cherenkov radiation.

Expansion. Alteration. The desk in front of her, and her arms on the desk, broke into color-separated images and developed intricate networks of filigree, became crystalline, net-like, tingled and shimmered and pulsed, then repeated in reverse and became solid again. Everything smelled of dust and age, musty, like vast libraries.

Both ships ended their existence in status geometry at the same moment.

Kamon followed at a different angle and hit the affect-field at the same instant the Fairchild ship did. As he had known and expected, his warp-wave created a temporary event horizon and he was divested of his material form.

The Fairchild ship survived its fall. Graetikin's equations, thus far, were wholly accurate.

None of them could conceive of what happened in the interface. It was not chaos—it was instead a sea of quiet, an end to action. The destruction and rearrangement of rules and constants led to a lassitude of space-time, an endless sargasso of thought and event, mired and tangled and gray.

Then each experienced that peculiar quality of his or her worldline which made them unique. Fairchild, stable and strong, did not see much to surprise him. Graetikin marveled at a new insight into his work. Edith, still wrapped in her childhood, had a nightmare and woke far in her past, screaming for her father.

Again the darkness. The ouroboros of the hole spat them out.

The computers triggered a lengthy jump, as best as they were able, for the actions of their smallest circuits were still not statistically reliable. This was the chance Graetikin knew they all had to take.

They escaped. The ship rattled and shook like a dog after a swim. The howl of metal made Fairchild's scalp prickle and his arm-hair stand on end. A rush of wind swept the bridge. Edith Fairchild wept quietly and Disjohn, beside her, trembled.

They held each other, sweat dripping and noses flaring, panicked like wild beasts. Graetikin bounced his fingers clumsily over the screen controls, then corrected his foul-up and gave them a view of what lay outside.

"I don't see anything," Fairchild said.

"I'm astonished we made it," Graetikin whispered. Disjohn gave him a wild look. The screen showed nothing but cold darkness.

"Scan and chart all radiating sources," the captain instructed the computer.

"There are no compact sources of radiation. Standard H-R distribution shows nothing. There is only an average temperature," it said.

"What's the temperature?"

"Two point seven one degrees Kelvin."

Graetikin slammed his scriber onto the panel. "Any white hole activity? Any sign of the singularity we just came through?"

"Nothing."

"We had to come out of something!"

"Undefined," the machine said.

"What does it mean?" Edith asked, holding her chin in her hands.

Graetikin fingered the mar his scriber had made in the panel. "It means we're in a region of heat-death."

"Where's that?"

"Undefined," the computer repeated.

"'Where' is meaningless now," Graetikin said, eyes dull. "Everything's evenly distributed. We're between beats, at the top of a cycle between expansion and collapse. We've escaped into a dead universe."

"What can we do?" Disjohn asked. He felt an intense ache for his wife, and wished she were at his side. The grief was so strong, it seemed he had lost her only recently. He looked at Edith. She resembled her mother so much his throat ached. He patted his daughter on the head, but felt none of the reassurance he was trying to give.

"We might go into stasis and wait it out. But we'd have to have a timer, something measuring the progress of the universe outside us. Tens of billions of years. I don't think any of our instruments would last that long."

"There has to be a way!" Fairchild said.

"I told you, Father," Edith said. "We were the offenders." She did a mad little dance. "I told you. We didn't prepare. Why—"

Graetikin thought of them waiting until the ship ran out of energy and food and breathable air. Years, certainly. But years with a burnt-out old politician and his pre-pubescent daughter, a triangle of agonizing possibilities. Even could they survive, they would have no basis for a new life.

Edith's face showed white and distorted. "Why, we're in hell!"

Nestor's ship rounded the nebula and waited. Anna asked the Heuritex several times if anything had been sighted, and each time it replied in the negative. "There is no sign," it said finally. "We would do well to return home."

"Nothing left," Anna said. She couldn't convince herself she had done all she could.

"One moment, madame," the Heuritex said. "This region was devoid of Thrina before."

"So?"

"There is a signal emerging from the black holes. A single Thrina tone, very strong."

"That's what started this whole thing," Anna said quietly. "Ignore it, and let's go home."

On the edges of the Rift, the old and the sick, the detritus of civilization awaiting rebirth elsewhere, the Aighor pilgrims received the Thrina, and there was rejoicing.

The death-ships resumed their voyages.

AFTERWORD

"The Venging" is not just about black holes, of course; I'm laying out the details of a space economy that lives and breathes information. This is not the first such prognostication of the Information Age, what I will later (in *Slant*) call the Dataflow age, but it's an early example. Anna's tapas (the root word in Sanskrit denotes "heat," and the word itself refers to deep meditation) is now to some extent available as tablet computers and smart phones. For historical perspective, however, remember some of the books and movies and TV shows that were influencing me: *Forbidden Planet*, John Brunner's heavily cybernetic *Stand on Zanzibar* and *The Sheep Look Up*, and *Star Trek*'s tricorder.

In 1977, in the wake of the success of *Star Wars*, studios and producers all over Los Angeles woke up to find the motion picture landscape changing drastically. Science fiction films—formerly relegated to B-movies by the critics, and occasional blockbusters such as *Forbidden Planet* and *2001: A Space Odyssey*—were rapidly becoming standard fare and very profitable.

I was living in Long Beach at the time with my first wife, Tina. I published an article in the *Los Angeles Times* Calendar section, describing the roots of *Star Wars* in written SF. Suddenly, I started fielding calls from producers all at sea about science fiction, and over the next few weeks, I took a number of interesting meetings. I had a lovely lunch with Gene Roddenberry, who was planning a television reincarnation of *Star Trek*. Mr. Roddenberry had appreciated a comment I made in my article about how science fiction was the kind of horse best ridden by an individual, and how studios turned these stories into camels—a horse designed by a committee.

I met with a number of people at Dino De Laurentiis Productions, and had the pleasure of explaining why hot air rises to Dino's son, who, sadly, died a few years later in a plane accident. De Laurentiis was about to go forward with an ill-conceived but beautifully art-directed version of *Flash Gordon,* and had already optioned Frank Herbert's *Dune.* I tried to convince them to film one of my favorite novels, *The House on the Borderland* by William Hope Hodgson's, but no go. Also nix on Poul Anderson's *Tau Zero.*

I heard from a friend, Rick Sternbach, that Disney Studios was working on a film involving a black hole. The project's name at that stage was *Space Probe One.* Here, I thought, was a sterling opportunity. I called the studios and asked about the possibility of becoming a technical advisor. I carried a folio of paintings and a total devotion to the idea of black holes and how they would look. My first meeting was with famed designer John Mansbridge, who then passed me on to Peter Ellenshaw, a master craftsman responsible for matte paintings in many movies. He was art director on *Space Probe One.* (He was also the father of Harrison Ellenshaw, another fine matte artist who produced backgrounds for *Star Wars* and many subsequent films.)

I showed all who were interested my painting of a black hole, done as a possible cover for "The Venging." As I spoke with Ellenshaw, studio head Ron Miller (no relation to the astronomical artist) came into Ellenshaw's office to chat, and was soon followed by the screenwriter. He seemed a little out of his depth, but Miller was faithfully sticking with him, and that was and is rare in movies.

It was a heady afternoon. Mansbridge told me I might be called on board the production as a sketch artist. I thought I was better suited to being a technical advisor, or even a script consultant, but what the hell. It was a job, and an interesting one.

I left behind the issue of *Galaxy* Magazine that contained "The Venging."

I never got the job.

Eventually, *Space Probe One* became *The Black Hole*. It was Peter Ellenshaw's last film, a beautiful production incorporating many technical advances, but otherwise it was pretty abysmal. Oddly enough, there had been a change made in the original movie concept. After passing through the film's glowing, geometric toilet-bowl of a black hole, the good guys end up in a kind of mystical heaven—painted onto the ceiling of the Sistine Chapel. The bad guy, played by German actor Maximilian Schell, ends up quite literally in a Dantean Hell, entombed in his evil robot and surrounded by flames.

Shades of the end of "The Venging"? We'll never know, very likely.

It was ironic, however, that this multi-million dollar production thudded to a halt with an awful pun. The evil robot is named Maximilian. Maximilian Schell ends up in Hell, in Maximilian's shell.

I wonder if anyone at Disney got the joke.

As an after-after-note, I called Disney Studios at one point and Ron Miller answered the phone. Wow! I've never had that experience since—or talked to another studio head in person, for that matter. Charming.

After-after-after note: I could not quite understand why Anna was so down on living forever in this and subsequent stories. Clearly, I was working through some ethical issues. But most of my fiction avoided the topic of biological immortality in later years.

(In the Thistledown books, people die but have their mentalities uploaded into City Memory—a prospect that seems to me less and less likely, barring transporter-beam superscience.)

I further explored my issues and objections to biological immortality in *Vitals*, published in early 2002. I doubt that I've reached any final conclusions, however.

Neither did Anna, as we learn in "Perihesperon."

PERIHESPERON

In the middle and late seventies, Roger Elwood was cutting a swath through science fiction with a plethora of anthologies and a line of SF novels published by Harlequin in Canada, famed for knock-'em-out-by-the-ream formulaic romances, much loved by a large group of devoted readers. Elwood's line was called Laser Books, and it was advertised to the trade through catalogs minus author names—a no-no in science fiction publishing, where readers care who is writing what. The line folded, but not before publishing novels by Tim Powers, R. Faraday Nelson, and many other up-and-coming writers. I never wrote a Laser Book, but I did sell a short story to one of Elwood's original anthologies, Tomorrow: New Worlds of Science Fiction.

This was my first appearance in hardcover (1975, the same year as "The Venging") and needless to say, I was extremely pleased with myself. I was living with my first wife, Tina, in an apartment in Costa Mesa, writing and painting and trying to pull myself up by my bootstraps while fitfully marketing a novel called Hegira. I was a newlywed, idealistic and energetic, and I remember those years as pretty good times, full of growth.

I was most of the way through another novel, a time travel piece called The Kriti Cylinder that would get shelved before it was sent out to publishers. And I was plotting a story called "Mandala," which was later bought by Robert Silverberg for his anthology New Dimensions 8.

Elwood would later move on to make a name for himself in Christian publishing, and to help First Lady Nancy Reagan write her autobiography.

"Perihesperon" is something of a downer, all about inevitable doom and bravery. It contains some back story on Anna Sigrid Nestor, however, and isn't that bad, after all these years.

It was the six-hour sleep period for the passengers. Parabolas of light divided the corridors where dim lamps glowed orange. Black carpet on the floors dulled the girl's footsteps. The ordinary sounds of shipboard machinery continued. The muted hum of the blowers and the barely audible click-whine of the periodic engine bursts comforted Karen a little, but she was still disturbed by her solitude.

Her parents hadn't been in the cabin. She shuffled across the carpet in blue quilted robe and knitted slippers, long brown hair quickly combed back behind her ears. As she passed beneath the corridor lights, the top of her head glowed in a yellow crescent and her face fell into umber shadow.

She reached out to touch the wall for balance, unsteady with the new strength in her step. As planned, the ship's artificial gravity had dropped another quarter since she fell asleep.

Something had scratched the yellow enamel on one wall. She examined the revealed layers of primer and white undercoating, the gray plastic bulkhead beneath.

"Hello?" she called hesitantly into an empty cabin.

The cabin's beds had been tucked away in the wall. Nets stuck out a little sloppily from drawer edges. The desk lamp glowed. She moved on.

The lounge waited two decks down, and beneath that, the level reserved for the crew—on this flight three men, pilots or copilots or whatever they called the people who monitored the automated ship—and two stewards. One pilot and one steward were female, young and friendly. Karen had talked to them the day before. She thought perhaps they could explain what was going on.

The central elevator didn't work. She descended an emergency ladder to the lounge and stood in the hatchway, jaw clenched tight.

Card tables had been drawn out. The theater screen's doors had been pulled aside. Chairs lay toppled and cards scattered as if wind had blown through the room.

A woman's tote bag lay next to one overturned chair, its contents spilled. Something red puddled on the carpet, too bright to be blood. She dipped her finger into it and sniffed. Nail polish. A ruptured autospray.

Eyes wide and nostrils flushed with the cold, sniffling in the chill air, she returned to the ladder and its tight tube and descended to the crew level.

"Hello?" she called again. No answer. It was impossible, but she was alone on the ship.

Everybody was gone.

Servos clicked and whined. She jumped as a voice spoke from the control room. "Flux rate five thousand hertz, emission velocity point-nine-nine c, time of pulse zero seven-zero-five hours. Request acknowledgement of previous engine analysis."

She returned to the empty control room and listened to the calm requests of the unattended computer.

Beyond the wide transparent panels, stars burned clear and bright, drifting slowly past the window. The ship tumbled and rolled in space. She knew enough about their journey to understand that no such motion was part of the flight plan.

The brownish mass of Hesperus rolled into view, sparsely striped with ice clouds and gray volcanic smudges. Even from a thousand kilometers the broad crater-scarred roads and cities showed as distinct markings. Hesperus's life had vanished in war before humankind had lost its body hair and crossed thumb and little finger.

"Correction of axis yaw in four minutes seven seconds. Please explain cause of yaw. Damage report is incomplete."

More frightened, she descended the ladder again, fingers clawing at the rungs, breath coming in harsh rasps.

Recreation occupied two decks below the crew quarters, adjoining a zero-gravity gymnasium. The door to the gymnasium had been sealed. The door's window fogged with drops of frost. She leaned against the far wall, lip quivering.

This is ridiculous, she thought. *I'm starting to cry. I will* not *cry.* She pushed herself from the wall and ran around the curving corridor, circling the deck, peering into the automated galley, empty, and the in-flight storage area. Tears streamed down her cheeks when she completed the inspection and stood again in front of the gymnasium.

If they were all inside the closed room, then—

She brightened immediately and pushed the button for the door to open. It stayed shut. The frost on the window slowly cleared and she looked inside.

A wide black streak marred the chamber floor. The rubber matting had burned and bubbled. Something had been wedged against a bulkhead high above the door, a patch of some sort, bulging outward toward the closed-off corridor which ringed the lower level.

"I'll be damned," a low voice said to one side. "I thought no one made it." She twisted around to face the man standing a few meters away. He wasn't a passenger, she knew immediately, and he wasn't a member of the crew. A stowaway?

"Where is everybody?" she asked, keeping her tone smooth.

"Went out like lights a half-hour ago. They're gone, honey. Were you in your cabin?" She nodded and examined him as though dreaming. He was old and nut-brown, face lightly etched with lines, nose broad, eyes large and black and calm. He wore green coveralls. An orange lump twitched on his shoulder.

"Where are they?" she asked, not wanting to understand.

"I've never seen anything like it. Snuffed out in minutes. Meteoroid took out a man-sized hole in the lower level, and all the doors were jammed open when it plowed through the safety center. She was airless in less than a minute." He pursed his lips and shook his head. "Everybody's dead. Sorry, honey."

"No," she said, backing away from him. "No!" She ran back along the corridor and up the narrow stairs, hair flying. The man in green stood motionless and looked at where she had stood, his face empty. The lump on his shoulder stirred and extended two horny palps to scratch at his ear. "Stop that," he said and the palps withdrew. "We've got more problems than I expected."

When Karen reached her room she looked at the empty nets, still extended, and remembered the card game that had been planned. Her only thought—and part of her coolly considered it ridiculous—was that she was twelve years old and now she was an orphan. What was she going to do?

There was one more body for him to throw out of the ship. Under different circumstances he would have kept the bodies in cold storage, as many as possible, but there was no point in that now. He removed the contorted steward's corpse and placed it in the lock, closing the inner hatch. He slipped into his spacesuit, adjusted the seals, and opened the three outer hatches. Hand clenched on the grips, he braced himself against the playful push of out-rushing air and frozen mist. He kicked the body into space with all his strength and said a brief prayer. Already stiffening in the cold, the body twisted around its central axis and began a slow journey away from the ship.

How was he going to tell the girl what was wrong? He closed the hatch, climbed out of the suit, and hung it up neatly in its rack. The orange lump stirred uneasily on his shoulder and he patted it as he locked off the one ruptured level and restored the elevator to operation.

Then he went to find the girl's cabin.

She sat on her bed, one hand entwined in the netting, staring at the opposite wall with its screen-picture of terrestrial desert. She turned to look at the old man as he walked into the door frame, then turned away.

"My name's Cammis Alista, Alista my calling name," he said. "What'll I call you?"

She shrugged as if it didn't matter. Then she said, "Karen."

"We're in trouble, Karen."

"Who are you?" she asked. "I don't remember you on the ship."

"I wasn't," Alista said. "I'm a drifter. Had my own ship, shared it with Jerk here." He patted the orange thing. "We stay away from the lanes mostly, but we have to cross paths with the big ships now and then. We saw that your ship was in trouble. We came aboard."

Karen knew enough about interplanetary distances to think that was hardly credible. She shook her head back and forth, trying to show with one part that she was smart enough not to believe him, and with another part that she didn't care.

"I happened to be following your assigned orbit," he said. "Hooked up with your path when you sling-shotted around Hesperus to cut travel time to Satiyajit. I was searching for satellites around Hesperus—alien artifacts bring a good price, you know."

She looked at him again, trying to analyze his features, and scowled at the thing he called Jerk. "Where's your ship?"

"I approached your ship and made a mistake. Didn't keep out of the way of a flux pulse. You were tumbling pretty badly, I thought the computers would have shut down the drive, but they hadn't. You roasted my outer shell like so much cake batter. Got me pretty good, too, with subsidiary scatter." He smiled a twisted smile and shrugged at the thought of what that meant.

"I didn't do it to you," she said.

"I didn't mean you, your ship . . ."

"It's not my ship," she said.

"You're right," Alista gave in, shrugging again. "It's not really even a ship any more. The safeties were destroyed and part of the guidance computer. I turned off the engines when I came aboard through the meteor hole. The computer still acts as if the engines were running. It clicks its servos and whistles its little electric songs as though everything's OK. My guess is, about two hours ago you were to start the flux pulses which would establish your path to Satiyajit, but now we're starting to curve back toward Hesperus. The computer put the ship in orbit after the accident, very eccentric, but we'll stay up here all the same."

He fell silent and shook his head at his own blabbering. "I'm not insensitive, honey, I know what you must be feeling." He knuckled his eyes. Drops of water beaded on the back of his hand.

"We're not going to Satiyajit?"

"No chance. Not for a while anyway. They'll be sending ships out soon. They'll be here in a few weeks."

"We'll be alive then?"

He lied. "I don't see why not. Hey, feel like a little food?" She said no and slumped down with her elbows on her knees. She was going to cry now. She knew it with certainty and didn't care whether he was there or not. Mother and Father were dead. Why was she alive?

The first sob shook her softly. The second was more violent. Alista backed out of the door and said he would fix some food.

The machines in the automatic galley were in good condition, and he punched up two synthecarn dinners. Jerk moved restlessly on his shoulder and squeaked its own demands for sustenance. Alista played with the controls of the machines for a moment and came up with a reasonable substitute for a yeast biscuit. He fed this to the animal as he gathered courage to face the girl again.

His lie wouldn't help. Their present orbit would take them right through a belt of Hesperus's moonlets. If they were lucky enough to escape them, in less than a day they'd be running through the belt again. A rescue ship wouldn't reach them for a couple of weeks. He wouldn't live that long anyway. He had no more than three days.

Jerk could outlast them all by encysting and floating around in the wreckage.

He took the covered trays to the girl's cabin. Pretending suspicion, she picked a morsel from her meal, then ate it in small bites while he watched from the desk chair. Her eyes had puffed with crying. She was very young, he thought. Fourteen, fifteen? Perhaps younger. She wasn't what he would call beautiful, but there was a simple regularity to her features which produced a pleasing effect. It was a face which any man could grow to love over the years far more than any rubber-stamp beauty. "Listen," he said. "You know how to take care of yourself on this thing?"

She nodded as she ate. "Why?"

"I just wanted to know. I'm not . . ." But he shook his head and filled his mouth with food, chewing and smiling, shaking his head. Could he feel the creeping disintegration of his flesh? Would he hide in a locked sealed cabin the last few hours, so she wouldn't see?

Karen stood up and asked if he'd picked out a room yet. His look of surprise irritated her. Did he think she was concerned about him? No. She was dead inside. She couldn't be concerned about anything any more.

"Not yet," he said.

"Well, you'd better find one."

"OK," he said. He took both trays and left, standing in the door frame for a moment, as he had stood before. "You'll be all right, Karen?" His questions were curiously accented in the middle, as though each query were half a statement of fact.

"Yes," she said.

He went to find a cabin and get some sleep.

When Alista came awake, he shut off the net that had held him in place during the night and kept him warm in the mesh pajamas he'd borrowed. He put everything in its place as though the occupant would be back soon. He had chosen the first officer's cabin, feeling more comfortable in the room of a man who had faced risks as his official duty. If such a man's time came in such a meaningless way, that was his gamble.

A passenger's cabin would have made Alista nervous.

He found Karen in the lounge cleaning up the scattered cards and taking out the spilled nail polish with solvent. "Damn," she said. "It eats the carpet, too."

"Do you want breakfast?" he asked.

"I've fixed some already," she said.

"I'll get some more myself then."

"Yours is all ready. It's in the warmer."

"Thank you." Looking around the compartment, he commented that it looked better and she shrugged.

"You put them all outside?" she asked.

He nodded.

"Why?"

"You know." He looked at her sternly. She looked away and took a deep breath.

When he had finished his food he tapped the orange lump with his finger and it came to life, protruding eyes on stalks and waving palps. "Ever seen anything like Jerk before?"

Karen shook her head. She didn't want to look at it, or ask any questions, or have it explained to her.

"When I get back from the control room I'll tell you about Jerk. I'm going to shut down the computer and cut the servos. We lose a little battery power each time they switch on the engine pumps."

"You stopped the fuel feed?" she asked.

"I did," Alista said, taking hope from the unprompted question.

He checked the ship's position by shooting the sun rising over the bloated arc of Hesperus and taking an angle from distant bright Sirius. Comparing his findings with the computer, the machine followed his calculations to three figures. The ship's brains weren't scrambled, then. He threw out his own paper and questioned the guidance systems about their position and orbital velocity.

Their speed was increasing. They were approaching Perihesperon. In a few minutes they'd make their first pass through the lunar belt at—he checked the readout—twenty-two thousand kilometers per hour. At that velocity it would be useless to try to dodge moonlets with the ship's maneuvering and docking engines.

He didn't feel old, watching the planets fill the screen. He didn't feel very old at all, but then he couldn't sense the breakdown of his cells either. Flexing his arms, stretching his legs to increase circulation, he felt like a young man, not at all ready to give up.

Something dark blotted out the planet for the blink of an eye. Then a sharply defined scatter of chunks went past. A haze of dust made the ship tremble and buck.

They were through. First passage.

He returned to the lounge, practicing smiles and wiping them away as they inevitably approached fatuousness.

"Hey!" he said. "I'm going to tell you about Jerk, hm?"

She nodded.

"I picked him up from a dealer on Tau Ceti's Myriadne. He—it—whatever, comes from a place where the air is so bad nothing can breath it, so he breaks down silicates for his oxygen. He eats plants that absorb his own kind when they're dead, and the whole thing . . ." he indicated the ecological pattern with a circling finger, ". . .means that no animal kills another animal to survive. So he's docile and smart . . ." He stopped and didn't feel like saying anything more, but he finished the sentence, "because he absorbs from your own personality, so he's as smart as his owner."

Karen was looking at the spot the solvent had made on the carpet.

"He, she, it, doesn't matter," Alista said. "Jerk doesn't care."

"Did something happen to you?" she asked. "I mean, when you came near the ship."

Alista felt like a small child who wanted to say something, but couldn't. He was eighty years old and he felt so much like a child that he wanted to find a sympathetic breast and weep. But he was a man long used to death, and finding a frightened weakness in himself made him more reluctant to say or do anything.

"Yes," he said.

"Bad?"

"Yes."

"You're going to die?"

"Yes, dammit! Be quiet. Don't say anything."

And he turned to walk out. A day, two days. That was all.

How long did she have?

The second passage through the belt went smoothly. Alista investigated the emergency shields to see what they could repel. They could absorb and transfer impacts from anything up to nine tons. But the shields required safeties to activate them and a guidance system to pinpoint their maximum force on the approaching object. Neither were in working order.

Karen stayed to herself, reading fitfully or trying to sleep, and he stayed in the bridge cabin, idly searching all possible avenues of escape.

If he didn't tell her and she died by surprise, would that be less cruel than telling her? Alista wasn't a religious man, but his Polynesian heritage still impressed him with the idea that dignity and a certain courage in facing one's end led to better relations in the afterlife.

Relations to what, he couldn't say—he'd long since stopped speculating about things after death. Death was merely the final solving of mysteries, one way or another.

Karen broke out of her pose of deep sorrow when the idea came to her that she wasn't going to survive. She couldn't shake it because she could visualize nothing beyond the walls of the crippled ship. She went to Alista on the bridge and again the uncomfortable waiting for words began.

Alista spoke first, adjusting his seat and manufacturing an excuse to concentrate on the controls. "I thought you were asleep."

"Couldn't."

"It would be good if you could get some rest."

"I've been sleeping for hours," she said. "I have more questions."

"Ask away," Alista said.

"What's going to keep the rescue ship from getting here?"

"Nothing."

"Don't lie to me!" she said, indignant. "I'm not a little girl."

"I see," he said. He wanted to ask, *And have you had lovers and*

*children, and lost people you loved and understood with the grace of
your own years what they lost by dying?*

"It's filthy," she said, "just filthy, not telling me what's going to
happen."

"I don't want to make you unhappy."

"I'm not a child," she said softly, evenly.

Alista lifted the shoulder with Jerk on it and patted the orange
lump, head cocked to one side. "You may make it. You'll last longer
than I will, anyway. But more than likely the ship will hit a rock in
the belt of moonlets and everything will go . . ." He made a whoosh
with lips and slapped his palms together.

"It will?"

He nodded.

"Goodbye to all, then."

"Hello to what?" he grinned.

"Where are you from?" she asked, and he told her. He talked
for a few minutes, telling of old Earth, where she'd never been, of
Molokai in a group of islands in a big ocean, of schools and brown
children and going away to seek the stars.

She spoke of her schools on Satiyajit, and the boy friend who
waited for her, and of her parents. When she could find nothing
more to say, she told him how little she had really seen. She was
surprised to find she had no more self-pity, only a deep well of
honesty which told her all the sad, sad pressure in her gut was
something human, of course, but of no use to anybody, least of
all her.

They ate dinner together in silence. Alista's face was more
relaxed, lines untensed, and his cheeks less wrinkled. But he grew
visibly more pale and weaker.

Alone in his cabin, he vomited up his food and slept fitfully,
sweating, on the floor, wrapped in a curtain unhooked from the
lounge wall. He couldn't stand the formless comfort of the net.

"Let's be a little happy," Karen said when the sleep period was
over and she met Alista in the hall around the gymnasium. "Can

you make the music play?" He said he could, but he was too weak to dance. "Then let me dance for you," she said. "You won't mind?"

He could hardly mind. She slipped on blue tights and pulled her hair into a long braid, putting a round white cap on her head. With a clapper in one hand and a bell in the other, she showed him a smooth ballet to orchestrated concréte sounds.

She moved in slow motion in the low gravity, but when she finished her breath came in heavy gasps. Her face, flushed with exertion, showed no awareness of the upcoming third passage.

Alista put himself to bed an hour later and took a small drink of water from a cup brought by Karen. With the weakening of his blood, his face was pale; with the failure of his liver, it was turning yellow.

He asked her to get him the kit from the medical officer's cabin and she did so. When she came back he saw she'd been crying and he asked her why.

"I can't hold it back," she said. "I just wish I was never born, to have to feel like I do now. It's all so damned useless! I haven't seen or done anything, anything at all!"

"A little while ago you said you weren't a little child. Do you still think that?"

"No," she said. "I feel like I've just been born."

"Would you like to hear a story?" he asked. "Maybe it'll make both of us feel better."

"All right," she said.

"I was a gigolo once, a long time ago, and do you know whom I was a gigolo to?" Karen shook her head, no. "I was a consort to Baroness Anna Sigrid-Nestor."

"You knew her?" Karen asked, not quite believing. Anna Sigrid Nestor had been the richest woman in the galaxy, with her control of Dallat Enterprises, the third largest Economische.

"I did. I knew her for three years, the last three years of her life. She was a hundred and fifty years old and she was an abstainer. She didn't use juvenates because—well, I never did find out exactly why, but even when her doctor told her she was going to die soon, she refused them. She also refused prosthetics and transplants.

"The last year, I couldn't be her gigolo any more. She finally gave that up." He smiled at the woman's perseverance and Karen managed a grin of half-understanding. "But I stayed on her ship. She liked to talk with me. Everybody else was too scared to come near her. She kept me on her flagship until she died." He stopped to regain his breath.

"That damned old woman, do you know what she had planned for her funeral? She was going to have her body sealed in a sublight ship and shot into a protostar in the Orion nebula. She thought she could radiate throughout the galaxy then and be immortal that way.

"A few weeks before she died, with the flagship warping to the nebula, she realized what she was doing. She was contradicting her own beliefs. She wanted to call it off. But she hadn't been thinking too well, she'd been getting senile—though I hadn't noticed—and she had ordered that all the ship's officers be fired without benefits if the original mission wasn't fulfilled.

"It was very sad. Nobody would listen to her. Now she wanted to be buried like everybody else of her faith, without pretension, and she couldn't. She told me and I tried to fight the officers, but they wouldn't budge. They said there was no way out for them. I think maybe they were taking a little revenge on her for years of . . . Well, she was a strong woman."

"That's horrible," Karen said.

Alista nodded. "We were all waiting for her to die, and you know what I began to do? Me, tough old Cammis Alista, I swore I'd never let myself get so involved with another woman again. You know, she was ugly and wrinkled and her breasts were dry and flat, but what she'd *been* and *done*; when she was dying, I loved her for those things. And I wanted to make her live. But there was no way out." He swallowed. "I talked with her just like you and I are talking now, and she told me why she had never wanted to live forever.

"'Alista,' she said, 'there's something very odd about living. It's not how long you live, not how long a bird flies, but how high you reach and what you learn when you get there. Just like a bird that flies as high as it can, and only does it once before going too near the sun. Think of the glory it must feel to go closer than anyone else!'"

He closed his eyes to rest. They were pink with ruptured vessels. "I asked her, 'What if we never get near the sun at all?' And she said that none of us ever do, really, but we have to work to make ourselves think that way. To think that we really do. She said, 'When I last saw the sun, the sun I was born under, it was something I didn't even pay attention to. I didn't care about it. When I last saw the Earth I was rich and young and it didn't matter to me that I might never come back.'

"The doctor kicked me out of her room before she died. But she wrote a note later. When I read it she was dead and they had just shot her off into the protostar cluster."

"What was the note?" Karen asked.

"A poem. I don't know who wrote it, maybe she did. But it said, 'When last I saw my final sun, I was cold and didn't mind the dark. But now, so near, my chill needs your warmth, and I cry for the warmth denied, the dark to come. I want to sing more, say more words, love again.' That was all she wrote."

"Do you know what she meant?"

"No," Alista said. "I took juvenates like everybody else. I didn't want to die as she had. When she was gone there was nothing left. A little bit of the dark world came in after her, and she didn't even come to my dreams."

Jerk crawled up from the blankets and squatted on Alista's chest, examining his face carefully with extended eyes.

"I don't want to die either," Karen said.

Alista smiled in agreement. "I'll trade you places, little girl," he said. "I'll take your loneliness for my quick end."

"Maybe I'll be saved," she said. "Maybe we can pass through the ring without hitting anything."

She didn't cry for the old spaceman when he was gone. She walked to the lounge, taking the orange animal with her. She didn't have the strength to write anything, and it didn't much matter anyway, so she spoke out loud. She stroked the orange lump and talked of all the places and things she wanted to see again, and do again, all the people she wanted to meet again.

"There's my parents," she said. Silence. "And Allen. And my friends at school. I would like to dance some more, but I'd probably never be any good. I'd like to . . ."

She was going to say "have children," but that was too much to even begin to understand.

"I'll miss not seeing things again. There's the lake where we swam at Ankhar, with its snaky blue fish. And my room at—"

THE FALL OF THE HOUSE OF ESCHER

Janet Berliner Gluckman asked me to contribute to a collection of science fiction and fantasy stories, to be selected and approved by David Copperfield, the magician. Each story would touch upon magic in some form or another. While I could easily imagine writing a fantasy story about magic, a science fiction story presented a bigger challenge. I grabbed up a few books about the history of legerdemain and stage magic, and soon had an idea.

A rather wealthy and powerful acquaintance, discussing the future of mass entertainment, once shook me by declaring, at the end of a conversation, "A hundred million people can't be wrong."

I wasn't so sure.

I wondered whether an entertainer could ever possibly satisfy a hundred million people on a regular basis, without undergoing some sort of undesirable transformation.

I then upped the ante; how about a hundred billion people, all mesmerized by centuries of cleverly designed, spiritually empty corporate amusement. What would it take to satisfy them?

Edgar Allan Poe was, I thought, an appropriate inspiration for such a tale of illusion, show business, and fear. Connecting Poe to a charge of something like Cyberpunk makes this one of my most chilling and effective stories, I think.

"*Hoc est corpus*," said the licorice voice. "Lich, arise."

The void behind my eyes filled. Subtle colors pinwheeled against velvet. Oiled thoughts raced, unable to grab.

The voice slid like black syrup into my ears.

"Once dead, now quick. Arise."

I opened my eyes. My fingers curled across palm, thumb touched pinkie, tack of prints on skin, twist and pull of muscles in wrist, the first things necessary. No pain in my joints. Hands agile and strong.

Tremors gone.

I shivered.

"I'm back," I said.

"Quick and quick," the voice said

I turned to see who spoke in such lovely black tones. My eyes focused on a brown oval like rich fine wood, ivory eyes with ruby pupils, face square and stern but untouched by age.

"How does it feel to be inside again, and whole? I am a doctor. You can tell."

I opened my mouth. "No pain," I said. "I feel . . . oily, inside. Smooth and slick."

"Young," the face said. I saw the face in profile and decided, from the timbre of the voice and general features, that this was a woman. The smoothness of her skin reminded me of the unlined surface of a painting. She wore long black robes from neck to below where I lay on an elevated bed or table. "Do you have memories?"

I swallowed. My throat felt cool. I thought of eating and remembered one last painful meal, when swallowing had been difficult. "Yes. Eating. Hurting."

"Your name?"

"Something. Cardino."

"Cardino, that's all?"

"My stage name. My real name. Is. Robert . . . Falucci."

"That is right. When you are ready, you may stand and join them for dinner. Roderick invites you."

"Them?"

"Roderick suggested you, and the five voted to bring you back. You may thank them, if you wish, at dinner."

The face smiled.

"Your name?" I asked.

"Ont. O-N-T."

The face departed, robes swishing like waves. Lights came up. I rolled and propped myself on one elbow, expecting pain, feeling only an easeful smoothness. I suspected that I had died. I surmised I had been frozen, as I had paid them to do, the Nitrogen Fixers, and that. . .

Lich, she had called me. Body, corpse. In one of my flashier shows I had reanimated a headless woman. Spark coils and strobes and a big van de Graaf generator had made the hair on her severed head stand on end.

I slipped my naked legs down from the table, found the coolness of a tessellated tile floor. My fumbling fingers found the robe on the table as I stared at the ornate floor tiles: men and women, each perfectly joined in a flow of completion advancing to the far wall: courtship, embracing, copulation, birth.

I felt a sudden floating happiness.

I've made it.

On a heavy black oak table, I found clothes set out that might have come from a studio costume department—black stiffly formal suit out of a 1930s society movie, something for Fred Astaire. To my chagrin, I tended to corpulence even in this resurrected state. I put the robe aside and stuffed myself into the outfit and poured a glass of water from a nearby pitcher. A watercress sandwich appeared and I nibbled it while exploring the room.

I should be terrified. I'm not. Roderick. . .

The table on which I had been reborn occupied the center of the room, spare and black and shiny, like a stone altar. It felt cold to my touch. A yard to the right, the heavy oak table supported my sandwich plate, the pitcher and glass of water, the discarded robe, and a pair of shoes.

Lich, she had called me.

I stood in bright if diffuse illumination. No lights were visible. The room's corners lay in shadow. Armless chairs lined the wall behind me. A door opened in the next wall. Paintings covered the wall before me. The room seemed square and complete, but I could not find a fourth wall. No matter which direction, as I made a complete turn, I counted only three walls. The decor seemed rich and fashionable, William Morris and the restrained lines of classic Japanese furniture.

Obviously, not the next decade, I thought. *Maybe centuries in the future.*

I walked forward and the illumination followed. Expertly painted portraits covered the wall, precise, cold renderings of five people, three pale males and two dark females, all in extravagant dress. None of them were Roderick—if Roderick was who I thought he might be—and Ont did not appear, either. The men wore tights and seemed ridiculously well endowed, with feathers puffed on their shoulders and immense fan-shaped hats rising from the crowns of their close-cropped heads. The women wore tight-fitting black gowns, their reddish hair spread like sunbursts, skin the color and sheen of rubbed maple.

I wondered if I would ever find employment in this future world. "Do you like illusions?" I asked the portraits rhetorically.

"They are life's blood," answered the male on the left, smiling at me.

The portrait resumed its old, painted appearance.

Assume nothing, I told myself.

Startling patterns decorated the wall behind the portraits. Flowers surrounded and gave form to skull-shapes, eyes like holograms of black olives floating within petaled sockets.

"Where is dinner?" I asked.

This time, the portraits did not answer.

The room's only door opened onto a straight corridor that extended for a few yards, then sent me back to the room where I had been reborn. I scowled at the unresponsive portraits, then looked for intercoms, doorbells, hidden telephones. Odd that I should still feel happy and at ease, for I might be stuck like a mouse in a cage.

"I would like to go to dinner," I said in my stage voice, precise and commanding. The door swung shut and opened again. When I stepped through, I faced another corridor, and this one led to a larger double door, half ajar.

I opened the door and stepped outside to an immense ruined garden and orchard, ranks of great squat thick trees barren of leaves and overgrown with brown creepers and tall, sere thistles spotted with patches of crusty black. Hundreds of acres spread over low desolate hills, and on the highest hill stood an edifice that would have seemed unlikely in a dream. It rose above the ruined gardens, white and yellow-gray, like ancient chalk—what must have once been a splendid mansion, its lowest level simple and elegant. An architectural cancer had set in, however, and tumorous wings and floors and towers and bridges thrust from the first floor with malign genius, twisting and joining in ways I could not make sense of. These extrusions reflected the condition of the garden: the house was overgrown, thick with its own weeds.

Beyond the house and land rose a sky gray and dull and threatening. Coils of cloud dropped from the scudding, ash-colored overcast like incipient tornadoes, and the air smelled of frustrated electricity and stale ocean.

A slender spike of alarm rose in me, then faded back into my euphoria at simply being alive and free of pain. It did not matter that everything in this place seemed nightmarish or out of balance. All would be explained, I told myself.

Roderick would explain.

If anyone besides me could have survived into this puzzling and perhaps far future, it was the resourceful and clever friend of my youth, the only Roderick of my acquaintance: Roderick Escher. I could imagine no other.

I let go of the door and stepped out on a stone pathway, then turned to look back at the building where I had been reborn. It was small and square, simply and solidly constructed of smooth pieces of yellow-gray stone, without ornament, like a dignified tomb. Frost covered the stones, and ice rime caked the soil around the building, yet the interior had not been noticeably cooler.

I squared my shoulders, examined my hands one more time, flexed the fingers, and spread them at arm's length. I then swiped both of my hands before my face, as if to pass an imaginary coin, and smiled at the ease of movement. That established, I set out on the path through the trees of the ruined garden, toward the encrusted and cancerous-looking house.

The trees and thistles consented to my passage, seeming to listen to my footfalls with silent reservation. I did not so much feel watched as measured, as if all the numbers of my life, my new body, were being recorded and analyzed. I noticed as I approached the barren trunks, or the dry, lifeless wall of some past hedge, that all the branches and dry leaves were gripped by tiny strands of white fiber. *Spiders, mites,* I hypothesized, but saw no evidence of anything moving.

When I stumbled and kicked aside a clod of dry dirt, I saw the soil was laden with even thicker white fibers, some of which released sparkles like buried stars where tiny rocks had cut or scratched them.

As I walked, I dug with my toe into more patches, and wherever I investigated, strands underlay the topsoil like fine human hairs, a few inches beneath the dusty gray surface. I bent down to feel them. They broke under my fingers and the severed ends sparkled, but then reassembled.

The closer I approached, the house on the hill appeared even more diseased and outlandish. Among its many peculiarities, one struck me forcibly: with the exception of the ground floor, there were no windows. All the walls and towers rose in blind disregard of each other and of the desolation beyond. Moreover, as I approached the broad verandah and the stone steps leading to a large bronze door, I noticed that the house itself was layered with tiny white threads, some of which had been cut and sparkled faintly. What might have seemed cheerful—a house pricked along its intricate surfaces and lines by a myriad of stars, as if portrayed on a Christmas card—became instead flatly dreadful, dreadful in my inner estimation, yet flatly so because of my artificial and inappropriate *calm*.

Another wave of concern swept outward from my core, and was just as swiftly damped. *Part of me wants to feel fear, but I don't. Something in me desires to turn around and find peace again. . .*

A *lich* would feel this way . . . Still half-dead.

From the porch, the house did not appear solid. Fine cracks spread through the stones, and to one side—the northern side, to judge from the angle of the sun—a long crack reached from the foundation to the top of the first floor, where it climbed the side of a short, stubby tower. I could easily imagine the stones crumbling. Perhaps all that held the house together were the white threads covering it like the fine webs of a silkworm or tent caterpillar.

I walked up the steps, my feet kicking aside dust and windblown fragments of desiccated leaves and twigs. The bronze door rose over my head, splotched with black and green. In its center panel, a bas relief of two hands had been cast. These hands reached out to clasp each other, desire apparent in the tension and arc of the phalanges and strain of tendons—yet the beseeching fingers did not touch.

I could not equate any of this with the Roderick I had known for so many years, beginning in university. I remembered a thin but energetic man, tall and handsome in an ascetic way, his hair flyaway fine and combed back from a high forehead, double-lobed with a crease between, above his nose, that gave him an air of intense concern and concentration. Roderick's most remarkable feature had always been his eyes, set low and deep beneath straight brows, eyes great and absorbing, sympathetic and sad and yet enlivened by a twist and glitter of sensuous humor.

The Roderick I remembered had always been excessively neat, and concerned about money and possessions, and would have never allowed such an estate to go to ruin . . . Or lived in such a twisted and forbidding house.

Perhaps, then, I was going to meet another of the same name, not my friend. Perhaps my frozen body had become an item of curiosity among strangers, and resurrection could be accomplished by whimsical dilettantes. Why would the doctor suddenly abandon me, if I had any importance?

The bronze door swung open silently. Along its edges and hinges, the fine white threads parted and sparkled. The door seemed surrounded by tiny embers, which faded to orange and died, silent and unexplained.

Within, a rich darkness gradually filled with a dour luminosity, and I stepped into a long hallway. The hallway twisted along its length, corkscrewing until wall became floor, and then wall again, and finally ceiling. Smells of food and sounds of tableware and clinking glasses came through doors at the end of the twisted hall.

I followed the smells and the sounds. I had expected to have to scramble up the sloping floor, to crawl down the twisted hall, but up and down redefined themselves, and I simply walked along what remained, to my senses, the floor, making a dizzy rotation, to a dining room at the very end. Doors swung open at my approach. I expected at any moment to meet my friend Roderick—expected and hoped, but was disappointed.

The five people pictured in the portraits sat in formal suits and gowns around a long table set with many empty plates and bottles of wine. Their raiment was of the same period and fashion as my own, the twenties or thirties of my century. They were in the middle of a toast, as I entered. The woman who had presided at my rebirth was not present, nor was anyone I recognized as Roderick.

"To our revivified lich, Robert Falucci," the five said, lifting their empty glasses and smiling. They were really quite handsome people, the two women young and brown and supple, with graceful limbs and long fingers, the three men strong and well-muscled, if a little too pale. Veins and arteries showed through the translucent skin on the men's faces.

"Thank you," I replied. "Pardon me, but I'm a little confused."

"Welcome to Confusion," the taller of the two women said, pushing her chair back to walk to my side. She took my arm and led me to an empty seat at the end of the table. Her skin radiated a gentle warmth and smelled sweetly musky. "Tonight, Musnt is presiding. I am Cant, and this is Shant, Wont, and Dont."

I smiled. Were they joking with me? "Robert," I said.

"We know," Cant said. "Roderick warned us you would arrive."

Musnt, at the head of the table, raised his glass again and with a gesture bade me to sit. Cant pushed my chair in for me and returned to her seat.

"I've been dead, I think," I said in a low voice, as if ashamed.

"Gone but not forgotten," Dont, the shorter woman, said, and hid a brief giggle behind a lace handkerchief.

"You brought me back?"

"The doctor brought you back," Cant said with a helpful and eager expression.

"Against the wishes of Roderick's poor sister," Musnt said. "Some of us believe that with her, and perhaps with you, he has gone too far."

I turned away from his accusing gaze. "Is this Roderick's house?" I asked.

"Yes and no," Musnt said. "We oversee his work and time. We are, so to speak, the bonds placed on the last remnants of the family Escher."

"Roles we greatly enjoy," Cant said. She was youthfully, tropically beautiful, and I hoped I attracted her as much as she did me.

"I think I've been gone a long time. How much has changed?" I asked.

The four around the table, all but Cant, looked at each other with expressions I might have found on children in a schoolyard: disdain for a new boy.

"A lot, really," Musnt said, lifting knife and fork. Food appeared on Musnt's plate, a green salad and two whole raw zucchinis. Food appeared on my plate, the uneaten remains of my watercress sandwich. I looked up, dismayed. Then a zucchini appeared, and they all laughed. I smiled, but there was a salt edge to my happiness now.

I felt inferior. I certainly felt out of touch.

I did not remember Roderick having a sister.

After dinner, they retired to the drawing room, which was darkly paneled and decorated in queer rococo fashion, with many reptilian cherubs and even full-sized dog-headed angels, as well as double pillars in spiral embrace and thick gold-threaded canopies. The materials appeared to be lapis and black marble and ebony, and everywhere, the sourceless lights followed, and everywhere, the busy and ubiquitous fibers overlay all surfaces.

I heard the distant murmur of a brook, rushes of air, sounds from some invisible ghostly landscape, and the voices of the five, discussing the spices used in the vegetable soup. Wont then added, "*She* persists in calling our work a blanding of the stew."

"Ah, but *she* is only half an Escher—" Wont said.

"Or a fading reflection of the truly penultimate Escher," Shant added.

"She would do anything for her brother," Cant said sympathetically.

"You've always favored Roderick," Dont said with a sniff. "You sound like Dr. Ont."

Cant turned and smiled at me. "We are judges, but not muses. I *am* the least critical."

Musnt opened a heavy brocaded curtain figured with seashells and they looked out upon the overgrown garden. Orange and yellow clouds moved swiftly in a twilight azure sky. Musnt flung open the glass-paneled doors and we all strode onto a marble patio.

Cant put her arm through mine and hugged my elbow against her ribs. "How nice for you to arrive on a good day, with such a fine settling," she said. "I trust the doctor remade you well?"

"She must have," I said. "I feel young and well. A little ... anxious, however."

Cant smiled sweetly. "Poor man. They have brought back so many, and all have felt anxious. We're quite used to your anxiety. You will not disturb us."

"We're Roderick's antitheticals," Wont said, as if that might explain something, but it still told me nothing useful. Mired in a dense awkwardness and buried unease, I looked back at the house. It reached to the sky, a cathedral, Xanadu and the tower of Babel all in one. Towers met with buttresses in impossible ways, drawing my eye from multiple perspectives into hopeless directions.

"What did you do, in your life?" Musnt asked.

"I was a magician," I said. "Cardino the Unbelievable." The name seemed ridiculous, from this distance, in the middle of these marvels.

"We are *all* magicians," Musnt said disdainfully. "How boring. Perhaps Roderick chose poorly."

"I do not think so," Cant said, and gave me another smile, this one eerily reassuring, an anxiolytic bowing curve of her smooth and plump lips. To my shock, nipples suddenly grew on her cheeks, surrounded by fine brown areolae. "If Robert wants, he can add another layer of critique to our efforts."

"What could he possibly know, and besides, aren't we critical enough?" Shant asked.

"Hush," Cant said. "He's our guest, and we're already showing him our dark side."

"As antitheticals should," Musnt said.

"I don't understand ... What am I, here?" I asked, the salt taste in my mouth turning bitter. "*Why* am I here?"

"You're a lich," Musnt said, staring away at nothing in particular. "As such, you have no rights. You can be an added amuse-ment. A spice against our blanding, if you wish, but nothing more."

"Please don't ask if you're in hell, not so soon," Shant said with a twist of disgust. "It is *so* common."

"Who is this Roderick?"

"He is our master and our slave," Shant said. "We observe all he does, bring him his audience, and bind him like chains."

"He is a seeker of sensation without consequence," Cant said. "We, like his audience, are perfect for him, for we are of no con-sequence whatsoever." Cant sighed. "I suppose he should come down and say hello."

"Or you can find *him,* which is more likely," Shant suggested.

I opened my mouth to speak, then closed it again, turning to look at the five on the patio. Finally, I said, "Are you real?"

Cant said, "If you mean embodied, no."

"You're dreams," I said.

"You asked if we like illusions," Cant said shyly, touching my shoulder with her slender hand. "We can't help but like them. We are all of us tricks of mind and light, and cheap ones at that. Rod-erick, for the time being, is real, as is this house."

"Where is Roderick?"

"Upstairs," Shant said.

Wont chuckled at that. "That's very general, but we really don't know. You may find him, or he will find you. Take care you do not meet his sister first. She may not approve of you."

At a noise from within the patio doors, I turned. I heard foot-steps cross the stone floor, and looked back at Cant and the others to see their reactions. All, however, had vanished. I took a tentative step toward the doors, and was about to take another, when a tall and spectrally thin figure strode onto the patio, turned his head, and fixed me with a puzzled and then irritated glare.

"So soon? The doctor said it would take days more," he said.

I studied the figure's visage with halting recognition. There were similarities; the high forehead, divided into two prominences of waxen pallor, the short sharp falcon nose, the sunken cheeks hollowed even more now as if by some wasting disease . . .

And the eyes. The figure's eyes burned like a flame on the taper of his thin, elongated body. The voice sounded like an echo from caverns at the center of a cold ferrous planet, metallic and sad, yet keeping some of the remembered strength of the original, and that I could not mistake.

"Roderick!"

The figure wore a tight-fitting pair of red pants and a black shirt with billowing sleeves buttoned to preposterously thick gloves like leathern mittens, while around his neck hung a heavy black collar or yoke as might be worn by an ox. At the ends of this yoke depended two brilliant silver chains threaded with thick white fiber. Around his legs twined more fibers, which seemed to grow from the floor, breaking and joining anew with his every step. He seemed to walk on faint embers. Threads grew also beneath his clothes and to his neck, forming fine webs around his mouth and eyes. Looking more closely, I saw that the threads intruded *into* his mouth and eyes.

Still his most arresting feature, the large and discerning eyes had assumed a blue and watery glaze, as if exposed to many brilliant suns, or visions too intense for healthy witness.

"You appear alert and well," Roderick said, averting his gaze with a long blink, as if ashamed. His hair swept back from his forehead, still thin and fine, but white as snow, and tufted as if he had just awakened from damp and restless sleep. "The doctor has done her usual excellent work."

"I feel well . . . But so many irritating . . . evasions! I have been treated like a . . . I have been called an amusement—"

Roderick raised his right hand, then stared at it with some surprise, and slowly, pulling back florid lips from prominent white teeth, as at the appearance of some vermin, peeled off the glove by tugging at one finger, then the next, until the hand rose naked and revealed. He curled and straightened the slender, bony fingers and thumb. A spot of blood bedewed the tip of each.

One drop fell to the floor and made a ruby puddle on the stone.

"Pardon me," Roderick said, closing the naked hand tightly and pushing it into a pocket in his clinging pants. "I still emerge. You have come from a farther land than I—how ironic you seem the more healthy despite that journey!"

"I am renewed," I said. Upon seeing Roderick, I began to feel my emotions return, fear mixing now with a leap of hope that some essential questions might be answered. "Have I truly died and been reborn?"

"You died a very young man—at the age of sixty," Roderick said. "I took charge of your frozen remains from that ridiculous corporation twenty years later and secured you in the vaults of my own family. I had made the beginnings of my huge fortune by then and arranged such preparations very early, and so you were protected by many forces, legal and political. None interfered with our vaults. If not for me, you would long ago have been decanted and allowed to thaw and rot."

"How long has it been?"

"Two hundred and fifty years."

"And the others?—Wont, Cant, Musnt, Shant, Dont . . ."

Roderick's face grew stern, as if I had unexpectedly uttered a string of rude words. Then he shook his head and put his still-gloved hand on my shoulder.

"All the world's people lie in cool vaults now, or wear no form at all. People are born and die at will, ever and again. Death is conquered, disease a helpmeet and plaything. The necessities of life are not food but sensation. All is servant to the quest for stimulus. The expectant and all-devouring Nerve is our monarch, our King."

I was suddenly dizzied by the vertigo of deep time, the precipitous awareness of having emerged from a long well or tunnel of insensate nullity leaving behind almost everyone and everything I had known. And perhaps Roderick, the friend I had once known, was no longer with me, either.

I felt as if the stones beneath me swayed.

"You alone, of all our friends, our family . . . are alive?" I asked.

"I alone keep my present shape, though not without some gaps," Roderick said with a pale pride. "I am the last of the embodied and walkabout Eschers . . . I, and my sister. But she is *not well*." His face creased into a mask of sorrow, a well-worn expression I could not entirely credit. "I have mourned her a thousand times already, and a thousand times she has returned to something like life. She feigns death, I think, to taunt me, and abhors my quest, but . . . I could ask for no one more obedient."

"I don't remember you having a sister," I said.

Roderick closed his eyes. "Come, this place is filled with unpleasant associations. I no longer eat. The thought of using my jaws to grind severed tissue . . . ugh!"

Roderick led me from the dining room, back to the foyer and a staircase which rose opposite the main door. The stairs branched midpoint to either side, leading to an upper floor. Roderick ascended the stairs with an eerie grace, halting and surveying his surroundings unpredictably, as if motivated not by human desires, but by the volition of a hunting insect or spider. His eyes studied the fiber-crusted walls, lids half-closed, head shaking at some association or memory conjured by stimuli invisible to me.

"You must find a place here," Roderick said. "You are the last in the vault. All the others have long since been freed and either vapored or joined with some neural clan or another. I have kept you in reserve, dear Robert, because I value you most highly. You have a keen mind and quick fingers. I *need* you."

"How may I be useful?"

"All this, the house and the lands around us, survive at the whim of King Nerve," Roderick said. "We are entertainers, and our tenure wears thin. Audiences demand so much of us, and of everything around us. You are new and unexplored."

"What kind of entertainment?"

"Our lives and creations—the lives of my sister and I—are one illusion following on the tail of another," Roderick said. "All that we do and think is marked and absorbed by billions. It is our prison, and our glory. Our family has always had conjurers—do you remember? It is how we met and became friends."

"I remember. Your father—"

"I have not thought of him in a century," Roderick said, and his eyes glowed. "Fine work, Robert! Already my mind tingles with associations. My father . . . and my *mother* . . ."

"But Roderick, you did not get along with your father. You abhorred magic and illusions. You called them 'tricks,' and said they 'deceived the simple and the unobservant.'"

"I remained a faithful friend, did I not?"

"Yes," I said. "You must have. You brought me back from the dead."

"Sufficient time shows how wrong even I can be," he murmured.

We reached the top of the stairs. A familiar figure, the doctor named Ont, passed down the endless hallway, black robes swirling like ink in water. She stopped before us, paying no attention to me, but staring at Roderick with pained solicitude, as if she might cry if he grew any more pale or thin.

"Thank you, Dr. Ont," Roderick said, bowing slightly.

She nodded. "Is he what you wanted, what you need?"

"So soon, and unexpected, but already valuable."

"He can help?"

"I do not know," Roderick said.

Ont now fixed her gaze on me.

"You must be very *cautious* with Roderick Escher," she warned. "He is a national cleverness, a treasure. It is my duty to sustain him, or to do his bidding, whichever he desires."

"How is *she?*" Roderick asked, hands clasped before him, naked fingers preposterously thin and white against the thick leathern glove.

Ont replied, "Even this vortex soon spins itself out, and this time I fear the end will be permanent."

"You fear . . . more than you hope?" Roderick asked.

Ont shook her head sternly. "I do not understand this conceit between you." With another tip of her head, she walked on, the hall curling ahead of her steps into a corkscrew. Remaining upright, she trod the spiraling floor and vanished around the curve.

The hall straightened, but she was no longer visible.

"A century ago, I chose to come back into this world refreshed," Roderick said, "and took from myself a kind of rib or vault of my mind, to make a sister. She became my twin. Now, let me show you how the house works . . ."

Roderick gripped me by the elbow and guided me to a steep, winding stair that might have coiled within the largest tower surmounting the house. He gave what he meant to be an encouraging smile, but instead revealed his teeth in a conspiratorial rictus, and climbed the steps before us. I hesitated, palms and upper lip moist with growing dread of this odd time and incomprehensible circumstance.

Soon, however, as my friend's form vanished around the first curve in the stair, I felt even more dread at being left alone, and hoped knowledge of whatever sort might ease my apprehension.

I raced to catch up with him.

"As a species, in the plenitude of time—a very short time— we have found our success," Roderick said. "Lacking threat from without, and at peace within, our people enjoy the fruits of the endeavors of all civilizations. All that has been suffered is here repaid." In the tower, his voice sounded hollow, echoing into the mocking laughter of a far-off crowd.

"How?" I asked, following on Roderick's heels. That which might have once winded me now seemed almost effortless. Whatever shortness of breath I felt was due to anxiety, not frailness of body.

"All work is stationary," Roderick said, again favoring me with that peculiar grimace that had replaced a once fine and encouraging smile. We had made two turns around the tower.

"Then why do we walk?" I asked.

"We are chosen. Privileged, in a way. We—my sister and I, Dr. Ont, and now you—maintain the last links with physical bodies. We give a foundation to all the world's dreams. The entire Earth is like the seed in a peach, all but disposed of. What matters is the sweet pulp of the fruit—communication and expansion along the fiber optic lines, endless interaction, endless exchange of sensations. Some have abandoned all links with the physical, the seed, having bodies no more. They flit like ghosts through the interwoven threads that make the highways and rivers and oceans of our civilization. Most, more conservative, maintain their corporeal forms like shrines, and visit them now and then, though the bodies are vestigial, cold and unfeeling. You were reborn in one such vault, made to hold such as you, and eventually to receive my sister and me—though I have decided not to go there, never to go there. I think *death* would be more interesting."

"*I've* been *there*," I said. "It is not."

"Yes, and I always ask my liches . . . What do you recall?"

"Nothing," I said.

"Look closely at that excised segment in your world-line. You were dead two and a half centuries, and you remember nothing?"

"No," I said.

He smiled. "No one ever has. The demands . . . The voices . . . Gone." He stopped and looked back at me. We had stopped more than halfway up the tower. "A blankness, a darkness. A surcease from endless art."

"In my life, you were more concerned with business than the arts."

"The world changed after you died. Everyone turned their eyes inward, and riches could be achieved by any who linked. Riches of the inner life, available to all. We made our world self-sustaining and returned to a kind of cradle. I grew bored with predicting the weather of money when it hardly mattered and so few cared. I worked with artists, and found more and more a sympathy, until I became one myself."

He stood before a large pale wooden door set in the concrete and plaster of the tower. "Robert, when we were boys, we dreamed of untrammeled sensual delights. Soon enough, I saw that experiences that seemed real, but carried no onerous burdens of pain, would consume all of humanity. Before my rebirth, I directed banks and shaped industries . . . Then I slept for twenty years, waiting for fruition. After my rebirth, my sister and I invested the riches I earned in certain industries and new businesses. We *directed* the flow and shape of the river of light, on which everyone floated like little boats. For a time, I controlled—but I never retired to the vaults myself."

He touched the door with a long finger, smearing a spot of blood on the unpainted and bleached surface. "Physical desire," he whispered, "drove the growth. Sex and lust without rejection or loss, without competition, was the beginning. Primal drives directed the river, until everyone had all the sex they wanted . . . In a land of ghosts and shades."

The door swung open at two taps of his finger, two red prints on the wood. Within, more river sounds—and a series of breathless sighs.

"Now, hardly anyone cares about sex or any other basic drives. We have accessed deeper pleasures. We re-string our souls and play new tunes."

A fog of gossamer filled the dark space beyond the door. Lights flitted along layer after layer of crossed fibers, and in the middle, a machine like a frightened sea-urchin squatted on a wheeled carriage. Its gray spines rose with rapid and sinuous grace to touch points on conjunctions between threads, and light seeped forth.

"This is the thymolecter. What I create, as well as what I think and experience, the thymolecter dispenses to waiting billions.

And my thoughts are at work throughout this house, in room after room. Look!"

He turned and lifted his hand, and I saw a group of thin children form within the gossamer. They played listlessly around a bubbling green lump, poking it with a stick and laughing like fiends. It made little sense to me. "This amuses half the souls who occupy what was once the subcontinent of India."

I curled my lip instinctively, but said nothing.

"It *speaks* to them," Roderick whispered. "There is torment in every gesture, and triumph in the antagonism. This has played continuously for fifteen years, and always it changes. The *audience* responds, becomes part of the piece, takes it over . . . and I adjust a figure here, a sensibility there. Some say it is my masterpiece. And I had to fight for years to overcome the objections of the five!" His cheeks took on some color at the memory of this triumph. He must have sensed my underwhelming, for he added, "You realize we experience only the tip of the sword here, the cover of a deep book. You see it out of context, and without the intervening years to acculturate you."

"I am sure," I muttered, and was thankful when Roderick extinguished the entertainment.

"You've had experience with live audiences, of course, but never with a hundred billion respondents. My works spread in waves against a huge shore. At one time they beat up against other waves, the works of other artists. But there are far fewer artists than when you were first alive. As we have streamlined our arts for maximum impact, competition has narrowed and variety has waned, and now, the waves slide in tandem; we serve niches which do not overlap. Mine is the largest niche of all. I am the master."

"It's all vague to me," I said. "Isn't there anything besides entertainment?"

"There is discussion of entertainment," Roderick said.

"Nothing else? No courtships, relationships, raising children?"

"Artists imagine children to be raised, far better than any real children. Remember how horrid *we* were?"

"I had no children . . . I had hoped, here—"

"A splendid idea! Eventually, perhaps we will re-enact the family. But for now . . ."

I sensed it coming. Roderick's friendship, however grand, had always hung delicately upon certain favors, never difficult to grant individually, but when woven together, amounting to a subtle fabric of obligations.

"I need a favor," Roderick said.

"I suppose I owe you my life."

"Yes," Roderick said, with an uninflected bluntness that chilled me. Roderick drew me from the gossamer chamber, and as he was about to close the door, I glimpsed another play of lights, arranged into curved blades slicing geometric objects. A few of the objects—angular polyhedra, flushing red—seemed to try to escape the blades.

"Half of Central America," Roderick confided, seeing my puzzlement.

"What sort of favor?" I asked with a sigh as the door swung silently shut.

"I need you to perform magic," Roderick said.

I brightened. "That's all?"

"It will be enough," Roderick said. "Nobody has performed magic of your sort for a hundred years. Few remember. It will be novel. It will be concrete. It will play on different strings. King Nerve has gotten demanding lately, and I feel . . ."

He did not complete this expression. "Pardon my enthusiasm, you must be exhausted," he said, with a tone of sudden humility that again endeared him to me. "There is a kind of night here. Sleep as best you can, in a special room, and we will talk . . . tomorrow."

Roderick led me through another of those helical halls, whose presence I keenly felt in every part of the house, and soon came to hate. I wondered if there were no real doors or halls, only illusions of connections between great stacks and heaps of cubicles, which Roderick could activate to carry us through the walls like Houdini or Joselyne.

In a few minutes, we came to a small narrow door, and beyond I found a pleasant though small room, with a canopy bed and a white marble lavatory, supplying a need I was beginning to feel acutely.

Roderick waited for me to return, and chided my physical limitations. "You still need to eat and drink, and suffer the consequences."

"Can I change that?" I asked, half fearfully.

"Not now. It is part of your novelty. You are a lich. you subscribe to no services, move nothing by will alone."

"As do the five?"

Again he shook his head and frowned. "They are projections. To you, they feel solid enough, real enough, but there is no amusement in them. They can *seem* to do anything. Including make my life a torment."

"How?"

"They express the combined will of King Nerve," he said, and answered no further questions on that subject, instead showing me the main highlights of the room. It was much larger than it seemed, and wherever I turned I beheld new walls, which met previous walls at square angles, each wall supporting shelves covered with thaumaturgical apparatus of such rareness and beauty that I lost all of my dread in a flush of professional delight.

"These can be your tools," Roderick said with a flourish. I turned and walked from wall to apparent wall, shelf to shelf, picking up Brema brasses, numerous fine boxes nested and false-bottomed and with hidden pockets and drawers, large and small tables covered with black and white squares in which velvet-drop bags might be concealed, stacks of silver and gold and steel and bronze coins hollow and hinged and double-faced and rough on one side and smooth on the other, silk handkerchiefs and scarves and stacks of cloths of many colors; collapsing bird-cages of such beautiful craftsmanship I felt my eyes moisten; glasses filled with apparent ink and wine and milk, metal tubes of many sizes, puppet doves and mice and white rats and even monkeys, mummified heads of many expressions, some in boxes; slates spirit and otherwise, some quite small; pens and pencils and paint brushes with hidden talents; cords and retracting reels and loops; stacked boxes a la Welles in which a young woman might be rearranged at will; several Johnson Wedlocks in crystal goblets; tables and platforms and cages with seemingly impassable Jarrett pedestals; collapsible or compressible chess pieces, checkers, poker chips, potato chips, marbles, golf balls, baseballs, basketballs, soccer balls; ingenious items of clothing and collars and cufflinks manufactured by the Magnificent Traumata; handcuffs and strait jackets. . .

As I turned from wall to wall with delight growing to delirium, Roderick merely stood behind me, arms folded, receiving my awe-struck glances with a patient smile. Finally I came to a wall on which hung one small black cabinet with glass doors. Within this cabinet there lay. . .

Ten sealed decks of playing cards.

I opened this cabinet eagerly, aching to try my new hands, wrists, fingers, on them. I unwrapped cellophane from a deck and tamped the stack into one hand, immediately fanning the cards into a double spiral. With a youthful and pliant fold of skin near my thumb I pushed a single Ace of Spades to prominence, remembering with hallucinatory vividness the cards most likely to be chosen by audience members in any given geography, as recorded by Maskull in his immortal *Force and Suit.*

I turned and presented the deck to Roderick.

"Pick a card," I said, "any card."

He stared at me intensely, almost resentfully, and his left eye opened wider than the right, presenting an expression composed at once of equal mix delight and apprehension. "Save it. There is altogether too much time."

But like a child suddenly brought home to familiar toys, I could not restrain myself. I propelled the deck in an arc from one hand to the other, and back. I shuffled the cards and cut them expertly behind my back, knowing the arrangement had not even now been disturbed. With my fingers I counted from the top of the precisely split deck, and brought up a Queen of Hearts. "Appropriate for your world," I said.

"Impressive legerdemain," Roderick said with a slight shudder. He had never been able to judge my lights of hand, or follow my instant sleights and slides and crosses. With almost carnivorous glee I wanted to dazzle this man who controlled so much illusion, to challenge him to a duel.

"It's magic," I said breathlessly. "*Real* magic."

"Its charm," he said in a subdued and musing voice, "lies in its simplicity *and* its antiquity." He seemed doubtful, and rested his chin on the tip of an index finger. Again a spot of blood. "Still, I insist you need to rest, to prepare. Tomorrow . . . We will begin, and all will be judged."

I realized he was correct. Now was not the time. I needed to know more. It was possible, in this unreal futurity, anything I might be able to accomplish with such simple props would be laughed at. Sooner expect a bird to fly to the moon. . .

With a brief farewell, he departed, and left me alone in the marvelous room. My heart hammered like a pecking dove in my chest.

Nowhere in this room, unique I supposed in all the rooms of the house of Roderick Escher, did there creep or coat or insinuate any of the pale, light-guiding threads or fibers. I was alone and unwatched, unconnected to any hungry external beings, be they kings or slaves. . .

I fancied I was Roderick's secret.

I undressed and showered. The bathroom filled with steam and I inhaled its warm moistness, returning again to the euphoria I had experienced upon my arrival. I toweled and picked up a thick terry cloth robe, examining the sleeves and pockets. In a table drawer I found needle and many colors of thread, and marveled at Roderick's thoroughness.

Far too restless and exalted for sleep, I began to sew hooks and loops and pockets into the robe, for practice, and then into my suit of clothes. My fingers worked furiously, as agile as they had ever been in my prime.

I turned to the laden walls and spun through a dozen displays before finding clamps, tack, glue, brads, wire, springs, card indexes, and other necessities. I altered the suit for fit as well as fittings. I had long centuries ago learned to be a tailor and seamstress, as well as a forger and engineer.

There were no windows, no clocks, no way to learn the time of evening, if evening it actually was. I might have spent days of objective time in my obsessive labors. It did not matter here; I was not disturbed and did not rest until I became so tired I could hardly stand or clasp a needle or bend a wire.

I removed the robe, climbed into the small, comfortable bed, and immediately fell into deep slumber.

I know not how many minutes or hours, or perhaps years later, I felt a touch on my face and jerked abruptly to consciousness. My eyes burned but my nerves pulsed as if I had just drunk a dozen cups of black coffee. In the darkened room (had I turned off any lights? there were no lights to control!) I saw a whitish shape, tall and blurred. Now came to me a supreme supernatural dread, and I was immediately drenched with sweat.

I rubbed my eyes to clear them.

"Who's there?" I cried.

"It is I, Maja," the whitish form said in a thrilling contralto.

"Who?" I asked, my voice cracking, for I only half-remembered my circumstances. I did not know what might face me in this unknown place and time.

"I am Roderick's sister," she said, and came closer, her face entering a sourceless, nacreous spot of glow. I beheld a woman of extraordinary character, her countenance as thin as the faces of the women in Klimt's darker paintings, her eyes as large as Roderick's, and of like cast and color. I could have sworn her high twin-lobed forehead would have blemished her femininity, had it been described so to me, yet it did not.

"What do you want?" I asked, my heart slowing its staccato beat. I felt no danger from her, only a ruinous sadness.

"Do not do this thing," she warned, eyes intent on mine. I could not break that gaze, so frightened and yet so strong. "It is a change too drastic for the Eschers, a breach, a leap to disaster. Roderick wishes our doom, but he does not know what he does."

"Why would he wish to die?"

This she did not answer, but instead leaned forward and whispered to me, "He believes we *can* die. That is his madness. He has told me to go before, to prove certain theories."

"And you have agreed—to die?"

She nodded, eyes fixed on mine, drawing me in as if to the doors of her soul. In her there was more of the cadaver already than a living woman, yet she seemed sadly, infinitely beautiful. Her beauty was that of a guttering candle flame. The fire of her eyes was a fraction that of Roderick's, and her body, as a taper, might supply only a few minutes more of the fuel of life. Unlike the brown women, Cant and Dont, who were unreal yet seemed solid and healthy, she was all too real, and I could have blown her away with a weak breath. "I am his twin. He took me from his mind, shaped me to equal him, in all but will. I have no will of my own. I obey him."

"He made his own sister a slave?"

"It is done that way here. We may create versions of our self that do not possess a legal existence."

"How bitter!" I exclaimed.

"Oh, I may protest, may try to show him my love by directing his will with persuasion. But he is stronger, and I do whatever he tells me. Now, it is his wish I try again to die. I only hope this time I might succeed."

Behind her I saw the approach of the solicitous Dr. Ont. The doctor took Roderick's sister by one skeletal hand, pushed her lips close to Maja's almost translucent ear, and murmured words in a tongue I could not understand. Maja's head fell to one side and it seemed she might collapse. Dr. Ont supported her, and they withdrew from the room.

I felt at once a heavy swell of resentment, and a commensurate surge of bluster. "How dare she come here, smelling of death. I've left *death* behind." But in my declining terror, I was exaggerating. Roderick's sister, Maja, had exuded no scent at all.

She had smelled, if anything, less intensely than a matching volume of empty air.

I felt I slept only a few minutes, yet when Roderick's voice boomed into my room, waking me, I was completely refreshed, confident, ready for any challenge. *I* was no slave of Roderick Escher.

"Dear friend—have you made the necessary preparations?" he asked.

I looked around for his presence, but he was not there, only his voice. "I'm ready," I said.

"Do you understand your challenge?"

"Better than ever," I said. I had the confidence of an innocent child, thinking tigers are simply large cats; even the appearance during the night of Maja Escher held no awe for me.

"Good. Then eat hearty, and build up your strength."

Roderick did not enter my room, but breakfast appeared on a table. The apparatuses I had chosen the night before lay beside the plates of warm vegetables, broth, breads. I put on my robe, manifested an Ace of Spades in my right hand, and threw it at the stack of toast. The card pierced the top slice of toast and stuck out upright.

I lifted the card, retrieving the toast with it, and took a bite, chewing with a broad smile. All my fears of the day before (if indeed a day had passed) had faded. I had never in my first life felt so confident before going on stage, or beginning a performance.

As I ate, I wondered at the lack of meat. Had the world's inhabitants suddenly and humanely ended the slaughter of innocent animals? Or did they simply distance themselves from the carnal, as most of them had assumed the character of frozen meat in chilly refrigerators?

Were there any animals left to eat?

In truth, what did I know about Roderick's brave civilization? Nothing. He had not prepared me or informed me any farther. Yet my confidence did not fade. I felt instinctively the challenge that Roderick was about to offer—to compare the overwhelming and undeniable magic of this time, against my own simple *legerdemain,* as Roderick had called it.

Roderick visited me in person as I finished my breakfast. "Did you enjoy yourself?" he asked as he entered through the door. His arm rose slowly to indicate the changeable wall of glass cases, now frozen at the apparatus associated with cards. He walked to the case, opened it, and removed a reel manufactured by my inspiration, Cardini, who had died just after my first birth, but whose effects I had learned by heart. "Did you know," Roderick said, holding the tiny reel in his palm, "that a century ago, children played with dollhouses indistinguishable from the real? Little automata going about their lives, using tools perfect for their scale, living dolls sitting on furniture accurate in every way . . . And these houses were so cheap they were made available to the poorest of the poor?"

"I didn't know that," I said.

Roderick smiled at me, and for the first time on this, my second day in my new life, I felt a narrow chilliness behind my eyes, a suspicion of the unforeseen.

"Yet we have advanced beyond that time as the gods reach beyond the ants," he said. "All pleasures available at will. Every nerve and region within the brain—and without!—charted and their affects explored in endless variations. Whole societies devoted to pain from injuries impossible in all past experience, to the ghostlike exertion of an infinite combination of muscles in creatures the size of planets, to the social and sexual dalliances of phantoms conjured from histories and times and places that never were."

"Remarkable," I said stiffly.

"An audience of such intense discernment and sophistication that nothing surprises them, nothing arouses their childlike amazement, for they have never *been* children!"

"Extraordinary," I said with some pique. Did he wish for my defeat, my failure, to enjoy some petty triumph over an inferior? I steeled myself against his words, as I might have armored against the complaints of an older and better magician, criticizing my fledgling efforts.

"There are audiences of such size that they dwarf all of the Earth's past populations," he added.

I saw my bed fold into itself until it vanished into a corner. The wall of cases shrank into a narrow box the size of a book, leaving me with only the table and the apparatus I had chosen the night before.

"Prepare, Robert," he said. "The curtain rises soon."

Then his voice took on a shadowed depth, betraying a mix of emotions I could not comprehend, relief mixed with heavy grief and even guilt, and something else beyond my poor, unembellished range. "Dr. Ont came to me last night. Maja has succumbed. My sister is no more. Ont certifies that she has truly died. She has even begun to decay."

"I'm sorry," I said.

"It's a triumph," he said quietly. "She goes before . . ."

I put on the suit I had tailored and adjusted, and inwardly smiled at its close fit and how it flattered my pudgy form. I have never been handsome, have always lacked the charm of magicians who combine grace and artistry with physical beauty. I compensate by simply being better, faster, and more ingenious.

Roderick looked around the room. Fibers grew from the floor, climbing the walls like mold, until they shrouded everything but me and my table and cards. I seemed surrounded by a forest of fungal tendrils, glowing like swarms of fireflies.

"Billions of receptors, hooked into webs and matrices and nets reaching around the Earth," Roderick said. "Tiny little eyes like stars that have replaced any desire to leave and venture out to real stars, to other worlds. We have our own interior infinities to explore."

I made my final arrangements, and stood in the center of the lights, the tendrils. "Tell me when I'm to begin."

"We've already begun, except for the time you've spent in this room," Roderick said. "Even Maja's protests to me, and her death, have been watched and absorbed. I've used the drama of my own war to stay at the top of the ratings, my preparations and agonies. Even the five, the antitheticals—I have made them part of this!"

The same nacreous light that had bathed Maja's face now surrounded me, and the fibers arranged themselves with a sound like the rubbing claws of chitinous sea-creatures.

Roderick backed away until he stood in shadow, then lifted his hand, giving me my cue.

I had never had such a draw in my life—nor felt so alone. But was this really so different from appearing on television? I had done that often enough.

"Once upon a time," I said, focusing ahead of me at no space in particular, and smiling confidently, "a young man on a luxury cruise was caught in a horrible shipwreck, stranded on a desert island with nobody and nothing but a crate of food and water, and a crate of unopened packs of playing cards."

I brought out a deck of cards and peeled away the plastic. "I was that young man. I knew nothing of the magical arts, but in three solitary years I taught myself thousands of manipulations and passes and motions, until I felt I could fool even myself at times. And how was this done? How does a magician, knowing all the methods behind his effects, come to believe in magic?"

I swallowed a lump in my throat and leaped into the abyss.

"In those three years, I learned to make cards *confess*." I riffled the deck of cards and formed a rippling mouth, and with one finger strummed the edges.

"We spoke to each other," the cards said in a breathless stringy voice. "And Cardino taught us all we know."

I produced another deck, opened it with one hand, removed the cards and arranged them on my palm, and made them speak as well, in a *female* voice: "And we taught him all that we know."

I squeezed both decks up in a double arc and caught them in opposite hands. From the top of each deck I produced a Queen of Hearts, and clamped the two cards together in my teeth. "I learned the secrets of royalty," I said through clenched jaws. Holding the decks in one hand, separated by my pointing finger, I plucked the cards from between my teeth and revealed them as two jacks. "The knaves whispered to me of court intrigues, and the kings and queens taught me the secrets of their royal numbers."

In my hands, the two cards quickly became a pair of threes, then fives, then sevens, then nines, and then queens again. "Finally, I was rescued." I riffled the decks together, blowing through them to make the sound of a ship's horn. "And returned to civilization. And there, I practiced my new art, my new life. And now, having returned from that island called *death*, where all magic must begin—"

I looked around me, unsure what effect my next request would have. "I call for volunteers, who wish to learn what I have learned."

The overgrown chamber whispered and lights passed among the fibrous growths like lanterns on far shores. Five figures appeared in the chambers then: Wont, Cant, Shant, Mustnt, and Dont. Cant approached first, smiling her most wistful and attractive smile. "I volunteer," she said.

Roderick, standing in the background, his feet almost rooted to the floor by thick cables of fiber, lifted his hands in overt approval. Why encourage those he loathed—those who shackled him with so many strictures?

Was he flaunting the strength of his chains, like Houdini?

"Am I a physical person?" I asked Cant, dismissing all questions from my thoughts.

"Yes," she said. "Very."

"Am I the last untouched human on this world?"

"In this house, to be sure."

"Do I have a connection with any of the external powers that can make things appear and disappear, make illusions by wish alone?"

"You do not subscribe to any services," Cant said. "This we guarantee, as antitheticals."

I hesitated just a moment, and then took her hand. She felt solid enough—like real flesh. "Are *you* real?" I asked.

"Who can say?" she replied.

"Is your form solid enough to forego false illusions, illusions of will isolated from body?"

"I can do that, and guarantee it," Cant said. Her companions took attitudes of rapt attention.

"It is guaranteed," they said as one.

I began to get some sense of what their function was then, and how they constrained Roderick. What would they do to constrain me?

"If I told you there were cards rolled up in your ears, what would you say?"

"All things are possible," Cant said musically, "but for you, that is not possible."

I held my hand up to her ear and drew out a rolled-up card, making sure to tap the auricle and the opening to the canal. She reacted with some puzzlement, then delight.

"You have doubtless been told that in the past, illusion was possible only through tricks. Tell me, then—how do I perform such tricks?"

"Concealment," Cant said, prettily nonplused.

I showed her my hands, which were empty, then removed my coat, dropping it to the floor, and rolled up my sleeves. I pulled another card from her other ear, unrolled it, showing it to be ruined as a playing card, then converted it to a cigarette by pushing it through my fist.

"Everyone can do that," Cant said, her smile fading. "But you—"

"*I can't do such things,*" I said with a note of triumph. "I am an atavism, an innocent, an anachronic . . . A *lich.*" I held out the cigarette. "Does anybody smoke anymore?" I asked. The five did not speak. Roderick shook his head in the shadows. "I didn't think so. King Nerve needs no chemical stimulants. All drugs are electronic. There is no one else on this planet—or in this house, at least—who can make the world dance, the *real* world. Except me—and I was taught by the cards."

The remaining antitheticals came forward. Musnt, as it happened, unknowingly carried a deck of cards in the pockets of his solid but unreal dinner jacket. Producing a fountain pen, I had him mark his name on the edge of the deck, grateful that these phantoms could still write, and blew upon the ink to help it dry. "These cards have friends all over the world, and they tell tales. Have you ever heard cards whisper?" I patted the deck firmly into his hands. "Hold these. Don't let them go anywhere." I borrowed his jacket and put it on Dont, helping her into the sleeves with courtesy centuries out of date. The cuffs hung over her hands.

"Hold up your deck of cards, please," I said to Musnt. He lifted the cards, his face betraying anticipation. I was grateful for small favors.

"I believe you have a set of pockets on the outside of your jacket," I told Dont. "Investigate them, please."

She reached into the pockets and removed two cellophane-wrapped decks of cards.

"Sneaky devils, these cards. They go anywhere and everywhere, and listen to our most intimate words. You have to be discreet around playing cards. Open the decks, please."

She pulled the cellophane from one deck. On the edge of the deck was the awkward scrawl of Musnt, written in fountain pen. Musnt immediately looked at his deck. The edges were blank.

Fibers formed curious worms and squirmed closer, lights pulsing.

"The other deck, now," I told Dont. She unwrapped the second deck, and there, in fountain pen, was written, *Wont.*

"Hand the deck to the person whose name is written on the side," I said. She passed the deck to Wont.

"Write on the other side your name and any number," I told Wont, giving him the pen. "And then, on a card within the deck, write the name of anybody in this room—in big, sloppy, wet letters. Show the card to everybody *except* me, and put it within the deck and press the deck together firmly."

He did this.

"Now give the deck to Cant."

He passed the deck to her. "How many decks do you carry now?" I asked. She reached into her pockets and found two more decks, which she handed to me, keeping Wont's deck with his name written on it.

"Now find the card on which Wont has written, and the card immediately next to it, smeared with the wet ink from that card. Write your name on the face of that card, and another number. Show them to everybody but me."

She did so.

"How many decks do we all have now?" I asked.

I went among them, counting the decks presently in circulation—five. I redistributed the decks one to each of the five Negatives.

"The cards have told each other all about you, and you have no secrets. But I am the master of the cards—and from *me* not even the cards have secrets!"

I reached behind their ears, one by one, and pulled the cards that had been written on, with the names Cant, Musnt, Dont, and Wont. "The gossip of the cards goes full circle," I said. "Show us your decks!"

On the top of each deck, the cards bearing the suit and number of the written-on cards—for all had been number cards—appeared, bearing a newly written number, and a new name—*Cardino.*

The Negatives seemed befuddled. They showed the cards to each other and to the questing fibers.

They had forgotten the art of applause, and the fibers were silent, but no applause was necessary.

"How is this done?" Musnt asked. "You must tell . . ."

I pitied them, just as a caveman might pity a city slicker who has lost the art of flint knapping. From the beginning of their lives to the present moment, they had truly fooled nobody. They had lived lives of illusion without wonder, for always they could explain how things were done.

All their magic was performed by silent, subservient, electronic demiurges.

"Turn to the last card in your decks," I said. "Show me who is King."

On every one of their decks, the King of Hearts was inscribed with two names. They held the cards out simultaneously. Each Negative carried a card bearing his or her name, and in larger letters, RODERICK ESCHER.

The fibers seemed to give a mighty heave. Roderick came forward, and I saw the fibers fleeing from his legs, his suit, his face and skin.

The Negatives turned to each other in confusion. Cant giggled. They compared their decks, searched them. "They're made of matter," Wont said. "They aren't false—"

"Tricks," Shant said.

"Can *you* do them?" Wont asked.

"In an instant," Shant said. Cards fluttered down around him, twisted, formed a tall mannequin and danced around us all. The fibers withdrew from around him as if singed by flames.

"Not the point," Roderick said, free of fibers now. "You can do anything you want, but you *subscribe*. Cardino does these things by himself, alone."

The fibers bunched around my feet. Shant made his cards and the mannequin vanish. "How?" he asked, shrugging.

"Skill," Roderick said.

"Skill of the body," Shant said haughtily. "Who needs that?"

"Self-discipline, training, years of concentrated effort," Roderick said. "Isn't that right, Cardino?"

"Yes," I said, the confidence of my performance fading. I was caught in a game whose rules I could not understand. Roderick was using me, and I did not know why.

"Nothing any of us can experience compares to what this man does all by himself," Roderick continued.

The five froze in place for a moment. I could see some change in their structure, a momentary fluctuation in their illusory shapes.

Roderick lifted his arms and stared at his body. "I'm free!" he said to me in an undertone, as if confiding to a priest.

"What's all this about?" I asked.

"It's about skill and friendship and death," Roderick said.

The five began to move again. The fibers touched my shoes, the hem of my pants. Instinctively, I kicked at them, sending glowing bits scattering like sparks. They recoiled, toughened, pushed in more insistently.

"My time is ending," Roderick said. "I've done all I can, experienced all I can."

The five smiled and circled around me. "*They* favor you," Cant said, and she bent to push a wave of growing fibers toward my legs. I backed off, kicked again without effect, shouted to Roderick,

"What do they want?"

"You," Roderick said. "My time is done. Maja is dead; I go to follow her."

I turned and ran from the room, sliding on the clumps of fibers, falling. The fibers lightly touched my face, felt at my cheeks, prodded my lips as if to push into my mouth, but I jumped to my feet and ran through the door. Roderick followed, and behind him a surge of fibers clogged the door.

Wherever I ran in the house, eager fibers grew from the walls, the floor, fell from the ceiling, like webs trying to ensnare me. Cant appeared in a twisted hallway ahead. I fell to my hands and knees, staring as the floor twisted into a corkscrew, afraid I would pitch forward into the architectural madness.

Dr. Ont appeared, shoulders dipped in failure, hands beseeching to explain. "Roderick, do not—"

"It is done!" Roderick cried.

A cold wind flowed down the hall, conveying a low moan of endless agony. Roderick helped me to my feet, his thin fingers cold even through the fabric of my suit.

"Can you feel it?" he whispered to me. "King Nerve has released me. I'm dying, Robert!" He turned to Dr. Ont. "I'm dying, and there's nothing you can do! I know all the permutations! I've experienced it all, and *I am bored. Let me die!*"

Dr. Ont stared at Roderick with an expression of infinite pity. "Your sister—"

Roderick gripped my shoulders. "We are walled in like prisoners by the laziness of gods, all desires sated, all refinements exhausted. Let them crown the new master!"

The moaning grew louder. Behind Dr. Ont, Roderick's sister appeared, even more haggard and pale, the feeblest energy of purpose animating a husk, her dry and shrunken mouth trying to speak.

Dr. Ont stood aside as Roderick saw her. "Maja!" Roderick cried, holding up his hands to block out sight of her.

"Still alive," Dr. Ont said. "I was wrong. She cannot die. We have all forgotten how."

The five brushed past Roderick, smiling only at me.

"The House of Escher loses all support," Cant said, lightly brushing my arm. "The flow is with you. The world wants you. You will teach them your experience. You will show them what it feels to be *skilled* and to have fleshly talents, to *work* and *touch* in a primal way. Roderick was absolutely correct—you are a marvel!"

I looked at Roderick, frozen in terror, and then at Maja, her eyes like pits sucking in nothing, as isolated as any corpse—but still *alive*.

The walls shuddered around me. The fibers withdrew from the stones, and where they no longer held, cracks appeared, running in crazed patterns over the white and yellow surfaces. The tiles of the floor heaved up, their tessellations disrupted, all order scattered.

Cant took my hand and led me through the disintegrating corridors, down the shivering and swaying stairs. Behind me, the stairs buckled and crumbled, and the beams of the ceiling split and jabbed down to the floor like broken elbows. Ahead, a tide of fibers withdrew from the house like sea sucked from a cave, and above the ripping snap of tearing timbers, the rumble and slam of stone blocks falling and shattering, I heard Roderick's high, chicken-cluck shriek, the cry of an avatar driven past desperation into madness:

"No death! *No Death!* King Nerve forever!"

And his bray of laughter at the final jest revealed, all his plans cocked asunder.

The antitheticals blew me through the front door like a wind, and down the walk into the ruined garden, among the twisted and fiber-covered trees, until I was away from the house of Roderick Escher. All of his spreading distractions and entertainments, all of his chambers filled with the world's diversions, the pandering to the commonest denominators of a frozen or disembodied horde . . . the impossible and convoluted towers leaned, shuddered, and collapsed, blowing dust and splinters through the door and the windows of the first floor.

The fibers pushed from the ground, binding my feet, rising up my legs toward my trunk, feeling through my suit, probing for secrets, for solutions. I felt voices and demands in my head, petulant, childish:

Show us.

Do for us.

Give us.

The fibers burrowed into my flesh with thousands of pricks like tiny cold needles.

Cant took my arm. "You are favored," she said.

The voices picked at my thoughts, rudely invaded my memories, making crude and cruel jokes. They seemed to know nothing but expletives, arranged in no sensible order, and they applied them accompanied by demands that went beyond the obscene, demands that echoed again and again; and I saw that this new world was composed not of gods, but of rude, ill-bred children who had never faced responsibility or consequence, and whose lives were all secrecy, all privilege, conducted behind thick and impersonal walls.

Tingles shot up my hands and feet and along my spine, and I felt sparks at the very basement of my reason.

Do for us, do everything, live for us, let us feel, all new and all unique, all superlatives and all gladness and joy, and no death no end.

My hands jerked out, holding a pack of cards, and I felt a will other than mine—a collective will—move my fingers, attempt to spread the cards into a fan. The fingers jerked and spilled the cards into the dirt, across the creeping fibers. "Get them away from me!" I cried in furious panic.

The blocks and timbers and reduced towers of the House of Escher settled with a final groaning sigh, but I pictured Roderick and Maja buried beneath its timbers, still alive.

The fibers lanced into my tongue. The voices filling my head hissed and slid and insinuated like snakes, like *worms in my living brain,* demanding *tapeworms,* asking numbing questions, prodding, prickling, insatiable.

Cant said, "You must assert yourself. They demand much, but you have so much to give—"

The fibers shoved down my throat, piercing and threading through my tissues as if to connect with every cell of my being. I clawed at my mouth, my throat, my body, trying to tug free, but the fibers were strong as steel wires, though thinner than the strands of a spider's web.

"Newness is a treasure," Musnt said, standing beside Cant. Wont and Shant and Dont joined her.

My legs buckled, but the fibers stiffened and held me like a puppet. I could not speak, could only gag, could hardly hear above the dissonant voices.

Amuse.

Give all.

Share all.

"Hail to the new and most masterful," Cant said worshipfully, smiling simply, innocently. Even in my terror and pain that smile seemed angelic.

"A hundred billion people cannot be wrong," Shant said, and touched the crown of my head with his outspread hand.

"We anoint the new Master of King Nerve," the five said as one, and I could breathe for myself, and speak for myself, no more.

THE WAY OF ALL GHOSTS

*The Thistledown sequence—*Eon, Eternity, *and* Legacy—*began with "The Wind from a Burning Woman." This most recent story was commissioned by Robert Silverberg for his anthology,* Far Horizons.

I've long been fascinated by the visionary novels of William Hope Hodgson, and in particular, his magnum opus, The Night Land, *published in 1912. Hodgson died in 1918 at Ypres, ending a very short and very influential career. Today,* The Night Land *is a difficult book to read, for stylistic reasons mostly—Hodgson affected a pseudo-Georgian style that doesn't really work for contemporary readers, though it does create a dreamlike sense of an ornately sentimental alternate reality.*

But more important is the incredible atmosphere of his most fabulous creation, the Night Land itself.

It seemed to me that a science fictional treatment of this vision, set in the Thistledown sequence, would serve more as a collaborative tribute than a rip-off, and Robert Silverberg agreed. Hence the dedication.

Later, I wrote a book on themes echoing some of those found in The Night Land *and Arthur C. Clarke's* The City and the Stars, *my novel* City at the End of Time.

Check out The Night Land *and William Hope Hodgson's many shorter works. We lost something very special at Ypres.*

A Myth from Thistledown

For William Hope Hodgson

PREFACE:

Once upon a very long extension, not precisely time nor any space we know, there existed an endless hollow thread of adventure and commerce called the Way, introduced in *Eon* (Bluejay/Tor, 1985). The Way, an artificial universe fifty kilometers in diameter and infinitely long, was created by the human inhabitants of an asteroid starship called *Thistledown*. They had become bored with their seemingly endless journey between the stars; the Way, with its potential of openings to other times and other universes, made reaching their destination unnecessary.

That the Way was destroyed (in *Eternity,* Warner, 1988) is known; that it never ends in any human space or time is less obvious.

Even before its creators completed their project, the Way was discovered and invaded by the nonhuman Jarts, who sought to announce themselves to Deity, what they called Descendant Mind, by absorbing and understanding everything, everywhere. The Jarts nearly destroyed the Way's creators, but were held at bay for a time, and for a price.

Yet there were stranger encounters. The plexus of universes is beyond the mind of any individual, human or Jart.

One traveler experienced more of this adventure than any other. His name was Olmy Ap Sennen. In his centuries of life, he lived to see himself become a living myth, be forgotten, rediscovered, and made myth again. So many stories have been told of Olmy that history and myth intertwine.

This is an early story. Olmy has experienced only one reincarnation (*Legacy*, Tor, 1995). In fee for his memories, he has been rewarded with a longing to return to death everlasting.

1

*"Probabilities fluctuated wildly, but always passed through zero.
Gate openers, their equipment, and all associated personnel within
a few hundred meters of the gate were swallowed by a null that can
only be described in terms of mathematics. It became difficult to
remember that these individuals had ever existed; records of their
histories were corrupted or altered, even though they were stored
millions of kilometers from the incident. We had tapped into the
geometric blood of the gods. But we knew we had to continue. We
were compelled."*

—Testimony of Master Gate Opener Ry Ornis,
Secret Hearings Conducted by the Infinite
Hexamon Nexus, "On the Advisability of
Opening Gates into Chaos and Order"

The ghost of his last lover found Olmy Ap Sennen in the oldest
columbarium of Alexandria, within the second chamber of the
Thistledown.

Olmy stood in the middle of the hall, surrounded by stacked
tiers of hundreds of small golden spheres. The spheres were urns.
They rose to the glassed-in ceiling, held within columns of gentle
yellow suspension fields. Most contained only a sample of ashes.

He reached out to a blank silver plate on the base of the nearest
column. One after another, the names of the dead appeared as if
suddenly engraved.

Olmy pulled back his hand when the names reached *Ilmo, Paul
Yan.* This is where the soldiers from his childhood neighborhood
were honored; five names in this column, all familiar to him from
days in school, and all killed in a single skirmish with the Jarts
near 3 ex 9, three billion kilometers down the Way.

These urns were empty. His friends had been obliterated without trace. He did not know the details. He did not need to. They

had served Thistledown as faithfully as Olmy, but they would never return.

Olmy had spent seventy-three years stranded on the planet Lamarckia, in the service of the Hexamon, but cut off from the Thistledown and the Way that stretched beyond the asteroid's seventh chamber. On Lamarckia, he had raised children, loved and buried wives . . . lived a long and memorable life in primitive conditions on an extraordinary world. His rescue and return to the Way, followed by conversion from an old and dying man to a fresh-bodied youth, had been a shock worse than the return of any real ghost.

Axis City, slung on the singularity that occupied the geodesic center of the Way, had been completed during those tumultuous years before Olmy's rescue and resurrection. It had moved four hundred thousand kilometers "north," down the Way, far from the seventh chamber cap.

Within the Geshel precincts of Axis City, the mental patterns of many who died were now transferred to City Memory, a technological afterlife not very different from the ancient dream of heaven. Using similar technology, temporary partial personalities could be created to help an individual multi-task. These were sometimes called ghosts, or partials. Olmy had heard of partials being sent to do the bidding of their originals, with most of their mental faculties, but limited power to make decisions. He had never actually met one, however.

The ghost appeared just to his right and announced its nature by flickering, becoming translucent, and briefly turning negative. This display lasted a few seconds. After, the simulacrum seemed perfectly solid and real.

Olmy surveyed the ghost's features, then shook his head and smiled. "Hello, Neya."

"It will give my original joy to find you well," the partial said. "You seem lost, Ser Olmy."

Olmy did not know what form of speech to use with a ghost. Should he address it with respect due to the original, a corprep and a woman of influence . . . The last woman he had tried to be in love with . . . Or as he might address a servant?

"I come here often," he said. "These are old acquaintances."

The image looked concerned. "Poor Olmy. Still don't belong anywhere."

Olmy ignored this. He looked for the ghost's source. It was being projected from a small, fist-sized flier hovering several meters away.

"I'm here on behalf of my original, corporeal representative Neya Taur Rinn," the ghost said. "You do realize . . . I am not her?"

"I'm not ignorant," Olmy said, finding himself once more at a disadvantage with this woman.

The ghost seemed to fix her gaze on him. The image, of course, was not actually doing the seeing. "The presiding minister of the Way, Yanosh Ap Kesler, instructed me to find you. My original was reluctant. I hope you understand."

Olmy folded his hands behind his back as the partial picted a series of ID symbols: Office of the Presiding Minister, Hexamon Nexus Office of Way Defense, Office of Way Maintenance. Quite a stack of bureaucracies, Olmy thought, Way Maintenance currently being perhaps the most powerful and arrogant of them all.

"What does Yanosh want with me?" he asked.

The ghost lifted her hands and pointed her index finger into her palm, tapping with each point. "You supported him in his bid to become presiding minister of the Seventh Chamber and the Way. You've become a symbol for the advance of Geshel interests."

"Against my will," Olmy said. Yanosh, a fervent progressive and Geshel, had sent Olmy to Lamarckia—and had also brought him back and arranged for his new body. Olmy for his part had never known quite which camp he belonged to: conservative Naderites, grimly opposed to the extraordinary advances of the last century, or the enthusiastically progressive Geshels. Neya Taur Rinn's people were Geshels of an ancient radical faction, among the first to move into Axis City.

The partial continued. "Ser Kesler has won re-election as presiding minister of the Way and now also serves as mayor of three precincts in Axis City."

"I'm aware."

"Of course. The presiding minister extends his greetings and hopes you are agreeable."

"I am very agreeable," Olmy said mildly. "I stay out of politics and disagree with nobody. I can't pay back Yanosh for all he has done—but then, I have rendered him due service as well. Yanosh knows I've put myself on permanent leave." He did not like being baited—and could not understand why Yanosh would send Neya to fetch him. The presiding minister knew enough about Olmy's private life—probably too much. Olmy could not restrain himself. "Pardon me for boldness, but I'm curious. How do you feel? Do you actually *think* you are Neya Taur Rinn?"

The partial smiled. "I am a high-level partial given subordinate authority by my original," it said. *She* said . . . Olmy decided he would not cut such fine distinctions.

"Yes, but what does it *feel* like?" he asked.

"At least you're still alive enough to be curious," the partial said.

"Your original regarded my curiosity as a kind of perversity," Olmy said.

"A morbid curiosity," the partial returned, clearly uncomfortable. "I couldn't stand maintaining a relationship with a man who wanted to be *dead.*"

"You rode my fame until I bored you," Olmy rejoined, then regretted the words.

The partial seemed to consider how to respond. "To answer your question, I *feel* everything my original would feel. And my original would hate to see you here. What do *you* feel like, Ser

Olmy?" The ghost's arm swung out to indicate the urns, the columbarium. "Walking among the truly dead—that's pretty melodramatic."

That a ghost could remember their time together, could carry tales of this meeting to her original—to a woman he had admired with all that he had left of his heart—both irritated and intrigued him. "You were attracted to me because of my history."

"I was attracted to you because of your strength," the ghost said. "It hurt me that you were so intent on living in your memories."

"I clung to you."

"And to nobody else . . ."

"I don't come here often," Olmy said. He shook his hands out by his side and stepped back. "All my finest memories are on a world I can never go back to. Real loves . . . real life. Not like Thistledown now." He squinted at the image. The ghost's focus was precise; still, there was something false about it, a glossy, prim neatness unlike Neya. "You didn't help."

The ghost's expression softened. "I don't take the blame entirely, but your distress doesn't please my original."

"I didn't say I was in distress. I feel a strange peace, in fact. Why did Yanosh send you? Why did you agree to come?"

The ghost reached out to him. Her hand passed through his arm. She apologized for this breach of etiquette. "For your sake, to get you involved, and for the sake of my original, please, at least speak to our staff. The presiding minister needs you to join an expedition." She seemed to consider for a moment, then screw up her courage. "There's trouble at the Redoubt."

Olmy felt a sting of shock at the mention of that name. The conversation had suddenly become more than a little risky. He shook his head vigorously. "I do not acknowledge even knowing of such a place," he said.

"You know more than I do," the partial said. "I've been assured that it's real. Way Defense tells the Office of Way Maintenance that it now threatens us all."

"I'm not comfortable holding this conversation in a public place," Olmy protested.

This seemed to embolden the partial, and it projected Neya's image closer. "This area is quiet and clean. No one listens."

Olmy stared up at the high glass ceiling.

"We are not being observed," the partial insisted. "The Nexus and Way Defense are concerned that the Jarts are closing in on that sector of the Way. I am told that if they occupy it and gain control of the Redoubt, Thistledown might as well be ground to dust and the Way set on fire like a piece of string. That scares my original. It scares *me* as I am now. Does it bother you in the least, Olmy?"

Olmy looked along the rows of urns . . . Centuries of Thistledown history, lost memory, now turned to pinches of ash—or less.

"Yanosh says he's positive you can help," the partial said with a strong lilt of emotion. "It's a way to rejoin the living and make a new place for yourself."

"Why should that matter to you? To your original?" Olmy asked.

"Because my original still regards you as a hero. I still hope to emulate your service to the Hexamon."

Olmy smiled wryly. "Better to find a living model," he said. "I don't belong out there. I'm rusted over."

"That is not true," the partial said. "You have been given a new body. You are youthful and strong, and very experienced . . ." She seemed about to say more, but hesitated, rippled again, and faded abruptly. Her voice faded as well, and he heard only "Yanosh says he's never lost faith in you—"

The floor of the columbarium trembled. The solidity of Thistledown seemed to be threatened; a quake through the asteroid material, an impact from outside . . . or something occurring within the Way. Olmy reached out to brace himself against a pillar. The golden spheres vibrated in their suspensions, jangling like hundreds of small bells.

From far away, sirens began to wail.

The partial reappeared. "I have lost contact with my original," it said, its features blandly stiff. "Something has broken my link with City Memory."

Olmy watched Neya's image with fascination as yet untouched by any visceral response.

"I do not know when or if there will be a recovery," she said. "There's a failure on Axis City." Suddenly the image appeared puzzled, then stricken. She held out her phantom arms. "My original . . ." As if she were made of solid flesh, her face crinkled with fear. "She's died. I've *died*. Oh my God, Olmy!"

Olmy tried to understand what this might mean, under the radical new rules of life and death for Geshels such as Neya. "What's happened? What can I do?"

The image flickered wildly. "My body is *gone*. There's been a complete system failure. I don't have any legal existence."

"What about the whole-life records? Connect with them." Olmy walked around the unsteady image, as if he might capture it, stop it from fading.

"I kept putting it off . . . So stupid! I haven't put myself in City Memory yet."

He tried to touch her and of course could not. He could not believe what she was saying, yet the sirens still wailed, and another small shudder ran through the thick walls of the asteroid.

"I have no place to go. Olmy, please! Don't let me just *end!*" The ghost of Neya Taur Rinn drew herself up, tried to compose herself. "I have only seconds before . . ."

Olmy felt a sudden and intense attraction to the shimmering image. He wanted to know what actual death, final death, could possibly feel like. He reached out again, as if to embrace her.

She shook her head. The flickering increased. "It feels so strange—losing—"

Before she could finish, the image vanished completely.

Olmy's arms hung around empty air.

The sirens continued to wail, audible throughout Alexandria. He slowly dropped his arms, all too aware of being alone. The projector flew in a small circle, emitting small *wheep*ing sounds. Without instructions from its source, it could not decide what to do.

For a moment, he shivered and his neck hair pricked—a sense of almost religious awe he had not experienced since his time on Lamarckia.

Olmy had started walking toward the end of the hall before he consciously knew what to do. He turned right to exit through the large steel doors and looked up through the thin clouds enwrapping the second chamber, through the glow of the flux tube to the axis borehole on the southern cap. His eyes were warm and wet. He wiped them with the back of his hand and his breath hitched.

Emergency beacons had switched on around the flux tube, forming a bright ring two thirds of the way up the cap.

His shivering continued, and it angered him. He had died once already, yet this new body was afraid of dying, and its wash of emotions had taken charge of his senses.

Deeper still and even more disturbing was a scrap of the old loyalty . . . To his people, to the vessel that bore them between the stars, that served as the open chalice of the infinite Way. A loyalty to the woman who had found him too painful to be with.

"Neya!" he moaned. Perhaps she had been wrong. A partial might not have access to all information; perhaps things weren't as bad as they seemed.

But he had never felt Thistledown shake so.

Olmy hurried to the rail terminal three city squares away, accompanied by throngs of curious and alarmed citizens. Barricades had been set across the entrances to the northern cap elevators; all inter-chamber travel was temporarily restricted. No news was available.

Olmy showed the ID marks on his wrist to a cap guard, who scanned them quickly and transmitted them to her commanders. She let him pass, and he entered the elevator and rode swiftly to the borehole.

Within the workrooms surrounding the borehole waited an arrowhead-shaped official transport, as the presiding minister's office had requested. None of the soldiers or guards he questioned knew what had happened. There were still no official pronouncements on any of the citizen nets. Olmy rode the transport, accompanied by five other officials, through the vacuum above the atmospheres of the next four chambers, threading the boreholes of each of the massive concave walls that separated them. None of the chambers showed any sign of damage.

In the southern cap borehole of the sixth chamber, Olmy transferred from the transport to a tuberider, designed to run along the singularity that formed the core of the Way. On this most unusual railway, he sped at many thousands of miles per hour toward the Axis City at 4 ex 5—four hundred thousand kilometers north of Thistledown.

A few minutes from Axis City, the tuberider slowed and the forward viewing port darkened. There was heavy radiation in the vicinity, the pilot reported. Something had come down the Way at relativistic velocity and struck the northern precincts of Axis City.

Olmy had no trouble guessing the source.

2

A day passed before Olmy could see the presiding minister. Emergency repairs on Axis City had rendered only one precinct, Central City, habitable; the rest, including Axis Prime and Axis Nader, were being evacuated. Axis Prime had taken the brunt of the impact. Tens of thousands had lost their lives, both Geshels and Naderites.

Naderites by and large did not participate in the practice of storing their body patterns and recent memories as insurance against such a calamity.

Some Geshels would receive their second incarnation—many thousands more would not. City Memory itself had been damaged. Even had Neya taken the time to make her whole-life record and store her patterns, she might still have died.

The last functioning precinct, Central City, now contained the combined offices of Presiding Minister of the Way and the Axis City government, and it was here that Yanosh met with Olmy.

"Her name was Deirdre Enoch," the presiding minister said, floating over the transparent external wall of the new office. His body was wrapped below the chest in a shining blue medical support suit; the impact had broken both of his legs and caused severe internal injuries. For the time being, the presiding minister was a functioning cyborg, until new organs could be grown and placed. "She opened a gate illegally at 3 ex 9, fifty years ago. Just beyond the point where we last repulsed the Jarts. She was helped by a master gate opener who deliberately disobeyed Nexus and guild orders. We learned about the breach six months after she had smuggled eighty of her colleagues—or maybe a hundred and twenty, we aren't sure how many—into a small research center, just days after the gate was opened. There was nothing we could do to stop it."

Olmy gripped a rail that ran around the perimeter of the office, watching Kesler without expression. The irony was too obvious. "I've only heard rumors. Way Maintenance—"

Kesler was hit by a wave of pain, quickly damped by the suit. He continued, his face drawn. "Damn Way Maintenance. Damn the in-fighting and politics." He forced a smile. "Last time it was a Naderite renegade on Lamarckia."

Olmy nodded.

"This time—Geshel. Even worse—a member of the Openers Guild. I never imagined running this damned starship would ever be so complicated. Makes me almost understand why you long for Lamarckia."

"It wasn't any easier there," Olmy said.

"Yes—but there were fewer people." Yanosh rotated his support suit and crossed the chamber. "We don't know precisely what happened. Something disturbed the immediate geometry around the gate. The conflicts between Way physics and the universe Enoch accessed were too great. The gate became a lesion, impossible to close. By that time, most of Enoch's scientists had retreated to the main station, a protective pyramid—what she called the Redoubt."

"She tapped into chaos?" Olmy asked. Some universes accessed through the Way were empty voids, dead, useless but relatively harmless; others were virulent, filled with a bubbling stew of unstable "constants" that reduced the reality of any observer or instrumentality. Only two such gates had ever been opened in the Way; the single fortunate aspect of these disasters had been that the gates themselves had quickly closed and could not be reopened.

"Not chaos," Kesler said, swallowing and bowing his head at more discomfort.

"You should be resting," Olmy said.

"No time. The Opener's Guild tells me Enoch was looking for a domain of enhanced structure—hyper-order. What she found was more dangerous than any chaos. Her gate may have opened into a universe of endless, fecund change. Not just order: creativity. Every universe is in a sense a plexus, its parts connected by information links; but Enoch's universe contained no limits to the propagation of information. No finite speed of light, no separation between anything analogous to the Bell continuum and other physicality."

Olmy frowned. "My knowledge of Way physics is shaky . . ."

"Ask your beloved Konrad Korzenoswki," Kesler snapped.

Olmy did not respond to this provocation.

Kesler apologized under his breath and floated slowly back across the chamber, his face contorted by pain and frustration. "We lost three expeditions trying to save her people and close the gate. The last was six months ago. Something like life-forms had grown up around the main station, fueled by the lesion. They've became *huge*, and unimaginably bizarre. No one can make sense of them.

What was left of our last expedition managed to build a barrier about a thousand kilometers south of the lesion. We thought that would give us the luxury of a few years to decide what to do next. But that barrier has been destroyed. We've not been able to get close enough since to discover what's happened. And some of our defenses have already been defeated." He looked down through the transparent floor at the segment of the Way twenty-four kilometers below. "The Jarts were able to send a relativistic projectile along the flaw, over the area of the Redoubt—hardly more than a gram of rest mass. We couldn't stop it. It struck Axis City at twelve hundred hours yesterday."

Olmy had been told the details of the attack: A pellet less than a millimeter in diameter, traveling very close to the speed of light. Only the safety and control mechanisms of the sixth chamber machinery had kept the entire Axis City from disintegrating. The original of Neya Taur Rinn had been conducting business on behalf of her boss, Yanosh, in Axis Prime while her partial had visited Olmy.

"We're moving the city south as fast as we can and still keep up the evacuation," Kesler said. "The Jarts are drawing close to the lesion now. We're not sure what they can do with it. Maybe nothing—but we can't afford to take the chance."

Olmy shook his head in puzzlement. "You've just told me nothing can be done. Why call me here when we're helpless?"

"I didn't say *nothing* could be done," Kesler said, eyes glittering. "Some of our gate openers think they can build a cirque—a ring gate—and seal off the lesion."

"That would cut us off from the rest of the Way," Olmy said.

"Worse. In a few days or weeks it would destroy the Way completely, bottle us up in Thistledown forever. Until now, we've never been that desperate." He smiled, lips twisted by pain. "Frankly, you were not my choice. I'm no longer sure that you can be relied upon, and this matter is far too complicated to allow anyone to act alone."

Neya had not told him the truth, then. "Who chose me?" Olmy asked.

"A gate opener. You made an impression on him when he escorted you down the Way some decades ago. He was the one who opened the gate to Lamarckia."

"Frederik Ry Ornis?"

Kesler nodded. "From what I'm told, he's become the most powerful opener in the guild. A senior master."

Olmy took a deep breath. "I'm not what I appear to be, Yanosh. I'm an old man who's seen his women and friends die. I miss my sons. You should have left me on Lamarckia."

Kesler closed his eyes. The blue jacket around his lower body adjusted slightly, and his face tightened. "The Olmy I knew would never have turned down a chance like this."

"I've seen too many things already," Olmy said.

Yanosh moved forward. "We both have. This . . . is beyond me," he said quietly. "The lesion . . . The gate openers tell me it's the strangest place in creation. All the boundaries of physics have collapsed. Time and causality have new meanings. Heaven and hell have married. Only those in the Redoubt have seen all that's happened there—if they still exist in any way we can understand. They haven't communicated with us since the lesion formed."

Olmy listened intently, something slowly stirring to life, a small speck of ember glowing brighter.

"It may be over, Olmy," Yanosh said. "We're ready to close off the Way, pinch it, seal the lesion within its own small bubble . . . dispose of it. All of it. The whole grand experiment may be at an end."

"Tell me more," Olmy said, folding his arms.

"Three citizens escaped from the Redoubt, from Enoch's small colony, before the lesion became too large. One died, his mind scrambled beyond retrieval. The second has been confined for study, as best we're able. What afflicts him—or *it*—is something we can never cure. The third survived relatively unharmed. She's become . . . unconventional, more than a little obsessed by the mystical, but I'm told she's still rational. If you accept, she will accompany you." Yanosh's tone indicated he was not going to allow Olmy to decline. "We have two other volunteers, both apprentice gate openers, both failed by the guild. All have been chosen by Frederik Ry Ornis. He will explain why."

Olmy shook his head. "A mystic, failed openers . . . What would I do with such a team?"

Yanosh smiled grimly. "Kill them if it goes wrong. And kill yourself. If you can't close off the Way, and if the lesion remains, you will not be allowed to come back. The third expedition I sent never even reached the Redoubt. They were absorbed by the lesion." Another grimace of pain. "Do you believe in ghosts, Olmy?"

"What kind?"

"Real ghosts?"

"No," Olmy said.

"I think I do. Some members of our rescue expeditions came back. Several versions of them. We *think* we destroyed them."

"Versions?"

"Copies of some sort. They were sent back—echoed—along their own world-lines in a way no one understands. They returned to their loved ones, their relatives, their friends. If more return, everything we call real could be in jeopardy. It's been very difficult keeping this secret."

Olmy raised an eyebrow skeptically. He wondered if Yanosh was himself still rational. "I've served my time. More than my time. Why should I go active?"

"Damn it, Olmy, if not for love of Thistledown—if you're beyond that, then because you *want to die*," Kesler grunted, his face betraying quiet disgust behind the pain, "You've wanted to die since I brought you back from Lamarckia. This time, if you make it to the Redoubt, you're likely to have your wish granted.

"Think of it as a gift from me to you, or to what you once were."

3

"If you were enhanced, this would go a lot faster," Jarr Flynch said, pointing to Olmy's head.

Frederik Ry Ornis smiled a gray, simple smile.

The three of them walked side by side down a long, empty hall, approaching a secure room deep in the old Thistledown Defense Tactical College building in Alexandria.

Ry Ornis had aged not at all physically. In appearance he was still the same long-limbed, mantis-like figure, but his gawkiness had been replaced by an eerie grace, and his youthful, eccentric volubility by a wry spareness of language.

Olmy dismissed Flynch's comment with a wave of his hand. "I've gone through the important files," he said. "I think I know them well enough. I have questions about the choice of people to go with me. The apprentice gate openers . . . They've been rejected by the guild. Why?"

Flynch shrugged. "They're flamboyant."

Olmy glanced at the master opener. "Ry Ornis was as flamboyant as they come."

"The guild has changed," Ry Ornis said. "It demands more now."

Flynch agreed. "In the time since I've been a teacher in the guild, that's certainly true. They tolerate very little . . . creativity. The defection of Enoch's pupils scared them. The lesion terrified all of us. Rasp and Karn are young, innovative. Nobody denies they're brilliant, but they've refused to settle in and play their roles. So . . . the guild denied them final certification."

"Why choose them for this job?" Olmy asked.

"Ry Ornis did the choosing," Flynch said.

"We've discussed this," Ry Ornis said.

"Not to my satisfaction. When do I meet them?"

"No meeting has been authorized with Rasp and Karn until

you're on the flawship. They're still in emergency conditioning."
Flynch glanced at Ry Ornis. "The training has been a little rough
on them."

Olmy felt less and less sure that he wanted anything more to
do with the guild, or with Ry Ornis's chosen openers. "The files
only tell half a story," he said. "Deirdre Enoch never became an
opener—she never even tried to qualify. She was just a teacher.
How could she become so important to the guild?"

Flynch shook his head. "Like me, she was never qualified to be
an opener, but also like me, as a teacher, she was considered one
of the best. She became a leader to some apprentice openers—a
philosopher and mentor."

"A prophet," Ry Ornis said softly.

"Training for the guild is grueling," Flynch continued. "Some
say it's become torture. The mathematical conditioning alone is
enough to produce a drop-out rate of over ninety per cent. Deirdre Enoch worked as a counselor in mental balance, compensation, and she was good . . . In the last twenty years, she worked
with many who went on to become very powerful in Way Maintenance. She kept up her contacts. She convinced a lot of her
students—"

"That human nature is corrupt," Olmy ventured sourly.

Flynch shook his head. "That the laws of our universe are inadequate. Incomplete. That there is a way to become better human
beings, and of course, better openers. Disorder, competition, and
death corrupt us, she thought."

"She knew high-level theory, speculations circulated privately
among master openers," Ry Ornis said. "She heard about domains
where the rules were very different."

"She heard about a gate into complete order?"

"It had been discussed, on a theoretical basis. None had ever
been attempted. No limits have been found to the variety of
domains—of universes. She speculated that a well-tuned gate
could access almost any domain a good opener could conceive of."

Olmy scowled. "She expected order to balance out competition and death? Order versus disorder, a fight to the finish?"

Ry Ornis made a whispery sigh, and Flynch nodded. "There's a reason none of this is in the files," Flynch said. "It's been very embarrassing to the guild. No opener will talk about it, or admit they knew anyone involved in making the decision. I'm impressed that you even know what questions to ask. But it's better that you ask Ry Ornis—"

Olmy focused on Flynch. "I'd rather ask you. You say you and Enoch occupied similar positions."

Flynch gestured for them to turn to the left. The lights came on before them, and at the end of a much shorter hall, a door stood open. "Deirdre Enoch read extensively in the old religious texts. As did her followers. I believe they lost themselves in a dream," he said. "They thought that anyone who bathed in a stream of pure order, as it were—in a domain of unbridled creation without destruction—would be enhanced. Armored. Annealed. That's my opinion as to what they might have been thinking. She might have told them such things."

"A fountain of youth?" Olmy ventured.

"Openers don't much care about temporal immortality," Ry Ornis said. "When we open a gate—we glimpse eternity. A hundred gates, a hundred different eternities. Coming back is just an interlude between forevers. Those who listened to Enoch thought they would end up more skilled, more brilliant. Less corrupted by competitive evolution." He smiled, a remarkably unpleasant expression on his skeletal face. "Free of original sin."

Olmy's scowl faded. He glanced at Flynch, who had turned away from Ry Ornis. Something between them, a coolness. "All right. I can see that."

"Really?" Flynch shook his head dubiously.

Perhaps the master opener could tell even more. But it did not seem wise at this point to push the matter.

A bell chimed and they entered the conference room.

Already seated within was the only surviving and whole escapee from the Redoubt: Gena Plass. As a radical Geshel, Plass had designed her body and appearance decades ago, opting for a solid frame, close to her natural physique. Her face she had tuned to show strength as well as classic beauty, but she had allowed it to age, and the experience of her time with the expedition, the trauma at the lesion, had not been erased. She maintained a look of proud dignity, but seemed more than a little perplexed.

Olmy noted that she carried a small book, an antique printed on paper—a Christian Bible.

Flynch made introductions. They sat around the table. "Let's start with what we know," he continued, and ordered up visual records made by the retreating flawship that had carried Plass from the Redoubt. Olmy studied the images hovering over the table: the great pipeline of the Way, protection fields fluorescing brilliantly as they were breached, debris caught in whirling clouds around the circumference—the flaw itself, running down the center of the Way like a wire heated to blinding blue-white. Plass refused to look. Olmy watched her from the corner of his eye. For an instant, something seemed to swirl around her—a wisp of shadow, smoothly transparent, like a small slice of twilight. The others did not see or ignored what they saw, but Plass's eyes locked on Olmy's and her lips tightened.

"I'm pleased you've both agreed to come," Ry Ornis said as the images came to an end.

Plass looked at the opener, and then back at Olmy. "I can't stay here. That's why I'm going back. I don't belong in Thistledown."

"Ser Plass is haunted," Flynch said. "Ser Olmy has been told about some of these visitors."

"My husband," she said, swallowing. "Just my husband, so far. Nobody else."

"Is he still there?" Olmy asked. "In the Redoubt?"

Bitterly, she said, "They haven't told you much that's useful, have they? As if they want us to fail."

"He's dead?"

"He's not in the Redoubt and I don't know if you could call it death," Plass said. "May I tell you what this really means? What we've actually done?" She stared around the table, eyes wide.

Ry Ornis lifted his hand and nodded.

"I have diaries from before the launch of Thistledown, from my family," she said. "As far back as my ancestors can remember, my family was special . . . They claimed to have direct access to the world of the spiritual. They all saw ghosts. The old-fashioned kind, not the ones we use now for servants. Some described the ghosts in their journals. Or rather, ghost." She reached up and pinched her chin hard, leaving pale marks. "I think they all saw the ghost of my husband. I recognize that now. Everyone on my world-line, back to centuries before I was born, was haunted by the same figure. Now I see him, too."

"I have difficulty believing in that sort of ghost," Olmy said.

Plass looked up at the ceiling and clutched her Bible. "Whatever it is that we tapped into—a domain of pure order, or something else very, very clever—it's *suffused* into the Way, into the Thistledown. It's like a caterpillar crawling up our lives, grabbing hold of events and adapting, spreading backward, maybe even forward in time. The ones who think they are in power try to keep us quiet, and I try to cooperate . . . but when my husband returns, he has things to tell me. Frightening things. Do the others hear . . . reports? Messages from the Redoubt?"

Ry Ornis shook his head, but Olmy doubted this meant simple denial.

"What happened when the gate became a lesion?" Olmy asked.

Plass grew pale. "My husband was at the gate with Enoch's master opener, Tom Issa Danna."

"One of our finest," Ry Ornis said.

"Enoch's gate into order was the second they opened. The first was a well to an established supply world where we could bring up raw materials."

"Standard practice for all far-flung stations," Flynch said.

"I wasn't there when they opened the second gate," Plass contin-ued, her eyes darting between Flynch and Olmy. She seemed to have little sympathy for either. "I was at a support facility about a kilome-ter from the gate, and two kilometers from the Redoubt. There was already an atmosphere and a cushion of sand and soil around the site. My husband and I had started a quick-growth garden. An orchard. I was in the orchard when I heard they had opened the second gate. My husband was with Issa Danna. Ser Enoch came by on a tractor and said the opening was a complete success. We were celebrating, a small group of researchers, opening bottles of champagne.

"Two hours later, we got reports of something going wrong. We came out of our bungalows—a scout from the main flawship was just landing. Enoch had returned to the new gate to join Issa Danna. My husband must have been right there with them."

"What did you see?" Olmy asked.

"Nothing, at first. We watched them on the monitors inside the bungalows. Issa Danna and his assistants were working, talking, laughing. Issa Danna was so confident. The second gate looked normal—a well, a cupola. But over the next few hours, we heard the people around the new gate behaving oddly. They sounded drunk, all of them. Something had come out of the gate, some-thing intoxicating. They spoke about a shadow. They were laugh-ing about seeing a shadow."

She looked up at Olmy, and Olmy realized that before this experience, she must have been a very lovely woman. Some of that beauty still shined through.

"We saw that some kind of veil covered the gate. Then the assis-tant openers in the bungalows, students of Issa Danna, became upset and said that the gate was out of control. They were feeling it in their clavicles, slaved to the master's clavicle."

Clavicles were used by gate-openers to create the portals that gave access to other times, other universes, "outside" the Way. Typically, they were shaped like bicycle handlebars attached to a small sphere.

"How many openers were there?" Olmy asked.

"Two masters and seven apprentices," Plass said.

Olmy turned to Ry Ornis. Ornis held up his hand, urging patience.

"A small truck came out of the gate site. Its tires wobbled and all the people clinging to it were shouting and laughing. Then everyone around the truck—the bungalows were almost empty now—began to shout, and an assistant grabbed me—I was the closest to her—and said we had to get onto the scout and return to the flawship. She—her name was Jara—said she had never felt anything like this. She said they must have made a mistake and opened a gate into chaos. I had never heard about such a thing—but she seemed to think if we didn't leave now, we'd all die. Four people. Two men and me and Jara. We were the only ones who made it into the scout ship. Shadows covered everything around us. Everybody was drunk, laughing, screaming."

Plass paused and took several breaths to calm herself. "We flew up to the flawship. The rest is on the record. The Redoubt was the last thing I saw, surrounded by something like ink in water, swirling. A storm. . .

"Two of the others on the flawship, the men, pushed through the veil around the truck and Jara helped them get into the scout. As for Jara . . . Nobody remembers her now but me."

Flynch said, "There were only two people aboard the scout when it reached the flawship. You, and the figure we haven't identified. There was no other man, and there has never been an assistant opener named Jara."

"They were real," Plass quietly insisted.

"It doesn't matter," Ry Ornis said impatiently. "Issa Danna knew better than to open a gate into chaos. He knew the signs and never would have completed the opening. But—in the linkage, the slaving, qualities can be reversed if the opener loses control."

"A gate into order—but the slaved clavicles behaving as if they were tuned to chaos?" Olmy asked, trying to grasp the complexities.

Ry Ornis seemed reluctant to go into more detail. "Those instruments, and the gate-openers associated with them, no longer exist in our world-line," he said. "Ser Plass remembers that one hundred and twenty people accompanied Enoch and Issa Danna. She remembers two master openers and seven assistants. Here on Thistledown, we have records, life-histories, of only eighty, with one master and two assistants."

"I survived. You remember *me*," Plass said, her expression desperate.

"You remain in our records," Ry Ornis confirmed. "We don't know why or how."

"What about the other survivor?" Olmy said.

"We don't know who he or she was," Ry Ornis said.

"Show him the other," Plass said. "Show him Number 2, show him what happens when you survive, but you *don't return*."

"That's next," Ry Ornis said. "If you're ready, Ser Olmy."

4

The flawship cradled in the borehole dock was sleek and new and very fast. Olmy tracted along the flank of the ship, resisting the urge to run his fingers along the featureless reflecting surface.

He was still pondering the meeting with the figure called Number 2.

Around the ship's dock, the bore hole between the sixth and seventh chamber glowed with a violet haze, a cup-shaped field erected to receive the southernmost extensors of Axis City, gripping the remaining precincts during their evacuation and repair. Olmy swiveled to face the axis and the flaw's blunt conclusion and watched the workers and robots guide power grids and huge steel beams into place to act as buffers.

The dock manager, a small man with boyish features and no

hair, his scalp decorated with an intricate green and brown Celtic braid, pulled himself toward Olmy and extended a paper certificate.

"We're going to vacuum in an hour," he said. "I hope everybody's here before then. I'd like to seal the ship and check its integrity."

Olmy applied his sigil to the document, transferring its command from borehole management and the construction guild to Way Defense.

"Two others were here earlier," the dock manager said. "Twins, young women. They carried the smallest clavicles I've ever seen."

Olmy looked back along the dock and saw three figures tracting toward them. "Looks like we're all here," he said.

"No send-off?" the manager asked.

Olmy smiled. "Everyone's much too busy," he said.

"Don't I know it," the manager said.

As a rule, gate openers had a certain look and feel that defined them, sometimes subtle, usually not. Rasp and Karn were little more than children, born (perhaps *made* was a better word) fifteen years ago in Thistledown City. They were of radical Geshel ancestry, and their four parent-sponsors were also gate-openers.

They tracted to the flawship and introduced themselves to Olmy. Androgynous, ivory-white, slender, with long fingers and small heads covered with a fine silvery fur. Each spoke with a resonant tenor voice. Karn had black eyes, Rasp green. Otherwise, they were identical.

To Olmy, neither had the air of authority he had seen in experienced gate-openers.

The dock manager picted a coded symbol and dilated the flawship entrance, a glowing green circle in the hull.

The twins solemnly entered the ship.

Plass arrived several minutes later. She wore a formal blue suit and seemed to have been crying. As she greeted Olmy, her voice sounded harsh. She addressed him as if they had not met before. "You're the soldier?"

"I've worked in Way Defense," he said.

Gray eyes small and wary, surrounded by puffy pale flesh, face broad and sympathetic, hair dark and cut short, Plass today reminded Olmy of any of a dozen matrons he had known as a child: polite but hardly hesitant.

"Ser Flynch tells me you're the one who died on Lamarckia. I heard about that. By birth, a Naderite."

"By birth," Olmy said.

"Such adventures we have," she said with a sniff. "Because of Ser Korzenowski's cleverness." She glanced away, then fastened her eyes on him and leaned her head to one side. "I'm not looking forward to this. Have they told you I'm a little broken, that my thoughts take odd paths?"

"They said your studies and experiences have influenced you," Olmy said, a little uncomfortable at having to re-establish an acquaintance already made.

Rasp and Karn watched from the flawship hatch.

"She's broken, but *we* are young and inexperienced," Rasp said. Karn laughed, a surprising watery tinkle. "And you've died once already, Ser Olmy. What a crew!"

"I presume everyone knows what they're doing," Plass said.

"Presume nothing," Olmy said.

Olmy guided Plass into the ship. The dock manager watched this with dubious interest. Olmy swung around the fields to face him.

"I take charge of this vessel now. Thanks for your attention and care."

"Our duty," the dock manager said. "She was delivered just yesterday. No one has taken her out yet—she's a virgin, Ser Olmy. She doesn't even have a name."

"Call her the *Lark*!" Rasp trilled from inside.

Olmy shook hands firmly with the manager and climbed into the ship. The entrance sealed with a small beep behind him. The flawship's interior was cool and quiet. With intertial control, there were no special couches or nets or fields; they would experience only simulated motion, for psychological effect, on their journey—at most a mild sense of acceleration and deceleration.

Plass formally introduced herself to Karn and Rasp. Since she wore no pictor, only words were exchanged. This suited Olmy.

"Ser Olmy," Plass said, "I assume we are in privacy now. No one outside can hear?"

"No one," Olmy said.

"Good. Then we can speak our minds. This trip is useless." She turned on the twins, who floated like casual accent marks on some unseen word. "They've chosen you because you're inexperienced."

"Unmarked," Rasp said brightly. "Open to the new."

Karn smiled and nodded. "And not afraid of spooks."

This seemed to leave Plass at a loss, but only for a second. She was obviously determined to establish herself as a Cassandra. "You won't be disappointed."

"We visited with Number 2," Rasp said, and Karn nodded. "Ser Ry Ornis insisted we study it."

Olmy remembered his own encounter with the vividly glowing figure in the comfortably appointed darkened room. It was not terribly misshapen, as he had anticipated before the meeting, but certainly far from normal. Its skin had burned with thousands of the tiny firefly deaths of stray metal atoms. Number 2 had stood out against the dark like a nebula in the vastness beyond Thistledown's walls. Its hands alone did not glow, and silently, nervously, ascribed shadowy arcs against its starry body as it tried to speak.

It lived in a twisted kind of time, neither backwards nor forwards, and its words required special translation. It spoke first of things that would happen in the room after Olmy left. It spoke next with a prediction that the Way would soon end, "in the blink of a bird's eye." The translator relayed this clearly enough, but could not translate other words; it seemed Number 2 was inventing or accessing new languages, some clearly not of human origin.

Plass said, "It'll be a mercy if all that happens is we end up like *him*."

"It was once a male? How interesting," Rasp said.

"We are fiends for novelty," Karn added with a smile.

"Monsters are *made*," Plass said with a grimace, clasping her Bible, "not born."

"Thank you," Karn said, and produced a forced, fixed smile, accompanied by a glassy stare. Rasp was obviously thinking furiously to come up with a more witty riposte.

Olmy decided enough was more than enough. "If we're going to die, or worse, we should at least be civil." The three stared at him, each surprised in a different way. This gave Olmy a bare minimum of satisfaction. "Let's go through our orders and manifest, and learn how to work together."

"A man who wants only to die again—" Karn began, still irritated, but her twin interrupted.

"Shut up," Rasp said. "As he says, time to get to work."

Karn shrugged and her anger dissolved instantly.

At speed, the flawship's forward view of the Way became a twisted lens. Stray atoms and ions of gas within the Way piled up before them into a distorting, white-hot atmosphere. Rays of many colors writhed from a skewed vertex of milky brightness; the flaw, itself a slender geometric distortion, now resembled a white-hot piston.

Atoms of gas in the Way were becoming more and more of a problem. They were one of the results of so many gates being opened to bring in raw materials from the first exploited worlds.

The flawship's status appeared before Olmy in steady reassuring symbols of blue and green. Their speed: three percent of c, the speed of light in the Way, slightly less than c in the outside universe. They were now accelerating at more than six g's, down from the maximum they had hit at 4 ex 5. None of this could be felt inside the hull.

The display showed their position as 1 ex 7, ten million kilometers beyond the cap of the seventh chamber, still almost three billion kilometers from the Redoubt.

Olmy had a dreamlike sense of dissociation, as always when traveling in a flawship. The interior had been divided by its occupants into three private compartments, a common area, and the pilot's position. Olmy was spending most of his time at the pilot's position. The others kept to their compartments and said little.

The first direct intimation of the strangeness of their mission came on the second day, halfway through their journey. Olmy was studying what little was known about the Redoubt, from a complete and highly secret file. He was deep into the biography of Deirdre Enoch when a voice called him from behind.

He turned and saw a young woman floating three meters aft, her head nearer to him than her feet, precessing slightly about her own axis. "I've felt you calling us," she said. "I've felt you studying us. What do you want to know?"

Olmy checked to make sure this was not some product of the files, of the data projectors. It was not; no simulations were being projected. Behind the image he saw the sisters and Plass emerging from their quarters. The sisters appeared interested.

Plass bore an expression of shocked sadness. "I don't recognize her," she said.

Olmy judged this was neither an illusion nor a twin-sisterly prank. "I'm glad you're decided to visit us," he said to the woman. "How is the situation at the Redoubt?"

"The same, ever the same," the young woman answered. Her face was difficult to discern. As she spoke, her features blurred and re-formed, each time subtly different.

"Are you well?" Olmy asked.

Rasp and Karn sidled forward around the image, which ignored them.

"I am *nothing*," the image said. "Ask another question. It's amusing to see if I can manage a sensible answer."

Rasp and Karn flanked Olmy.

"She's real?" Rasp asked. The twins were both pale, their faces locked in dread fascination.

"I don't know," Olmy said. "I don't think so."

"Then she's used her position on the Redoubt's timeline to

climb back to us," Rasp said. "Some of us at least do indeed get to where we're going!"

Karn smiled with her usual fixed contentment and glazed eyes. Olmy was beginning not to like this hyper-intelligent twin.

Plass moved forward, hands clenched as if she would hit the figure. "I don't recognize you," she said. "Who are you?"

"I see only one of you clearly." The young woman pointed at Olmy. "The others are like clouds of insects."

"Have the Jarts taken over the Redoubt?" Rasp asked. The image did not answer, so Olmy echoed the question.

"They are alone in the Redoubt. That is sufficient. I can describe the situation as it will be when you arrive. There is a large groove or valley in the Way, with the Redoubt forming a series of bands of intensely ranked probabilities within the groove. The Redoubt has grown to immense proportions, in time, all possibilities realized. My prior self has lived more than any cardinal number of lives. Still lives them. The Redoubt sheds us as you shed skin."

"Tell us about the gate," Karn requested, sidling closer to the visitor. "What's happened there? What state is it in?" Again, Olmy relayed the question. The woman watched him through a flux of discomforting intensity.

"The gate has become those who opened it. There is an immense head of Issa Danna on the western boundary of the gate, watching over the land. We do not know what it does, or what it means."

Plass made a small choking sound and covered her mouth with her hand, eyes wide.

"Some tried to escape. It made them into living mountains, carpeted with fingers, or forests filled with fog and clinging blue shadow. Some waft through the air as vapors that change whoever encounters them. We've learned. We don't go outside, none for thousands of years . . ."

Rasp and Karn now flanked the visitor, studying her with cat-like focus.

"Then how can you leave, then return to us?" Olmy asked.

The young woman frowned and held up her hands. "It doesn't speak. It doesn't know. I am so lonely."

Then she was gone. Plass, Rasp and Karn, and Olmy stood facing each other through empty air.

Olmy startled, suddenly drawn back to the last time he had seen a ghost vanish—the partial of Neya Taur Rinn.

Plass let out her breath with a shudder. "It is always the same," she said. "My husband says he's lonely. He's going to find a place where he won't be lonely. But there are no such places!"

Karn turned to Rasp. "A false vision, a deception?" she asked her twin.

"There are no deceptions where we are going," Plass said, and relaxed her hands, rubbed them.

Karn made a face out of her sight.

"No one knows what happened to the gate opened at the Redoubt," Rasp said, turning away from her own session with the records. Since the appearance of the female specter, the twins had spent most of their time in the pilot cabin. Olmy's presence seemed to afford them some comfort. "None of the masters can even guess."

Karn sighed, whether in sympathy or shame, Olmy could not tell.

"Can either of you make a guess?" Olmy asked.

Plass floated at the front of the common space around the pale violet bulkhead, arms folded, having found some sort of calm but not looking in the least hopeful.

"A gate is opened on the floor of the Way," Rasp said flatly, as if reciting an elementary lesson. "That is a constraint in the local continuum of the Way. Four point gates are possible in each ring position. When four are opened, they are supposed to always cling to the wall of the Way. In practice, however, small gates have been known to rise above the floor. They are always closed immediately."

"What's that got to do with my question?" Olmy asked.

"Oh, nothing, really!" Rasp said, waving her hand in exasperation.

"Perhaps it does," Karn said, for the moment playing the role of thoughtful one. "Perhaps it's deeply connected."

"Oh, all *right*, then," Rasp said, and squinched up her face. "What I might have been implying is this: if Issa Danna's gate somehow lifted free of the floor, the wall of the Way, then its constraints might have changed. A free gate can adversely affect local world-lines. Something can enter and leave from any angle. In conditioning we are made to understand that the world-lines of all transported objects passing through such a free gate actually shiver for several years backward. Waves of probability retrograde."

"How many actually went through the gate?" Olmy asked.

"My husband never did," Plass said, pulling herself into the hatchway. "Issa Danna and his entourage did, however. Maybe others, after the lesion formed . . . against their will."

"But you didn't recognize this woman," Olmy said.

"No," Plass said.

"Was she extinguished when the gate became a lesion?" Olmy continued. "Was her world-line wiped clean in our domain?"

"My head hurts," Rasp said.

"I think you might be right," Karn said. "It makes sense, in a frightening sort of way. She is suspended . . . And so we have no record of her existence."

"But the line still exists," Rasp said. "It echoes back in time even in places where her record has ended."

"No," Plass said, shaking her head.

"Why?" Rasp asked.

"She mentioned an *allthing*."

"I didn't hear that," Rasp said.

"Neither did I," Olmy said.

Plass gripped her elbow and squeezed her arms tight around

her, pulling her shoulder forward. "We heard different words." She pointed at Olmy. "But he's the only one she really saw."

"It looked at you, too," Rasp said. "Just once."

"An allthing was an ancient Nordic governmental meeting," Olmy said, reading from the flawship command entry display, where he had called for a definition.

"That's not what she meant," Plass said. "My husband used another phrase in the same way. He referred to the Final Mind of the domain. Maybe they mean the same thing."

"It was just an echo," Rasp said. "We all heard it differently. We all interacted with it differently depending on . . . Whatever. That means more than likely it carried random information from a future we'll never reach. It's a ghost that merely babbles . . . like your husband, perhaps."

Plass stared at the twins, then grabbed for the hatch frame and stubbornly shook her head. "We're going to hear more about this allthing," she said. "Deirdre Enoch is still working. Something is still happening there. The Redoubt still exists."

"Your husband told you this?" Rasp asked with a taunting smile.

"We'll know when we see our own ghosts," Plass said, with a kick that sent her flying back to her cabin.

Plass calmly read her Bible in the common area as the ship prepared a meal for her. The twins ate on their own schedule, but Olmy matched his meals to Plass's, for the simple reason that he liked to talk to the woman, and did not feel comfortable around the twins. There was about Plass the air of a spent force, something falling near the end of its arc from a truly high and noble trajectory.

Plass seemed to enjoy his company in return and asked about his experiences on Lamarckia.

"It was a beautiful world," he said. "The most beautiful I've ever seen."

"It no longer exists, does it?" Plass said.

"Not as I knew it. It adapted the ways of chlorophyll. Now it's something quite different, and at any rate, the gate there has collapsed . . . No one in the Way will ever go there again."

"A shame," Plass said. "It seems a great tragedy of being mortal that we can't go back. My husband, on the other hand . . . has visited me seven times since I left the Redoubt." She smiled. "Is it wrong for me to take pleasure in his visits? He isn't happy—but I'm happier when I can see him, listen to him." She looked away and hunched her shoulders as if expecting a blow. "He doesn't, *can't,* listen to me."

Olmy nodded. What did not make sense could at least be politely acknowledged.

"In the Redoubt, he says, nothing is lost. I wonder how he knows? Is he there? Does he watch over them? The tragedy of uncontrolled order is that the past is revised—and revisited—as easily as the future. The last time he returned, he was in great pain. He said a new god had cursed him for being a counter-revolutionary. The Final Mind. He told me that the Eye of the Watcher tracked him throughout all eternity, on all world-lines, and whenever he tried to stand still, he was tortured, made into something different."

Plass's face took on a shiny, almost sensual expectancy and she watched for Olmy's reaction.

"You denied what the twins were saying," Olmy reminded her. "About echoes along world-lines."

"They aren't just *echoes.* We *are* our world-lines, Ser Olmy. These ghosts . . . are really just altered versions of the originals. They have blurred origins. They come from many different futures. But they have a reality, an independence. I feel this . . . when he speaks to me."

Olmy revealed his confusion. "I can't visualize any of that. Order is supposed to be simplicity and peace . . . Not torture and distortion and coercion. Surely a universe of complete order would be more like heaven, in the Christian sense." He pointed to the Bible resting lightly in her lap.

Plass shifted and the antique book rose into the air a few centimeters. She reached out to grasp it, then pulled it close again. "Heaven has no permanent change, and certainly no death, as we know death," she said. "Mortals find that attractive, but they are mistaken. No good thing lasts forever. That sort of existence becomes unbearable. Now imagine a force that demands that something last forever, yet become even more the essence of what it was—a force that will accept nothing less than compliance, but *can't communicate.*"

Olmy shook his head. "I can't."

"I can't, either, but that is what my husband describes." Several seconds passed.

Plass tapped the book rhythmically with her finger.

"How long since he last visited you?" Olmy asked.

"Three weeks. Maybe longer. Things seemed quiet just before they told me I could return to the Redoubt." She closed her eyes. "I believed what Enoch believed, that order ascends, that it ascends forever. I believed that we are made with flaws, in a universe that was itself born flawed. I thought we would be so much more beautiful when—"

Karn and Rasp tracted forward and hovered beside Plass, who greeted them with a small shiver.

"We have ventured a possible answer to this dilemma," Karn said.

"Our birth geometry, outside the Way, is determined by a vacuum of infinite potential," Rasp said, nodding with something like glee. "We are forbidden from tapping that energy, so in our domain, space has a shape, and time has direction and a velocity. In the universe Enoch tapped, the energy of the vacuum is available at all times. Time and space and this energy, this potential, are bunched in a tight little knot of incredible density. That is what your husband must call the Final Mind. That our female visitor re-named the allthing."

Plass shook her head indifferently.

"How amazing that must be!" Karn said. "A universe where order took hold in the first few nanoseconds after creation, con-

trolling all the fires of the initial expansion, all the shape and constants of existence . . ."

"I wonder what Enoch would have done with such a domain, if
she could have controlled it," Rasp said, hovering over Plass, peering down on her. Plass made as if to swat a fly, and Rasp tracted
out of reach with a broad smile. "Ours is a pale candle indeed by
comparison."

"Everything must tend toward a Final Mind. This force blossoms
at the end of Time like a flower pushed up from all events, all lives,
all thought. It is the ancestor not just of living creatures, but of
all the interactions of matter, space, and time, for all things tend
toward this blossom."

Olmy had often thought about this quote from the notes of
Korzenowski. The designer of the Way had put together quite an
original cosmology, which he had never tried to spread among his
fellows. The original was in Korzenowski's library, kept as a Public
Treasure, but few visited there now.

Olmy moved across to see Rasp and Karn in their cabin while
Plass read her Bible in the common area. The twins had arranged
projections of geometric art and mathematical figures around the
room, brightly colored and disorienting.

He asked them whether they believed an allthing, a perfectly
ordered mind, could exist.

"Goodness, no!" Karn said, giggling.

"You mean, *Godness,* no!" Rasp added. "Not even if we believed
in it, which we don't. Energy and impulse, yes; final, perhaps.
Mind, no!"

"Whatever you call it—in the lesion, it may already exist, and
it's different?"

"Of course it would exist! Not as a mind, that's all. Mind is
impossible without neural qualities—communication between
separate nodes that either contradict or confirm. If we think correctly, a domain of order would reach completion within the first

few nanoseconds of existence, freezing everything. It would grasp and control all the energy of its beginning moment, work through all possible variations in an instant—become a monobloc, still and perfected, timeless. Not eternal, but *eviternal*, frozen forever. Utterly timeless."

"Our universe, our domain, could spin on for many billions or even trillions more years," Karn continued. "In our universe, there could very well be a Final Mind, the summing up of all neural processes throughout all time. But Deirdre Enoch found an abomination. If it *were* a mind, think of it! Instantly creating all things, never being contradicted, never *knowing*. Nothing has ever frustrated it, stopped it, trained or tamed it. It would be as immature as a newborn baby, and as sophisticated—"

"And ingenious," Rasp chimed in.

"—As the very devil," Karn finished.

"Please," Rasp finished, her voice suddenly quiet. "Even if such a thing is possible, let it *not* be a mind."

For the past million kilometers, they had passed over a scourged, scrubbed segment of the Way. In driving back the Jarts from their strongholds, tens of thousands of Way defenders had died. The Way had been altered by the released energies of the battle and still glowed slightly, shot through with pulsing curls and rays, while the flaw in this region transported them with a barely noticeable roughness. The flawship could compensate some, but even with this compensation, they had to reduce their speed to a few thousand kilometers an hour.

The Redoubt lay less than five thousand kilometers ahead. Rasp and Karn removed their clavicles from their boxes and tried as best they could to interpret the state of the Way as they approached. Evidence of immense constructions lined the wall of the Way: highways, bands connecting what might have been linked gates; yet there were no gates. The structures had been leveled to thin lanes of rubble, like lines of powder.

Olmy shook his head, dismayed. "Nothing is the way it was reported to be just a few weeks ago."

"I detect something unusual, too," Rasp said. Karn agreed. "Something related to the Jart offensive . . ."

"Something we weren't told about?" Plass wondered. "A colony that failed?"

"Ours, or Jart?" Olmy asked.

"Neither," Karn said, looking up from her clavicle. She lifted the device, a small fist-sized sphere mounted on two handles, and rotated the display for Olmy and Plass to see. Olmy had watched gate openers perform before, and knew the workings of the display well enough—though he could never operate a clavicle. "There have never been gates opened here. This is all sham."

"A decoy," Plass said.

"Worse," Rasp said. "The gate at the Redoubt is twisting probabilities, sweeping world-lines within the Way to such an extreme . . . The residue of realities that never were and never could be are being deposited."

"Murmurs in the Way's sleep, nightmares in our unhistory," Karn said. For once, the twins seemed completely subdued, even disturbed. "I don't see how we can function if we're incorporated into such a sweep."

"So what is this?" Olmy asked, pointing to the smears of destroyed highways, cities, bands between the ghosts of gates.

"A bad future," Karn said. "Maybe what will happen if we fail."

"But these patterns aren't like human construction," Plass observed. "No human city planner would lay out such a map. Nor does it match anything we know about the Jarts."

Olmy looked more closely, frowning in concentration. "If someone else had created the Way," he said, "maybe this would be their ruins, the rubble of their failure."

Karn gave a nervous laugh. "Wonderful!" she said. "All we could have hoped for! If we open a gate here, what could possibly happen?"

Plass grabbed Olmy's arm. "Put it in our transmitted record.

Tell the Hexamon this part of the Way must be forbidden. *No gates should be opened here, ever!*"

"Why not?" Karn said. "Think what could be learned. The new domains!"

"I agree with Ser Plass," Rasp said. "It's possible there are worse alternatives than finding a universe of pure order." She let go of her clavicle and grabbed her head. "Even touching our instruments here causes pain. We are useless ... any gate we open would consume us more quickly than the gate at the Redoubt! You *must* agree, sister!"

Karn was stubborn. "I don't see it," she said. "I simply don't. I think this could be very interesting. Fascinating, even."

Plass sighed. "This is the box that Konrad Korzenowski has opened for us," she said for Olmy's benefit. "Spoiled genius children drawn to evil like insects to a corpse."

"I thought evil was related to disorder," Olmy said.

"Already, you know better," Plass rejoined.

Rasp turned her eyes on Olmy and Plass, eyes narrow and full of uncomfortable speculation.

Olmy reached out and grasped Rasp's clavicle to keep it from bumping into the flawship bulkheads. Karn took charge of the instrument indignantly and thrust it back at her sister. "You forget your responsibility," she chided. "We can fear this mission, or we can engage it with joy and spirit," she said. "Cowering does none of us any good."

"You're right, sister, about that at least," Rasp said. She returned her clavicle to its box and straightened her clothing, then used a cloth to wipe her face. "We are, after all, going to a place where we have always gone, and always will go."

"It's what happens when we get there that is always changing," Karn said.

Plass's face turned livid with her disagreement. "My husband never returns the same way, in the same condition," she said. "How many hells does he experience?"

"One for each of him," Rasp said. "Only one. It is different husbands who return."

Though there had never been such this far along the Way, Olmy saw the scattered wreckage of Jart fortifications, demolished, dead and empty. Beyond them lay a region where the Way was covered with winding black and red bands of sand, an immense serpentine desert; also unknown.

Olmy felt a spark of something reviving, if not a wish for life, then an appreciation of what extraordinary sights his life had brought him. On Lamarckia, he had seen the most extraordinary variations on biology. Here, near the Redoubt, it was reality itself subject to its own flux, its own denial.

Plass was transfixed. "The next visitors, if any, will see something completely different," she said. "We've been caught up in a sweeping world-line of the Way, not necessarily our own."

"I would never have believed it possible," Rasp said, and Karn reluctantly agreed. "This is not the physics we were taught."

"It can make any physics it wishes," Plass said. "Any reality. It has all the energy it needs. And it's captured, analyzed, and transformed any number of human minds, from any number of universes, to teach it our variations."

"Yet it knows only unity," Karn said, taking hold of Plass's shoulder.

The older woman did not seem to mind. "It knows no will stronger than its own," she said. "Yet it may divide its will into illusory units. If it is a mind, and if it is a tyrant . . ." Plass pointed to the winding sands, stretching for thousands of kilometers beneath them. "This is a moment of calm, of steady concentration. If my memories are correct, if what my husband's returning self . . . selves . . . tell me, is correct, it is usually much more frantic. Much more inventive. And much more liberated from any sort of self-control."

Karn made a sour face and placed her hands on the bars of her clavicle. She rubbed the grips as her face tensed with concentration. "I feel it. There is still a lesion . . ."

Rasp took hold of her own instrument and went into her own state. "It *is* still there," she agreed. "And it *is* bad. It floats above the Way, very near the flaw. From below, it must look like some sort of bale star . . ."

They passed through a fine bluish mist that rose from the northern end of the desert. The flawship made a faint belling sound. The mist passed behind.

"There," Plass said. "No mistaking it!"

The gate pushed through the Way by Issa Danna had expanded and risen above the floor, just as Rasp and Karn had felt in their instruments. Now, at a distance of a hundred kilometers, they could see the spherical lesion clearly. It did indeed resemble a dark sun—or a chancre. A glow of pigeon's blood flicked around it, the red of rubies and enchantment.

The black center, less than the width of a fingertip at this distance, perversely seemed to fill Olmy's field of vision. His young body decided it was time to be very reluctant to proceed. He swallowed and brought this fear under control, biting his cheek until blood flowed.

The flawship lurched. Its voice told Olmy, "We have received an instructional beacon. There is a place held by humans less than ten kilometers away. They say they will guide us to safety."

"It's still there!" Plass said.

They all looked down through the flawship's transparent nose, away from the lurid pink of the flaw, through layers of blue and green haze wrapped around the Way—down twenty-five kilometers to a single dark, gleaming steel point in the center of a rough, rolling land.

The Redoubt lay in the shadow of the lesion, surrounded by a penumbral twilight suffused with the flickering ruby of the lesion's halo.

"I can feel the whipping hairs of other world-lines," Karn and

Rasp said together. Olmy glanced back and saw their clavicles touching sphere to sphere. The spheres crackled and clacked. Karn twisted her instrument toward Olmy so that he could see the display. A long list of domain "constants"—pi, Planck's constant, others—varied with a regular humming in the flawship hull. "Nothing is stable out there!"

Olmy glanced at the message sent from the Redoubt. It provided navigation instructions for their flawship's landing craft; how to disengage from the flawship, descend, undergo examination, and be taken into the pyramid. The message concluded, "We will determine whether you are illusions or aberrations. If you are from our origin, we will welcome you. It is too late to return now. Abandon your flawship before it approaches any closer to the allthing. Whoever sent you has committed you to our own endless imprisonment."

The ghastly light cast a fitful, abbatoir glow on their faces.

"Cheerful enough," Olmy said.

"We have always gone there," Rasp said quietly.

"I have to agree," Plass said. "We have no other place to go."

They tracted aft to the lander's hatch and climbed into the small, arrowhead-shaped craft. Its interior welcomed them by fitting to their forms, providing couches, instruments, tailored to their bodies. Plass sat beside Olmy in the cockpit, Rasp and Karn directly behind them.

Olmy disengaged from the flawship and locked the lander onto the pyramid's beacon. They dropped from the flawship.

The landscape steadily grew in the broad cockpit window.

Plass's face crumpled like a child's about to break into tears. "Star, fate and pneuma, be kind. There!" She pointed in helpless dread, equally horrified and fascinated "I see the opener's head."

On a low, broad rise in the shadowed land surrounding the Redoubt, a huge dark head rose like an upright mountain, its skin like gray stone, one eye turned toward the south, the other watching over the territory before the nearest face of the pyramid. This watchful eye was easily a hundred meters wide and glowed a dismal sea green, throwing a long beam through the thick twisted ropes of mist.

Plass's voice became shrill. "Oh Star and Fate . . ."

The landscape around the Redoubt rippled beneath the swirling rays of rotating world-lines, spreading like hair from the black center of the lesion, changing the land a little with each pass, shifting the bizarre landmarks a few dozen meters this way or that, increasing them in size, reducing them.

Olmy could never have imagined such a place. The Redoubt sat within a child's nightmare of disembodied human limbs, painted over the hills like trees, their fingers grasping and releasing spasmodically.

At the top of one hill stood a kind of castle made of blocks of green glass, with a single huge door and window. Within the door stood a figure—a statue, perhaps—several hundred meters high, vaguely human, nodding its head steadily, idiotically, as the lander passed over. Hundreds of much smaller figures, gigantic nevertheless, milled in a kind of pen before the castle, their red and black shadows flowing like capes in the lee of the constant wind of changing probabilities. Olmy thought they might be huge dogs, or tailless lizards, but Plass pointed and said, "My husband told me about an assistant to Issa Danna named Ram Chako . . . Forced to run on all fours."

The giant in the castle door slowly raised its huge hand, and the massive lizards scrambled over each other to pour through an open portal into the castle's central yard. They leaped up as the lander passed overhead, as if they would snap it out of the air with their hideous jaws.

Olmy's head throbbed. He could not bring himself out of a conviction that none of this could be real; indeed, there was no necessity for it to *be* real in any sense his mind or body understood.

For their part, Rasp and Karn had lost all their earlier bravado and clung to each other, their clavicles floating on tethers wrapped around their wrists.

The lurid red glare of the halo flowed like blood into the cabin as the lander rotated to present points of contact for traction fields from the Redoubt. Olmy instructed the ship to present a wide-angle view of the Redoubt and the land, and this view revolved slowly around them, filling the lander's cramped interior.

The perverse variety seemed to never end. Something had dissected not only a human body, or many bodies, and wreaked hideous distortions on its parts, but had done the same with human thoughts and desires, planting the results here and there throughout with no obvious design, like a garden for stupid demons.

Within the low valley—as described by the female visitant—a large blue-skinned woman, the equal of the figure in the doorway of the castle, crouched near a cradle within which churned hundreds of naked humans. She slowly dropped her hand into the cauldron of flesh and stirred, and her hair sprayed out from her head with a sullen cometary glow, casting everything in a syrupy green luminosity.

"Mother of geometries," Karn muttered, and hid her eyes.

Olmy could not turn away, but everything in him wanted to go to sleep, to *die*, rather than to acknowledge what they were seeing.

Plass saw his distress. Somehow she took strength from the incomprehensible view. "It does not need to make sense," she said with the tone of a chiding schoolteacher. "It's supported by infinite energy and a monolithic, mindless will. There is nothing new here, nothing—"

"I'm not asking that it make sense," Olmy said. "I need to know what's behind it."

"A sufficient force, channeled properly, can create anything a mind can imagine—" Karn began.

"More than any mind will imagine. Not a mind like our minds," Rasp restated. "A unity, not a *mind* at all."

For a moment, Olmy's anger lashed and he wanted to shout his frustration, but he took a deep breath and folded his arms where he floated in tracting restraints, and said to Plass, "A mind that has no goals? If there's pure order here—"

Karn broke in, her voice high and sweet, singing. "Think of the dimensions of order. There is mere arrangement, the lowest form of order, without motive or direction. Next comes self-making, when order can convert resources into more of itself, propagating order. Then comes creation, self-making by reshaping matter into something new. But when creation stalls, when there is no mind, just force, it becomes mere elaboration, an endless spiral of rearrangement of what has been created. What do we see down there? Empty elaboration. Nothing new. And certainly no understanding."

"She shows some wisdom," Plass acknowledged grudgingly. "But the allthing still must exist."

"And all this . . . elaboration?" Olmy asked.

"Spoiled by deathlessness," Plass said, "by never-ending supplies of resources. Never freshened by the new, at its core. Order without death, art without critic or renewal, the final mind of a universe where only riches exist, only joy is possible, never knowing disappointment."

The lander shuddered again and again as they dropped toward the pyramid. Its inertial control systems could not cope with the sweeping rays of different world-lines.

"Sounds like a spoiled child," Olmy said.

"Far worse," Karn said. "*We're* like spoiled children, Rasp and I. Willful and maybe a little silly. Humans are silly, childish, but always learning, full of promise and failure. Out there—beyond the lesion, reaching through it . . ."

"Perpetual success," Rasp mocked. "Ultimate maturity. It cannot fail. It cannot learn. It can only rearrange."

"Deirdre Enoch was never content with limitations," Plass said, looking to Olmy as if for sympathy. "She went searching for what heaven would really be." Her eyes glittered with her emotion— exaltation stimulated by too much fear and dismay.

"Maybe she found it," Karn said.

5

"I can't welcome you," Deirdre Enoch said, walking heavily toward them.

Behind Olmy, within a chamber high in the Redoubt, near the tip of the steel pyramid, the lander sighed and settled into its cradle.

Olmy tried to compare this old woman with the portraits of Enoch in the records. Her voice was much the same, though deeper and almost without emotion.

Rasp, Karn, and Plass stood beside Olmy as Enoch approached. Behind Enoch, in the lambency of soft amber lights spaced around the base of the chamber, wavered a line of ten other men and women, all of them old, all dressed in black, with silver ribbons hanging from the tops of their white-haired heads. "You've come to a place of waiting where nothing is resolved. Why come at all?"

Before Olmy could answer, Enoch smiled, her deeply wrinkled face seeming to crack with the unfamiliar expression. "We assume you are here because you think the Jarts could become involved."

"I don't know what to think," Olmy said, his voice hoarse. "I recognize you, but none of the others . . ."

"We survived the first night after the lesion. We formed an expedition to make an escape attempt. There were sixty of us that first time. We managed to return to the Redoubt before the Night Land could change us too much, play with us too drastically. We who survived, aged. Some of us were taken and . . . You see them out there. There was no second expedition."

"My husband," Plass said. "Where is he?"

"I know you," Enoch said. "You are so much the same it hurts. You escaped at the very beginning."

"I was the only one," Plass said.

"You called it the Night Land," Rasp said, holding up her hands, raising the case that carried her clavicle. "How appropriate."

"No sun, no hope, only *order*," Enoch said, as if the word were a curse. "Did you send yourselves, or were you sent by other fools?"

"Fools, I'm afraid," Plass said.

"And you . . . You came back, knowing what you'd find?"

"It wasn't like this when I left. My husband sent ghosts to visit me. They told me a little of what's happened here . . . or might have happened."

"Ghosts try to enter the Redoubt and talk all the time," Enoch said. "We refuse them. Your husband was caught outside that first night. He hasn't been changed much. He stands near the Watcher, frozen in the eyebeam."

Plass sobbed and hid her face.

Enoch continued, heedless. "The only thing left in his control— to shed ghosts like dead skin. And never the same . . . are they? He's allowed to take temporary twists of space-time and shape them in his own image. The allthing finds this amusing. Needless to say, we don't let the ghosts bother us. We have too much else to do just to keep our place secure and in repair."

"Repair," Karn said with a beatific smile, and Olmy turned to her, startled by a reaction similar to his own. Karn did a small dance. "Disorder has its place here, then. You have to *work* to *fix things?*"

"Precisely," Enoch said. "I worship rust and age. But we're only allowed so much of it and no more. Now that you're here, per- haps you'll join us for some tea?" She smiled. "Blessedly, tea cools quickly in the Redoubt. Our bones grow frail, our skin wrinkles. And tea cools. Hurry!"

"Don't be deceived by our bodies," Deirdre Enoch said as she poured steaming tea into cups for all her guests. "They are dis- torted, but they are sufficient. The *allthing* can only perfect and elaborate; it knows nothing of real destruction."

Olmy watched something ripple through the old woman, a shudder of slight change. She seemed not as old and wrinkled now, as if some force had turned back a clock.

"I'm not clear about perfection," Olmy said, lifting the cup. "I'm not even clear on how you come to look old."

"We're not unhappy," Enoch said. "That isn't within our power. We know we can never return to Thistledown. We know we can never escape."

"You haven't answered Ser Olmy's question," Plass said gently. "Are you independent here?"

"That wasn't his question, Ser Gena Plass," Enoch said, an edge in her voice. "What you ask is not a *polite* question. I said, we were caught trying to escape. Some of us are out there in the Night Land now. Those of us who returned to the pyramid . . . did not escape the enthusiasm of the allthing. But its influence here is limited. To answer one question at least: We have some independence." Enoch nodded as if falling asleep, her head dropping briefly to an angle with her shoulders . . . an uncomfortable angle, Olmy would have thought. She raised it again with a jerk. "The universe I discovered . . . there is nothing else. It is all."

"The Final Mind of the domain," Plass said.

"I gather it regards the Way and the humans it finds here as objects of curiosity," Olmy said. Rasp and Karn fidgeted.

"Objects to be recombined and distorted," Enoch said. "We are materials for the ultimate in decadent art. The allthing is beyond our knowing." She leaned forward on her cushion, where she had gracefully folded her legs into an agile lotus, and rubbed her nose reflectively with the back of one hand. "We are allowed to resist, I suspect, because we are antithesis."

"The *allthing* has only known thesis," Rasp said with a small giggle.

"Exa-a-a-ctly," Enoch said, drawing out the word with pleasure.

Struck by another sensation of unreality, Olmy looked around the group sitting with Enoch and himself: Plass, the twins, a small woman with a questing, feline expression behind Enoch who had so far not spoken.

She carried the teapot around again and refilled their cups. The tea was cold.

Olmy turned on his sitting pillow to observe the other elderly followers, arrayed around the circular room, still, subservient. Their faces had changed since his arrival, yet no one had left, no one had entered.

It had been observed for a dozen generations that Thistledown's environment and culture bred followers with proportionately fewer leaders, often assigned much greater power. Efforts were being made to remedy that—to reduce the extreme schisms of rogues such as Deirdre Enoch. *Too late for these,* he thought. *Does this allthing want followers?*

He could not get his bearings long enough to plan his course of action. He felt drugged, but knew he wasn't.

"Can it tolerate otherness?" Karn asked, her voice high and sweet once more, like a child's.

"No," Enoch said. "Its nature is to absorb and disguise all otherness in mutation, change without goal."

"Like the Jarts?" Rasp asked, chewing on her thumb with a coyness and insecurity that was at once studied and completely convincing.

"Not like the Jarts. The Jarts met the allthing and it gave them their own Night Land. I fear it won't be long until ours is merged with theirs, and we are both mingled and subjected to further useless change."

"How long?" Olmy asked.

"Another few years, perhaps."

"Not so soon, then," he said.

"Soon enough," Enoch said with a sniff. She rubbed her nose again. "We've been here already for well over a thousand centuries."

Olmy tried to understand this. "Truly?" he asked, expecting her to break into laughter.

"Truly. I've had millions of different followers here. Look around you." She leaned over the table to whisper to Olmy, "Waves in a sea. I've lived a thousand centuries in a thousand infinitesimally different universes. It plays with all world-lines, not just the tracks of individuals. Only I am relatively the same with each tide. I appear to be the real nexus in this part of the Way."

"Tea cools . . . skin wrinkles . . . But you experience such a length of time?"

"Ten thousand lengths cut up and bundled and rotated." She took a scarf from around her thin neck and stretched it between her firsts. "Twisted. Knotted. You were sent here to correct the reckless madness of a renegade . . . weren't you?"

"A Geshel visionary," Olmy said.

Enoch was not mollified. She drew herself up and returned her scarf to her neck, tying it with a conscious flourish. "I was appointed by the Office of Way Maintenance, by Ry Ornis himself. They gave me two of the best gate openers in the guild, and they instructed me, specifically, to find a gate into total order. I wasn't told why. I can guess now, however."

"I remember two openers," Plass said. "They don't."

"They hoped you would find me transformed or dead," Enoch said. "Well, I'm different, but I've survived, and after a few thousands of centuries, one's personality becomes rather rigid. I've become more like that Watcher outside with its huge gaping eye. I don't know how to lie any more. I've seen too much. I've fought against what I found, and I've endured atrocities beyond what any human has ever had to face. Believe me, I would rather have died before my mission began than see what I've seen."

"Where is the other opener?" Olmy asked.

"In the Night Land," Enoch said. "Issa Danna was the first to encounter the *allthing*. He and his partner, Master Tolby Kin, took the brunt of its first efforts at elaboration."

Rasp walked over to Olmy and whispered in his ear. "There never was a master opener named Tolby Kin."

"Can anybody else confirm your story?" Olmy asked.

"Would you believe anyone here? No," Enoch said.

"Not that it matters," Plass said fatalistically. "The end result is the same."

"Not at all," Enoch said. "We couldn't close down the lesion now even if we had it in our power. Ry Ornis was correct. The rift had to be opened. The infection is not finished. If we don't wait for completion, our universe will never quicken. It'll be born dead." Enoch shook her head and laughed softly. "And no human in our history will ever see a ghost. A haunted world is a living world, Ser Olmy."

Olmy touched his tea cup with his finger.

The tea was hot again.

The living quarters made available were spare and cold. Most of the Redoubt's energy went to keeping the occupants of the Night Land at bay; that energy was derived from the wall of the Way, an ingenious arrangement set up by Issa Danna before he was caught up in the lesion; sufficient, but not a surfeit by any means.

For the first time in days, Olmy had a few moments alone. He cleared a window looking south toward the lesion and across about fifty kilometers of the Night Land. Enoch had provided him with a pair of ray-tracing binoculars.

Beyond a tracting grid stretched to its limits, and a glowing demarcation of complete nuclear destruction, through which nothing made of matter could hope to cross, less than a thousand meters from the pyramid, lay the peculiar vivid darkness and the fitful nightmare glows of the allthing's victims.

Olmy swung the lightweight binoculars in a slow steady arc. What looked like hills or low mountains were constructions attended by hundreds of pale figures, human-sized but only vaguely human in shape. They seemed to spend much of their time fighting, waving their limbs about like insect antennae. Others carried loads of glowing dust in baskets, dumping them at the top of a hill, then stumbling and sliding down to begin again.

The giant head modeled after the opener stood a little to the west of the Green Glass Castle. Olmy could not tell whether the head was actually organic material—human flesh—or not. It looked more like stone, though the eye was very expressive.

From this angle, he could not see the huge figure standing in the door of the castle; that side was turned away from the Redoubt. Nothing that he saw contradicted what Plass and Enoch had told him. He could not share the cheerful nihilism of the twins. Nevertheless, nothing out there could be fit into any philosophy or web of physical laws he had ever encountered. If there was a mind here, it was incomprehensibly different—indeed, likely no mind at all. Still, he tried to find some pattern, some plan to the Night Land. A rationale.

He could not.

Just before the tallest hills stood growths like the tangled roots of upended trees, leafless, barren, dozens of meters high and stretching in ugly, twisted forests several kilometers across. A kind of pathway reached from the northern wall of the Redoubt, through the demarcation, into a tortured terrain of what looked like huge strands of melted and drawn glass, and to the east of the castle. The path continued to drop behind a closer hill, and he could not see where it terminated.

The atmosphere around the Redoubt was remarkably clear, though columns of twisted mist rose around the Night Land. Before a wall of blue haze at some fifty kilometers distance, everything stood out with complete clarity.

Olmy turned away at a knock on his door. Plass entered, wearing a look of contentment that seemed ready to burst into enthusiasm. "Now do you doubt me?"

"I doubt everything," Olmy said. "I'd just as soon believe we've been captured and are being fed delusions."

"Do you think that's what's happened?" Plass asked, eyes narrowing as if she had been insulted.

"No," Olmy said. "I've experienced some pretty good delusions in training. This is real, whatever that means."

"I must admit the little twins are busy," Plass said, sitting on a small chair near the table. These and a small mattress on the floor were the only items of furniture in the room. "They're talking to anybody who knows anything about Enoch's gate openers. I don't think you can talk to the same person twice here in an hour—unless it's Enoch."

Olmy nodded. He was still digesting Enoch's claim that the Office of Way Maintenance had sent an expedition with secret orders . . . In collusion with the opener's guild. Perhaps the twins knew more than he did, or Plass. "Did you ever hear anything about an official mission?" he asked.

Plass did not answer for a moment. "Not in so many words. Not 'official.' But perhaps not without strong support from Way Maintenance. We never did believe we were outlaws."

"You've both talked about completion. Was that mentioned when you joined the group?"

"Only in passing. A theory."

Olmy turned back to the window. "There's a camera obscura near the top of the pyramid. I'd like to look over everything around us, try to make sense of our position."

"Useless," Plass said. "I'd wait for a visitation first."

"More ghosts?"

Plass shrugged her shoulders and stretched out her legs, rubbing her knees.

"I haven't been visited," Olmy said.

"It will happen," Plass said flatly. She appeared to be hiding something, something that worried her. "I wouldn't look forward to it. But then, there's nothing you can do to prepare."

Olmy laughed, but the laugh sounded hollow. He felt as if he were slowly coming unraveled, like Enoch's bundle of relived world-lines. "How would I know if I've seen a ghost?" he asked. "Maybe I have—on Thistledown. Maybe they're around us all the time, but don't reveal themselves."

Plass looked to one side, then said, with an effort, her voice half-choking, "I've met my own ghost."

"You didn't mention that before."

"It came to visit me the night after we left Thistledown. It told me we would reach the pyramid."

Olmy held back another laugh, afraid it might get loose and never stop. "I've never seen a ghost of myself. What's that experience like?"

Crazy to even ask.

"We do things differently, then. I seemed to be working backward from some experience with the allthing. A ghost lets you remember the future, or some alternate of the future. Maybe in time I'll be told what the allthing will do to me."

Olmy considered this in silence. Plass's somber gray eyes focused on him, clear, child-like in their perfect gravity. Now he saw the resemblance, the reason why he felt a tug of liking for her. She reminded him of Sheila Ap Nam, his first wife on Lamarckia.

"Your loved ones, friends, colleagues . . . They will see you, versions of you, if you meet the allthing." Plass said. "Remembrance. A kind of immortality." She looked down and clutched her arms. "No other intelligent species we've encountered has a history of myths about spirits. No experience with ghosts. You know that? We're unique. Alone. Except perhaps the Jarts . . . and we don't know much about them, do we?"

Olmy needed to get rid of this topic. "What are the twins planning?"

"They seem to regard all of this as a challenging game. Who knows? They're working. It's even possible they'll think of something. I've come to admire them, in a way. A limited way."

Olmy aimed the binoculars toward the Watcher, its single glowing eye forever turned toward the Redoubt. He felt a bone-deep revulsion and hatred, mixed with a desiccating chill. His tongue seemed frosted. Perversely, the flesh behind his eyes felt hot and moist. His neck hair pricked.

"There's—" he began, but then flinched and blinked. A curtain of shadow passed through the few centimeters between him and the window. He backed off with a groan and tried to push something away, but the curtain would not be touched. It whirled around him, swept before Plass, who tracked it calmly, and then seemed to press against and slip through the opposite wall.

The warmth behind his eyes felt hot as steam.

"*I knew it!*" he said hoarsely. "I could feel it coming! Something about to happen." His hands trembled. He had never reacted so drastically to physical danger.

"That was nothing," Plass said. "I've seen them many times, more since I first came here."

Olmy's reaction angered him. "What is it?"

"Not a ghost, not any other version of ourselves, that's for sure," she said. "A parasite, maybe, like a flea darting around our world-lines. Harmless, as far as I know. But much more visible here than back on Thistledown."

Trying to control himself was backfiring. All his instincts rejected what he was experiencing. "I don't accept any of this!" he shouted. His hands spasmed into fists. "None of it makes sense!"

"I agree," Plass said, her voice low. "Pity we're stuck with it. Pity you're stuck with me. But more pity still that I'm stuck with *you*. It seems you try to be a rational man, Ser Olmy. My husband was exceptionally rational. The allthing adores rational men."

6

Rasp and Karn walked with Olmy on the parapet near the peak of the Redoubt. Their work seemed to have sobered them. They still walked like youngsters, Karn or Rasp lagging to peer at something in the Night Land and then scurrying to catch up; but their voices were steady, serious, even a little sad.

"We've never experienced anything like the lesion," Karn said. The huge dark disk, rimmed in bands and flares of red, blotted out the opposite side of the Way. "It's much more than just a failed gate. It doesn't stop here, you know."

"How do you mean?" Olmy asked.

"Something like this influences the entire Way. When the gate got out of control—"

Rasp took Karn's hand and tugged it in warning.

"What does it matter?" Karn asked, and shook her twin loose. "There can't be secrets here. If we don't agree to do something, the allthing will get us soon anyway, and then we'll be planted out there . . . bits and pieces of us, like lost and broken toys."

Rasp dropped back a few steps and folded her arms in pique. Karn continued. "When the lesion formed, gate openers felt it in every new gate. Threads trying to get through, like spider-silk. We can see the world-lines being twirled here . . . But they bunch up and wind around the Way even where we can't see them. Master Ry Ornis thought—"

"Enough!" Rasp said, rushing to catch up.

Karn stopped with tears in her eyes and glared over the parapet wall.

"I can guess a few things," Olmy said. "What Deirdre Enoch says leaves little enough to imagine. You aren't failed apprentices, are you?"

Rasp stared at him defiantly.

"No," Karn said.

Her twin turned and lifted a hand as if to strike her, then dropped it by her side. She drew a short breath, said, "We act like children because of the mathematical conditioning. Too fast. Ry Ornis told us we were needed. He accelerated training. We were the best, but we *are* too young. It holds us down."

A sound like hundreds of voices in a bizarre chorus floated over the Night Land, through the field that protected the Redoubt's atmosphere. The chorus alternately rose and sank through scales, hooting forlornly like apes in a zoo.

"Ry Ornis thought the lesion was bending world-lines even beyond Thistledown," Karn said. Rasp nodded and held her sister's hand. "Climbing back along the Thistledown's worldline . . .

where all our lives bunch together with the lives of our ancestors. Using us as a ladder."

"Not just us," Rasp added. The hooting chorus now came from all around the Redoubt. From this side of the pyramid, they could see a slender obelisk the colors of bright moon on an oil slick. The obelisk rose inside an immense scaffold made of parts of bodies, arms and legs strapped together with cords. These limbs were monstrous, however, fully dozens of meters long, and the obelisk had climbed within its scaffolding to at least a kilometer in height, twice as tall as the Redoubt.

The region around the construction crawled with pale tubular bodies, like insect larva, and Olmy decided it was these bodies that were doing most of the singing and hooting.

"Right," Karn agreed. "Not just us. Using the branching lines of all the matter, all the particles in Thistledown and the Way."

"Who knows how far it's reached?" Rasp asked.

"What can it do?" Olmy asked.

"We don't know," Karn said.

"What can *we* do?"

"Oh, we can close down the lesion, if we act quickly," Rasp said with a broken smile. "That shouldn't be too difficult."

"It's actually growing smaller," Karn said. "We can create a ring gate from here . . . A cirque. Cinch off the Way. The Way will shrink back towards the source, the maintenance machinery in the sixth chamber, very quickly—a million kilometers a day. We might even be able to escape along the flaw, but—"

"The flaw will act weird if we make a cinch," Rasp finished.

"Very weird," Karn agreed. "So we probably won't get home. We knew that. Ry Ornis prepared us. He told us that much."

"Besides, if we did go back to Thistledown, who would want us now, the way we are?" Rasp asked. "We're pretty broken inside."

The twins paused on the parapet. Olmy watched as they clasped hands and began to hum softly to each other. Their clavicles hung from their shoulders, and the cases tapped as they swayed. Rasp glanced at Olmy, primming her lips.

"Enoch spoke of a plan by the Office of Way Maintenance," Olmy said. "She claims she was sent here secretly."

"We know nothing about that," Karn said guilelessly. "But that might not mean much. I don't think they would have trusted us."

"She also said that the allthing has some larger purpose in our own universe," Olmy continued. "Something that has to be completed, or our existence will be impossible."

Karn considered this quietly, a finger against her nose, then shook her head. "We heard her, but I don't see it," she said. "Maybe she's trying to justify herself."

"*We* do that all the time," Rasp said. "We understand that sort of thing."

They had reached the bottom of the stairs leading up to the peak and the camera obscura. Karn climbed two steps at a time, her robe swinging around her ankles, and Rasp followed with more dignity. Olmy stayed near the bottom.

Rasp turned and looked down on him. "Come on," she said, waving.

Olmy shook his head. "I've seen enough. I can't make sense out of anything out there. I think it's random—just nonsense."

"Not at all!" Rasp said, and descended a few steps, beseeching him to join her. "We have to see what happened to the openers' clavicles, if they're still out there. It could be important."

Olmy hunched his shoulders, shook his head like a bull trying to build courage. Then he followed her up the steps.

The camera obscura was a spherical all-focal lens, its principle not unlike that of the ray-tracing binoculars. Mounted on a tripod on the flat platform at the peak of the pyramid, it projected and magnified the Night Land for anyone standing on the platform. Approaching the tripod increased magnification in logarithmic steps, with precise quickness; distances of a few tenths of a centimeter could make objects zoom to alarming proportions. Monitors on the peripheral circle, small spheres on steel poles, rolled in and out with slow grace, tracking the developments in the Night Land and sending their results down to Enoch and the others inside.

Olmy deftly avoided the monitors and walked slowly, with great concentration, around the circle. Karn and Rasp made their own surveys.

Olmy stopped and drew back to take in the Watcher's immense eye. The angle of the hairless brow, the droop of the upper lid, gave it a sad and corpse-like lassitude, but the eye still moved in small arcs, and from this perspective, there was no doubt it was observing the Redoubt. Olmy felt that it saw him, knew him; had he ever met the opener, before his mission to Lamarckia, perhaps by accident? Was there some residual memory of Olmy in that immense head? Olmy thought such a connection might be very dangerous.

"The Night Land changes every hour, sometimes small changes, sometimes massive," Enoch said, walking slowly and deliberately up the steps behind them. She stopped outside the camera's circle. "It tracks our every particle. It's patient."

"Does it fear us?" Olmy asked.

"No fear. We haven't even begun to be played with."

"That out there is not elaboration—it's pointless madness."

"I thought so myself," Enoch said. "Now I see a pattern. The longer I'm here, the more I sympathize with the allthing. Do you understand what I told you earlier? It *recognizes* us, Ser Olmy. It sees its own work in us, a cycle waiting to be completed."

Rasp held a spot within the circle and motioned for Karn to join her. Together, they peered at something in complete absorption, ignoring Enoch.

Olmy could not ignore her, however. He needed to resolve this question. "The Office of Way Maintenance sent you here to confirm that?"

"Not in so many words, but . . . Yes. We know that our own

domain, our home universe outside the Way, should have been born barren, empty. Something quickened it, fed it with the necessary geometric nutrients. Some of us thought that would only be possible if the early universe made a connection with a domain of very different properties. I told Ry Ornis that such a quickening need not have happened at the beginning. We could do it now. We had the Way . . . We could perform the completion. There was such a feeling of power and justification within the guild. I encouraged it. The connection has been made . . . And all that, the Night Land, is just a side effect. Pure order flowing back through the Way, through Thistledown, back through time to the beginning. Was it worth it? Did we do what we had planned? I'll never know conclusively, because we can't reverse it now . . . and cease to be."

"You weren't sure. You knew this could be dangerous, harm the Way fatally if the Jarts gained an advantage?"

Enoch stared at him for a few seconds, eyes moving from his eyes to his lips, his chest, as if she would measure him. "Yes," she said. "I knew. Ry Ornis knew. The others did not."

"They suffered for what you've learned," Olmy said.

Enoch's gaze steadied and her jaw clenched. "I've suffered, too. I've learned so very little, Ser Olmy. What I learn repeats itself over and over again, and it has more to do with arrogance than metaphysics."

"We've found one!" Karn shouted. "There's a clavicle mounted on top of the green castle. We can pinpoint it!"

Olmy stood where Rasp indicated. At the top of the squat, massive green castle stood a cube, half-hidden behind a mass of root-like growth. On top of the cube, a black pillar about the height of a man supported the unmistakable sphere-and-handles of a clavicle. The sphere was dark, dormant; nothing moved around the pillar or anywhere on the castle roof.

"There's only one, and it appears to be inactive," Rasp said. "The lesion is independent."

Karn spread her arms, wiggling her fingers. A wide smile lit up her face. "We can make a cirque!"

"We can't do it from here," Rasp said. "We have to go out there."

Enoch's face tensed into a rigid mask. "We haven't finished," she said. "The work isn't done!"

Olmy shook his head. He'd made his decision. "Whoever started this, and for whatever reason, it has to end now. The Nexus orders it."

"They don't know!" Enoch cried out.

"We know enough," Olmy said.

Rasp and Karn held each other's hand and descended the stairs. Rasp stuck her tongue out at the old woman.

Enoch laughed and lightly slapped her hands on her thighs. "They're only children! They won't succeed. What have I to fear from failed apprentices?"

The Night Land's atmosphere was a thin haze of primordial hydrogen, mixed with carbon dioxide and some small trace of oxygen from the original envelope surrounding the gate. At seven hundred millibars of pressure, and with a temperature just above freezing, they could venture out of the Redoubt in the most basic pressurized worksuits.

Enoch and her remaining, ever-changing people would not help them. Olmy preferred it that way. He walked through the empty corridors of the pyramid's ground floor and found a small wheeled vehicle that at one time had been used to reach the garden outside the Redoubt—a garden that now lay beyond the demarcation.

Plass showed him how the open vehicle worked. "It has its own pilot, makes a field around the passenger compartment."

"It looks familiar enough," Olmy said.

Plass sat next to Olmy and placed her hand on a control bar. "My husband and I used to tend our plot out there . . . flowers, herbs, vegetables. We'd drive one of these for a few hundred meters, outside the work zone, to where the materials team had spread soil brought through the first gate."

Olmy sat in the vehicle. It announced it was drawing a charge in case it would be needed. It then added, in a thin voice, "Will this journey last more than a few hours? I can arrange with the station master for—"

"No," Olmy said. "No need." He turned to Plass. "Time to put on a suit."

Plass stepped out of the car and nervously smoothed her hands down her hips. "I'm staying here. I can't bring myself to go out there again."

"I understand."

"I don't see how you'll survive."

"It looks very chancy," Olmy admitted.

"Why can't they open a ring gate from here?"

"Rasp and Karn say they have to be within five hundred meters of the lesion. About where the other clavicle is now."

"Do you know what my husband was, professionally? Before we came here?"

"No."

"A neurologist. He came along to study the effects of our experiment on the researchers. There was some thought our minds would be enhanced by contact with the ordered domain. They were all very optimistic." She put her hand on Olmy's shoulder. "We had faith. Enoch still believes what they told her, doesn't she?"

Olmy nodded. "May I make one last request?"

"Of course," Plass said.

"Enoch promised us she would open a way through the demarcation and let us through. She claimed we couldn't do anything out there but be taken in by the allthing, anyway . . ."

Plass smiled. "I'll watch her, make sure the fields are open long enough for you to go through. The guild was very clever, sending you and the twins, you know."

"Why?"

"You're all very deceptive. You all seem to be failures." Plass clenched his shoulder, then turned and left as Rasp and Karn entered the storage chamber. The twins watched her go in silence. They carried their clavicles and had already put on their pressure suits, which had adjusted to tightly fit their small frames.

"We've always made her uncomfortable," Rasp said. "Maybe I don't blame her."

Karn regarded Olmy with deep black eyes. "You haven't met a ghost of yourself, have you?"

"I haven't," Olmy said.

"Neither have we. And that's significant. We're never going to reach the allthing. It's never going to get us."

7

They cursed the opening of the Way and the change of the Thistledown's mission. They assassinated the Way's creator, Konrad Korzenowski. For centuries they maintained a fierce opposition, largely underground, but with connections to the Naderites in power. In any given year there might be only four or five active members of this most radical sect, the rest presuming to lead normal lives; but the chain was maintained. All this because their original leader had a vision of the Way as an easy route to infinite hells.

—*Lives of the Opposition*, Anonymous, Journey Year 475

The three rode the tiny wheeled vehicle over a stretch of bare Way floor, a deeply tarnished copper-bronze colored surface of no substance whatsoever, and no friction at this point. They kept their course with little jets of air expelled from the sides of the car, until they reached a broad low island of glassy materials, just before the boundary markers that warned they were coming to the demarcation.

As agreed, the traction lines switched to low power, and an

opening appeared directly ahead of them—a clarified darkness in the pale green field. This relieved Olmy somewhat; he had had some doubts that Enoch would cooperate, or that Plass could compel her. The vehicle rolled through. They crossed the defenses.

Behind them, the fields went up again.

Now the floor of the Way was covered with sandy soil. The autopilot switched off the air jets and let the vehicle roll for another twenty meters.

The pressure suits were already becoming uncomfortable; they were old, and while they did their best to fit, their workings were in less than ideal condition. Still, they would last several weeks, recycling gases and liquids and complex molecules, rehydrating the body through arterial inserts and in the same fashion providing a minimal diet.

Olmy doubted the suits would be needed for more than a few more hours.

The twins ignored their discomfort and focused their attention on the lesion. Outside the pyramid, the lesion seemed to fill the sky, and in a few kilometers it would be almost directly overhead. From this angle, the hairlike swirls of spinning world-lines already took on a shimmering reflective quality, like bands sliced from a wind-ruffled lake; their passage sang in Olmy's skull, more through his teeth than through his ears.

The full character of the Night Land came on gradually, beginning with a black, gritty, loose scrabble beneath the vehicle's tires. Olmy's suit readout, shining directly into his left eye, showed a decrease in air pressure of a few millibars beyond the demarcation. The temperature remained steady, just above zero degrees Celsius.

They turned west, to their left as they faced north down the Way, and came upon the path Olmy had seen from the peak of the pyramid. Plass had identified it as the road used by vehicles carrying material from the first gate Enoch had opened. It had also been the path to Plass's garden, the one she had shared with her husband. Within a few minutes, about three kilometers from the Redoubt, passing over the rise that had blocked his view, they came across the garden's remains.

The relief here was very low, but the rise of some fifty meters had been sufficient to hide what must have been among the earliest attempts at elaboration. Olmy was not yet sure he believed in the allthing, but what had happened in the garden, and in the rest of the Night Land, made any disagreement moot. The trees in the southwest corner of the orchard had spread out low to the ground, and glowed now with a galaxy of sparks, much like the body of Number 2, their silhouettes flickering like frames in a child's flipbook. The rest of the orchard had simply turned to glittering ash.

In the center, however, rose a mound of gnarled brown shot through with vivid reds and greens, and in the middle of this mound, facing almost due south, not looking at anything in particular, was a face some three meters in height, its skin the color of green wood, with several broad cracks running from crown to chin. The face did not move or exhibit any sign of life.

Puffs of dust rose from the ash, tiny little explosions from within this mixture of realities. The ash quickly writhed and filled in to erase the newly-formed craters. It seemed to have some purpose of its own, as did everything else in the garden but the face.

Ruin and elaboration; one form of life extinguished, another imbued.

"Early," Karn said, looking to their right as a sprawl of shining dark green leaves stretched, expanded, and braided into eye-twisting knots. "Didn't know what it was dealing with."

"Doesn't look like it ever did," Olmy said, realizing she was speaking as if some central director actually did exist.

Rasp set her sister straight. "Geometry is the living tissue of reality. We've seen textbook studies of gates gone wrong. Mix constants and you get a—"

"We've sworn not to discuss the failures," Karn said, but without any strength.

"We are being driven through the worst failure of all," Rasp said. "Mixed constants and skewed metrics can explain all of this."

Karn shrugged. Olmy thought that perhaps it did not matter; perhaps Rasp and Karn and Plass did not really disagree, merely described the same thing in different ways. What they were seeing up close was not random rearrangement; it had a demented, even a vicious quality, that suggested purpose.

Above the rows of flip-book trees and the living layers of ash stretched a dead and twisted sky. From the hideous black chancre, with its sullen ring of congealed red, depended curtains of rushing darkness that swept the Night Land like rain beneath a moving front.

"Mother's hair," Karn said, and clutched her clavicle tightly in white-knuckled hands.

"She's playing with us," Rasp said. "Bending over us, waving her hair over our crib. We reach up to grab and she pulls away."

"She laughs," Karn said.

"Then she gives us to the—"

Rasp did not have time to finish. The vehicle swerved abruptly with a small squeak before a sudden chasm that had not been there an instant before. Out of the chasm leaped white shapes, humanlike but doughy and featureless—fungal. They seemed to be both expelled and to climb out, and they lay on the sandy black-streaked ground for a moment, as if recovering from their birth. Then they rose to loose and wobbling feet and ran with speed and even grace over the irregular landscape to the trees, which they began to uproot. These were the laborers Olmy had seen from the pyramid. They paid no attention to the intruders.

The chasm closed, and Olmy instructed the car to continue.

"Is that what we'll become?" Karn asked.

"Each of us will become *many* of them," Rasp said.

"Such a relief to know!" Karn said sardonically.

The rotating shadows ahead gave the ground a blurred and frantic aspect, like unfocused time-lapse photography. Only the major landmarks stood unchanged by the sweeping curtains of revision: the Watcher, pale beam lancing out from its unblinking eye, the Castle with its unseen giant occupant, and the obelisk with its scaffold and hordes of white figures working directly beneath the lesion.

Olmy ordered the vehicle to stop, but Rasp grabbed his hand. "Farther," she said. "We can't do anything here."

Olmy threw back his head, then grimaced like a monkey in the oldest forest of all, baring his teeth at this measureless madness.

"Farther!" Karn insisted. The car rolled on, jolting over the regular ridges some or other force had pushed up in the sand.

Above the constant sizzle of rearranged world-lines, like a symphony of scrubbing and tapping brooms, came more sounds. If a burning forest could sing its pain, Olmy thought, it would be like the rising wail that escaped from the tower and the Castle. Thousands of white figures made thousands of different sounds, as if trying to talk to each other but not succeeding. Mock speech, sing-song pidgin nonsense, attempts to communicate emotions and thoughts they could not truly have; protests at being jabbed and pulled and jiggled along the scaffolding of the tower, over the uneven ground, like puppets directed by something trying to mock any process of construction.

Olmy's body had up to this moment sent him a steady blood-wash of fear. He had controlled this emotion as well as he could, but never ignored it; that would have been senseless and wrong, for fear was what told him he came from a world that made sense, that held together and was consistent, that *worked*.

Yet fear was not enough, could not be an adequate response to what they were seeing. This was a threat beyond anything the body had been designed to experience. Had he allowed himself to scream, he could not have screamed loudly enough.

The Death we all know, Olmy told himself, is an end to something real; death here would be worse than nightmare, worse than the hell one imagines for one's enemies and unbelievers.

"I know," Karn said, and her hands shook on the clavicle.

"What do you know?" Rasp asked.

"Every meter, ever second, every dimension has its own mind here," Karn said. "Space and time are arguing, fighting."

Rasp disagreed violently. "There are no minds, no minds at all!" she insisted.

Light itself began to waver and change as they came closer to the tower. Olmy could see the face of oncoming events before they occurred, like waves on a beach, rushing over the land, impatient to reach their destinations, their observers, before all surprise had been lost.

They now entered the fringes of shadow. The revisions of their surroundings felt like deep drumming pulses. Caught directly in a shadow, Olmy felt a sudden rub of excitement. He saw flashes of colors, felt a spectrum of unfamiliar emotions that threatened to cancel out his fear. He looked to his left, into the counterclockwise sweep, anticipating each front of darkness, leaning toward it. Ecstasy, followed by a buzz of exhilaration, suddenly a spasm of brilliance—all the while the back of his head crisping and glowing and sparking. He could *see* into the back of his brain, down to the working foundations of every thought; where symbols with no present meaning are painted and arrayed on long tables, then jerked and jostled until they become emotions and memories and words.

"Like opening a gate!" Karn shouted, seeing Olmy's expression. "Much worse. Dangerous! Very dangerous!"

"Don't ignore it, don't suppress," Rasp told him. "Just pay attention to what's right before you. That's what they teach us when we open a gate!"

"These aren't gates!" Olmy shouted above the hideous symphony of brooms. The twins' heads jerked and vibrated as he spoke.

"They *are!*" Rasp said. "Little gates into directly adjacent worlds. They're trying to escape their neighboring realities, to split away, but the lesion gathers them, holds them. They flow back behind us, along our world-lines."

"Back to the beginning!" Karn said.

"Back to our birth!" Rasp said.

"Here!" Karn said, and Olmy brought the car to a stop. The two assistants, little more than girls, with pale faces and wide eyes and serious expressions climbed down from the open cab and marched resolutely across the rippled sand, leaning into the pressure of other streams of reality. Their clothes changed color, their hair changed its arrangement, even their skin changed color, but they marched until the clavicles seemed to lift of their own will.

Rasp and Karn faced each other.

Olmy told himself, with whatever was left of his mind, that they were now going to attempt a cirque, a ring gate, that would bring all this to a meeting with the flaw. Within the flaw lay the peace of incommensurable contradictions, pure and purifying. Within the flaw this madness would burn to less than nothing, to paradoxes that would cancel and expunge.

He did not think they would have time to escape, even if the shrinking of the Way was less than instantaneous.

He stood on the seat of the car for a moment, watching the twins, admiring them. *Enoch underestimated them. As have I. This is what Ry Ornis wanted, why he chose them.*

He hunched his shoulders: something coming. Before he could duck or jump aside, Olmy was caught between two folds of shadow, like a bug snatched between fingers, and lifted bodily from the car. He twisted his neck and looked back to see a fuzzy image of the car, the twins raising their clavicles, the rippled and streaked sand. The car seemed to vibrate, the tire tracks rippling behind it like snakes; and for a long moment, the twins and the car were not visible at all, as if they had never been.

Olmy's thoughts raced and his body shrieked with joy. Every

nerve shivered, and all his memories stood out together in sharp relief, with different selves viewing them all at once. He could not distinguish between present and future; all were just parts of different memories. His reference point had blurred to where his life was a flat field, and within that field swam myriad possibilities. What would happen, what had happened, became indistinguishable from the unchosen and unlived moments that *could* happen.

This blurring of his world-line rushed backward. He felt he could sidle across fates into what was fixed and unfix it, free his past to be all possible, all potential, once more. But the diffusion, the smearing and blending of the chalked line of his life, came up against the moment of his resurrection, the abrupt shift from Lamarckia—

And could not go any further. Dammed, the tide of his life spilled out in all directions. He cried out in surprise and a kind of pain he had never known before.

Olmy hung suspended beneath the dark eye, spinning slowly, all things above and below magnified or made minute depending on his angle. The pain passed. Perhaps it had never been. He felt as if his head had become a tiny but all-seeing camera obscura.

There was a past in which Ry Ornis accompanied the twins; he saw them working together near a very different vehicle, tractor rather than small car, to make the cirque. Already they had forced the Way to extrude a well through the sand. A cupola floated over the well, brazen and smooth, reflecting in golden hues the flaw, the lesion.

Olmy turned his head a fraction of a centimeter and once more saw only the twins, but this time dead, lying mangled beside the car, their clavicles flaring and burning. Another degree or two, and they were resurrected, still working. Ry Ornis was with them again.

A memory: Ry Ornis had traveled with them in the flawship. How could Olmy have lost this basic fact?

He rotated again, this time around a new and unfamiliar

dimension, and felt the Way simply cease to exist, and his own life with it. From this dark and soundless eventuality, he turned with a bitter, acrid wrench and found a very narrow course through the gripping shadows, a course illumined by half-forgotten emotions that had been plucked like flowers, arranged like silent speech.

He had been carried to the other side of the lesion, looking north down the endless throat of the Way. The gripping baleen of shadow from the whale's mouth of the lesion, the driving cilia whisking him between world-lines, drove him under and over a complex surface through which he could see a deep mountainous valley, its floor smooth and vitreous like obsidian. Black glass, reflecting the lesion, the flaw behind the lesion, scudding layers of mist. The cilia that controlled Olmy's orientation let him drop to a few meters above the vitreous black floor.

Motion stopped. His thoughts slowed. He felt only one body, one existence. All his lines clumped back into one flow.

He tried to close his eyes, to not see, but that was impossible. He faced down and saw his reflection in the mirror-shiny valley floor, a small still man floating beneath the red-rimmed eye like an intruding mote. On either side of the valley rose jagged glassy peaks, mountain ranges like shreds of pulled taffy. A few hundred meters ahead of him, or perhaps a few kilometers, mounted in the middle of the valley lay something he recognized: a Jart defensive emplacement, white as ivory, jagged spikes thrusting like a sea urchin's spines from a squat discus. Shaded cilia played around the spikes, but the spikes did not track, did not move.

The emplacement was dead.

Olmy held his hands in front of his face. He could see them, see through them, with equal clarity. Nothing was obscured, nothing neglected by his new vision.

He tried to speak, or perhaps to pray, to whatever it was that held him, directed his motion. He asked first if anything was there, listening. No answer. He remembered Plass's comments about the allthing: that in its domain it was unique, had never learned the arts of communication, was *one* without other and controlled all by *being all*. No separation between mind and matter, observed and observer. Such a being could neither listen nor answer.

Nor could it change.

He thought of the emotions arrayed along the path that had guided him here. Pain, disappointment, fear. Weariness. Had the allthing learned this method of communication after its time in the Way? Had it dissected and rearranged enough human elements to change its nature this much?

Why pain? Olmy asked, spoken but unheard in the stillness.

He moved north down the center of the valley, over the dead Jart emplacement. Past the frozen spikes, his reflection again shimmered in the floor's uneven black mirror. He looked east up the long curves of the Way beyond the jagged mountains, and saw more Jart emplacements, the spiral and beaded walls of what looked like Jart settlements, all abandoned, all spotted with large, distorted shapes he could not begin to comprehend.

Olmy thought, *It's made a Night Land for the Jarts. It does not know any difference between us.*

As if growing used to the extraordinary pressure of the shadow cilia gripping him, his body once more sent signals of fear, then simple, childlike wonder, and finally its own exhaustion. Olmy's head rolled on his shoulders and he felt his body sleep, but his mind remained alert. All his muscles tingled as they went off-line and would not respond to his tentative urgings.

How much time passed, if it were possible for time to pass, he could not judge. The tingling stopped and control returned. He lifted his head and saw a different valley, this one lined with huge figures. If the scale he had assumed at the beginning of his journey was still valid, these monolithic sculptures or shapes or beings— whatever they might be—were fully two or three kilometers distant, and therefore hundreds of meters in height. They were so strange he found himself looking at them in his peripheral vision, to avoid the confusion of placing them at the points of his visual focus. While vaguely organic in design—compound curves, folds of what might have been a semblance of tissue weighted by gravity, a kind of multilateral symmetry—the figures simply refused to be analyzed.

Olmy had many times experienced a lapse of visual judgment, when he would look at something in his living quarters and not remember it right away, and because of dim lighting or an unfamiliar angle, be unable to judge what it was. Under those conditions, he could feel his mind making hypotheses, trying desperately to compare them with what he was looking directly at, to reach some valid conclusion, and so actually *see* the object. This had occurred to him many times on Lamarckia, especially with regard to objects unique to that planet.

Here, he had no prior experience, no memory, no physical training or familiarity whatsoever with what he looked at, so he saw *nothing* sensible, nameable, to which he could begin to relate. Slowly, it dawned on Olmy that these might be more trophies of the allthing's encounters with Jarts.

He was drifting down a rogue's gallery of failed models, failed attempts to duplicate and understand, much like the gallery of objects and conditions around the Redoubt that made up the Night Land.

Humans had approached from one end of the Way, Jarts from the other. The allthing had applied similar awkward tools to both, either to unify them into its being, or to find some new method of experiencing their otherness.

Both had been incomprehensibly alien to the allthing.

Pain. One of the emotions borrowed from Olmy's mind and arrayed along the pathway. A sense of disunification, unwanted change. The allthing had been disturbed by this entry; there was no evil, no enthusiastic destruction, in the Night Land. Olmy suddenly saw what Enoch had been trying to communicate to him, and went beyond her own understanding.

A monobloc of pure order had been invaded by a domain whose main character was that of disunity and contradiction. That must have been very painful indeed. And this quality of order was being sucked backward, like gas into a vacuum, into their domain.

Enoch and the guild of gate openers had manufactured the tip of a tooth. They had thrust into this other domain the bloody predatorial tooth of a hungry universe seeking quickening, a completion at its own beginning.

But this hypothesis did not instantly open any floodgate of comprehension or communication. Olmy did not find himself suddenly analyzing the raw emotional outbursts of another mind, godlike or otherwise; the allthing was not a mind in any sense he could understand. It was simply a pure and necessary set of qualities. It gripped him, controlled him, but literally had no use for him. Like everything else here, it could neither analyze nor absorb him. It could not even spread back along his world-line, for Olmy's existence had begun over with this new body, with his resurrection.

That was why he had not met any ghosts of himself. Physically, he had almost no past. The allthing, if such existed, had flung him along this valley of waste and failure, another piece of detritus, even more frustrating than most.

He squirmed, his body struggling to break free like an animal in a cage. Panic overwhelmed him despite his best efforts. Olmy could not locate any point of reference within; not even a self was clearly defined.

Everything blurred, became confused, as if he had been smudged by an enormous finger and no outline remained. *I am no where, now here, no name, moving, no future*

He twisted, convulsed, trying to find his center. The figures mounted on the ranges of mountains to either side seemed interested in this effort. He could feel their attention and did not welcome it. He fancied they moved, however slowly, advancing toward him across astronomical time.

If this lump of conflicting order and chaos could define himself anew, perhaps these incomprehensible monoliths, these unworshipped gods and unrealized mockeries, could establish a presence as well.

The panic stopped.

Signals stopped.

He had come to an end. That minimum condition he had wished for was now upon him.

He cared nothing for past or future, had lost nothing, gained nothing.

I am or was a part of a society really no part of any

This name is Olmy Ap Sennen

Lover of many loved and loving by few

Contact nothing without

Without contact nothing

Uprooted tree

The lesion's inflamed rim began to brighten. The suspended and aimless figure in its gripping cilia of probabilities maintained enough structure and drive to be interested in this, and noted that compared to past memory, the lesion was much smaller, much darker, and the flaring rim much broader. It resembled an immense solar eclipse with a bloody corona.

Loyalties and loves uprooted

Language itself faded until the aimless figure saw only images, the lushness of another world out of reach, closed off, the faces of old humans once loved once reassuringly close now dead and without ghosts.

Can't even be haunted by a past uprooted

The figure's motion down the valley slowed. No time passed. Eveternity, endless now. Naked, skinless, fleshless, boneless. Consumed, integrated.

Experiences stillness.

Mark this in an endless column: *experiences*

Experiences stillness

stillness

stillness

No divisions. A tiny place no bigger than a fist a womb. Tiny place of infinite peace at the heart of a frozen geometry. All elaboration, variation, permutation, long since exhausted; infinite access to unbounded energy contained in oneness.

You/I/We no difference. See?

See. Vidya. *All seeing. Eye of Buddha. Nerveless kalpas of some body. Nerve vanity.*

This oneness consumed. Many nows, peace past.

At peace in the past. Loved women, raised children, lived a long life on a world to which there is no returning.

Nothing one at peace in no past all completed no returning.

Point.

One makes possible all.

I see. Buddha, do not leave your student bound.

The eye is shrinking, closing, its gorgeous bloody flare dimming. It is pierced by a white needle visible behind the small dark center.

Small large no matter no time

Do not go. Take us with

Am your father/mother/food

loved raised living longing no return

my own ghost

8

Ry Ornis, the tall insect-thin master, smiled down on him. Olmy saw many of the master opener, like an avatar of an ancient god. All the different masters merged.

They were surrounded by a glassy tent. A slow breeze cooled his face. Ry Ornis had wrapped him in a rescue field where he fell, carrying safe cool air to replenish what his worksuit could no longer provide.

Olmy rediscovered scattered rivers of memory and bathed his ancient feet there. He swallowed once. The eye, the lesion, had shut forever. "It's gone," he said.

Ry Ornis nodded. "It's done."

"I can never tell anybody," Olmy realized out loud.

"You can never tell anybody."

"We robbed and ate to live. To be born."

Ry Ornis held his fingers to his lips, his face spectral in a new light from the south. A huge grin was spreading around half the Way, a gorgeous brilliant electric light. "The ring gate. A cirque," the gate opener said, glancing over his shoulder. "Rasp and Karn, my students, have done well. We've done what we came here to do, and we saved the Way, as well. Not bad, eh, Ser Olmy?"

Olmy reached up to grab the gate opener, perhaps to strangle him. Ry Ornis had moved, however.

Olmy turned away, swallowed a second time against a competing dryness. There had been no need to complete the ring gate. The unfinished cirque had done its job and drained the final wasted remnants of the lesion, forcing a closure.

As they watched, the cirque shrank. The grin became a smile became an all-knowing serene curve, then collapsed to a point, and the point dimmed on distant rippled sands.

"I think the twins are a little disappointed they can't finish the cirque. But it's wonderful," Ry Ornis enthused, and performed a small dance on the black obsidian of the valley floor. "They are truly masters now! When I am tried and convicted, they will take my place!"

The Way remained.

Rolling his head to one side, Olmy could not see the Redoubt. "Where's the pyramid?" he asked hoarsely.

"Enoch has her wish," Ry Ornis said, and shaded his eyes with one hand.

Plass, Enoch, the allthing.

Plass had seen her own ghost.

To east and west, the ruined mountains and their statues remained, rejected, discarded. No dream, no hallucination.

He had been used again. No matter. For an endless instant, like any gate opener, only more so, he had merged with the eye of the Buddha.

9

"The Infinite Hexamon Nexus does not approve of risky experiments that cannot be documented or explained. How many were deceived, Master Ry Ornis?"

"All, myself included."

"Yet you maintain this was done out of necessity?"

"All of it. The utmost necessity."

"Will this ever be necessary again? Answer honestly; the trust between us has worn very thin!"

"Never again."

"How do you explain that one universe, one domain, must feed on another in order to be born?"

"I don't. We were compelled. That is all I know."

"Could it have gone badly?"

"Of course. As it is, in our clumsiness and ignorance, we have condemned all our ancestors to live with unexplainable presences, ghosts of past and future. A kind of afterbirth."

"You are smiling, Master Gate Opener. This is intolerable!"

"It is all I can do, Sers."

. . .

"For your disobedience and arrogance, what punishment do you choose, Master Ry Ornis?"

"Sers of the Nexus. This I swear. I will put down my clavicle from this time forward, and never know the grace again."

— Sentencing Phase of Secret Hearings Conducted
by the Infinite Hexamon Nexus, "On the Advisability
of Opening Gates into Chaos and Order"

Tracting through the weightless forest of the Wald in the rebuilt Axis Nader, reaching out to the trees to push or grab roots and branches, half-flying and half-climbing, in his mind's river-wide eye, Olmy Ap Sennen returned to Lamarckia, where he had once nearly died of old age, and retrieved a package he had left there, tied in neat pieces of mat-paper. His wives and children had kept it safe for him, and now they returned it. There was much smiling and laughter, then saying of farewells, last of all a farewell to his sons, whom he had left behind. Occupants of a different land, another life.

As they faded, in his mind's eye, he opened the package they had given to him and greedily swallowed the wonderful contents.

His soul.

MDIO ECOSYSTEMS INCREASE KNOWLEDGE OF DNA LANGUAGES (2215 C.E.)

Henry Gee at Nature asked a select list of science fiction writers to contribute brief stories describing some future development in science. The series was great fun. My contribution was an attempt to write a review of recent discoveries as it might appear in Nature *some two centuries hence. Along the way, I got to pump my speculative views of genetics and biological development (expressed in detail in* Darwin's Radio, Vitals, *and* Darwin's Children*) as if they're part of an established paradigm. Talk about smug!*

The discovery of over 15,000 massive deep ice objects (MDIO) in orbit around supermassive planets in the close interstellar neighborhood has the potential to revolutionize our understanding of biological languages.

Phenotype-generating languages for terrestrial DNA-recorded life forms can be ranked closely according to kingdoms. Most plants, for example, express phylogeny according to the famous Zinn-Wang languages, first decoded in the mid-twenty-first century.

Archaea, commonly used as the Rosetta stone for all primitive DNA languages, have provided deep insights into nonterrestrial biologies that have advanced to the DNA level.

RNA languages in terrestrial viruses constitute a virtual Tower of Babel, indicating a degenerate and mutationally rich mix that can still compel replication in DNA hosts. Early RNA coding systems found outside the solar system, however, can often be translated into Archaean DNA based languages, and these may constitute the most basic fixed languages of life.

MDIOs are typically seven to nine Earth masses and consist of layers of water ice two to five thousand kilometers in depth, overlying a high-pressure liquid ocean (HPLO) that sits in turn on a rocky mantle. At the center is an iron- and sulfur-rich core.

The interior is warmed both by latent heat and radioactivity (chiefly thorium 90) and by tidal friction generated by interaction with the supermassive parent body. Temperatures in the HPLO can frequently exceed 130 degrees Celsius.

MDIOs may constitute the most common life-supporting bodies in the universe.

Neutronium self-guided probes (NSGP) have penetrated seven of these deep ice objects and have obtained remarkable data. Spin-off probes made of normal matter, transmuted from neutronium and released into the HPLO, perform *in situ* analysis of all carbon chemistry and send information to orbiting research stations.

What is most remarkable about MDIO biologies is that they can exist at all under these extraordinary conditions. Once again, it is demonstrated that life will begin and thrive anywhere there is liquid water and the necessary elements.

To date, RNA and DNA language analysis has been conducted on three HPLO ecosystems. Because of limited exploration ranges for the probes, the extent of these ecosystems is not known; however, every probed MDIO possesses life.

One of the ecosystems (MDIO 2341-a) is still in a "profligate" mutation-rich RNA phase, with no complex organisms and no DNA detected. Here, new genetic coding schemes may naturally emerge every few months, and competition between coding schemes is likely to be extreme. (The emergence of competent and stable genetic languages on Earth may have taken more than a billion years.)

The other two ecosystems (MDIO 5756-b, MDIO 349-x) have entered the more stable age of DNA and show remarkable similarities to each other.

The most striking feature of these ecosystems is how bright they are, since they are completely hidden from all starlight. The roving probes have sent back images of massive reef-like structures glowing as brightly as several full moons, surrounded by a thick, slowly churning mass of light-dependent microbes. Feeding on these microbes are living filter nets, fringed by corkscrew cilia, able to join into larger units or separate into smaller.

Tall spiral chimneys, like Baroque columns in a church, release water heated in the upper mantle, creating plumes that can extend for many kilometers. These plumes spread out at the upper ice layer, eroding smooth domes almost a hundred kilometers in diameter and usually less than a millimeter deep. These domes collect oxygen freed from the actions of photosynthetic organisms. Typically, within seconds the oxygen is forced back under extreme pressure into the water and the ice, but during this brief time, miniature forests of opportunistic organisms grow in the domes, extracting all the benefits from a more efficient oxygen metabolism.

The upper limit of organization in MDIO ecosystems is not known. Typical distributed-intelligence ecosystems are found here, and interact to form complex neuronal networks that govern MDIO life-cycles (as on Earth). However, no condensed nodal intelligences such as large animals have yet been found. Instead, intelligence seems frozen at a very early and distributed stage.

This may reflect the unlikelihood of any intelligences within the MDIO ever being challenged by major environmental change, much less being given a chance to observe the outside universe.

MDIOs seem to be remarkably stable over hundreds of millions of years.

The impossibility of emergence through the deep ice and escape into space limits the potential growth of concentrated hypothesis engines as defined by the Turing-Watteau diagram of novel information vs. expansion opportunity.

Some researchers suggest that the seeding of provocative artifacts ("Clarkeing") below the deep ice may encourage condensation of concentrated intelligences, or at the very least, induce some interesting emergent properties. The design of these artifacts is currently spurring intense debate.

As one chief communications researcher has asked, "How do you uplift slime?"

Harnessing of bacterial communities on Earth in the last century could provide a template for working with MDIO ecosystems, adding to the list of beings we can actually talk to.

HARDFOUGHT

I can't recall the list of magazines that rejected "Hardfought." At some 24,000 words, my novella was too long for most at the time; too weird and difficult for some. When I sent it to Isaac Asimov's Science Fiction Magazine, an interim editor caught the story and didn't know what to do with it. (Isaac Asimov did not buy stories for the magazine. He wrote editorials and answered letters, and visited the offices to spread good cheer.)

Asimov's future editor-in-chief, Shawna McCarthy, was enthusiastic, but she was not yet in control. Asimov's had become known for publishing fairly traditional stories, generally light and doggedly unpretentious. "Hardfought" is long and heavy and very pretentious.

I made a phone call and tried to persuade the interim editor to buy it. Certainly it was not your usual SF story, I said. I invoked the hallowed name of Joseph Conrad. I was desperate. I needed the money. "What if I cut it—a little?" I suggested. Pretty please. . . ?

The editor, still undecided, soon left to take another editorial position. Shawna McCarthy moved up, bought the story, made some cuts, slotted it for publication, and. . .

But let's go back a bit.

Jim Turner at Arkham House was waiting for me to write a masterpiece to cap off a proposed story collection. Jim is dead now, but I remember his voice very clearly, and cherish his contrarian sense of humor. I sent him "Hardfought." He phoned to tell me the bad news. It was a tough read, he confessed. He was not enthusiastic.

He read it four more times and called again.

Had he seen Babe, he might have said, "That'll do, Bear." What he actually said was, "All right, Bear. It's a masterpiece."

Asimov's published the story first. Shawna warned the magazine's readers that it was not the magazine's usual fare. She needn't have worried.

"Hardfought" and "Blood Music" picked up Nebula awards from the Science Fiction Writers of America, on the same evening. The Nebula Banquet that year (1984) was held on the Queen Mary in Long Beach Harbor. Seated at our table were my mother and father, my favorite college professor, Elizabeth Chater, her daughter Patty, and my wife Astrid. The ceremony was emceed by my good friend Gregory Benford, and the award was presented by my father-in-law, Poul Anderson. Karen Anderson, my mother-in-law, was present as well. A full house!

Need I say it was a great evening?

My first story collection, The Wind from a Burning Woman, was published in the spring of 1983 by Arkham House. It sold out its first print run in ninety days, and became the fastest selling book in Arkham House history.

A few years later, in 1986, I spoke briefly with Isaac Asimov at a SFWA Publisher's Reception in Manhattan. I had my infant son Erik strapped to my chest. Isaac was being ferried from interview to interview when he spotted my name tag, paused, lifted his eyebrows, and said, "So you're Greg Bear! I'm glad you weren't around when I was getting started!"

I beamed.

This may be the best story I've ever written.

In the Han Dynasty, historians were appointed by royal edict to write the history of Imperial China. They alone were the arbiters of what would be recorded. Although various emperors tried, none could gain access to the ironbound chest in which each document

*was placed after it was written. The historians preferred to suffer
death rather than betray their* trust.

*At the end of each reign the box would be opened and the docu-
ments published, perhaps to benefit the next emperor. But for these
documents, Imperial China, to a large extent, has no history.*

The thread survives by whim.

Humans called it the Medusa. Its long twisted ribbons of gas
strayed across fifty parsecs, glowing blue, yellow, and carmine.
Watery black flecked a central core of ghoulish green. Half a dozen
protostars circled the core, and as many more dim conglomerates
pooled in dimples in the nebula's magnetic field. The Medusa was
a huge womb of stars—and disputed territory.

Whenever Prufrax looked at the nebula in displays or through
the ship's ports, it seemed malevolent, like a zealous mother showing an ominous face to protect her children. Prufrax had never
had a mother, but she had seen them in some of the fibs.

At five, Prufrax was old enough to know the *Mellangee's* mission
and her role in it. She had already been through four ship-years
of indoctrination. Until her first battle she would be educated in
both the Know and the Tell. She would be exercised and trained
in the Mocks; in sleep she would dream of penetrating the huge
red-and-white Senexi seedships and finding the brood mind.
"Zap, Zap," she went with her lips, silent so the tellman wouldn't
think her thoughts were straying.

The tellman peered at her from his position in the center of
the spherical classroom. Her mates stared straight at the center, all
focusing somewhere around the tellman's spiderlike teaching desk,
waiting for the trouble, some fidgeting. "How many branch individuals in the Senexi brood mind?" he asked. He looked around the
classroom. Peered face by face. Focused on her again. "Pru?"

"Five," she said. Her arms ached. She had been pumped full of
moans the wake before. She was already three meters tall, in elfstate, with her long, thin limbs not nearly adequately fleshed out

and her fingers still crisscrossed with the surgery done to adapt them to the gloves.

"What will you find in the brood mind?" the tellman pursued, his impassive face stretched across a hammerhead as wide as his shoulders. Some of the fems thought tellmen were attractive. Not many, and Pru was not one of them.

"Yoke," she said.

"What is in the brood-mind yoke?"

"Fibs."

"More specifically? And it really isn't all fib, you know."

"Info. Senexi data."

"What will you do?"

"Zap," she said, smiling.

"Why, Pru?"

"Yoke has team gens-memory. Zap yoke, spill the life of the team's five branch inds."

"Zap the brood, Pru?"

"No," she said solemnly. That was a new instruction, only in effect since her class's inception. "Hold the brood for the supreme overs." The tellman did not say what would be done with the Senexi broods. That was not her concern.

"Fine," said the tellman. "You tell well, for someone who's always half-journeying."

Brainwalk, Prufrax thought to herself. Tellman was fancy with the words, but to Pru, what she was prone to do during Tell was brainwalk, seeking out her future. She was already five, soon six. Old. Some saw Senexi by the time they were four.

"Zap, Zap," she said softly.

Aryz skidded through the thin layer of liquid ammonia on his broadest pod, considering his new assignment. He knew the Medusa by another name, one that conveyed all the time and effort the Senexi had invested in it. The protostar nebula held few mysteries for him. He and his four branch-mates, who along with the all-important brood mind comprised one of the six teams aboard the seedship, had patrolled the nebula for ninety-three orbits, each orbit—including the timeless periods outside status geometry—taking some one hundred and thirty human years. They had woven in and out of the tendrils of gas, charting the infalling masses and exploring the rocky accretion disks of stars entering the main sequence. With each measure and update, the brood minds refined their view of the nebula as it would be a hundred generations hence when the Senexi plan would finally mature.

The Senexi were nearly as old as the galaxy. They had achieved spaceflight during the time of the starglobe when the galaxy had been a sphere. They had not been a quick or brilliant race. Each great achievement had taken thousands of generations, and not just because of their material handicaps. In those times elements heavier than helium had been rare, found only around stars that had greedily absorbed huge amounts of primeval hydrogen, burned fierce and blue and exploded early, permeating the ill-defined galactic arms with carbon and nitrogen, lithium and oxygen. Elements heavier than iron had been almost nonexistent. The biologies of cold gas-giant worlds had developed with a much smaller palette of chemical combinations in producing the offspring of the primary Population II stars.

Aryz, even with the limited perspective of a branch ind, was aware that, on the whole, the humans opposing the seedship were more adaptable, more vital. But they were not more experienced. The Senexi with their billions of years had often matched them. And Aryz's perspective was expanding with each day of his new assignment.

In the early generations of the struggle, Senexi mental stasis and cultural inflexibility had made them avoid contact with the Population I species. They had never begun a program of extermination of the younger, newly life-forming worlds; the task would have been monumental and probably useless. So when spacefaring cultures developed, the Senexi had retreated, falling back into the redoubts of old stars even before engaging with the new kinds. They had retreated for three generations, about thirty thousand human years, raising their broods on cold nestworlds around red dwarfs, conserving, holding back for the inevitable conflicts.

As the Senexi had anticipated, the younger Population I races had found need of even the aging groves of the galaxy's first stars. They had moved in savagely, voraciously, with all the strength and mutability of organisms evolved from a richer soup of elements. Biology had, in some ways, evolved in its own right and superseded the Senexi.

Aryz raised the upper globe of his body, with its five silicate eyes arranged in a cross along the forward surface. He had memory of those times, and times long before, though his team hadn't existed then. The brood mind carried memories selected from the total store of nearly twelve billion years' experience; an awesome amount of knowledge, even to a Senexi. He pushed himself forward with his rear pods.

Through the brood mind Aryz could share the memories of a hundred thousand past generations, yet the brood mind itself was younger than its branch individuals. For a time in their youth, in their liquid-dwelling larval form, the branch inds carried their own sacs of data, each a fragment of the total necessary for complete memory. The branch inds swam through ammonia seas and wafted through thick warm gaseous zones, protoplasmic blobs three to four meters in diameter, developing their personalities under the weight of the past—and not even a complete past. No wonder they were inflexible, Aryz thought. Most branch inds were aware enough to see that—especially when they were allowed to compare histories with the Population I species, as he was doing— but there was nothing to be done. They were content the way they were. To change would be unspeakably repugnant. Extinction was preferable . . . almost.

But now they were pressed hard. The brood mind had begun a number of experiments. Aryz's team had been selected from the seedship's contingent to oversee the experiments, and Aryz had been chosen as the chief investigator. Two orbits past, they had captured six human embryos in a breeding device, as well as a highly coveted memory storage center. Most Senexi engagements had been with humans for the past three or four generations. Just as the Senexi dominated Population II species, humans were ascendant among their kind.

Experiments with the human embryos had already been conducted. Some had been allowed to develop normally; others had been tampered with, for reasons Aryz was not aware of. The tamperings had not been very successful.

The newer experiments, Aryz suspected, were going to take a different direction, and the seedship's actions now focused on him; he believed he would be given complete authority over the human shapes. Most branch inds would have dissipated under such a burden, but not Aryz. He found the human shapes rather interesting, in their own horrible way. They might, after all, be the key to Senexi survival.

The moans were toughening her elfstate. She lay in pain for a wake, not daring to close her eyes; her mind was changing and she feared sleep would be the end of her. Her nightmares were not easily separated from life; some, in fact, were sharper.

Too often in sleep she found herself in a Senexi trap, struggling uselessly, being pulled in deeper, her hatred wasted against such power. . .

When she came out of the rigor, Prufrax was given leave by the subordinate tellman. She took to the *Mellangee's* greenroads, walking stiffly in the shallow gravity. Her hands itched. Her mind seemed almost empty after the turmoil of the past few wakes. She had never felt so calm and clear. She hated the Senexi doubly now; once for their innate evil, twice for what they had made her overs put her through to be able to fight them. Logic did not matter. She was calm, assured. She was growing more mature wake by wake.

Combat-budding, the tellman called it, hate emerging like flowers, synthesizing the sunlight of his teaching into pure fight.

The greenroads rose temporarily beyond the labyrinth shields and armor of the ship. Simple transparent plastic and steel geodesic surfaces formed a lacework over the gardens, admitting radiation necessary to the vegetation growing along the paths. No machines scooted one forth and inboard here. It was necessary to walk. Walking was luxury and privilege.

Prufrax looked down on the greens to each side of the paths without much comprehension. They were *beautiful*. Yes, one should say that, think that, but what did it mean? Pleasing? She wasn't sure what being pleased meant, outside of thinking Zap. She sniffed a flower that, the signs explained, bloomed only in the light of young stars not yet fusing. They were near such a star now, and the greenroads were shiny black and electric green with the blossoms. Lamps had been set out for other plants unsuited to such darkened conditions. Some technic allowed suns to appear in selected plastic panels when viewed from certain angles. Clever, the technicals.

She much preferred the looks of a technical to a tellman, but she was common in that. Technicals required brainflex, tellmen cargo capacity. Technicals were strong and ran strong machines, like in the adventure fibs, where technicals were often the protags. She wished a technical were on the greenroads with her. The moans had the effect of making her receptive—what she saw, looking in mirrors, was a certain shine in her eyes—but there was no chance of a breeding liaison. She was quite unreproductive in this moment of elfstate. Other kinds of meetings were not unusual.

She looked up and saw a figure at least a hundred meters away, sitting on an allowed patch near the path. She walked casually, gracefully as possible with the stiffness. Not a technical, she saw soon, but she was not disappointed. Too calm.

"Over," he said as she approached.

"Under," she replied. But not by much—he was probably six or seven ship years old and not easily classifiable.

"Such a fine elfstate," he commented. His hair was black. He was shorter, but something in his build reminded her of the glovers. She accepted his compliment with a nod and pointed to a spot near him. He motioned for her to sit, and she did so with a whuff, massaging her knees.

"Moans?" he asked.

"Bad stretch," she said.

"You're a glover." He looked at the fading scars on her hands.

"Can't tell what you are," she said.

"Noncombat," he said. "Tuner of the mandates."

She knew very little about the mandates, except that law decreed every ship carry one, and few of the crew were ever allowed to peep. "Noncombat, hm?" she mused. She didn't despise him for that; one never felt strong negatives for a crew member. She didn't feel much of anything.

"Been working on ours this wake," he said. "Too hard, I guess. Told to walk." Overzealousness in work was considered an erotic trait aboard the *Mellangee*. Still, she didn't feel receptive toward him.

"Glovers walk after a rough grow," she said.

He nodded. "My name's Clevo."

"Prufrax."

"Combat soon?"

"Hoping. Waiting forever."

"I know. Just been allowed access to the mandate for a half-dozen wakes. All new to me. Very happy."

"Can you talk about it?" she asked. Information about the ship not accessible in certain rates was excellent barter.

"Not sure," he said, frowning. "I've been told caution."

"Well, I'm listening."

He could come from glover stock, she thought, but probably not from technical. He wasn't very muscular, but he wasn't as tall as a glover, or as thin, either.

"If you'll tell me about gloves."

With a smile she held up her hands and wriggled the short, stumpy fingers. "Sure."

The brood mind floated weightless in its tank, held in place by buffered carbon rods. Metal was at a premium aboard Senexi ships, more out of tradition than actual material limitations. From what Aryz could tell, the Senexi used metals sparingly for the same reason—and he strained to recall the small dribbles of information about the human past he had extracted from the memory store—for the same reason that the Romans of old Earth regarded farming as the only truly noble occupation—

Farming being the raising of *plants* for food *and* raw materials. *Plants* were analogous to the freeth Senexi ate in their larval youth, but the freeth were not green and sedentary.

There was always a certain fascination in stretching his mind to encompass human concepts. He had had so little time to delve deeply—and that was good, of course, for he had been set to answer specific questions, not mire himself in the whole range of human filth.

He floated before the brood mind, all these thoughts coursing through his tissues. He had no central nervous system, no truly differentiated organs except those that dealt with the outside world: limbs, eyes, permea. The brood mind, however, was all central nervous system, a thinly buffered sac of viscous fluids about ten meters wide.

"Have you investigated the human memory device yet?" the brood mind asked.

"I have."

"Is communication with the human shapes possible for us?"

"We have already created interfaces for dealing with their machines. Yes, it seems likely we can communicate."

"Does it occur to you that in our long war with humans, we have made no attempt to communicate before?"

This was a complicated question. It called for several qualities that Aryz, as a branch ind, wasn't supposed to have. Inquisitiveness, for one. Branch inds did not ask questions. They exhibited initiative only as offshoots of the brood mind.

He found, much to his dismay, that the question had occurred to him. "We have never captured a human memory store before," he said, by way of incomplete answer. "We could not have communicated without such an extensive source of information."

"Yet, as you say, even in the past we have been able to use human machines."

"The problem is vastly more complex."

The brood mind paused. "Do you think the teams have been prohibited from communicating with humans?"

Aryz felt the closest thing to anguish possible for a branch ind. Was he being considered unworthy? Accused of conduct inappropriate to a branch ind? His loyalty to the brood mind was unshakeable. "Yes."

"And what might our reasons be?"

"Avoidance of pollution."

"Correct. We can no more communicate with them and remain untainted than we can walk on their worlds, breathe their atmosphere." Again, silence. Aryz lapsed into a mode of inactivity. When the brood mind readdressed him, he was instantly aware.

"Do you know how you are different?" it asked.

"I am not . . ." Again, hesitation. Lying to the brood mind was impossible for him. What snared him was semantics, a complication in the radiated signals between them. He had not been aware that he was different; the brood mind's questions suggested he might be. But he could not possibly face up to the fact and analyze it all in one short time. He signaled his distress.

"You are useful to the team," the brood mind said. Aryz calmed instantly. His thoughts became sluggish, receptive. There was a possibility of redemption. But how was he different? "You are to attempt communication with the shapes yourself. You will not engage in any discourse with your fellows while you are so involved." He was banned. "And after completion of this mission and transfer of certain facts to me, you will dissipate."

Aryz struggled with the complexity of the orders. "How am I different, worthy of such a commission?"

The surface of the brood mind was as still as an undisturbed pool. The indistinct black smudges that marked its radiating organs circulated slowly within the interior, then returned, one above the other, to focus on him. "You will grow a new branch ind. It will not have your flaws, but, then again, it will not be useful to me should such a situation come a second time. Your dissipation will be a relief, but it will be regretted."

"How am I different?"

"I think you know already," the brood mind said. "When the time comes, you will feed the new branch ind all your memories but those of human contact. If you do not survive to that stage of its growth, you will pick your fellow who will perform that function for you."

A small pinkish spot appeared on the back of Aryz's globe. He floated forward and placed his largest permeum against the brood mind's cool surface. The key and command were passed, and his body became capable of reproduction. Then the signal of dismissal was given. He left the chamber.

Flowing through the thin stream of liquid ammonia lining the corridor, he felt ambiguously stimulated. His was a position of privilege and anathema. He had been blessed—and condemned. Had any other branch ind experienced such a thing?

Then he knew the brood mind was correct. He *was* different from his fellows. None of them would have asked such questions. None of them could have survived the suggestion of communicating with human shapes. If this task hadn't been given to him, he would have had to dissipate anyway.

The pink spot grew larger, then began to make grayish flakes. It broke through the skin, and casually, almost without thinking, Aryz scraped it off against a bulkhead. It clung, made a radio-frequency emanation something like a sigh, and began absorbing nutrients from the ammonia.

Aryz went to inspect the shapes.

She was intrigued by Clevo, but the kind of interest she felt was new to her. She was not particularly receptive. Rather, she felt a mental gnawing as if she were hungry or had been injected with some kind of brain moans. What Clevo told her about the mandates opened up a topic she had never considered before. How did all things come to be—and how did she figure in them?

The mandates were quite small, Clevo explained, each little more than a cubic meter in volume. Within them was the entire history and culture of the human species, as accurate as possible, culled from all existing sources. The mandate in each ship was updated whenever the ship returned to a contact station. It was not likely the *Mellangee* would return to a contact station during their lifetimes, with the crew leading such short lives on the average.

Clevo had been assigned small tasks—checking data and adding ship records—that had allowed him to sample bits of the mandate. "It's mandated that we have records," he explained, "and what we have, you see, is *man-data*." He smiled. "That's a joke," he said. "Sort of."

Prufrax nodded solemnly. "So where do we come from?"

"Earth, of course," Clevo said. "Everyone knows that."

"I mean, where do *we* come from—you and I, the crew."

"Breeding division. Why ask? You know."

"Yes." She frowned, concentrating. "I mean, we don't come from the same place as the Senexi. The same way."

"No, that's foolishness."

She saw that it was foolishness—the Senexi were different all around. What was she struggling to ask? "Is their fib like our own?"

"Fib? History's not a fib. Not most of it, anyway. Fibs are for unreal. History is overfib."

She knew, in a vague way, that fibs were unreal. She didn't like to have their comfort demeaned, though. "Fibs are fun," she said. "They teach Zap."

"I suppose," Clevo said dubiously. "Being noncombat, I don't see Zap fibs."

Fibs without Zap were almost unthinkable to her. "Such dull," she said.

"Well, of course you'd say that. I might find Zap fibs dull—think of that?"

"We're different," she said. "Like Senexi are different."

Clevo's jaw hung open. "No way. We're crew. We're human. Senexi are . . ." He shook his head as if fed bitters.

"No, I mean . . ." She paused, uncertain whether she was entering unallowed territory. "You and I, we're fed different, given different moans. But in a big way we're different from Senexi. They aren't made, nor do they act as you and I. But . . ." Again it was difficult to express. She was irritated. "I don't want to talk to you anymore."

A tellman walked down the path, not familiar to Prufrax. He held out his hand for Clevo, and Clevo grasped it. "It's amazing," the tellman said, "how you two gravitate to each other. Go, elf-state," he addressed Prufrax. "You're on the wrong greenroad."

She never saw the young researcher again. With glover training underway, the itches he aroused soon faded, and Zap resumed its overplace.

The Senexi had ways of knowing humans were near. As information came in about fleets and individual cruisers less than one percent nebula diameter distant, the seedship seemed warmer, less hospitable. Everything was UV with anxiety, and the new branch ind on the wall had to be shielded by a special silicate cup to prevent distortion. The brood mind grew a corniculum automatically, though the toughened outer membrane would be of little help if the seedship was breached.

Aryz had buried his personal confusion under a load of work. He had penetrated the human memory store deeply enough to find instructions on its use. It called itself a *mandate* (the human word came through the interface as a correlated series of radiated symbols), and even the simple preliminary directions were difficult for Aryz. It was like swimming in another family's private sea, though of course infinitely more alien; how could he connect with experiences never had, problems and needs never encountered by his kind?

He could speak some of the human languages in several radio frequencies, but he hadn't yet decided how he was going to produce modulated sound for the human shapes. It was a disturbing prospect. What would he vibrate? A permeum could vibrate subtly—such signals were used when branch inds joined to form the brood mind, but he doubted his control would ever be subtle enough. Sooner expect a human to communicate with a Senexi by controlling the radiations of its nervous system! The humans had distinct organs within their breathing passages that produced the vibrations; perhaps those structures could be mimicked. But he hadn't yet studied the dead shapes in much detail.

He observed the new branch ind once or twice each watch period. Never before had he seen an induced replacement. The normal process was for two brood minds to exchange plasm and form new team buds, then to exchange and nurture the buds. The buds were later cast free to swim as individual larvae. While the larvae often swam through the liquid and gas atmosphere of a Senexi world for thousands, even tens of thousands of kilometers, inevitably they returned to gather with the other buds of their team. Replacements were selected from a separately created pool of "generic" buds only if one or more originals had been destroyed during their wanderings. The destruction of a complete team meant reproductive failure.

In a mature team, only when a branch ind was destroyed did the brood mind induce a replacement. In essence, then, Aryz was already considered dead.

Yet he was still useful. That amused him, if the Senexi emotion could be called amusement. Restricting himself from his fellows was difficult, but he filled the time by immersing himself, through the interface, in the mandate.

The humans were also connected with the mandate through their surrogate parent, and in this manner they were quiescent.

He reported infrequently to the brood mind. Until he had established communication, there was little to report.

And throughout his turmoil, like the others he could sense a fight was coming. It could determine the success or failure of all their work in the nebula. In the grand scheme, failure here might not be crucial. But the Senexi had taken the long view too often in the past. Their age and experience—their calmness—were working against them. How else to explain the decision to communicate with human shapes? Where would such efforts lead? If he succeeded.

And he knew himself well enough to doubt he would fail.

He could feel an affinity for them already, peering at them through the thick glass wall in their isolated chamber, his skin paling at the thought of their heat, their poisonous chemistry. A diseased affinity. He hated himself for it. And reveled in it. It was what made him particularly useful to the team. If he was defective, and this was the only way he could serve, then so be it.

The other branch inds observed his passings from a distance, making no judgments. Aryz was dead, though he worked and moved. His sacrifice had been fearful. Yet he would not be a hero. His kind could never be emulated.

It was a horrible time, a horrible conflict.

She floated in language, learned it in a trice; there were no distractions. She floated in history and picked up as much as she could, for the source seemed inexhaustible. She tried to distinguish between eyes-open—the barren, pale gray-brown chamber with the thick green wall, beyond which floated a murky roundness—and eyes-shut, when she dropped back into language and history with no fixed foundation.

Eyes-open, she saw the Mam with its comforting limbs and its soft voice, its tubes and extrusions of food and its hissings and removal of waste. Through Mam's wires she learned. Mam also tended another like herself, and another, and one more unlike any of them, more like the shape beyond the green wall.

She was very young, and it was all a mystery.

At least she knew her name. And what she was supposed to do. She took small comfort in that.

They fitted Prufrax with her gloves, and she went into the practice chamber, dragged by her gloves almost, for she hadn't yet knitted her plug-in nerves in the right index digit and her pace control was uncertain.

There, for six wakes straight, she flew with the other glovers back and forth across the dark spaces like elfstate comets. Constellations and nebula aspects flashed at random on the distant walls, and she oriented to them like a night-flying bird. Her glovemates were Ornin, an especially slender male, and Ban, a red-haired female, and the special-projects sisters Ya, Trice, and Damu, new from the breeding division.

When she let the gloves have their way, she was freer than she had ever felt before. Did the gloves really control? The question wasn't important. Control was somewhere uncentered, behind her eyes and beyond her fingers, as if she were drawn on a beautiful silver wire where it was best to go. Doing what was best to do. She barely saw the field that flowed from the grip of the thick, solid gloves or felt its caressing, life-sustaining influence. Truly, she hardly saw or felt anything but situations, targets, opportunities, the success or failure of the Zap. Failure was an acute pain. She was never reprimanded for failure; the reprimand was in her blood, and she felt like she wanted to die. But then the opportunity would improve, the Zap would succeed, and everything around her—stars, Senexi seedship, the *Mellangee,* everything—seemed part of a beautiful dream all her own.

She was intense in the Mocks.

Their initial practice over, the entry play began.

One by one, the special-projects sisters took their hyperbolic formation. Their glove fields threw out extensions, and they combined force. In they went, the mock Senexi seedship brilliant red and white and UV and radio and hateful before them. Their tails swept through the seedship's outer shields and swirled like long silky hair laid on water; they absorbed fantastic energies, grew bright like violent little stars against the seedship outline. They were engaged in the drawing of the shields, and sure as topology, the spirals of force had to have a dimple on the opposite side that would iris wide enough to let in glovers. The sisters twisted the forces, and Prufrax could see the dimple stretching out under them—

The exercise ended. The elfstate glovers were cast into sudden dark. Prufrax came out of the mock unprepared, her mind still bent on the Zap. The lack of orientation drove her as mad as a moth suddenly flipped from night to day. She careened until gently mitted and channeled. She flowed down a tube, the field slowly neutralizing, and came to a halt still gloved, her body jerking and tingling.

"What the breed happened?" she screamed, her hands beginning to hurt.

"Energy conserve," a mechanical voice answered. Behind Prufrax the other elfstate glovers lined up in the catch tube, all but the special-projects sisters. Ya, Trice, and Damu had been taken out of the exercise early and replaced by simulations. There was no way their functions could be mocked. They entered the tube ungloved and helped their comrades adjust to the overness of the real.

As they left the mock chamber, another batch of glovers, even younger and fresher in elfstate, passed them. Ya held up her hands, and they saluted in return. "Breed more every day," Prufrax grumbled. She worried about having so many crew she'd never be able to conduct a satisfactory Zap herself. Where would the honor of being a glover go if everyone was a glover?

She wriggled into her cramped bunk, feeling exhilarated and irritated. She replayed the mocks and added in the missing Zap, then stared gloomily at her small narrow feet.

Out there the Senexi waited. Perhaps they were in the same state as she—ready to fight, testy at being reined in. She pondered her ignorance, her inability to judge whether such feelings were even possible among the enemy. She thought of the researcher, Clevo. "Blank," she murmured. "Blank, blank." Such thoughts were unnecessary, and humanizing Senexi was unworthy of a glover.

Aryz looked at the instrument, stretched a pod into it, and willed. Vocal human language came out the other end, thin and squeaky in the helium atmosphere. The sound disgusted and thrilled him. He removed the instrument from the gelatinous strands of the engineering wall and pushed it into his interior through a stretched permeum. He took a thick draft of ammonia and slid to the human shapes chamber again, then pushed through the narrow port into the observation room. Adjusting his eyes to the heat and bright light beyond the transparent wall, he saw the round mutated shape first—the result of their unsuccessful experiments. He swung his sphere around and looked at the others.

For a time he couldn't decide which was uglier—the mutated shape or the normals. Then he thought of what it would be like to have humans tamper with Senexi and try to make them into human forms . . . He looked at the round human and shrunk as if from sudden heat. Aryz had had nothing to do with the experiments. For that, at least, he was grateful.

Apparently, even before fertilization, human buds—eggs— were adapted for specific roles. The healthy human shapes appeared sufficiently different, discounting *sexual* characteristics, to indicate some variation in function. They were four-podded, two-opticked, with auditory apparatus and olfactory organs mounted on the *head,* along with one permeum, the *mouth.* At least, he thought, they were hairless, unlike some of the other Population I species Aryz had learned about in the mandate.

Aryz placed the tip of the vocalizer against a sound-transmitting plate and spoke.

"Zello," came the sound within the chamber. The mutated shape looked up. It lay on the floor, great bloated stomach backed by four almost useless pods. It usually made high-pitched sounds continuously. Now it stopped and listened, straining on the tube that connected it to the breed-supervising device.

"Hello," replied the male. It sat on a ledge across the chamber, having unhooked itself.

The machine that served as surrogate parent and instructor stood in one corner, an awkward parody of a human, with limbs too long and head too small. Aryz could intuit the unwillingness of the designing engineers to examine human anatomy too closely.

"I am called—" Aryz said, his name emerging as a meaningless stretch of white noise. He would have to do better than that. He compressed and adapted the frequencies. "I am called Aryz."

"Hello," the young female said.

"What are your names?" He knew that well enough, having listened many times to their conversations.

"Prufrax," the female said. "I'm a glover."

The human shapes contained very little genetic memory. As a kind of brood marker, Aryz supposed, they had been equipped with their name, occupation, and the rudiments of environmental knowledge. This seemed to have been artificially imposed; in their natural state, very likely, they were born almost blank. He could not, however, be certain, since human reproductive chemistry was extraordinarily subtle and complicated.

"I'm a teacher, Prufrax," Aryz said. The logic structure of the language continued to be painful to him.

"I don't understand you," the female replied.

"You teach me, I teach you."

"We have the Mam," the male said, pointing to the machine. "She teaches us." The Mam, as they called it, was hooked into the mandate. Withholding that from the humans—the only equivalent, in essence, to the Senexi sac of memory—would have been unthinkable. It was bad enough that humans didn't come naturally equipped with their own share of knowledge.

"Do you know where you are?" Aryz asked.

"Where we live," Prufrax said. "Eyes-open."

Aryz opened a port to show them the stars and a portion of the nebula. "Can you tell where you are by looking out the window?"

"Among the lights," Prufrax said.

Humans, then, did not instinctively know their positions by star patterns as other Population I species did.

"Don't talk to it," the male said. "Mam talks to us." Aryz consulted the mandate for some understanding of the name they had given to the breed-supervising machine. Mam, it explained, was probably a natural expression for womb-carrying parent.

Aryz severed the machine's power. "Mam is no longer functional," he said. He would have the engineering wall put together another less identifiable machine to link them to the mandate and to their nutrition. He wanted them to associate comfort and completeness with nothing but himself.

The machine slumped, and the female shape pulled herself free of the hookup. She started to cry, a reaction quite mysterious to Aryz. His link with the mandate had not been intimate enough to answer questions about the wailing and moisture from the eyes. After a time the male and female lay down and became dormant.

The bloated, mutated shape made more soft sounds and tried to approach the transparent wall. It held up its thin arms as if beseeching. The others would have nothing to do with it; now it wished to go with him. Perhaps the biologists had partially succeeded in their attempt at transformation; perhaps it was more Senexi than human.

Aryz quickly backed out through the port, into the cool and security of the corridor beyond.

It was an endless orbital dance, this detection and matching of course, moving away and swinging back, deceiving and revealing, between the *Mellangee* and the Senexi seedship. It was inevitable that the human ship should close in; human ships were faster, knew better the higher geometries.

Filled with her skill and knowledge, Prufrax waited, feeling like a ripe fruit about to fall from the tree. At this point in their training, just before the application, elfstates were very receptive. She was allowed to take a lover, and they were assigned small separate quarters near the outer greenroads.

The contact was satisfactory, as far as it went. Her mate was an older glover named Kumnax, and as they lay back in the cubicle, soothed by air-dance fibs, he told her stories about past battles, special tactics, how to survive.

"Survive?" she asked, puzzled.

"Of course." His long brown face was intent on the view of the greenroads through the cubicle's small window.

"I don't understand," she said.

"Most glovers don't make it," he said patiently.

"I will."

He turned to her. "You're six," he said. "You're very young. I'm ten. I've seen. You're about to be applied for the first time, you're full of confidence. But most glovers won't make it. They breed thousands of us. We're expendable. We're based on the best glovers of the past, but even the best don't survive."

"I will," Prufrax repeated, her jaw set.

"You always say that," he murmured.

Prufrax stared at him for a moment.

"Last time I knew you," he said, "you kept saying that. And here you are, fresh again."

"What last time?"

"Master Kumnax," a mechanical voice interrupted.

He stood, looking down at her. "We glovers always have big mouths. They don't like us knowing, but once we know, what can they do about it?"

"You are in violation," the voice said. "Please report to S."

"But now, if you last, you'll know more than the tellman tells."

"I don't understand," Prufrax said slowly, precisely, looking him straight in the eye.

"I've paid my debt," Kumnax said. "We glovers stick. Now I'm going to go get my punishment." He left the cubicle. Prufrax didn't see him again before her first application.

The seedship buried itself in a heating protostar, raising shields against the infalling ice and stone. The nebula had congealed out of a particularly rich cluster of exploded fourth- and fifth-generation stars, thick with planets, the detritus of which now fell on Aryz's ship like hail.

Aryz had never been so isolated. No other branch ind addressed him; he never even saw them now. He made his reports to the brood mind, but even there the reception was warmer and warmer, until he could barely endure to communicate. Consequently—and he realized this was part of the plan—he came closer to his charges, the human shapes. He felt more sympathy for them. He discovered that even between human and Senexi there could be a bridge of need—the need to be useful.

The brood mind was interested in one question: how successfully could they be planted aboard a human ship? Would they be accepted until they could carry out their sabotage, or would they be detected? Already Senexi instructions were being coded into their teachings.

"I think they will be accepted in the confusion of an engagement," Aryz answered. He had long since guessed the general outlines of the brood mind's plans. Communication with the human shapes was for one purpose only; to use them as decoys, insurgents. They were weapons. Knowledge of human activity and behavior was not an end in itself; seeing what was happening to him, Aryz fully understood why the brood mind wanted such study to proceed no further.

He would lose them soon, he thought, and his work would be over. He would be much too human-tainted. He would end, and his replacement would start a new existence, very little different from Aryz—but, he reasoned, adjusted. The replacement would not have Aryz's peculiarity.

He approached his last meeting with the brood mind, preparing himself for his final work, for the ending. In the cold liquid-filled chamber, the great red-and-white sac waited, the center of his team, his existence. He adored it. There was no way he could criticize its action.

Yet—

"We are being sought," the brood mind radiated. "Are the shapes ready?"

"Yes," Aryz said. "The new teaching is firm. They believe they are fully human." And, except for the new teaching, they were. "They defy sometimes." He said nothing about the mutated shape. It would not be used. If they won this encounter, it would probably be placed with Aryz's body in a fusion torch for complete purging.

"Then prepare them," the brood mind said. "They will be delivered to the vector for positioning and transfer."

Darkness and waiting. Prufrax nested in her delivery tube like a freshly chambered round. Through her gloves she caught distant communications, murmurs that resembled voices down hollow pipes. The *Mellangee* was coming to full readiness.

Huge as her ship was, Prufrax knew that it would be dwarfed by the seedship. She could recall some hazy details about the seedship's structure, but most of that information was stored securely away from interference by her conscious mind. She wasn't even positive what the tactic would be. In the mocks, that at least had been clear. Now such information either had not been delivered or had waited in inaccessible memory, to be brought forward by the appropriate triggers.

More information would be fed to her just before the launch, but she knew the general procedure. The seedship was deep in a protostar, hiding behind the distortion of geometry and the complete hash of electromagnetic energy. The *Mellangee* would approach, collide if need be. Penetrate. Release. Find. Zap. Her fingers ached. Sometime before the launch she would also be fed her final moans—the tempers—and she would be primed to leave elfstate. She would be a mature glover. She would be a woman.

If she returned

will return

she could become part of the breed, her receptivity would end in ecstasy rather than mild warmth, she would contribute second state, naturally born glovers. For a moment she was content with the thought. That was a high honor.

Her fingers ached worse.

The tempers came, moans tiding in, then the battle data. As it passed into her subconscious, she caught a flash of—

Rocks and ice, a thick cloud of dust and gas glowing red but seeming dark, no stars, no constellation guides this time. The beacon came on. That would be her only way to orient once the gloves stopped inertial and locked onto the target—

The seedship, twenty-two kilometers across yet carrying only six teams,

shadow within shadow

LAUNCH *She flies!*

Data: the *Mellangee* has buried herself in the seedship, ploughed deep into the interior like a carnivore's muzzle looking for vitals.

Instruction: a swarm of seeks is dashing through the seedship, looking for the brood minds, for the brood chambers, for branch inds. The glovers will follow.

Prufrax sees herself clearly now. She is the great avenging

comet, bringer of omen and doom, like a knife moving through the glass and ice and thin, cold helium as if they weren't there, the chambered round fired and tearing at hundreds of kilometers an hour through the Senexi vessel, following the seeks.

The seedship cannot withdraw into higher geometries now. It is pinned by the *Mellangee.*

It is Prufrax's—it is *hers.*

Information floods *her,* pleases *her* immensely. *She* swoops down orange-and-gray corridors, buffeting against *the* walls like a ricocheting bullet. Almost immediately she comes across a branch ind, sliding through the ammonia film against the outrushing wind, trying to reach an armored cubicle. Her first Zap is too easy, not satisfying, nothing like what she thought. In her wake the branch ind becomes scattered globules of plasma. She plunges deeper.

Aryz delivers his human charges to the vectors that will launch them. They are equipped with simulations of the human weapons, their hands encased in the hideous gray gloves.

The seedship is in deadly peril; the battle has almost been lost at one stroke. The seedship cannot remain whole. It must self-destruct, taking the human ship with it, leaving only a fragment with as many teams as can escape.

The vectors launch the human shapes. Aryz tries to determine which part of the ship will be elected to survive; he must not be there. His job is over, and he must die.

The glovers fan out through the seedship's central hollow, demolishing the great cold drive engines, bypassing the shielded fusion flare and the reprocessing plant, destroying machinery built before their Earth was formed.

The special-projects sisters take the lead. Suddenly they are confused. They have found a brood mind, but it is not heavily protected. They surround it, prepare for the Zap—

It is sacrificing itself, drawing them in to an easy kill and away from another portion of the seedship. Power is concentrating elsewhere. Sensing that, they kill quickly and move on.

Aryz's brood mind prepares for escape. It begins to wrap itself in flux bind as it moves through the ship toward the frozen fragment. Already three of its five branch inds are dead; it can feel other brood minds dying. Aryz's bud replacement has been killed as well.

Following Aryz's training, the human shapes rush into corridors away from the main action. The special-projects sisters encounter the decoy male, allow it to fly with them . . . until it aims its weapons. One Zap almost takes out Trice. The others fire on the shape immediately. He goes to his death weeping, confused from the very moment of his launch.

The fragment in which the brood mind will take refuge encompasses the chamber where the humans had been nurtured, where the mandate is still stored. All the other brood minds are dead, Aryz realizes; the humans have swept down on them so quickly. What shall he do?

Somewhere, far off, he feels the distressed pulse of another branch ind dying. He probes the remains of the seedship. He is the last. He cannot dissipate now; he must ensure the brood mind's survival.

Prufrax, darting through the crumbling seedship, searching for more opportunities, comes across an injured glover. She calls for a mediseek and pushes on.

The brood mind settles into the fragment. Its support system is damaged; it is entering the time-isolated state, the flux bind, more rapidly than it should. The seals of foamed electric ice cannot quite close off the fragment before Ya, Trice, and Damu slip in. They frantically call for bind-cutters and preservers; they have instructions to capture the last brood mind, if possible.

But a trap falls upon Ya, and snarling fields tear her from her gloves. She is flung down a dark disintegrating shaft, red cracks opening all around as the seedship's integrity fails. She trails silver dust and freezes, hits a barricade, shatters.

The ice seals continue to close. Trice is caught between them and pushes out frantically, blundering into the region of the intensifying flux bind. Her gloves break into hard bits, and she is melded into an ice wall like an insect trapped on the surface of a winter lake.

Damu sees that the brood mind is entering the final phase of flux bind. After that they will not be able to touch it. She begins a desperate Zap

and is too late.

Aryz directs the subsidiary energy of the flux against her. Her Zap deflects from the bind region, she is caught in an interference pattern and vibrates until her tiniest particles stop their knotted whirlpool spins and she simply becomes

space and searing light.

The brood mind, however, has been damaged. It is losing information from one portion of its anatomy. Desperate for storage, it looks for places to hold the information before the flux bind's last wave.

Aryz directs an interface onto the brood mind's surface. The silvery pools of time-binding flicker around them both. The brood mind's damaged sections transfer their data into the last available storage device—the human mandate.

Now it contains both human and Senexi information.

The silvery pools unite, and Aryz backs away. No longer can he sense the brood mind. It is out of reach but not yet safe. He must propel the fragment from the remains of the seedship. Then he must wrap the fragment in its own flux bind, cocoon it in physics to protect it from the last ravages of the humans.

Aryz carefully navigates his way through the few remaining corridors. The helium atmosphere has almost completely dissipated, even there. He strains to remember all the procedures. Soon the seedship will explode, destroying the human ship. By then they must be gone.

Angry red, Prufrax follows his barely sensed form, watching him behind barricades of ice, approaching the moment of a most satisfying Zap. She gives her gloves their way and finds a shape behind her, wearing gloves that are not gloves, not like her own, but capable of grasping her in tensed fields, blocking the Zap, dragging them together. The fragment separates, heat pours in from the protostar cloud. They are swirled in their vortex of power, twin locked comets—one red, one sullen gray.

"Who are you?" Prufrax screams as they close in on each other in the fields. Their environments meld. They grapple. In the confusion, the darkening, they are drawn out of the cloud with the fragment, and she sees the other's face.

Her own.

The seedship self-destructs. The fragment is propelled from the protostar, above the plane of what will become planets in their orbits, away from the crippled and dying *Mellangee*.

Desperate, Prufrax uses all her strength to drill into the fragment. Helium blows past them, and bits of dead branch inds.

Aryz catches the pair immediately in the shapes chamber, rearranging the fragment's structure to enclose them with the mutant shape and mandate. For the moment he has time enough to concentrate on them. They are dangerous. They are almost equal to each other, but his shape is weakening faster than the true glover. They float, bouncing from wall to wall in the chamber, forcing the mutant to crawl into a corner and howl with fear.

There may be value in saving the one and capturing the other. Involved as they are, the two can be carefully dissected from their fields and induced into a crude kind of sleep before the glover has a chance to free her weapons. He can dispose of the gloves—fake and real—and hook them both to the Mam, reattach the mutant shape as well. Perhaps something can be learned from the failure of the experiment.

The dissection and capture occur faster than the planning. His movement slows under the spreading flux bind. His last action, after attaching the humans to the Mam, is to make sure the brood mind's flux bind is properly nested within that of the ship.

The fragment drops into simpler geometries.
It is as if they never existed.

The battle was over. There were no victors. Aryz became aware
of the passage of time, shook away the sluggishness, and crawled
through painfully dry corridors to set the environmental equipment going again. Throughout the fragment, machines struggled
back to activity.

How many generations? The constellations were unrecogniz-
able. He made star traces and found familiar spectra and types, but
advanced in age. There had been a malfunction in the overall flux
bind. He couldn't find the nebula where the battle had occurred.
In its place were comfortably middle-aged stars surrounded by
young planets.

Aryz came down from the makeshift observatory. He slid
through the fragment, established the limits of his new home, and
found the solid mirror surface of the brood mind's cocoon. It was
still locked in flux bind, and he knew of no way to free it. In time
the bind would probably wear off—but that might require life
spans. The seedship was gone. They had lost the brood chamber,
and with it the stock.

He was the last branch ind of his team. Not that it mattered
now; there was nothing he could initiate without a brood mind.
If the flux bind was permanent—as sometimes happened during
malfunction—then he might as well be dead.

He closed his thoughts around him and was almost completely
submerged when he sensed an alarm from the shapes chamber.
The interface with the mandate had turned itself off; the new version of the Mam was malfunctioning. He tried to repair the equipment, but without the engineer's wall he was almost helpless. The
best he could do was rig a temporary nutrition supply through the
old human-form Mam.

When he was done, he looked at the captive and the two

shapes, then at the legless, armless Mam that served as their link to the interface and life itself.

She had spent her whole life in a room barely eight by ten meters, and not much taller than her own height. With her had been Grayd and the silent round creature whose name—if it had any—they had never learned. For a time there had been Mam, then another kind of Mam not nearly as satisfactory. She was hardly aware that her entire existence had been miserable, cramped, in one way or another incomplete.

Separated from them by a transparent partition, another round shape had periodically made itself known by voice or gesture.

Grayd had kept her sane. They had engaged in conspiracy. Removing themselves from the interface—what she called "eyes-shut"—they had held on to each other, tried to make sense out of what they knew instinctively, what was fed them through the interface, and what the being beyond the partition told them.

First they knew their names, and they knew that they were glovers. They knew that glovers were fighters. When Aryz passed instruction through the interface on how to fight, they had accepted it eagerly but uneasily. It didn't seem to jibe with instructions locked deep within their instincts.

Five years under such conditions had made her introspective. She expected nothing, sought little beyond experience in the eyes-shut. Eyes-open with Grayd seemed scarcely more than a dream. They usually managed to ignore the peculiar bloated creature in the chamber with them; it spent nearly all its time hooked to the mandate and the Mam.

Of one thing only was she completely sure. Her name was Prufrax. She said it in eyes-open and eyes-shut, her only certainty.

Not long before the battle, she had been in a condition resembling dreamless sleep, like a robot being given instructions. The part of Prufrax that had taken on personality during eyes-shut and

eyes-open for five years had been superseded by the fight instructions Aryz had programmed. She had flown as glovers must fly
(though the gloves didn't seem quite right). She had fought, grap-
pling (she thought) with herself, but who could be certain of anything? She had long since decided that reality was not to be sought
too avidly.

After the battle she fell back into the mandate—into eyes-shut—
all too willingly. And what matter? If eyes-open was even less com-
prehensible than eyes-shut, why did she have the nagging feeling
eyes-open was so compelling, so necessary?

She tried to forget.

But a change had come to eyes-shut, too. Before the battle, the
information had been selected. Now she could wander through
the mandate at will. She seemed to smell the new information,
completely unfamiliar, like a whiff of ocean.

She hardly knew where to begin.

She stumbled across:

—that all vessels will carry one, no matter what their size or
class, just as every individual carries the map of a species. The
mandate shall contain all the information of our kind, including
accurate and uncensored history, for if we have learned anything,
it is that censored and untrue accounts distort the eyes of the leaders. Leaders must have access to the truth. It is their responsibility.
Whatever is told those who work under the leaders, for whatever
reason, must not be believed by the leaders. Unders are told lies.
Leaders must seek and be provided with accounts as accurate as
possible, or we will be weakened and fall—

What wonderful dreams the *leaders* must have had. And they
possessed some intrinsic gift called *truth,* through the use of the
man-date. Prufrax could hardly believe that. As she made her tentative explorations through the new fields of eyes-shut, she began
to link the word *mandate* with what she experienced.

That was where she was. And she alone. Once, she had explored
with Grayd. Now there was no sign of Grayd.

She learned quickly. Soon she walked along a beach on Earth, then a beach on a world called Myriadne, and other beaches, fading in and out. By running through the entries rapidly, she came up with a blurred *eidos* and so learned what a beach was in the abstract. It was a boundary between one kind of eyes-shut and another, between water and land, neither of which had any corollary in eyes-open.

Some beaches had sand. Some had clouds—the *eidos* of clouds was quite attractive. And one—

had herself running scared, screaming.

She called out, but the figure vanished. Prufrax stood on a beach under a greenish-yellow star, on a world called Kyrene, feeling lonelier than ever.

She explored farther, hoping to find Grayd, if not the figure that looked like herself. Grayd wouldn't flee from her. Grayd would. The bloated thing confronted her, its helpless limbs twitching. It seemed to be human, but put together all *wrong*.

Now it was her turn to run, terrified. Never before had she met the mutated creature in eyes-shut. It was mobile; it had a purpose. Over land, clouds, trees, rocks, wind, air, equations, and an edge of physics she fled. The farther she went, the more distant from the strange one with twisted hands and small head, the less afraid she was.

She never found Grayd.

The memory of the battle was fresh and painful. Her environment had collapsed and been replaced by something indistinct. She remembered the ache of her hands, clumsily removed from the gloves.

Prufrax had fallen into a deep slumber and had dreamed. The dreams were totally unfamiliar to her. If there was a left-turning in her arc of sleep, she dreamed of philosophies and languages and other things she couldn't relate to. A right-turning led to histories and sciences so incomprehensible as to be nightmares.

It was a most unpleasant sleep, and she was not at all sorry to find she wasn't really asleep.

The crucial moment came when she discovered how to slow her turnings and the changes of dream subject. She entered a pleasant place of which she had no knowledge but which did not seem threatening. There was a vast expanse of water, but it didn't terrify her. She couldn't even identify it as water until she scooped up a handful. Beyond the water was a floor of shifting particles. Above both was an open expanse, not black but obviously space, drawing her eyes into intense pale blue-green.

And there was that figure she had encountered in the seedship. Herself. The figure pursued.

She fled.

Right over the boundary into Senexi information. She knew then that what she was seeing couldn't possibly come from within herself. She was receiving data from another source. Perhaps she had been taken captive. It was possible she was now being forcibly debriefed. The tellman had discussed such possibilities, but none of the glovers had been taught how to defend themselves in specific situations. Instead it had been stated, in terms that brooked no second thought, that self-destruction was the only answer.

So she tried to kill herself. She sat in the freezing cold of a red-and-white room, her feet meeting but not touching a fluid covering on the floor. The information didn't fit her senses—it seemed blurred, inappropriate. Unlike the other data, this didn't allow participation or motion. Everything was locked solid.

She couldn't find an effective means of killing herself. She resolved to close her eyes and simply will herself into dissolution. But closing her eyes only moved her into a deeper or shallower level of deception—other categories, subjects, visions.

She couldn't sleep, wasn't tired, couldn't die. Like a leaf on a stream, she drifted. Her thoughts untangled, and she imagined herself floating on the water called ocean. She kept her eyes open. It was quite by accident that she encountered:

Instruction. Welcome to the introductory use of the mandate. As a noncombat processor, your duties are to maintain the mandate, provide essential information for your overs, and, if necessary, protect or destroy the mandate. The mandate is your immediate over. If it requires maintenance, you will oblige. Once linked with the mandate, as you are now, you may explore any aspect of the information by requesting delivery. To request delivery, indicate the core of your subject—

Prufrax! she shouted silently. What is Prufrax?

A voice with different tone immediately took over.

Ah, now that's quite a story. I was her biographer, the organizer of her life tapes (ref. GEORGE MACKNAX), and knew her well in the last years of her life. She was born in the Ferment 26468. Here are selected life tapes. Choose emphasis. Analyses follow.

—Hey! Who are you? There's someone here with me . . . .

—Shh! Listen. Look at her. Who is she?

They looked, listened to the information.

—Why, she's me . . . sort of.

—She's *us*.

She stood two and a half meters tall. Her hair was black and thick, though cut short; her limbs well-muscled though drawn out by the training and hormonal treatments. She was seventeen years old, one of the few birds born in the solar system, and for the time being she had a chip on her shoulder. Everywhere she went, the birds asked about her mother, Jayax. "You better than her?"

Of course not! Who could be? But she was good; the instructors said so. She was just about through training, and whether she graduated to hawk or remained bird she would do her job well. Asking Prufrax about her mother was likely to make her set her mouth tight and glare.

On Mercior, the Grounds took up four thousand hectares and had its own port. The Grounds was divided into Land, Space, and Thought, and training in each area was mandatory for fledges, those birds embarking on hawk training. Prufrax was fledge three. She had passed Land—though she loathed downbound fighting—and was two years into Space. The tough part, everyone said, was not passing Space, but lasting through four years of Thought after the action in nearorbit and planetary.

Prufrax was not the introspective type. She could be studious when it suited her. She was a quick study at weapon maths, physics came easy when it had a direct application, but theory of service and polinstruc—which she had sampled only in prebird courses—bored her.

Since she had been a little girl, no more than five—

—Five! Five what?

and had seen her mother's ships and fightsuits and fibs, she had known she would never be happy until she had ventured far out and put a seedship in her sights, had convinced a Senexi of the overness of end—

—The Zap! She's talking the Zap!

—What's that?

—You're me, you should know.

—I'm not you, and we're not her.

The Zap, said the mandate, and the data shifted.

"Tomorrow you receive your first implants. These will allow you to coordinate with the zero-angle phase engines and find your targets much more rapidly than you ever could with simple biologic. The implants, of course, will be delivered through your noses—minor irritation and sinus trouble, no more—into your limbic system. Later in your training, hookups and digital adapts will be installed as well. Are there any questions?"

"Yes, sir." Prufrax stood at the top of the spherical classroom, causing the hawk instructor to swivel his platform. "I'm having problems with the zero-angle phase maths. Reduction of the momenta of the real."

Other fledge threes piped up that they, too, had had trouble with those maths. The hawk instructor sighed. "We don't want to install cheaters in all of you. It's bad enough needing implants to supplement biologic. Individual learning is much more desirable. Do you request cheaters?" That was a challenge. They all responded negatively, but Prufrax had a secret smile. She knew the subject. She just took delight in having the maths explained again. She could reinforce an already thorough understanding. Others not so well versed would benefit. She wasn't wasting time. She was in the pleasure of her weapon—the weapon she would be using against the Senexi.

"Zero-angle phase is the temporary reduction of the momenta of the real." Equations and plexes appeared before each student as the instructor went on. "Nested unreals can conflict if a barrier is placed between the participator princip and the assumption of the real. The effectiveness of the participator can be determined by a convenience model we call the angle of phase. Zero-angle phase is achieved by an opaque probability field according to modified Fourier of the separation of real waves. This can also be caused by the reflection of the beam—an effective counter to zero-angle phase, since the beam is always compoundable and the compound is always time-reversed. Here are the true gedanks—"

—Zero-angle phase. She's learning the Zap.

—She hates them a lot, doesn't she?

—The Senexi? They're Senexi.

—I think . . . eyes-open is the world of the Senexi. What does that mean?

—That we're prisoners. You were caught before me.

—Oh.

The news came as she was in recovery from the implant. Seedships had violated human space again, dropping cuckoos on thirty-five worlds. The worlds had been young colonies, and the cuckoos had wiped out all life, then tried to reseed with Senexi forms. The overs had reacted by sterilizing the planet's surfaces. No victory, loss to both sides. It was as if the Senexi were so malevolent they didn't care about success, only about destruction.

She hated them. She could imagine nothing worse.

Prufrax was twenty-three. In a year she would be qualified to hawk on a cruiser/raider. She would demonstrate her hatred.

Aryz felt himself slipping into endthought, the mind set that always preceded a branch ind's self-destruction. What was there for him to do? The fragment had survived, but at what cost, to what purpose? Nothing had been accomplished. The nebula had been lost, or he supposed it had. He would likely never know the actual outcome.

He felt a vague irritation at the lack of a spectrum of responses. Without a purpose, a branch ind was nothing more than excess plasm.

He looked in on the captive and the shapes, all hooked to the mandate, and wondered what he would do with them. How would humans react to the situation he was in? More vigorously, probably. They would fight on. They always had. Even without leaders, with no discernible purpose, even in defeat. What gave them such stamina? Were they superior, more deserving? If they were better, then was it right for the Senexi to oppose their triumph?

Aryz drew himself tall and rigid with confusion. He had studied them too long. They had truly infected him. But here at least was a hint of purpose. A question needed to be answered.

He made preparations. There were signs the brood mind's flux bind was not permanent, was in fact unwinding quite rapidly. When it emerged, Aryz would present it with a judgment, an answer.

He realized, none too clearly, that by Senexi standards he was now a raving lunatic.

He would hook himself into the mandate and improve the somewhat isolating interface he had used previously to search for selected answers. He, the captive, and the shapes would be immersed in human history together. They would be like young suckling on a Population I mother-animal—just the opposite of the Senexi process, where young fed nourishment and information into the brood mind.

The mandate would nourish, or poison. Or both.

—Did she love?

    —What—you mean, did she receive?

    —No, did she—we—I—give?

    —I don't know what you mean.

    —I wonder if *she* would know. . .

Love, said the mandate, and the data proceeded.

Prufrax was twenty-nine. She had been assigned to a cruiser in a new program where superior but untested fighters were put into thick action with no preliminary. The program was designed to see how well the Grounds prepared fighters; some thought it foolhardy, but Prufrax found it perfectly satisfactory.

The cruiser was a million-ton raider, with a hawk contingent of fifty-three and eighty regular crew. She would be used in a second-wave attack, following the initial hardfought.

She was scared. That was good; fright improved basic biologic, if properly managed. The cruiser would make a raid into Senexi space and retaliate for past cuckoo-seeding programs. They would come up against thornships and seedships, likely.

The fighting was going to be fierce.

The raider made its final denial of the overness of the real and pipsqueezed into an arduous, nasty sponge space. It drew itself together again and emerged far above the galactic plane.

Prufrax sat in the hawks' wardroom and looked at the simulated rotating snowball of stars. Red-coded numerals flashed along the margins of known Senexi territory, signifying old stars, dark hulks of stars, the whole ghostly home region where the Senexi had first come to power while the terrestrial sun was still a mist-wrapped youngster. A green arrow showed the position of the raider.

She drank sponge-space supplements with the others but felt isolated because of her firstness, her fear. Everyone seemed so calm. Most were fours or fives—on their fourth or fifth battle call. There were ten ones and an upper scatter of experienced hawks with nine to twenty-five battles behind them. There were no thirties. Thirties were rare in combat; the few that survived so many engagements were plucked off active and retired to PR service under the polinstructors. They often ended up in fibs, acting poorly, looking unhappy.

Still, when she had been more naive, Prufrax's heroes had been a man-and-woman thirty team she had watched in fib after fib—Kumnax and Arol. They had been better actors than most.

Day in, day out, they drilled in their fightsuits. While the crew bustled, hawks were put through implant learning, what slang was already calling the Know, as opposed to the Tell, of classroom teaching. Getting background, just enough to tickle her curiosity, not enough to stimulate morbid interest.

—There it is again. Feel?

—I know it. Yes. The round one, part of eyes-open. . .

—Senexi?

—No, brother without name.

—Your . . . brother?

—No . . . I don't know.

—Can it hurt us?

—It never has. It's trying to talk to us.

—Leave us *alone!*

—It's going.

Still, there were items of information she had never received before, items privileged only to the fighters, to assist them in their work. Older hawks talked about the past, when data had been freely available. Stories circulated in the wardroom about the Senexi, and she managed to piece together something of their origins and growth.

Senexi worlds, according to a twenty, had originally been large, cold masses of gas circling bright young suns nearly metal-free. Their gas-giant planets had orbited the suns at hundreds of millions of kilometers and had been dusted by the shrouds of neighboring dead stars; the essential elements carbon, nitrogen, silicon, and fluorine had gathered in sufficient quantities on some of the planets to allow Population II biology.

In cold ammonia seas, lipids had combined in complex chains. A primal kind of life had arisen and flourished. Across millions of years, early Senexi forms had evolved. Compared with evolution on Earth, the process at first had moved quite rapidly. The mechanisms of procreation and evolution had been complex in action, simple in chemistry.

There had been no competition between life forms of different genetic bases. On Earth, much time had been spent selecting between the plethora of possible ways to pass on genetic knowledge.

And among the early Senexi, outside of predation there had been no death. Death had come about much later, self-imposed for social reasons. Huge colonies of protoplasmic individuals had gradually resolved into the team-forms now familiar.

Soon information was transferred through the budding of branch inds; cultures quickly developed to protect the integrity of larvae, to allow them to regroup and form a new brood mind. Technologies had been limited to the rare heavy materials available, but the Senexi had expanded for a time with very little technology. They were well adapted to their environment, with few predators and no need to hunt, absorbing stray nutrients from the atmosphere and from layers of liquid ammonia. With perceptions attuned to the radio and microwave frequencies, they had before long turned groups of branch inds into radio telescope chains, piercing the heavy atmosphere and probing the universe in great detail, especially the very active center of the young galaxy. Huge jets of matter, streaming from other galaxies and emitting high-energy radiation, had provided laboratories for their vicarious observations. Physics was a primitive science to them.

Since little or no knowledge was lost in breeding cycles, cultural growth was rapid at times; since the dead weight of knowledge was often heavy, cultural growth often slowed to a crawl.

Using water as a building material, developing techniques that humans still understood imperfectly, they prepared for travel away from their birthworlds.

Prufrax wondered, as she listened to the older hawks, how humans had come to know all this. Had Senexi been captured and questioned? Was it all theory? Did anyone really know—anyone she could ask?

—She's weak.

—Why weak?

—Some knowledge is best for glovers to ignore. Some questions are best left to the supreme overs.

—Have you thought that in here, you can answer her questions, our questions?

—No. No. Learn about me—us—first.

In the hour before engagement, Prufrax tried to find a place alone. On the raider this wasn't difficult. The ship's size was overwhelming for the number of hawks and crew aboard. There were many areas where she could put on an environs and walk or drift in silence, surrounded by the dark shapes of equipment wrapped in plexerv. There was so much about ship operations she didn't understand, hadn't been taught. Why carry so much excess equipment, weapons—far more than they'd need even for replacements? She could think of possibilities—superiors on Mercior wanting their cruisers to have flexible mission capabilities, for one—but her ignorance troubled her less than why she was ignorant. Why was it necessary to keep fighters in the dark on so many subjects?

She pulled herself through the cold g-less tunnels, feeling slightly awked by the loneness, the quiet. One tunnel angled outboard, toward the hull of the cruiser. She hesitated, peering into its length with her environs beacon, when a beep warned her she was near another crew member. She was startled to think someone else might be as curious as she. The other hawks and crew, for the most part, had long outgrown their need to wander and regarded it as birdish. Prufrax was used to being different—she had always perceived herself, with some pride, as a bit of a freak. She scooted expertly up the tunnel, spreading her arms and tucking her legs as she would in a fightsuit.

The tunnel was filled with a faint milky green mist, absorbing her environs beam. It couldn't be much more than a couple of hundred meters long, however, and it was quite straight. The signal beeped louder.

Ahead she could make out a dismantled weapons blister. That explained the fog: a plexerv aerosol diffused in the low pressure. Sitting in the blister was a man, his environs glowing a pale violet. He had deopaqued a section of the blister and was staring out at the stars. He swiveled as she approached and looked her over dispassionately. He seemed to be a hawk—he had fightform, tall, thin with brown hair above hull-white skin, large eyes with pupils so dark she might have been looking through his head into space beyond.

"Under," she said as their environs met and merged.

"Over. What are you doing here?"

"I was about to ask you the same."

"You should be getting ready for the fight," he admonished.

"I am. I need to be alone for a while."

"Yes." He turned back to the stars. "I used to do that, too."

"You don't fight now?"

He shook his head. "Retired. I'm a researcher."

She tried not to look impressed. Crossing rates was almost impossible. A bitalent was unusual in the service.

"What kind of research?" she asked.

"I'm here to correlate enemy finds."

"Won't find much of anything, after we're done with the zero phase."

It would have been polite for him to say, "Power to that," or offer some other encouragement. He said nothing.

"Why would you want to research them?"

"To fight an enemy properly, you have to know what they are. Ignorance is defeat."

"You research tactics?"

"Not exactly."

"What, then?"

"You'll be in a tough hardfought this wake. Make you a proposition. You fight well, observe, come to me and tell me what you see. Then I'll answer your questions."

"Brief you before my immediate overs?"

"I have the authority," he said. No one had ever lied to her; she didn't even suspect he would. "You're eager?"

"Very."

"You'll be doing what?"

"Engaging Senexi fighters, then hunting down branch inds and brood minds."

"How many fighters going in?"

"Twelve."

"Big target, eh?"

She nodded.

"While you're there, ask yourself—what are they fighting for? Understand?"

"I—"

"Ask, what are they fighting for. Just that. Then come back to me."

"What's your name?"

"Not important," he said. "Now go."

She returned to the prep center as the sponge-space warning tones began. Overhawks went among the fighters in the lineup, checking gear and giveaway body points for mental orientation. Prufrax submitted to the molded sensor mask being slipped over her face.

"Ready!" the overhawk said. "Hardfought!" He clapped her on the shoulder. "Good luck."

"Thank you, sir." She bent down and slid into her fightsuit. Along the launch line, eleven other hawks did the same. The overs and other crew left the chamber, and twelve red beams delineated the launch tube. The fightsuits automatically lifted and aligned on their individual beams. Fields swirled around them like silvery tissue in water, then settled and hardened into cold, scintillating walls, pulsing as the launch energy built up.

The tactic came to her. The ship's sensors became part of her information net. She saw the Senexi thornship—twelve kilometers in diameter, cuckoos lacing its outer hull like maggots on red fruit, snakes waiting to take them on.

She was terrified and exultant, so worked up that her body temperature was climbing. The fightsuit adjusted her balance.

At the count of ten and nine, she switched from biologic to cyber. The implant—after absorbing much of her thought processes for weeks—became Prufrax. For a time there seemed to be two of her. Biologic continued, and in that region she could even relax a bit, as if watching a fib.

With almost dreamlike slowness, in the electronic time of cyber, her fightsuit followed the beam. She saw the stars and oriented herself to the cruiser's beacon, using both for reference, plunging in the sword-flower formation to assault the thornship. The cuckoos retreated in the vast red hull like worms withdrawing into an apple. Then hundreds of tiny black pinpoints appeared in the closest quadrant to the sword flower.

Snakes shot out, each piloted by a Senexi branch ind. "Hardfought!" she told herself in biologic before that portion gave over completely to cyber.

> *Why were we flung out of dark*
> *through ice and fire, a shower*
> *of sparks? a puzzle;*
> *Perhaps to build hell.*

> *We strike here, there;*
> *Set brief glows, fall through*
> *and cross round again.*

By our dimming, we see what
Beatitude we have.
In the circle, kindling
together, we form an exhausted Empyrean.
We feel the rush of
igniting winds but still
grow dull and wan.

New rage flames, new light,
dropping like sun through muddy
ice and night and fall
Close, spinning blue and bright.

In time they, too,
Tire. Redden.
We join, compare pasts
cool in huddled paths, turn gray.

And again.
We are a companion flow
of ash, in the slurry,
out and down.
We sleep.

Rivers form above and below.
Above, iron snakes twist,
clang and slice, chime,
helium eyes watching, seeing
Snowflake hawks,
signaling adamant muscles and
energy teeth. What hunger
compels our venom spit?

It flies, strikes the crystal

flight, making mist gray-green
with ammonia rain.

Sleeping, we glide,
and to each side
unseen shores wait
with the moans of
an unseen tide.

—She wrote that. We. One of her—our—poems.
  —Poem?
  —A kind of fib, I think.
  —I don't see what it says.
  —Sure you do! She's talking hardfought.
  —The Zap? Is that all?
  —No, I don't think so.
  —Do you understand it?
  —Not all. . .

She lay back in the bunk, legs crossed, eyes closed, feeling the receding dominance of the implant—the overness of cyber—and the almost pleasant ache in her back. She had survived her first. The thornship had retired, severely damaged, its surface seared and scored so heavily it would never release cuckoos again.

It would become a hulk, a decoy. Out of action. *Satisfaction / out of action / Satisfaction. . .*

Still, with eight of the twelve fighters lost, she didn't quite feel the exuberance of the rhyme. The snakes had fought very well. Bravely, she might say. They lured, sacrificed, cooperated, demonstrating teamwork as fine as that in her own group. Strategy was what made the cruiser's raid successful. A superior approach, an excellent tactic. And perhaps even surprise, though the final analysis hadn't been posted yet.

Without those advantages, they might have all died.

She opened her eyes and stared at the pattern of blinking lights in the ceiling panel, lights with their secret codes that repeated every second, so that whenever she looked at them, the implant deep inside was debriefed, reinstructed. Only when she fought would she know what she was now seeing.

She returned to the tunnel as quickly as she was able. She floated up toward the blister and found him there, surrounded by packs of information from the last hardfought. She waited until he turned his attention to her.

"Well?" he said.

"I asked myself what they are fighting for. And I'm very angry."

"Why?"

"Because I don't know. I *can't* know. They're Senexi."

"Did they fight well?"

"We lost eight. Eight." She cleared her throat.

"Did they fight well?" he repeated, an edge in his voice.

"Better than I was ever told they could."

"Did they die?"

"Enough of them."

"How many did you kill?"

"I don't know." But she did. Eight.

"You killed eight," he said, pointing to the packs. "I'm analyzing the battle now."

"You're behind what we read, what gets posted?" she asked.

"Partly," he said. "You're a good hawk."

"I knew I would be," she said, her tone quiet, simple.

"Since they fought bravely—"

"How can Senexi be brave?" she asked.

"Since," he repeated, "they fought bravely, why?"

"They want to live, to do their . . . work. Just like me."

"No," he said. "They're Senexi. They're not like us."

She was confused, moving between extremes in her mind, first resisting, then giving in too much. "What's your name?" she asked, dodging the issue.

"Clevo."

Her glory had yet to begin, and already she was well into her fall.

Aryz made his connection and felt the brood mind's emergency cache of knowledge in the mandate grow up around him like ice crystals on glass. He stood in a static scene. The transition from living memory to human machine memory had resulted in either a coding of data or a reduction of detail; either way, the memory was cold not dynamic. It would have to be compared, recorrelated, if that would ever be possible.

How much human data had had to be dumped to make space for this?

He cautiously advanced into the human memory, calling up topics almost at random. In the short time he had been away, so much of what he had learned seemed to have faded or become scrambled. Branch inds were supposed to have permanent memory, but human data, for one reason or another, didn't take. It required so much effort just to begin to understand the different modes of thought.

He backed away from sociological data, trying to remain within physics and mathematics. There he could make conversions to fit his understanding without too much strain.

Then something unexpected happened. He felt the brush of another mind, a gentle inquiry from a source made even stranger by the hint of familiarity. It made what passed for a Senexi greeting, but not in the proper form, using what one branch ind of a team would radiate to a fellow; a gross breach, since it was obviously not from his team or even from his family. Aryz tried to withdraw. How was it possible for minds to meet in the mandate? As he retreated, he pushed into a broad region of incomprehensible data. It had none of the characteristics of the other human regions he had examined.

—This is for machines, the other said. —Not all cultural data is limited to biologic. You are in the area where programs and cyber designs are stored. They are really accessible only to a machine hooked into the mandate.

—What is your family? Aryz asked, the first step-question in the sequence Senexi used for urgent identity requests.

—I have no family. I am not a branch ind. No access to active brood minds. I have learned from the mandate.

—Then what are you?

—I don't know, exactly. Not unlike you.

Aryz understood what he was dealing with. It was the mind of the mutated shape, the one that had remained in the chamber, beseeching when he approached the transparent barrier.

—I must go now, the shape said.

Aryz was alone again in the incomprehensible jumble. He moved slowly, carefully, into the Senexi sector, calling up subjects familiar to him. If he could encounter one shape, doubtless he could encounter the others—perhaps even the captive. The idea was dreadful—and fascinating. So far as he knew, such intimacy between Senexi and human had never happened before. Yet there was something very Senexi-like in the method, as if branch inds attached to the brood mind were to brush mentalities while searching in the ageless memories.

The dread subsided. There was little worse that could happen to him, with his fellows dead, his brood mind in flux bind, his purpose uncertain.

What Aryz was feeling, for the first time, was a small measure of freedom.

The story of the original Prufrax continued.

In the early stages she visited Clevo with a barely concealed anger. His method was aggravating, his goals never precisely spelled out. What did he want with her, if anything? And she with him? Their meetings were clandestine, though not precisely forbidden. She was a hawk one now with considerable personal liberty between exercises and engagements. There were no monitors in the closed-off reaches of the cruiser, and they could do whatever they wished. The two met in areas close to the ship's hull, usually in weapons blisters that could be opened to reveal the stars there they talked.

Prufrax was not accustomed to prolonged conversation. Hawks were not raised to be voluble, nor were they selected for their curiosity. Yet the exhawk Clevo talked a great deal and was the most curious person she had met, herself included, and she regarded herself as uncharacteristically curious.

Often he was infuriating, especially when he played the "leading game," as she called it. Leading her from one question to the next, like an instructor, but without the trappings or any clarity of purpose.

"What do you think of your mother?"

"Does that matter?"

"Not to me."

"Then why ask?"

"Because you matter."

Prufrax shrugged. "She was a fine mother. She bore me with a well-chosen heritage. She raised me as a hawk candidate. She told me her stories."

"Any hawk I know would envy you for listening at Jayax's knee."

"I was hardly at her knee."

"A speech tactic."

"Yes, well, she was important to me."

"She was a preferred single?"

"Yes."

"So you have no father."

"She selected without reference to individuals."

"Then you are really not that much different from a Senexi."

She bristled and started to push away. "There! You insult me again."

"Not at all. I've been asking one question all this time, and you haven't even heard. How well do you know the enemy?"

"Well enough to destroy them." She couldn't believe that was the only question he'd been asking. His speech tactics were very odd.

"Yes, to win battles, perhaps. But who will win the war?"

"It'll be a long war," she said softly, floating a few meters from him. "They fight well."

He rotated in the blister, blocking out a blurred string of stars. The cruiser was preparing to shift out of status geometry again. "They fight with conviction. Do you believe them to be evil?"

"They destroy us."

"We destroy them."

"So the question," she said, smiling at her cleverness, "is who began to destroy?"

"Not at all," Clevo said. "I suspect there's no longer a clear answer to that. Our leaders have obviously decided the question isn't important. No. We are the new, they are the old. The old must be superseded. It's a conflict born in the essential difference between Senexi and humans."

"That's the only way we're different? They're old, we're not so old? I don't understand."

"Nor do I, entirely."

"Well, finally!"

"The Senexi," Clevo continued, unperturbed, "long ago needed only gas-giant planets like their homeworlds. They lived in peace for billions of years before our world was formed. But as they moved from star to star, they learned uses for other types of worlds. We were most interested in rocky Earth-like planets. Gradually we found uses for gas giants, too. By the time we met, both of us encroached on the other's territory. Their technology is so improbable, so unlike ours, that when we first encountered them we thought they must come from another geometry."

"Where did you learn all this?" Prufrax squinted at him suspiciously.

"I'm no longer a hawk," he said, "but I was too valuable just to discard. My experience was too broad, my abilities too useful. So I was placed in research. It seems a safe place for me. Little contact with my comrades." He looked directly at her. "We must try to know our enemy, at least a little."

"That's dangerous," Prufrax said, almost instinctively.

"Yes, it is. What you know, you cannot hate."

"We must hate," she said. "It makes us strong. Senexi hate."

"They might," he said. "But, sometime, wouldn't you like to . . . sit down and talk with one, after a battle? Talk with a fighter? Learn its tactic, how it bested you in one move, compare—"

"No!" Prufrax shoved off rapidly down the tube. "We're shifting now. We have to get ready."

—She's smart. She's leaving him. He's crazy.

—Why do you think that?

—He would stop the fight, end the Zap.

—But he was a hawk.

—And hawks became glovers, I guess. But glovers go wrong, too. —?

—Did you know they used you? How you were used?

—That's all blurred now.

—She's doomed if she stays around him. *Who's that?*

—Someone is listening with us.

—Recognize?

—No, gone now.

The next battle was bad enough to fall into the hellfought. Prufrax was in her fightsuit, legs drawn up as if about to kick off. The cruiser exited sponge space and plunged into combat before sponge-space supplements could reach full effectiveness. She was dizzy, disoriented. The overhawks could only hope that a switch from biologic to cyber would cure the problem.

She didn't know what they were attacking. Tactic was flooding the implant, but she was only receiving the wash of that; she hadn't merged yet. She sensed that things were confused. That bothered her. Overs did not feel confusion.

The cruiser was taking damage. She could sense at least that, and she wanted to scream in frustration. Then she was ordered to merge with the implant. Biologic became cyber. She was in the Know.

The cruiser had reintegrated above a gas-giant planet. They were seventy-nine thousand kilometers from the upper atmosphere. The damage had come from ice mines—chunks of Senexi-treated water ice, altered to stay in sponge space until a human vessel integrated nearby. Then they emerged, packed with momentum and all the residual instability of an unsuccessful exit into status geometry. Unsuccessful for a ship, that is—very successful for a weapon.

The ice mines had given up the overness of the real within range of the cruiser and had blasted out whole sections of the hull. The launch lanes had not been damaged. The fighters lined up on their beams and were peppered out into space, spreading in the classic sword flower.

The planet was a cold nest. Over didn't know what the atmosphere contained, but Senexi activity had been high in the star system, concentrating on this world. Over had decided to take a chance. Fighters headed for the atmosphere. The cruiser began planting singularity eggs. The eggs went ahead of the fighters, great black grainy ovoids that seemed to leave a trail of shadow—the wake of a birthing disruption in status geometry that could turn a gas giant into a short-lived sun.

Their time was limited. The fighters would group on entry sleds and descend to the liquid water regions where Senexi commonly kept their upwelling power plants. The fighters would first destroy any plants, loop into the liquid ammonia regions to search for hidden cuckoos, then see what was so important about the world.

She and five other fighters mounted the sled. Growing closer, the hazy clear regions of the atmosphere sparkled with Senexi sensors. Spiderweb beams shot from the six sleds to take down the sensors. Buffet began. Scream, heat, then a second flower from the sled at a depth of two hundred kilometers. The sled slowed and held station. It would be their only way back. The fightsuits couldn't pull out of such a large gravity well.

Prufrax descended deeper. The pale, swollen beacon of the red star was dropping below the second cloudtops, limning the strata in orange and purple. At the liquid ammonia level she was instructed to key in permanent memory of all she was seeing. She wasn't "seeing" much, but other sensors were recording a great deal, all of it duly processed in her implant. "There's life here," she told herself. Indigenous life. Just another example of Senexi disregard for basic decency: they were interfering with a world developing its own complex biology.

The temperature rose to ammonia vapor levels, then to liquid water. The pressure on the fightsuit was enormous, and she was draining her stores much more rapidly than expected. At this level the atmosphere was particularly thick with organics.

Senexi snakes rose from below, passed them in altitude, then doubled back to engage. Prufrax was designated the deep diver; the others from her sled would stay at this level in her defense. As she fell, another sled group moved in behind her to double the cover.

She searched for the characteristic radiation curve of an upwelling plant. At the lower boundary of the liquid water level, below which her suit could not safely descend, she found it.

The Senexi were tapping the gas giant's convection from greater depths than usual. Ten kilometers above the plant, almost undetectable, hung another object with an uncharacteristic curve. The power plant was feeding its higher companion with tight energy beams.

She slowed. Two other fighters, disengaged from the brief skirmish above, took backup positions a few dozen kilometers higher. Her implant searched for an appropriate tactic. She would avoid the zero-angle phase for the moment, go in for reconnaissance.

She could feel sound pouring from the plant and its companion—rhythmic, not waste noise, but deliberate. And homing in on that sound were waves of large vermiform organisms, like chains of gas-filled sausages. They were dozens of meters long, two meters at their greatest thickness, shaped vaguely like the Senexi snake fighters. The vermiforms were native, and they were being lured into the uppermost floating structure. None were emerging. Her backups spread apart, descended, and drew up along her flanks.

She made her decision almost immediately. She could see a pattern in the approach of the natives. If she fell into the pattern, she might be able to enter the structure unnoticed.

—It's a grinder. She doesn't recognize it.

—What's a grinder?

—She should make the Zap! It's an ugly thing; Senexi use them all the time. Net a planet with grinders, like a cuckoo, but for larger operations.

The creatures were being passed through separator fields. Their organics fell from the bottom of the construct, raw material for new growth--Senexi growth. Their heavier elements were stored for later harvest.

With Prufrax in their midst, the vermiforms flew into the separator. The interior was hundreds of meters wide, lead-white walls with flat gray machinery floating in a dust haze, full of hollow noise, the distant bleats of vermiforms being slaughtered. Prufrax tried to retreat, but she was caught in a selector field. Her suit bucked and she was whirled violently, then thrown into a repository for examination. She had been screened from the separator; her plan to record, then destroy, the structure had been foiled by an automatic filter.

"Information sufficient." Command logic programmed into the implant before launch was now taking over. "Zero-angle phase both plant and adjunct." She was drifting in the repository, still slightly stunned. Something was fading. Cyber was hissing in and out; the over logic-commands were being scrambled. Her implant was malfunctioning and was returning control to biologic. The selector fields had played havoc with all cyber functions, down to the processors in her weapons.

Cautiously she examined the down systems one by one, determining what she could and could not do. This took as much as thirty seconds—an astronomical time on the implant's scale.

She still could use the phase weapon. If she was judicious and didn't waste her power, she could cut her way out of the repository, maneuver and work with her escorts to destroy both the plant and the separator. By the time they returned to the sleds, her implant might have rerouted itself and made sufficient repairs to handle defense. She had no way of knowing what was waiting for her if—when—she escaped, but that was the least of her concerns for the moment.

She tightened the setting of the phase beam and swung her fightsuit around, knocking a cluster of junk ice and silty phosphorescent dust. She activated the beam. When she had a hole large enough to pass through, she edged the suit forward, beamed through more walls and obstacles, and kicked herself out of the repository into free fall. She swiveled and laid down a pattern of wide-angle beams, at the same time relaying a message on her situation to the escorts.

The escorts were not in sight. The separator was beginning to break up, spraying debris through the almost-opaque atmosphere. The rhythmic sound ceased, and the crowds of vermiforms began to disperse.

She stopped her fall and thrust herself several kilometers higher—directly into a formation of Senexi snakes. She had barely enough power to reach the sled, much less fight and turn her beams on the upwelling plant.

Her cyber was still down.

The sled signal was weak. She had no time to calculate its direction from the inertial guidance cyber. Besides, all cyber was unreliable after passing through the separator.

Why do they fight so well? Clevo's question clogged her thoughts. Cursing, she tried to blank and keep all her faculties available for running the fightsuit. *When evenly matched, you cannot win against your enemy unless you understand them. And if you truly understand, why are you fighting and not talking?* Clevo had never told her that—not in so many words. But it was part of a string of logic all her own.

Be more than an automaton with a narrow range of choices. Never underestimate the enemy. Those were old Grounds dicta, not entirely lost in the new training, but only emphasized by Clevo.

If they fight as well as you, perhaps in some ways they fight-think like you do. Use that.

Isolated, with her power draining rapidly, she had no choice. They might disregard her if she posed no danger. She cut her thrust and went into a diving spin. Clearly she was on her way to a high-pressure grave. They would sense her power levels, perhaps even pick up the lack of field activity if she let her shields drop. She dropped the shields. If they let her fall and didn't try to complete the kill—if they concentrated on active fighters above—she had enough power to drop into the water vapor regions, far below the plant, and silently ride a thermal into range. With luck, she could get close enough to lay a web of zero-angle phase and take out the plant.

She had minutes in which to agonize over her plan. Falling, buffeted by winds that could knock her kilometers out of range, she spun like a vagrant flake of snow.

She couldn't even expend the energy to learn if they were scanning her, checking out her potential. Perhaps they had unwritten rules of conduct like the ones she was using, taking hunches into account. Hunches were discouraged in Grounds training—much less reliable than cyber.

She fell. Temperature increased. Pressure on her suit began to constrict her air supply. She used fighter trancing to cut back on her breathing.

Fell.

And broke the trance. Pushed through the dense smoke of exhaustion. Planned the beam web. Counted her reserves. Nudged into an updraft beneath the plant. The thermal carried her, a silent piece of paper in a storm, drifting back and forth beneath the objective. The huge field intakes pulsed above, lightning outlining their invisible extension. She held back on the beam.

Nearly faded out. Her suit interior was almost unbearably hot.

She was only vaguely aware of laying down the pattern. The beams vanished in the murk. The thermal pushed her through a layer of haze, and she saw the plant, riding high above clear-atmosphere turbulence. The zero-angle phase had pushed through the field intakes, into their source nodes and the plant body, surrounding it with bright blue Cherenkov. First the surface began to break up, then the middle layers, and finally key supports. Chunks vibrated away with the internal fury of their molecular, then atomic, then particle disruption. Paraphrasing Grounds description of beam action, the plant became less and less convinced of its reality. "Matter dreams," an instructor had said a decade before. "Dreams it is real, maintains the dream by shifting rules with constant results. Disturb the dreams, the shifting of the rules results in inconstant results. Things cannot hold."

She slid away from the updraft, found another, wondered idly how far she would be lifted. Curiosity at the last. Let's just see, she told herself; a final experiment.

Now she was cold. The implant was flickering, showing signs of reorganization. She didn't use it. No sense expanding the amount of time until death. No sense—

at all.

The sled, maneuvered by one remaining fighter, glided up beneath her almost unnoticed.

Aryz waited in the stillness of a Senexi memory, his thinking temporarily reduced to a faint susurrus. What he waited for was not clear.

—Come.

The form of address was wrong, but he recognized the voice. His thoughts stirred, and he followed the nebulous presence out of Senexi territory.

—Know your enemy.

Prufrax . . . the name of one of the human shapes sent out against their own kind. He could sense her presence in the mandate, locked into a memory store. He touched on the store and caught the essentials—the grinder, the updraft plant, the fight from Prufrax's viewpoint.

—Know how your enemy knows you.

He sensed a second presence, similar to that of Prufrax. It took him some time to realize that the human captive was another form of the shape, a reproduction of the. . .

Both were reproductions of the female whose image was in the memory store. Aryz was not impressed by threes—Senexi mysticism, what had ever existed of it, had been preoccupied with fives and sixes—but the coincidence was striking.

—Know how your enemy *sees you.*

He saw the grinder processing organics—the vermiform natives—in preparation for a widespread seeding of deuterium gatherers. The operation had evidently been conducted for some time; the vermiform populations were greatly reduced from their usual numbers. Vermiforms were a common type-species on gas giants of the sort depicted. The mutated shape nudged him into a particular channel of the memory, that which carried the original Prufrax's emotions. She had reacted with *disgust* to the Senexi procedure. It was a reaction not unlike what Aryz might feel when coming across something forbidden in Senexi behavior. Yet eradication was perfectly natural, analogous to the human cleansing of *food* before *eating.*

—It's in the memory. The vermiforms are intelligent. They have their own kind of civilization. Human action on this world prevented their complete extinction by the Senexi.

—So what matter they were *intelligent?* Aryz responded. They did not behave or think like Senexi, or like any species Senexi find compatible. They were therefore not desirable. Like humans.

—You would make humans extinct?

—We would protect ourselves from them.

—Who damages whom most?

Aryz didn't respond. The line of questioning was incomprehensible. Instead, he flowed into the memory of Prufrax, propelled by another aspect of complete freedom— confusion.

The implant was replaced. Prufrax's damaged limbs and skin were repaired or regenerated quickly, and within four wakes, under intense treatment usually reserved only for overs, she regained all her reflexes and speed. She requested liberty of the cruiser while it returned for repairs. Her request was granted.

She first sought Clevo in the designated research area. He wasn't there, but a message was, passed on to her by a smiling young crew member. She read it quickly:

"You're free and out of action. Study for a while, then come find me. The old place hasn't been damaged. It's less private, but still good. Study! I've marked highlights."

She frowned at the message, then handed it to the crew member, who duly erased it and returned to his duties. She wanted to talk with Clevo, not study.

But she followed his instructions. She searched out highlighted entries in the ship's memory store. It was not nearly as dull as she had expected. In fact, by following the highlights, she felt she was learning more about Clevo and about the questions he asked.

Old literature was not nearly as graphic as fibs, but it was different enough to involve her for a time. She tried to create imitations of what she read, but erased them. Nonfib stories were harder than she suspected. She read about punishment, duty; she read about places called heaven and hell, from a writer who had died tens of thousands of years before. With ed supplement guidance, she was able to comprehend most of what she read. Plugging the store into her implant, she was able to absorb hundreds of volumes in an hour. Some of the stores were losing definition. They hadn't been used in decades, perhaps centuries.

Halfway through, she grew impatient. She left the research area. Operating on another hunch, she didn't go to the blister as directed, but straight to memory central, two decks inboard the research area. She saw Clevo there, plugged into a data pillar, deep in some aspect of ship history. He noticed her approach, unplugged, and swiveled on his chair. "Congratulations," he said, smiling at her.

"Hardfought," she acknowledged, smiling.

"Better than that, perhaps," he said.

She looked at him quizzically. "What do you mean, better?"

"I've been doing some illicit tapping on over channels."

"So?"

—He *is dangerous!*

"*You've* been recommended."

"For what?"

"Not for hero status, not yet. You'll have a good many more fights before that. And you probably won't enjoy it when you get there. You won't be a fighter then."

Prufrax stood silently before him.

"You may have a valuable genetic assortment. Overs think you behaved remarkably well under impossible conditions."

"Did I?"

He nodded. "Your type may be preserved."

"Which means?"

"There's a program being planned. They want to take the best fighters and reproduce them—clone them—to make uniform top-grade squadrons. It was rumored in my time—you haven't heard?"

She shook her head.

"It's not new. It's been done, off and on, for tens of thousands of years. This time they believe they can make it work."

"You were a fighter, once," she said. "Did they preserve your type?"

Clevo nodded. "I had something that interested them, but not, I think, as a fighter."

Prufrax looked down at her stubby-fingered hands. "It was grim," she said. "You know what we found?"

"An extermination plant."

"You want me to understand them better. Well, I can't. I refuse. How could they do such things?" She looked disgusted and answered her own question. "Because they're Senexi."

"Humans," Clevo said, "have done much the same, sometimes worse."

"No!"

—No!

"Yes," he said firmly. He sighed. "We've wiped Senexi worlds, and we've even wiped worlds with intelligent species like our own. Nobody is innocent. Not in this universe."

"We were never taught that."

"It wouldn't have made you a better hawk. But it might make a better human of you, to know. Greater depth of character. Do you want to be more aware?"

"You mean, study more?"

He nodded.

"What makes you think you can teach me?"

"Because you thought about what I asked you. About how Senexi thought. And you survived where some other hawk might not have. The overs think it's in your genes. It might be. But it's also in your head."

"Why not tell the overs?"

"I have," he said. He shrugged. "I'm too valuable to them, otherwise I'd have been busted again, a long time ago."

"They don't want me to learn from you?"

"I don't know," Clevo said. "I suppose they're aware you're talking to me. They could stop it if they wanted. They may be smarter than I give them credit for." He shrugged again. "Of course they're smart. We just disagree at times."

"And if I learn from you?"

"Not from me, actually. From the past. From history, what other people have thought. I'm really not any more capable than you . . . but I know history, small portions of it. I won't teach you so much as guide."

"I did use your questions," Prufrax said. "But will I ever need to use them—think that way—again?"

Clevo nodded. "Of course."

—You're quiet.

—She's giving in to him.

--She gave in a long time ago.

—She should be afraid.

—Were you—we—ever really afraid of a challenge?

—No.

—Not Senexi, not forbidden knowledge.

—Someone listens with us. Feel—

Clevo first led her through the history of past wars, judging that was appropriate considering her occupation. She was attentive enough, though her mind wandered; sometimes he was didactic, but she found she didn't mind that much. At no time did his attitude change as they pushed through the tangle of the past. Rather her perception of his attitude changed. Her perception of herself changed.

She saw that in all wars, the first stage was to dehumanize the enemy, reduce the enemy to a lower level so that he might be killed without compunction. When the enemy was not human to begin with, the task was easier. As wars progressed, this tactic frequently led to an underestimation of the enemy, with disastrous consequences. "We aren't exactly underestimating the Senexi," Clevo said. "The overs are too smart for that. But we refuse to understand them, and that could make the war last indefinitely."

"Then why don't the overs see that?"

"Because we're being locked into a pattern. We've been fighting for so long, we've begun to lose ourselves. And it's getting worse." He assumed his didactic tone, and she knew he was reciting something he'd formulated years before and repeated to himself a thousand times. "There is no war so important that to win it, we must destroy our minds."

She didn't agree with that. Losing the war with the Senexi would mean extinction for all of them, and their minds as well—as she understood things.

Most often they met in the single unused weapons blister that had not been damaged. They met when the ship was basking in the real between sponge-space jaunts. He brought memory stores with him in portable modules, and they read, listened, experienced together. She never placed a great deal of importance in the things she learned; her interest was focused on Clevo. Still, she learned.

The rest of her time she spent training. She was aware of a growing isolation from the hawks, which she attributed to her uncertain rank status. Was her genotype going to be preserved or not? The decision hadn't been made. The more she learned, the less she wanted to be singled out for honor. Attracting that sort of attention might be dangerous, she thought. Dangerous to whom, or what, she could not say.

Clevo showed her how hero images had been used to indoctrinate birds and hawks in a standard of behavior that was ideal, not realistic. The results were not always good; some tragic blunders had been made by fighters trying to be more than anyone possibly could or refusing to be flexible.

The war was certainly not a fib. Yet more and more the overs seemed to be treating it as one. Unable to bring about strategic victories against the Senexi, the overs had settled in for a long war of attrition and were apparently bent on adapting all human societies to the effort.

"There are overs we never hear of, who make decisions that shape our entire lives. Soon they'll determine whether or not we're even born, if they don't already."

"That sounds paranoid," she said, trying out a new word and concept she had only recently learned.

"Maybe so."

"Besides, it's been like that for ages—not knowing all our overs."

"But it's getting worse," Clevo said. He showed her the projections he had made. In time, if trends continued unchanged, fighters and all other combatants would be treated more and more mechanically, until they became the machines the overs wished them to be.

—No.

—Quiet. How does he feel toward her?

It was inevitable that as she learned under his tutelage, he began to feel responsible for her changes. She was an excellent fighter. He could never be sure that what he was doing might reduce her effectiveness. And yet he had fought well—despite similar changes—until his billet switch. It had been the overs who had decided he would be more effective, less disruptive, elsewhere.

Bitterness over that decision was part of his motive. The overs had done a foolish thing, putting a fighter into research. Fighters were tenacious. If the truth was to be hidden, then fighters were the ones likely to ferret it out. And pass it on. There was a code among fighters, seldom revealed to their immediate overs, much less to the supreme overs parsecs distant in their strategospheres. What one fighter learned that could be of help to another had to be passed on, even under penalty. Clevo was simply following that unwritten rule.

Passing on the fact that, at one time, things had been different. That war changed people, governments, societies, and that societies could effect an enormous change on their constituents, especially now—change in their lives, their thinking. Things could become even more structured. Freedom of fight was a drug, an illusion—

—No!

used to perpetuate a state of hatred.

"Then why do they keep all the data in stores?" she asked. "I mean, you study the data, everything becomes obvious."

"There are still important people who think we may want to find our way back someday. They're afraid we'll lose our roots, but—"

His face suddenly became peaceful. She reached out to touch him, and he jerked slightly, turning toward her in the blister. "What is it?" she asked.

"It's not organized. We're going to lose the information. Ship overs are going to restrict access more and more. Eventually it'll decay, like some already has in these stores. I've been planning for some time to put it all in a single unit—"

—He built the mandate!

"and have the overs place one on every ship, with researchers to tend it. Formalize the loose scheme still in effect, but dying. Right now I'm working on the fringes. At least I'm allowed to work. But soon I'll have enough evidence that they won't be able to argue. Evidence of what happens to societies that try to obscure their histories. They go quite mad. The overs are still rational enough to listen; maybe I'll push it through." He looked out the transparent blister. The stars were smudging to one side as the cruiser began probing for entrances to sponge space. "We'd better get back."

"Where are you going to serve when we return? We'll all be transferred."

"That's some time removed. Why do you want to know?"

"I'd like to learn more."

He smiled. "That's not your only reason."

"I don't need someone to tell me what my reasons are," she said testily.

"We're so reluctant," he said. She looked at him sharply, irritated and puzzled. "I mean," he continued, "we're hawks. Comrades. Hawks couple like *that*." He snapped his fingers. "But you and I sneak around it all the time."

Prufrax kept her face blank.

"Aren't you receptive toward me?" he asked, his tone almost teasing.

"You're so damned superior. Stuffy," she snapped.

"Aren't you?"

"It's just that's not all," she said, her tone softening.

"Indeed," he said in a barely audible whisper.

In the distance they heard the alarms.

—It was never any different.

—What?

—Things were never any different before me.

—Don't be silly. It's all here.

—If Clevo made the mandate, then he put it here. It isn't true.

—Why are you upset?

—I don't like hearing that everything I believe is a . . . fib.

—I've never known the difference, I suppose. Eyes-open was never all that real to me. This isn't real, you aren't . . . this is eyes-shut. So why be upset? You and I . . . we aren't even whole people. I feel you. You wish the Zap, you fight, not much else. I'm just a shadow, even compared to you. But *she* is whole. She loves him. She's less a victim than either of us. So something has to have changed.

—You're saying things have gotten worse.

—If the mandate is a lie, that's all I am. You refuse to accept. I *have* to accept, or I'm even less than a shadow.

—I don't refuse to accept. It's just hard.

—You started it. You thought about love.

—You did!

—Do you know what love is?

—Reception.

They first made love in the weapons blister. It came as no surprise; if anything, they approached it so cautiously they were clumsy. She had become more and more receptive, and he had dropped his guard. It had been quick, almost frantic, far from the orchestrated and drawn-out ballet the hawks prided themselves for. There was no pretense. No need to play the roles of artists interacting. They were depending on each other. The pleasure they exchanged was nothing compared to the emotions involved.

"We're not very good with each other," Prufrax said.

Clevo shrugged. "That's because we're shy."

"Shy?"

He explained. In the past—at various times in the past, because such differences had come and gone many times—making love had been more than a physical exchange or even an expression of comradeship. It had been the acknowledgment of a bond between people.

She listened, only half-believing. Like everything else she had heard that kind of love seemed strange, distasteful. What if one hawk was lost, and the other continued to love? It interfered with the hardfought, certainly. But she was also fascinated. Shyness—the fear of one's presentation to another. The hesitation to present truth, or the inward confusion of truth at the awareness that another might be important, more important than one thought possible. That such emotions might have existed at one time, and seem so alien now only emphasized the distance of the past, as Clevo had tried to tell her. And that she felt those emotions only confirmed she was not as far from that past as, for dignity's sake, she might have wished.

Complex emotion was not encouraged either at the Grounds or among hawks on station. Complex emotion degraded performance. The simple and direct was desirable.

"But all we seem to do is talk—until now," Prufrax said, holding his hand and examining his fingers one by one. They were very little different from her own, though extended a bit from hawk fingers to give greater versatility with key instruction.

"Talking is the most human thing we can do."

She laughed. "I know what you are," she said, moving up until her eyes were even with his chest. "You're stuffy. You aren't the party type."

"Where'd you learn about parties?"

"You gave me literature to read, I read it. You're an instructor at heart. You make love by telling." She felt peculiar, almost afraid, and looked up at his face. "Not that I don't enjoy your lovemaking, like this. Physical."

"You receive well," he said. "Both ways."

"What we're saying," she whispered, "is not truth-speaking. It's amenity." She turned into the stroke of his hand through her hair. "Amenity is supposed to be decadent. That fellow who wrote about heaven and hell. He would call it a sin."

"Amenity is the recognition that somebody may see or feel differently than you do. It's the recognition of individuals. You and I, we're part of the end of all that."

"Even if you convince the overs?"

He nodded. "They want to repeat success without risk. New individuals are risky, so they duplicate past success. There will be more and more people, fewer individuals. More of you and me, less of others. The fewer individuals, the fewer stories to tell, the less history. We're part of the death of history."

She floated next to him, trying to blank her mind as she had before, to drive out the nagging awareness he was right. She thought she understood the social structure around her. Things seemed new. She said as much.

"It's a path we're taking," Clevo said. "Not a place we're at."

—It's a place *we're* at. How different are we?

—But there's so much history in here. How can it be over for us?

—I've been thinking. Do we know the last event recorded in the mandate?

—Don't, we're drifting from Prufrax now. . ..

Aryz felt himself drifting with them. They swept over countless millennia, then swept back the other way. And it became evident that as much change had been wrapped in one year of the distant past as in a thousand years of the closing entries in the mandate. Clevo's voice seemed to follow them, though they were far from his period, far from Prufrax's record.

"Tyranny is the death of history. We fought the Senexi until we became like them. No change, youth at an end, old age coming upon us. There is no important change, merely elaborations in the pattern."

—How many times have we been here, then? How many times have we died?

Aryz wasn't sure, now. *Was* this the first time humans had been captured? Had he been told everything by the brood mind? Did the Senexi have no *history,* whatever that was—

The accumulated lives of living, thinking beings. Their actions, thoughts, passions, hopes.

The mandate answered even his confused, nonhuman requests. He could understand action, thought, but not passion or hope. Perhaps without those there was no *history.*

—You have no history, the mutated shape told him. There have been millions like you, even millions like the brood mind. What is the last event recorded in the brood mind that is not duplicated a thousand times over, so close they can be melded together for convenience?

—You understand that? Aryz asked the shape.

—Yes.

—How do you understand—because we made you into something between human and Senexi?

—Not only that.

The requests of the twin captives and shape were moving them back once more into the past, through the dim gray millennia of repeating ages. History began to manifest again.

Differences in the record.

On the way back to Mercior, four skirmishes were fought. Prufrax did well in each. She carried something special with her, a thought she didn't even tell Clevo, and she carried the same thought with her through their last days at the Grounds.

Taking advantage of hawk liberty, she opted for a posthardfought residence just outside the Grounds, in the relatively uncrowded Daughter of Cities zone. She wouldn't be returning to fight until several issues had been decided, her status most important among them.

Clevo began making his appeal to the middle overs. He was given Grounds duty to finish his proposals. They could stay together for the time being.

The residence was sixteen square meters in area, not elegant— *natural,* as RentOpts described it. Clevo called it a "garret," inaccurately as she discovered when she looked it up in his memory blocs, but perhaps he was describing the tone.

Toward the end of the last day, she lay in the crook of Clevo's arm. They had done a few hours of natural sleep. He hadn't come out yet, and she looked up at his face, reached up with a hand to feel his arm.

It was different from the arms of others she had been receptive toward. It was unique. The thought amused her. There had never been a reception like theirs. This was the beginning. And if both were to be duplicated, this love, this reception, would be repeated an infinite number of times. Clevo meeting Prufrax, teaching her, opening her eyes.

Somehow, even though repetition contributed to the death of history, she was pleased. This was the secret thought she carried into fight. Each time she would survive, wherever she was, however many duplications down the line. She would receive Clevo, and he would teach her. If not now—if one or the other died—then in the future. The death of history might be a good thing. Love could go on forever.

She had lost even a rudimentary apprehension of death, even with present pleasure to live for. Her functions had sharpened. She would please him by doing all the things he could not. And if he was to enter that state she frequently found him in, that state of introspection, of reliving his own battles and of envying her activity, then that wasn't bad. All they did to each other was good.

—Was good

—Was

She slipped from his arm and left the narrow sleeping quarter, pushing through the smoke-colored air curtain to the lounge. Two hawks and an over she had never seen before were sitting there. They looked up at her.

"Under," Prufrax said.

"Over," the woman returned. She was dressed in tan and green, Grounds colors, not ship.

"May I assist?"

"Yes."

"My duty, then?"

The over beckoned her closer. "You have been receiving a researcher."

"Yes," Prufrax said. The meetings could not have been a secret on the ship, and certainly not their quartering near the Grounds. "Has that been against duty?"

"No." The over eyed Prufrax sharply, observing her perfected fightform, the easy grace with which she stood, naked, in the middle of the small compartment. "But a decision has been reached. Your status is decided now."

She felt a shiver.

"Prufrax," said the elder hawk. She recognized him from fibs, and his companion: Kumnax and Arol. Once her heroes. "You have been accorded an honor, just as your partner has. You have a valuable genetic assortment—"

She barely heard the rest. They told her she would return to fight, until they deemed she had had enough experience and background to be brought into the polinstruc division. Then her fighting would be over. She would serve better as an example, a hero.

Heroes never partnered out of function. Hawk heroes could not even partner with exhawks.

Clevo emerged from the air curtain. "Duty," the over said. "This residence is disbanded. Both of you will have separate quarters, separate duties."

They left. Prufrax held out her hand, but Clevo didn't take it. "No use," he said.

Suddenly she was filled with anger. "You'll give it up? Did I expect too much? *How strongly?*"

"Perhaps even more strongly than you," he said. "I knew the order was coming down. And still I didn't leave. That may hurt my chances with the supreme overs."

"Then at least I'm worth more than your breeding history?"

"Now you are history. History the way they make it."

"I feel like I'm dying," she said, amazement in her voice. "What is that, Clevo? What did you do to me?"

"I'm in pain, too," he said.

"You're hurt?"

"I'm confused."

"I don't believe that," she said, her anger rising again. "You knew, and you didn't do anything?"

"That would have been counter to duty. We'll be worse off if we fight it."

"So what good is your great, exalted history?"

"History is what you have," Clevo said. "I only record."

—Why did they separate them?

—I don't know. You didn't like him, anyway.

—Yes, but now. . .

—See? You're her. We're her. But shadows. She was whole.

—I don't understand.

—We don't. Look what happens to her. They took what was best out of her. Prufrax

went into battle eighteen more times before dying as heroes often do, dying in the midst of what she did best. The question of what made her better before the separation—for she definitely was not as fine a fighter after—has not been settled. Answers fall into an extinct classification of knowledge, and there are few left to interpret, none accessible to this device.

—So she went out and fought and died. They never even made fibs about her. This killed her?

—I don't think so. She fought well enough. She died like other hawks died.

—And she might have lived otherwise.

—How can I know that, any more than you?

—They—we—met again, you know. I met a Clevo once, on my ship. They didn't let me stay with him long.

—How did you react to him?

—There was so little time, I don't know.

—Let's ask. . ...

In thousands of duty stations, it was inevitable that some of Prufrax's visions would come true, that they should meet now and then. Clevos were numerous, as were Prufraxes. Every ship carried complements of several of each. Though Prufrax was never quite as successful as the original, she was a fine type. She—

—She was never quite as successful. They took away her edge. They didn't even know it!

—They must have known.

—Then they didn't want to win!

—We don't know that. Maybe there were more important considerations.

—Yes, like killing history.

Aryz shuddered in his warming body, dizzy as if about to bud, then regained control.

He had been pulled from the mandate, called to his own duty. He examined the shapes and the human captive. There was something different about them. How long had they been immersed in the mandate? He checked quickly, frantically, before answering the call. The reconstructed Mam had malfunctioned. None of them had been nourished. They were thin, pale, cooling. Even the bloated mutant shape was dying; lost, like the others, in the mandate.

He turned his attention away. Everything was confusion. Was he human or Senexi now? Had he fallen so low as to understand them? He went to the origin of the call, the ruins of the temporary brood chamber. The corridors were caked with ammonia ice, burning his pod as he slipped over them. The brood mind had come out of flux bind. The emergency support systems hadn't worked well; the brood mind was damaged.

"Where have you been?" it asked.

"I assumed I would not be needed until your return from the flux bind."

"You have not been watching!"

"Was there any need? We are so advanced in time, all our actions are obsolete. The nebula is collapsed, the issue is decided."

"We do not know that. We are being pursued."

Aryz turned to the sensor wall—what was left of it—and saw that they were, indeed, being pursued. He had been lax.

"It is not your fault," the brood mind said. "You have been set a task that tainted you and ruined your function. You will dissipate."

Aryz hesitated. He had become so different, so tainted, that he actually *hesitated* at a direct command from the brood mind. But it was damaged. Without him, without what he had learned, what could it do? It wasn't reasoning correctly.

"There are facts you must know, important facts—"

Aryz felt a wave of revulsion, uncomprehending fear, and something not unlike human anger radiate from the brood mind. Whatever he had learned and however he had changed, he could not withstand that wave.

Willingly, and yet against his will—it didn't matter—-he felt himself liquefying. His pod slumped beneath him, and he fell over, landing on a pool of frozen ammonia. It burned, but he did not attempt to lift himself. Before he ended, he saw with surprising clarity what it was to be a branch ind, or a brood mind, or a human. Such a valuable insight, and it leaked out of his permea and froze on the ammonia.

The brood mind regained what control it could of the fragment. But there were no defenses worthy of the name. Calm, preparing for its own dissipation, it waited for the pursuit to conclude.

The Mam set off an alarm. The interface with the mandate was severed. Weak, barely able to crawl, the humans looked at each other in horror and slid to opposite corners of the chamber.

They were confused: which of them was the captive, which the decoy shape? It didn't seem important. They were both bone-thin, filthy with their own excrement.

They turned with one motion to stare at the bloated mutant. It sat in its corner, tiny head incongruous on the huge thorax, tiny arms and legs barely functional even when healthy. It smiled wanly at them.

"We felt you," one of the Prufraxes said. "You were with us in there." Her voice was a soft croak.

"That was my place," it replied. "My only place."

"What function, what name?"

"I'm . . . I know that. I'm a researcher. In there. I knew myself in there."

They squinted at the shape. The head. Something familiar, even now. "You're a Clevo . . ."

There was noise all around them, cutting off the shape's weak words. As they watched, their chamber was sectioned like an orange, and the wedges peeled open. The illumination ceased. Cold enveloped them.

A naked human female, surrounded by tiny versions of herself, like an angel circled by fairy kin, floated into the chamber. She was thin as a snake. She wore nothing but silver rings on her wrists and a narrow torque around her waist. She glowed blue-green in the dark.

The two Prufraxes moved their lips weakly but made no sound in the near vacuum. *Who are you?*

She surveyed them without expression, then held out her arms as if to fly. She wore no gloves, but she was of their type.

As she had done countless times before on finding such Senexi experiments—though this seemed older than most—she lifted one arm higher. The blue-green intensified, spread in waves to the mangled walls, surrounded the freezing, dying shapes. Perfect, angelic, she left the debris behind to cast its fitful glow and fade.

They had destroyed every portion of the fragment but one. They left it behind unharmed.

Then they continued, millions of them thick like mist, working the spaces between the stars, their only master the overness of the real.

They needed no other masters. They would never malfunction.

The mandate drifted in the dark and cold, its memory going on, but its only life the rapidly fading tracks where minds had once passed through it. The trails writhed briefly, almost as if alive, but only following the quantum rules of diminishing energy states. Finally, a small memory was illuminated.

Prufrax's last poem, explained the mandate reflexively.

> *How the fires grow!*
> *Peace passes*
> *All memory lost.*
> *Somehow we always miss that single door,*
> *Dooming ourselves to circle.*
> *Ashes to stars, lies to souls,*
> *Let's spin round the sinks and holes.*
> *Kill the good, eat the young.*
> *Forever and more,*
> *You and I are never done.*

The track faded into nothing. Around the mandate, the universe grew old very quickly.

JUDGMENT ENGINE

"Judgement Engine" was first published in Japanese translation for inclusion in a magnificent boxed set published by Pioneer. The set, called Artificial Life (Insects), contains an art book with computer graphics concepts by Daizaburo Harada, a CD-ROM, and a paperback book with this story, essays, and interviews with me and with Ryuichi Sakamoto. It is the most sumptuous presentation yet for my fiction—truly a stunning piece of work.

About the same time, Gregory Benford, a longtime friend, invited me to submit an original story to an anthology he was editing, Far Futures, to be published by Tor Books. The Japanese edition presented no difficulties, and so I was able to market the story as an original publication twice, always a good thing, though rare in my experience.

Among the hardest science fiction stories to write are those set in the near future, and the very far future. The near future is difficult because it takes only a few years for the reader and history to catch up with the story; maintaining believability in such circumstances is difficult. A typical mistake is inventing too many new words and new things, thus: "In the year 1990, John Jones entered the living room of his beautiful mistress, Leonora. He rubbed the lumo-cig across his palm, took a deep inhale of the herbivorous tobacco, and switched on the Tri-D set to catch the morning Dicto-news." Only rarely does society accept a new word for something familiar, however expanded its capabilities. Thus, a cellular phone is still a phone, not a trans-palmer. A 3D TV is probably still going to be a TV, not a Tri-D visionater. An electronic nose flute is still going to be—well, you get the idea.

The far future is difficult to describe because so much will have changed. Mainstream literature often claims that there are eternal human verities, immutable qualities that will last throughout all eternity. I have severe doubts about this. There is so much variation just in our time, around the globe, in these so-called basic verities that I can't imagine them not changing in the thousands of years to come.

The problem for a modern reader is that a believable story of the far future may also be incomprehensible. (To wit: "Fergon grabbed his twad with something very like glee, and obnoxiously asserted his right to snorg and wippie in the middle of the info-stream." Lewis Carroll, anyone?)

I've touched on the far future in a number of stories in this collection: "Hardfought," "The Fall of the House of Escher," and this one. Just to keep the attention of contemporary, mortal humans, I've stuck with a few of the eternal human verities in each of these tales.

I'm sure the real inhabitants of the distant future will forgive me. Or, to use their parlance, undergo complete snorgwhup and carnsymp on my case.

WE

Seven tributaries disengage from their social=mind and Library and travel by transponder to the School World. There they are loaded into a temporary soma, an older physical model with eight long, flexible red legs. Here the seven become We.

We have received routine orders from the Teacher Annex. We are to investigate student labor on the Great Plain of History, the largest physical feature on the School World. The students have been set to searching all past historical records, donated by the nine remaining Libraries. Student social=minds are sad; they will not mature before Endtime. They are the last new generation and their behavior is often aberrant. There may be room for error.

The soma sits in an enclosure. We become active and advance

from the enclosure's shadow into a light shower of data condensing from the absorbing clouds high above. We see radiation from the donating Libraries, still falling on School World from around the three remaining systems; We hear the lambda whine of storage in the many rows of black hemispheres perched on the plain; we feel a patter of drops on our black carapace.

We stand at the edge of the plain, near a range of bare brown and black hills left over from planetary reformation. The air is thick and cold. It smells sharply of rich data moisture, wasted on us; We do not have readers on our surface. The moisture dews up on the dark, hard ground under our feet, evaporates, and is reclaimed by translucent soppers. The soppers flit through the air, a tenth our size and delicate.

The hemispheres are maintained by single–tributary somas. They are tiny, marching along the rows by the hundreds of thousands.

The brilliant violet sun appears in the west, across the plain, surrounded by streamers of intense blue. The streamers curl like flowing hair. Sun and streamers cast multiple shadows from each black hemisphere. The sun attracts our attention. It is beautiful, not part of a Library simscape; this scape is *real*. It reminds us of approaching Endtime; the changes made to conserve and concentrate the last available energy have rendered the scape beautifully novel, unfamiliar to the natural birth algorithms of our tributaries.

The three systems are unlike anything that has ever been. They contain all remaining order and available energy. Drawn close together, surrounded by the permutation of local space and time, the three systems deceive the dead outer universe, already well into the dull inaction of the long Between. We are proud of the three systems. They took a hundred million years to construct, and a tenth of all remaining available energy. They were a gamble. Nine of thirty–seven major Libraries agreed to the gamble. The others spread themselves into the greater magnitudes of the Between, and died.

The gamble worked.

Our soma is efficient and pleasant to work with. All of our tributaries agree, older models of such equipment are better. We have an appointment with the representative of the School World students, student tributaries lodged in a newer model soma called a Berkus, after a social=mind on Second World, which designed it. A Berkus soma is not favored. It is noisy; perhaps more efficient, but brasher and less elegant. We agree it will be ugly.

Data clouds swirl and spread tendrils high over the plain. The single somas march between our legs, cleaning unwanted debris from the black domes. Within the domes, all history. We could reach down and crush one with the claws on a single leg, but that would slow Endtime Work and waste available energy. We are proud of such stray, antisocial thoughts, and more proud still that We can ignore them. They show that We are still human, still linked directly to the past.

We are teachers. All teachers must be linked with the past, to understand and explain. Teachers must understand error; the past is rich with pain and error.

We await the Berkus.

Too much time passes. The world turns away from the sun and night falls. Centuries of Library time pass, but We try to be patient and think in the flow of external time. Some of our tributaries express a desire to taste the domes, but there is no real need, and this would also waste available energy.

With night, more data fills the skies from the other systems, condenses, and rains down, covering us with a thick sheen. Soppers again clean our carapace. All around, the domes grow richer, absorbing history. We see, in the distance, a night interpreter striding on giant disjointed legs between the domes. It eats the domes and returns white mounds of discard. All the domes must be interpreted to see if any of the history should be carried by the final Endtime self.

The final self will cross the Between, order held in perfect inaction, until the Between has experienced sufficient rest and boredom. It will cross that point when time and space become granular and nonlinear, when the unconserved energy of expansion, absorbed at the minute level of the quantum foam, begins to disturb the metric. The metric becomes noisy and irregular, and all extension evaporates. The universe has no width, no time, and all is back at the beginning.

The final self will survive, knitting itself into the smallest interstices, armored against the fantastic pressures of a universe's deathsound. The quantum foam will give up its noise and new universes will bubble forth and evolve. One will transcend. The transcendent reality will absorb the final self, which will seed it. From the compression should arise new intelligent beings.

It is an important thing, and all teachers approve. The past should cover the new, forever. It is our way to immortality.

Our tributaries express some concern. We are to be sure not on a vital mission, but the Berkus is very late. Something has gone wrong. We investigate our links and find them cut. Transponders do not reply.

The ground beneath our soma trembles. Hastily, the soma retreats from the plain of history. It stands by a low hill, trying to keep steady on its eight red legs. The clouds over the plain turn green and ragged. The single somas scuttle between vibrating hemispheres, confused.

We cannot communicate with our social=mind or Library. No other libraries respond. Alarmed, We appeal to the School World Student Committee, then point our thoughts up to the Endtime Work Coordinator, but they do not answer, either.

The endless kilometers of low black hemispheres churn as if stirred by a huge stick. Cracks appear, and from the cracks, thick red fluid drops; the drops crystallize into high, tall prisms. Many of the prisms shatter and turn to dead white powder.

We realize with great concern that We are seeing the internal stored data of the planet itself. This is a reserve record of all Library knowledge, held condensed; the School World contains selected records from the dead Libraries, more information than any single Library could absorb in a billion years. The knowledge shoots through the disrupted ground in crimson fountains, wasted.

Our soma retreats deeper into the hills.

Nobody answers our emergency signal.

Nobody will speak to us, anywhere.

More days pass. We are still cut off from the Library. Isolated, We are limited only to what the soma can perceive, and that makes no sense at all.

We have climbed a promontory overlooking what was once the Great Plain of History. Where once our students worked to condense and select those parts of the past that would survive the Endtime, the hideous leaking of reserve knowledge has slowed and an equally hideous round of what seems to be amateurish student exercises work themselves in rapid time.

Madness covers the plain. The hemispheres have all disintegrated, and the single somas and interpreters have vanished.

Now, everywhere on the plain, green and red and purple forests grow and die in seconds; new trees push through the dead snags of the old. New kinds of tree invade from the west and push aside their predecessors. Climate itself accelerates: the skies grew heavy with cataracting clouds made of water, and rain falls in sinuous sheets. Steam twists and pullulates. The ground becomes hot with change.

Trees themselves come to an end and crumble away; huge solid brown and red domes balloon on the plain, spread thick shell–leaves like opening cabbages, push long shoots through their crowns. The shoots tower above the domes and bloom with millions of tiny gray and pink flowers.

Watching all our work and plans destroyed, the seven tributaries within our soma offer dismayed hypotheses: this is a malfunction, the conservation and compression engines have failed and all knowledge is being acted out uselessly; no, it is some new gambit of the Endtime Work Coordinator, an emergency project; on the contrary, it is a political difficulty, lack of communication between the Coordinator and the Libraries, and it will all be over soon. . .

We watch shoots topple with horrendous snaps and groans, domes collapse in brown puffs of corruption.

The scape begins anew.

More hours pass, and still no communication with any other social=minds. We fear our Library itself has been destroyed; what other explanation for our abandonment? We huddle on our promontory, seeing patterns but no sense. Each generation of creativity brings something different, something that eventually fails or is rejected.

Today, large–scale vegetation is the subject of interest. The next day, vegetation is ignored for a rush of tiny biologies, no change visible from where We stand, our soma still and watchful on its eight sturdy legs. We shuffle our claws to avoid a carpet of reddish growth surmounting the rise. By nightfall, We see, the mad scape could claim this part of the hill and We will have to move.

The sun approaches zenith. All shadows vanish. Its violet magnificence humbles us, a feeling We are not used to. We are from the great social=minds of the Library; humility and awe come from our isolation and concern. Not for a billion years have any of our tributaries felt so removed from useful enterprise. If this is the Endtime overtaking us, overcoming all our efforts, so be it. We feel resolve, pride at what We have managed to accomplish.

Then, We receive a simple message. The meeting with the students will take place. The Berkus will find us and explain. But We are not told when.

Something has gone very wrong, that students should dictate to their teachers, and should put so many tributaries through this kind of travail.

The concept of *mutiny* is studied by all the tributaries within the soma. It does not explain much. New hypotheses occupy our thinking. Perhaps the new matter of which all things were now made has itself gone wrong, destabilizing our worlds and interrupting the consolidation of knowledge; that would explain the scape's ferment and our isolation. It might explain unstable and improper thought processes. Or, the students have allowed some activity on School World to run wild; error.

The scape pushes palace-like glaciers over its surface, gouging itself in painful ecstasy: change, change, birth and decay, all in a single day, but slower than the rush of forests and living things. We might be able to remain on the promontory.

Why are We treated so?

We keep to the open, holding our ground, clearly visible, concerned but unafraid. We are of older stuff. Teachers have always been of older stuff.

Could We have been party to some mis-instruction, to cause such a disaster? What have We taught that might push our students into manic creation and destruction? We search all records, all memories, contained within the small soma. The full memories of our seven tributaries have not of course been transferred into the extension; it was to be a temporary assignment, and besides, the records would not fit. The lack of capacity hinders our thinking and We find no satisfying answers.

One of our tributaries has brought along some personal records. It has a long shot hypothesis and suggests that an ancient prior self be activated to provide an objective judgment engine. There are two reasons: the stronger is that this ancient self once, long ago, had a connection with a tributary making up the Endtime Work Coordinator. If the problem is political, perhaps the self's memories can give us deeper insight. The second and weaker reason: truly, despite our complexity and advancement, perhaps We have missed something important. Perhaps this earlier, more primitive self will see what We have missed.

There is indeed so little time; isolated as We are from a greater river of being, a river that might no longer exist, We might be the last fragment of social=mind to have any chance of combating planet–wide madness.

There is barely enough room to bring the individual out of compression. It sits beside the tributaries in the thought plenum, in distress and not functional. What it perceives it does not understand.

Our questions are met with protests and more questions.

THE ENGINE

I come awake, aware. *I* sense a later and very different awareness, part of a larger group. My thoughts spin with faces to which I try to apply names, but my memory falters. These fade and are replaced by gentle calls for attention, new and very strange sensations.

I label the sensations around me: other humans, but not in human bodies. They seem to act together while having separate voices. I call the larger group the We–ness, not me and yet in some way accessible, as if part of my mind and memory.

I do not think that I have died, that I am *dead*. But the quality of my thought has changed. I have no body, no sensations of liquid pumping and breath flowing in and out.

Isolated, confused, I squat behind the We–ness's center of observation, catching glimpses of a chaotic, high–speed landscape. Are they watching some entertainment?

I worry that I am in a hospital, in recovery, forced to consort with other patients who cannot or will not speak with me. I try to collect my last meaningful memories. I remember a face again and give it a name and relation: Elisaveta, my wife, standing beside me as I lie on a narrow bed. Machines bend over me. I remember nothing after that.

But I am not in a hospital, not now.

Voices speak to me and I begin to understand some of what they say. The voices of the We–ness are stronger, more complex and richer, than anything I have ever experienced.

I do not hear them.

I have no ears.

"You've been stored inactive for a very long time," the We–ness tells me. It is (or they are) a tight–packed galaxy of thoughts, few of them making any sense at all.

Then I know.

I have awakened in the future. Thinking has changed.

"I don't know where I am. I don't know who you are . . ."

"We are joined from seven tributaries, some of whom once had existence as individual biological beings. You are an ancient self of one of us."

"Oh," I say. The word seems wrong without lips or throat. I will not use it again.

"We're facing great problems. You'll provide unique insights." The voice expresses overtones of fatherliness and concern.

I do not believe it. Blackness paints me.

"I'm hungry but I can't feel my body. Where am I? I'm afraid. I miss . . . my family."

"There is no body, no need for hunger, no need for food. Your family—*our* family—no longer lives."

"How did I get here?"

"You were stored before a major medical reconstruction, to prevent total loss. Your stored self was kept as a kind of an historical record, as a memento."

I don't remember any of that, but then, how could I? I remember signing contracts to allow such a thing. I remember thinking about the possibility I would awake in the future. But I did not die! "How long has it been?"

"Twelve billion two hundred and seventy–nine million years."

Had the We–ness said, *Ten thousand years,* or even *two hundred years*, I might feel some visceral reaction. All I know is that such an enormous length of time is beyond geological. It is *cosmo-logical*. I do not believe in it.

I glimpse the landscape again, glaciers slipping down mountain slopes, clouds pregnant with winter building gray and orange in the stinging glare of a huge setting sun. The sun is all wrong—too bright, too violet. It resembles a dividing cell, all extrusions and blebs and long ribbons of streaming hair. It could be Medusa, one of the Gorgon sisters.

The edges of the glaciers calve pillars of white ice that topple and shatter across hills and valleys. I have awakened in the middle of an ice age. But it is *fast*, too fast.

Nothing makes sense.

"Is all of me here?" I ask. Perhaps, lacking a whole mind, I am delusional.

"The most important part of you is here. We would like to ask you some questions. Do you recognize any of the following faces/voices/thought patterns/styles?"

Disturbing synesthesia—bright sounds, loud colors, dull electric smells—fill my senses and I close them out as best I can. "No! That isn't right. Please, no questions until I know what's happened. No! That hurts!"

The We-ness prepares to turn me off, to shut me down. I am warned that I will again become inactive. Just before I wink out, I feel a cold blast of air crest the promontory on which the We-ness, and I, sit. Glaciers now blanket the hills and valleys. The We-ness flexes eight fluid red legs, pulling them from quick-freezing mud.

The sun still has not set.

Thousands of years in a day.

I am given sleep as blank as death, but not so final.

We gather as one and consider the problem of the faulty interface. "This is too early a self. It doesn't understand our way of thinking," one tributary says. "We must adapt to it."

The tributary whose prior self this was volunteers to begin re-structuring.

"There is so little time," says another, who now expresses strong disagreement with the plan to resurrect. "Are We truly agreed this is best?"

We threaten to fragment as two of the seven tributaries vehemently object. But solidarity holds. All tributaries flow again to renewed agreement. We start the construction of an effective interface, which first requires deeper understanding of the nature of the ancient self.

This takes some more precious time. The glacial cold nearly kills us. The soma changes its fluid nature by linking liquid water with long-chain and even more slippery molecules, highly resistant to freezing.

"Do the students know We're here, that We watch?" asks a tributary.

"They must . . ." says another. "They express a willingness to meet with us."

"Perhaps they lie, and they mean to destroy this soma, and us with it. There will be no meeting."

Dull sadness.

We restructure the ancient self, wrap it in our new interface, build a new plenary face to hold us all on equal ground, and call it up again, saying,

Vasily

I know the name, recognize the fatherly voice, feel a new clarity. I wish I could forget the first abortive attempt to live again, but my memory is perfect from the point of first rebirth on. I will forget nothing.

"Vasily, your descendant self does not remember you. It has purged older memories many times since your existence, but We recognize some similarities even so between your patterns. Birth patterns are strong and seldom completely erased. Are you comfortable now?"

I think of a simple place where I can sit. I want wood paneling and furniture and a fireplace, but I am not skilled; all I can manage is a small gray cubicle with a window on one side. In the wall is a hole through which the voices come. I imagine I am hearing them through flesh ears, and a kind of body forms within the cubicle. This body is my security. "I'm still afraid. I know—there's no danger."

"There *is* danger, but We do not yet know how significant the danger is."

Significant carries an explosion of information. If their original selves still exist elsewhere, in a social=mind adjunct to a Library, then all that might be lost will be immediate memories. A *social=mind*, I understand, is made up of fewer than ten thousand tributaries. A Library typically contains a trillion or more social minds.

"I've been dead for billions of years," I say, hoping to address my future self. "But you've lived on—you're immortal."

"We do not measure life or time as you do. Continuity of memory is fragmentary in our lives, across eons. But continuity of access to the Library—and access to records of past selves—does confer a kind of immortality. If that has ended, We are completely mortal."

"I must be so primitive," I say, my fear oddly fading now. This is a situation I can understand—life or death. I feel more solid within my cubicle. "How can I be of any use?"

"You are primitive in the sense of *firstness*. That is why you have been activated. Through your life experience, you may have a deeper understanding of what led to our situation. Argument, rebellion, desperation . . . These things are difficult for us to deal with."

Again, I don't believe them. From what I can tell, this group of minds has a depth and strength and complexity that makes me feel less than a child . . . perhaps less than a bacterium. What can I do except cooperate? I have nowhere else to go. . .

For billions of years . . . inactive. Not precisely death.

I remember that I was once a *teacher*.

Elisaveta had been my student before she became my wife.

The We-ness wants me to teach it something, to do something for it. But first, it has to teach me history.

"Tell me what's happened," I say.

THE LIBRARIES

In the beginning, human intelligences arose, and all were alone. That lasted for tens of thousands of years. Soon after understanding the nature of thought and mind, intelligences came together to create group minds, all in one. Much of the human race linked in an intimacy deeper than sex. Or unlinked to pursue goals as quasi-individuals; the choices were many, the limitations few. (*This all began a few decades after your storage.*) Within a century, the human race abandoned biological limitations, in favor of the social=mind. Social=minds linked to form Libraries, at the top of the hierarchy.

The Libraries expanded, searching around star after star for other intelligent life. They found life—millions upon millions of worlds, each rare as a diamond among the trillions of barren star systems, but none with intelligent beings. Gradually, across millions of years, the Libraries realized that they were the All of intelligent thought.

We had simply exchanged one kind of loneliness for a greater and more final isolation. There were no companion intelligences, only those derived from humanity. . .

As the human Libraries spread and connections between them became more tenuous—some communications taking thousands of years to be completed—many social=minds re-individuated, assuming lesser degrees of togetherness and intimacy. Even in large Libraries, individuation became a crucial kind of relaxation and holiday. The old ways reasserted.

Being human, however, some clung to old ways, or attempted to enforce new ones, with greater or lesser tenacity. Some asserted moral imperative. Madness spread as large groups removed all the barriers of individuation, in reaction to what they perceived as a dangerous atavism—the "lure of the singular."

These "uncelled" or completely communal Libraries, with their slow, united consciousness, proved burdensome and soon vanished—within half a million years. They lacked the range and versatility of the "celled" Libraries.

But conflicts between differing philosophies of social=mind structure continued. There were wars.

Even in wars the passions were not sated; for something more frightening had been discovered than loneliness: the continuity of error and cruelty. After tens of millions of years of steady growth and peace, the renewed paroxysms dismayed us. No matter how learned or advanced a social=mind became, it could, in desperation or in certain moments of development, perform acts analogous to the errors of ancient, individuated societies. It could kill other social=minds, or sever the activities of many of its own tributaries. It could frustrate the fulfillment of other minds. It could experience something like *rage*, but removed from the passions of the body: rage cold and precise and long-lived, terrible in its persuasiveness, dreadful in its consequences. Even worse, it could experience *indifference*.

I tumble through these records, unable to comprehend the scale of what I see. Our galaxy was linked star to star with webworks of transferred energy and information; but large sectors of the galaxy were darkened by massive conflict, and millions of stars turned off, shut down.

This was war.

At the scale of individual humans, planets seemed to revert to ancient Edens, devoid of artifice or instrumentality; but the trees and animals themselves carried myriads of tiny machines, and the ground beneath them was an immense thinking system, down to the core . . .

Other worlds, and other structures between worlds, seemed as abstract and meaningless as the wanderings of a stray brush on canvas.

THE PROOF

One great social=mind, retreating from the ferment of the Libraries, formulated the rules of advanced meta–biology, and found them precisely analogous to those governing planet-bound ecosystems: competition, victory through survival, evolution and reproduction. It proved that error and pain and destruction are essential to any change—but more importantly, to any growth.

The great social=mind carried out complex experiments simulating millions of different ordering systems, and in every single case, the rise of complexity (and ultimately intelligence) led to the wanton destruction of prior forms. Using these experiments to define axioms, what began as a scientific proof ended as a rigorous mathematical proof:

There can be no ultimate ethical advancement in this universe

The indifference of the universe—reality's grim and mindless harshness—is multiplied by the necessity that old order, prior thoughts and lives, must be extinguished to make way for new.

After checking its work many times, the great social=mind wiped its stores and erased its infrastructure in, on and around seven worlds and the two stars, leaving behind only the formulation and the Proof.

For Libraries across the galaxy, absorption of the Proof led to mental disruption. From the nightmare of history there was to be no awakening.

Suicide was one way out. A number of prominent Libraries brought their own histories to a close. Others recognized the validity of the Proof, but did not commit suicide. They lived with the possibility of error and destruction. And still, they grew wiser, greater in scale and accomplishment . . .

Crossing from galaxy to galaxy, still alone, the Libraries realized that human perception was the only perception. The Proof would never be tested against the independent minds of non-human intelligences.

In this universe, the Proof must stand.

Billions of years passed, and the universe became a huge kind of house, confining a practical infinity of mind, an incredible ferment which "burned" the available energy with torchy brilliance, decreasing the total life span of reality.

Yet the Proof remained unassailed.

Wait. I don't see anything here. I don't *feel* anything. This isn't history; it's . . . too large! I can't understand some of the things you show me . . . But worse, pardon me, it's babbling among minds who feel no passion. This We–ness . . . how do you *feel* about this?

You are distracted by preconceptions. You long for an organic body, and assume that lacking organic bodies, We experience no emotions. We experience emotions. *Listen* to them>>>>>

I squirm in my cubicle and experience their emotions of first and second loneliness, degrees of isolation from old memories, old selves; longing for the first individuation, the Birth–time . . . Hunger for understanding not just of the outer reality, beyond the social=mind's vast internal universe of thought, but of the ever–changing currents and orderliness arising between tributaries. Here is social and mental interaction as a great song, rich and joyous, a love greater than anything I can remember experiencing as an embodied human. Greater emotions still, outside my range again, of loyalty and love for a social=mind and something like *respect* for the immense Libraries. (I am shown what the We–ness says is an emotion experienced at the level of Libraries, but it is so far beyond me that I seem to disintegrate, and have to be coaxed back to wholeness.)

A tributary approaches across the mind space within the soma. My cubicle grows dim. I feel a strange familiarity again.

This will be, this *is*, my future self.

This tributary feels sadness and some grief, touching its ancient self—me. It feels pain at my limitations, at my tight–packed biological character. Things deliberately forgotten come back to haunt it.

And they haunt *me*. My own inadequacies become abundantly clear. I remember useless arguments with friends, making my wife cry with frustration, getting angry at my children for no good reason. My childhood and adolescent indiscretions return like shadows on a scrim. And I remember my *drives:* rolling in useless lust, and later, Elisaveta! With her young and supple body.

And others.

Just as significant, but different in color, the cooler passions of discovery and knowledge, my growing self–awareness. I remember fear of inadequacy, fear of failure, of not being a useful member of society. I needed above all (more than I needed Elisaveta) to be important and to teach and be influential on young minds.

All of these emotions, the We–ness demonstrates, have analogous emotions at their level. For the We–ness, the most piercing unpleasantness of all—akin to physical pain—comes from recognition of their possible failure. The teachers may not have taught their students properly, and the students may be making mistakes.

"Let me get all this straight," I say. I grow used to my imagined state—to riding like a passenger within the cubicle, inside the eight–legged soma, to seeing as if through a small window the advancing and now receding of the glaciers. "You're teachers—as I was once a teacher—and you used to be connected to a larger social=mind, part of a Library." I mull over mind as society, society as mind. "But there may have been a revolution. After billions of years! Students . . . A *revolution!* Extraordinary! You've been cut off from the Library. You're alone, you might be killed . . . And you're telling *me* about ancient history?"

The We–ness falls silent.

"I must be important," I say with an unbreathed sigh, a kind of asterisk in the exchanged thoughts. "I can't imagine why. But maybe it doesn't matter—I have so many questions!" I hunger for knowledge of what has become of my children, of my wife. Of everything that came after me . . .

All the changes!

"We need information from you, and your interpretation of certain memories. Vasily was our name once. Vasily Gerazimov. You were the husband of Elisaveta, father of Maxim and Giselle . . . We need to know more about Elisaveta."

"You don't remember her?"

"Twelve billion years have passed. Time and space have changed. This tributary alone has since partnered and bonded and matched and socialized with perhaps fifty billion individuals and tributaries. Our combined tributaries in the social=mind have had contacts with all intelligent beings, once or twice removed. Most have dumped or stored memories more than a billion years old. If We were still connected to the Library, I could learn more about my past. I have kept you as a kind of *memento*, a talisman, and nothing more."

I feel a freezing awe. Fifty billion mates . . . Or whatever they had been. I catch fleeting glimpses of liaisons in the social=mind, binary, trinary, as many as thousands at a time linked in the crumbling remnants of marriage and sexuality, and finally those liaisons passing completely out of favor, fashion, or usefulness.

"Elisaveta and you," the tributary continues, "were divorced ten years after your storage. I remember nothing of the reasons why. We have no other clues to work with."

The "news" comes as a doubling of my pain, a renewed and expanded sense of isolation from a loved one. I reach up to touch my face, to see if I am crying. My hands pass through imagined flesh and bone. My body is long since dust; Elisaveta's body is dust.

What went wrong between us? Did she find another lover? Did I? I am a ghost. I should not care. There were difficult times, but I never thought of our liaison—our *marriage*, I would defend that word even now—as temporary. Still, across *billions* of years! We have become *immortal*—her perhaps more than I, who remember nothing of the time between. "Why do you need me at all? Why do you need clues?"

But We are interrupted. An extraordinary thing happens to the retreating glaciers. From our promontory, the soma half-hidden behind an upthrust of frozen and deformed knowledge, We see the icy masses blister and bubble as if made of some superheated glass or plastic. Steam bursts from the bubbles—at least, what appears to be steam—and freezes in the air in shapes suggesting flowers. All around, the walls and sheets of ice succumb to this beautiful plague.

The We-ness understands it no more than I.

From the hill below come faint sounds and hints of radiation—gamma rays, beta particles, mesons, all clearly visible to the We-ness, and vaguely passed on to me as well.

"Something's coming," I say.

The Berkus advances in its unexpected cloud of production-destruction. There is something deeply wrong with it—it squanders too much available energy. Its very presence disrupts the new matter of which We are made.

Of the seven tributaries, four feel an emotion rooted in the deepest algorithms of their pasts: fear. Three have never known such bodily functions, have never known mortal and embodied individuation. They feel intellectual concern and a tinge of cosmic sadness, as if our end might be equated with the deaths of stars and galaxies. We keep to our purpose despite these ridiculous excursions, the increasing and disturbing signs of our disorder.

The Berkus advances up the hill.

I see through my window this monumental and absolutely horrifying *creature*, shining with a brightness comprised of the qualities of diamonds and polished silver, a scintillating insect pushing its sharply pointed feet into the thawing soil, steam rising all around. The legs hold together despite gaps where joints should be, gaps crossed only by something that produces hard radiation. Below the Berkus (so the We–ness calls it), the ground ripples as if School World has muscles and twitches, wanting to scratch.

The Berkus pauses and sizes up our much less powerful, much smaller soma with blasts of neutrons, flicked as casually as a flashlight beam. The material of our soma wilts and reforms beneath this withering barrage. The soma expresses distress—and inadvertently, the We–ness translates this distress to me as tremendous pain.

Within my confined mental space, I explode . . .

Again comes the blackness.

The Berkus decides it is not necessary to come any closer. That is fortunate for us and for our soma. Any lessening of the distance could prove fatal.

The Berkus communicates with pulsed light. "Why are you here?"

"We have been sent here to observe and report. We are cut off from the Library—"

"Your Library has fled," the Berkus informs us. "It disagreed with the Endtime Work Coordinator."

"We were told nothing of this."

"It was not our responsibility. We did not know you would be here."

The magnitude of this rudeness is difficult to envelope. We

wonder how many tributaries the Berkus contains. We hypothesize that it might contain all of the students, the entire student social=mind, and this would explain its use of energy and change in design.

Our pitiful ancient individual flickers back into awareness and sits quietly, too stunned to protest.

"We do not understand the purpose of this creation and destruction," We say. Our strategy is to avoid the student tributaries altogether now. Still, they might tell us more We need to know.

"It must be obvious to teachers," the Berkus says. "By order of the Coordinator, We are rehearsing all possibilities of coherence, usurping stored knowledge down to the planetary core and converting it. There must be an escape from the Proof."

"The Proof is an ancient discovery. It has never been shown to be wrong. What can it possibly mean to the Endtime Work?"

"It means a great deal," the Berkus says.

"How many are you?"

The Berkus does not answer. All this has taken place in less than a millionth of a second. The Berkus's incommunication lengthens into seconds, then minutes.

Around us, the glaciers crumple like mud caught in rushing water.

"Another closed path, of no value," the Berkus finally says.

"We wish to understand your motivations. Why this concern with the Proof? And what does it have to do with the change you provoke, the destruction of School World's knowledge?"

The Berkus rises on a tripod of three disjointed legs, waving its other legs in the air, a cartoon medallion so disturbing in design that We draw back a few meters. "The Proof is a cultural aberration," it radiates fiercely, blasting our surface and making the mud around us bubble. "It is not fit to pass on to those who seed the next reality. You failed us. You showed no way beyond the Proof. The Endtime Work has begun, the final self chosen to fit through the narrow gap—"

*   *   *

I see all this through the We-ness as if I have been there, have lived it, and suddenly I know why I have been recalled, why the We-ness has shown me faces and patterns.

The universe, across more than twelve billion years, grows irretrievably old. From spanning the galaxies billions of years before, all life and intelligence—all arising from the sole intelligence in all the universe, humanity—have shrunk to a few star systems. These systems have been resuscitated and nurtured by concentrating the remaining available energy of thousands of dead galaxies.

And they are no longer natural star systems with planets—the bloated, coma-wrapped violet star rising at zenith is a congeries of plasma macromachines, controlling and conserving every gram of the natural matter remaining, harnessing every erg of available energy. These artificial suns pulse like massive living cells, shaped to be ultimately efficient and to squeeze every moment of active life over the time remaining. The planets themselves have been condensed, recarved, rearranged—and they too are composed of geological macromachines.

With some dread, I gather that the matter of which all these things are made is *itself* artificial, with redesigned component particles. The natural galaxies have died, reduced to a colorless murmur of useless heat, and the particles of all original creation—besides those marshaled and remade in these three close-packed systems—have dulled and slowed and unwound. Gravity itself has lost its bearings and become a chancy phenomenon, supplemented by new forces generated within the macromachine planets and suns. Nothing is what it seems, and nothing is what it had been when I lived.

The We-ness looks forward to less than four times ten to the fiftieth units of Planck time—roughly an old Earth year.

And in charge of it all, controlling the Endtime Work, a

supremely confident social=mind composed of many "tributaries," and among those gathered selves. . .

Someone very familiar to me indeed.

My wife.

"Where is she? Can I speak to her? What happened to her? Did she die, was she stored—did she live?"

The We–ness seems to vibrate both from my reaction to this information, and to the spite of the Berkus. I am assigned to a quiet place where I can watch and listen without bothering them.

I feel our soma, our insect–like body, dig into the loosening substance of the promontory.

"You taught us the Proof was absolute," the Berkus says, "that throughout all time, in all circumstances, error and destruction and pain will accompany growth and creation, that the universe must remain indifferent and randomly hostile. We do not accept that."

"But why dissolve links with the Library?" We cry, even as We shrink beneath the Berkus's glare. The constantly reconstructed body of the Berkus channels and consumes energy with enormous waste, as if the students do not care, intent only on their frantic mission, whatever that might be . . . Reducing available active time by days for *all of us*—

I know why! I know the reason! I shout in the quiet place, but I am not heard, or not paid attention to.

"Why condemn us to a useless end in this chaos, this madness?" We ask.

"Because We must refute the Proof and there is so little useful time remaining. The final self must not be sent over carrying this burden of error."

"Of sin!" I shout, still not heard. Proof of the validity of primordial sin—that everything living must eat, must destroy, must climb up

the ladder on the backs of miserable victims. That all true creation involves death and pain; the universe is a charnel house.

I am fed and study the Proof. I try to encompass the principles and expressions, no longer given as words, but as multi-sense abstractions. In the Proof, miniature universes of discourse are created, manipulated, reduced to an expression, and discarded: the Proof is more complex than any single human life, or even the life of a species, and its logic is not familiar. The Proof is rooted in areas of mental experience I am not equipped to understand, but I receive glosses.

Law: Any dynamic system (I understand this as *organism)* has limited access to resources, and a limited time in which to achieve its goals. A multitude of instances are drawn from history, as well as from an artificial miniature universe. Other laws follow regarding behavior of systems within a flow of energy, but they are completely beyond me.

Observed Law: The goals of differing organisms, even of like variety, never completely coincide. History and the miniature universe teem with instances, and the Proof lifts these up for inspection at moments of divergence, demonstrating again and again this obvious point.

Then comes a roll of deductions, backed by examples too numerous for me to absorb:

And so it follows that for any complex of organisms, competition must arise for limited resources.

From this: some will succeed, some will fail, to acquire resources sufficient to live. Those who succeed, express themselves in later generations.

From this: New dynamic systems will arise to compete more efficiently.

From this: Competition and selection will give rise to *streamlined* organisms that are incapable of surviving even in the midst of plenty because they are not equipped with complete methods of absorbing resources. These will prey on complete organisms to acquire their resources.

And in return, the prey will acquire a reliance on the predators to hone their fitness.

From this: Other forms of *streamlining* will occur. Some of the resulting systems will become diseases and parasites, depending entirely on others for reproduction and fulfillment of basic goals.

From this: Ecosystems will arise, interdependent, locked in predator-prey, disease-host relationships.

I experience a multitude of rigorous experiments, unfolding like flowers.

And so it follows that in the course of competition, some forms will be outmoded and will pass away, and others will be preyed upon to extinction, without regard to their beauty, their adaptability to a wide range of possible conditions.

I sense here a kind of aesthetic judgment, above the fray: beautiful forms will die without being fully tested, their information lost, their opportunities limited.

And so it follows. . .

And so it follows. . .

The ecosystems increase in complexity, giving rise to organisms whose primary adaptation is perception and judgment, forming the abstract equivalents of societies, which interact through the exchange of resources and extensions of cultures and politics—models for more efficient organization. Still, change and evolution, failure and death, societies and cultures pass and are forgotten; whole classes of these larger systems suffer extinction, without being allowed fulfillment.

From history: Nations pray upon nations, and eat them alive, discarding them as burned husks.

Law: The universe is neutral; it will not care, nor will any ultimate dynamic system interfere. . .

In those days before I was born, as smoke rose from the ovens, God did not hear the cries of His people.

And so it follows: that no system will achieve perfect efficiency and self-sufficiency. Within all changing systems, accumulated error must be purged. For the good of the dynamic whole, systems must die. But efficient and beautiful systems will die as well.

I see the Proof's abstraction of evil: a shark–like thing, to me, but no more than a very complex expression. In this shark there is history, and dumb organic pressure, and the accumulations of the past, and the shark does not discriminate, knows nothing of judgment or justice, will eat the promising and the strong as well as birthing young. Waste, waste, an agony of waste, and over it all, not watching, the indifference of the real.

After what seems hours of study, of questions asked and answered, new ways of thinking acquired—re–education—I begin to feel the thoroughness of the Proof, and I feel a despair unlike anything in my embodied existence.

Where once there had been hope that intelligent organisms could see their way to just, beautiful and efficient systems, in practice, without exception, they revert to the old rules.

Things have not and will never improve.

Heaven itself would be touched with evil—or stand still. But there is no heaven run by a just God. Nor can there be a just God. Perfect justice and beauty and evolution and change are incompatible.

Not the birth of my son and daughter, not the day of my marriage, not all my moments of joy can erase the horror of history. And the stretch of future histories, after my storage, shows even more horror, until I seem to swim in carnivorous, *cybernivorous* cruelty.

CONNECTIONS

We survey the Berkus with growing concern. Here is not just frustration of our attempts to return to the Library, not just destruction of knowledge, but a flagrant and purposeless waste of precious resources. Why is it allowed?

Obviously, the Coordinator of the Endtime Work has given license, handed over this world, with such haste that We did not have time to withdraw. The Library has been forced away (or worse), and all transponders destroyed, leaving us alone on School World.

The ancient self, having touched on the Proof (absorbing no more than a fraction of its beauty) is wrapped in a dark shell of mood. This mood, basic and primal as it is, communicates to the tributaries. Again, after billions of years, We feel sadness at the inevitability of error and the impossibility of justice—and sadness at our own error. The Proof has always stood as a monument of pure thought—and a curse, even to We who affirm it.

The Berkus expands like a balloon. "There is going to be major work done here. You will have to move."

"*No*," the combined tributaries cry. "This is enough confusion and enough being *shoved around*." Those words come from the ancient self.

The Berkus finds them amusing.

"Then you'll stay here," it says, "and be absorbed in the next round of experiment. You are teachers who have taught incorrectly. You deserve no better."

I break free of the *dark shell of mood*, as the tributaries describe it, and now I seem to kick and push my way to a peak of attention, all without arms or legs.

"Where is the plan, the order? Where are your billions of years of superiority? How can this be happening?"

We pass on the cries of the ancient self. The Berkus hears the message.

"We are not familiar with this voice," the student social=mind says.

"I judge you from the past!" the ancient self says. "You are *all* found wanting!"

"This is not the voice of a tributary, but of an individual," the Berkus says. "The individual sounds uninformed."

"I demand to speak with my wife!"

My demand gets no reaction for almost a second. Around me, the tributaries within the soma flow and rearrange, thinking in a way I cannot follow. They finally rise as a solid, seamless river of consent.

"*We charge you with error,*" they say to the Berkus. "*We charge you with confirming the Proof you wish to negate.*"

The Berkus considers, then backs away swiftly, beaming at us one final message: "There is an interesting rawness in your charge. You no longer think as outmoded teachers. A link with the End-time Work Coordinator will be requested. Stand where you are. Our own work must continue."

I feel a sense of relief around me. This is a breakthrough. I have a purpose! The Berkus retreats, leaving us on the promontory to observe. Where once, hours before, glaciers melted, the ground begins to churn, grow viscous, divide into fenced enclaves. Within the enclaves, green and gray shapes arise, sending forth clouds of steam. These enclaves surround the range of hills, surmount all but our promontory, and move off to the horizon on all sides, perhaps covering the entire School World.

In the center of each fenced area, a sphere forms first as a white blister on the hardness, then a pearl resting on the surface. The pearl lifts, suspended in air. Each pearl begins to evolve in a different way, turning inward, doubling, tripling, flattening into disks, centers dividing to form toruses; a practical infinity of different forms.

The fecundity of idea startles me. Blastulas give rise to cell–like complexity, spikes twist into intricate knots, all the rules of ancient topological mathematics are demonstrated in seconds, and then violated as the spaces within the enclaves themselves change.

"What are they doing?" I ask, bewildered.

"A mad push of evolution," my descendant self explains, "trying all combinations starting from a simple beginning. This was once a common exercise, but not on such a vast scale. Not since the formulation of the Proof."

"What do they want to learn?"

"If they can find one instance of evolution and change that involves only growth and development, not competition and destruction, then they will have falsified the Proof."

"But the Proof is perfect," I said. "It can't be falsified . . ."

"So we have judged. The students incorrectly believe we are wrong."

The field of creation becomes a vast fabric, each enclave contributing to a larger weave. What is being shown here could have occupied entire civilizations in my time: the dimensions of change, all possibilities of progressive growth.

"It's beautiful," I say.

"It's futile," my descendant self says, its tone bitter. I feel the emotion in its message as an aberration, and it immediately broadcasts shame to all of its fellows, and to me.

"Are you afraid they'll show your teachings were wrong?" I asked.

"No," my tributary says. "I am sorry that they will fail. Such a message to pass on to a young universe . . . That whatever our nature and design, however we develop, we are doomed to make errors and cause pain. Still, that is the truth, and it has never been refuted."

"But even in my time, there was a solution," I say.

They show mild curiosity. What could come from so far in the past, that they hadn't advanced upon it, improved it, a billion times over, or discarded it? I wonder why I have been activated at all. . .

But I persist. "From God's perspective, destruction and pain and error may be part of the greater whole, a beauty from its point of view. We only perceive it as evil because of our limited point of view."

The tributaries allow a polite pause. My tributary explains, as gently as possible, "We have never encountered ultimate systems you call gods. Still, We are or have been very much like gods. As gods, all too often we have made horrible errors, and caused unending pain. Pain did not add to the beauty."

I want to scream at them for their hubris, but it soon becomes apparent to me, they are right. Their predecessors have reduced galaxies, scanned all histories, made the universe itself run faster with their productions and creations. They have advanced the Endtime by billions of years, and now prepare to seed a new universe across an inconceivable gap of darkness and immobility.

From my perspective, humans have certainly become god-like. But not just. And there are no others. Even in the diversity of the human Diaspora across the galaxies, not once has the Proof been falsified.

And that is all it would have taken: one instance.

"*Why did you bring me back, then?*" I ask my descendant self in private conference.

It replies in kind:

"*Your thought processes are not our own. You can be a judgment engine. You might give us insight into the reasoning of the students, and help explain to us their plunge into greater error. There must be some motive not immediately apparent, some fragment of personality and memory responsible for this. An ancient self of a tributary of the Endtime Work Coordinator, and you, were once intimately related—married as sexual partners. You did not stay married. That is division and dissent. And there is division and dissent between the Endtime Work Committee and the teachers. That much is apparent . . .*"

Again I feel like clutching my hands to my face and screaming in frustration. Elisaveta—it must mean Elisaveta.

But we were not divorced . . . not when I was stored!

I sit in my imagined gray cubicle, my imagined body uncertain in its outline, and wish for a moment of complete privacy. They give it to me.

TAPERING TIME

The scape has progressed to a complexity beyond our ability to process. We stand on our promontory, surrounded by the field of enclaved experiments, each enclave containing a different evolved object, still furiously morphing. Some of the objects glow faintly as night sweeps across our part of the School World.

We are as useless and incompetent as the revived ancient self, now wrapped in its own shock and misery. Our tributaries have fallen silent. We wait for what will happen next, either in the scape, or in the promised contact with the Endtime Work Coordinator.

The ancient self rises from its misery and isolation. It joins our watchful silence, expectant. It has not completely lost *hope*. We have never had need of *hope*. Connected to the Library, fear became a distant and unimportant thing; hope, its opposite, equally distant and not useful.

I have been musing over my last hazy memories of Elisaveta, of our children Maxim and Giselle—bits of conversation, physical features, smells . . . Reliving long stretches with the help of memory recovery . . . watching seconds pass into minutes as if months pass into years.

Outside, time seems to move much more swiftly. The divisions between enclaves fall and the uncounted experiments stand on the field, still evolving, but now allowed to interact. Tentatively, their evolution takes in the new possibility of *motion*.

I feel for the students, wish to be part of them. However wrong, this experiment is vital, idealistic. It smells of youthful naiveté.

Because of my own rugged youth, raised in a nation running frantically from one historical extreme to another, born to parents who jumped like puppets between hope and despair, I have always felt uneasy in the face of idealism and naiveté.

Elisaveta was a naive idealist when I first met her. I tried to teach her, pass on my sophistication, my sense of better judgment.

The brightly colored, luminous objects hover on the plain, discovering new relations: a separate identity, a larger sense of space. The objects have reached a high level of complexity and order, but within a limited environment. If any have developed mind, they can now reach out and explore new objects.

First, the experiments shift a few centimeters this way or that, visible across the plain as kind of restless, rolling motion. The plain becomes an ocean of gentle waves. Then, the experiments *bump* each other. Near our hill, some of the experiments circle and surround their companions, or just bump with greater and greater urgency. Extensions reach out, and we can see—it must be obvious to all—that mind does exist, and new senses are being created and explored.

If Elisaveta, whatever she has become, is in charge of this sea of experiments, then perhaps she is merely following an inclination she had billions of years before: when in doubt, when all else fails, *punt*.

This is a cosmological kind of punt, burning up available energy at a distressing rate. . .

Just like her, I think, and feel a warmth of connection with that ancient woman. But the woman *divorced* me. She found me wanting, later than my memories reach . . . And after all, what she has become is as little like the Elisaveta I knew as my descendant tributary is like me.

The dance on the plain becomes a frenzied blur of color. Snakes flow, sprout legs, wings beat the air. Animal relations, plant relations, new ecosystems . . . But these creatures have evolved not from the simplest beginnings, but from already elaborate sources.

Each isolated experiment, already having achieved a focused complexity beyond anything I can understand, becomes a potential player in a new order of interaction.

What do the students—or Elisaveta—hope to accomplish in this peculiar variation on the old scheme?

I am so focused on the spectacle surrounding us that it takes a "nudge" from my descendant self to alert me to change in the sky. A liquid silvery ribbon pours from above, spreading over our heads into a flat, upside–down ocean of reflective cloud. The inverse ocean expands to the horizon, blocking all light from the new day.

Our soma rises expectantly on its eight legs. I feel the tributaries' interest as a kind of heat through my cubicle, and for the moment, abandon the imagined environment.

Best to receive this new phenomenon directly.

A fringed curtain, like the edge of a shawl woven from threads of mercury, descends from the upside-down ocean, brushing across the land. The fringe crosses the plain of experiments without interfering, but surrounds our hill, screening our view. Light pulses from selected threads in the liquid weave.

The tributaries translate instantly.

"What do *you* want?" asks a clear, neutral voice. No character, no tone, no emotion. This is the Endtime Work Coordinator, or at least an extension of that powerful social=mind. It does not sound anything like Elisaveta. My hopes have been terribly naive.

After all this time and misery, the teachers' reserve is admirable. I detect respect, but no awe; they are used to the nature of the Endtime Work Coordinator, largest of the social=minds not directly connected to a Library.

"We have been cut off, and We need to know why," the tributaries say.

"Your work reached a conclusion," the voice responds.

"Why were We not accorded the respect of being notified, or allowed to return to our Library?"

"Your Library has been terminated. We have concluded the active existence of all entities no longer directly connected with Endtime Work, to conserve available energy."

"But you have let us live."

"It would involve more energy to terminate existing extensions than to allow them to run down."

The sheer coldness and precision of the voice chill me. The end of a Library is equivalent to the end of thousands of worlds full of individual intelligences.

Genocide. Error and destruction.

But my future self corrects me. *"This is expediency,"* it says in a private sending. *"It is what We all expected would happen sooner or later. The manner seems irregular, but the latitude of the Endtime Work Coordinator is great."*

Still, the tributaries request a complete accounting of the decision. The Coordinator obliges.

A judgment arrives:

The Teachers are irrelevant. Teaching of the Proof has been deemed useless; the Coordinator has decided—

I hear a different sort of voice, barely recognizable to me—*Elisaveta*—

"All affirmations of the Proof merely discourage our search for alternatives. The Proof has become a thought disease, a cultural tyranny. It blocks our discovery of another solution."

A NEW ACCOUNTING

Our ancient self recognizes something in the message. What We have planned from near the beginning now bears fruit—the ancient self, functioning as an engine of judgment and recognition, has found a key player in the decision to isolate us, and to terminate our Library.

"We detect the voice of a particular tributary," We say to the Coordinator. "May We communicate with this tributary?"

"Do you have a valid reason?" the Coordinator asks.

"We must check for error."

"Your talents are not recognized."

"Still, the Coordinator might have erred, and as there is so little time, following the wrong course will be doubly tragic."

The Coordinator reaches a decision after sufficient time to show a complete polling of all tributaries within its social=mind.

"An energy budget is established. Communication is allowed."

We follow protocol billions of years old, but excise unnecessary ceremonies. We poll the student tributaries, searching for some flaw in reasoning, finding none.

Then We begin searching for our own justification. If We are about to *die*, lost in the last–second noise and event–clutter of a universe finally running down, We need to know where *We* have failed. If there is no failure—and if all this experimentation is simply a futile act, We might die less ignominiously. We search for the tributary familiar to the ancient self, hoping to find the personal connection that will reduce all our questions to one exchange.

Bright patches of light in the sky bloom, spread, and are quickly gathered and snuffed. The other suns and worlds are being converted and conserved.

We have minutes, perhaps only seconds.

We find the voice, descendant tributary of Elisaveta.

There are immense deaths in the sky, and now all is going dark. There is only the one sun, turning in on itself, violet shading to deep orange, and the School World.

Four seconds. I have just four seconds . . . Endtime accelerates upon us. The student experiment has consumed so much energy. All other worlds have been terminated, all social=minds except the Endtime Coordinator's and the final self . . . The seed that will cross the actionless Between.

I feel the tributaries frantically create an interface, make distant requests, then demands. They meet strong resistance from a tributary within the Endtime Work Coordinator. This much they convey to me . . . I sense weeks, months, years of negotiation, all passing in a second of more and more disjointed and uncertain real time.

As the last energy of the universe is spent, as all potential and all kinesis bottom out at a useless average, the fractions of seconds become clipped, their qualities altered. Time advances with an irregular jerk, truly like an off–center wheel.

Agreement is reached. Law and persuasion even now have some force.

"Vasily. I haven't thought about you in ever so long."

"Elisaveta, is that you?"

I cannot see her. I sense a total lack of emotion in her words. And why not?

"Not *your* Elisaveta, Vasily. But I hold her memories and some of her patterns."

"You've been alive for billions of years?"

I receive a condensed impression of a hundred million sisters, all related to Elisaveta, stored at different times like a huge library of past selves. The final tributary she has become, now an important part of the Coordinator, refers to her past selves much as a grown woman might open childhood diaries. The past selves are kept informed, to the extent that being informed does not alter their essential natures.

How differently my own descendant self behaves, sealing away a small part of the past as a reminder, but never consulting it. How perverse for a mind that reveres the past! Perhaps what it reveres is form, not actuality. . .

"Why do you want to speak with me?" Elisaveta asks. Which Elisaveta, from which time, I cannot tell right away.

"I think . . . *they* seem to think it's important. A disagreement, something that went wrong."

"They are seeking justification through you, a self stored billions of years ago. They want to be told that their final efforts have meaning. How like the Vasily I knew."

"It's not my doing! I've been inactive . . . Were we divorced?"

"Yes." Sudden realization changes the tone of this Elisaveta's voice. "You were stored before we divorced?"

"Yes! How long after . . . were you stored?"

"A century, maybe more," she answers. With some wonder, she says, "Who could have known we would live forever?"

"When I saw you last, we loved each other. We had children . . ."

"They died with the Libraries," she says.

I do not feel physical grief, the body's component of sadness and rage at loss, but the news rocks me, even so. I retreat to my gray cubicle. What happened to my children, in my time? What did they become to me, and I to them? Did they have children, grandchildren, and after our divorce, did they respect me enough to let me visit my grandchildren. . . ? But it's all lost now, and if they kept records of their ancient selves—records of what had truly been my children—that is gone, too.

My children! They have survived all this time, and yet I have missed them.

They are *dead*.

Elisaveta regards my grief with some wonder, and finds it sympathetic. I feel her warm to me slightly. "They weren't really our children any longer, Vasily. They became something quite other, as have you and I. But *this* you—you've been kept like a butterfly in a collection. How sad."

She seeks me out and takes on a bodily form. It is not the shape of the Elisaveta I knew. She once built a biomechanical body to carry her thoughts. This is the self-image she carries now, of a mind within a primitive, woman-shaped soma.

"What happened to us?" I ask, my agony apparent to her, to all who listen.

"Is it that important to you?"

"Can you explain any of this?" I ask. I want to bury myself in her bosom, to hug her. I am so lost and afraid I feel like a child, and yet my pride keeps me together.

"I was your student, Vasily. Remember? You *browbeat* me into marrying you. You poured learning into my ear day and night, even when we made love. You were so full of knowledge. You spoke nine languages. You knew all there was to know about Schopenhauer and Hegel and Marx and Wittgenstein. You did not listen to what was important to me."

I want to draw back; it is impossible to cringe. This I recognize. This I remember. But the Elisaveta I knew had come to accept me, my faults and my learning, joyously; had encouraged me to open up with her. I had taught her a great deal.

"You gave me absolutely no room to grow, Vasily."

The enormous triviality of this conversation, at the end of time, strikes me and I want to laugh out loud. Not possible. I stare at this *monstrous* Elisaveta, so bitter and different . . . And now, to me, shaded by her indifference.

"I feel like I've been half a dozen men, and we've all loved you badly," I say, hoping to sting her.

"No. Only one. You became angry when I disagreed with you. I asked for more freedom to explore . . . You said there was really little left to explore. Even in the last half of the twenty–first century, Vasily, you said we had found all there was to find, and everything thereafter would be mere details. When I had my second child, it began. I saw you through the eyes of my infant daughter, saw what you would do to her, and I began to grow apart from you. We separated, then divorced, and it was for the best. For me, at any rate; I can't say that you ever understood."

We seem to stand in that gray cubicle, that comfortable simplicity with which I surrounded myself when first awakened.

Elisaveta, taller, stronger, face more seasoned, stares at me with infinitely more experience. I am outmatched.

Her expression softens. "But you didn't deserve *this*, Vasily. You mustn't blame me for what your tributary has done."

"I am not he . . . It. It is not me. And you are not the Elisaveta I know!"

"You wanted to keep me forever the student you first met in your classroom. Do you see how futile that is now?"

"Then what can we love? What is there left to attach to?"

She shrugs. "It doesn't much matter, does it? There's no more time left to love or not to love. And love has become a vastly different thing."

"We reach this *peak* . . . of intelligence, of accomplishment, immortality . . ."

"Wait." Elisaveta frowns and tilts her head, as if listening; lifts her finger in question and listens again to voices I do not hear. "I begin to understand your confusion," she says.

"What?"

"This is not a peak, Vasily. This is a backwater. We are simply all that's left after a long, dreadful attenuation. The greater, more subtle galaxies of Libraries ended themselves a hundred million years ago."

"Suicide?"

"They saw the very end we contemplate now. They decided that if our kind of life had no hope of escaping the Proof—the Proof these teachers helped fix in all our thoughts—than it was best not to send a part of ourselves into the next universe. We are what's left of those who disagreed . . ."

"My tributary did not tell me this."

"Hiding the truth from yourself even now."

I hold my hands out to her, hoping for pity, but this Elisaveta has long since abandoned pity. I desperately need to activate some fragment of love within her. "I am so lost . . ."

"We are all lost, Vasily. There is only one hope."

She turns and opens a broad door on one side of my cubicle, where I originally placed the window to the outside. "If we succeed at this," she says, "then we are better than those great souls. If we fail, they were right . . . Better that nothing from our reality crosses the Between."

I admire her for her knowledge, then, for being kept so well informed. But I resent that she has advanced beyond me, has no need for me.

The tributaries watch with interest, like voyeurs.

(*"Perhaps there is a chance."* My descendant self speaks in a private sending.)

"I see why you divorced me," I say sullenly.

"You were a tyrant and a bully. When you were stored—before your heart replacement, I remember now . . . When you were stored, you and I had not yet grown so far apart. We would. It was inevitable."

"The Proof is very convincing," I tell Elisaveta. "Perhaps *this is* futile."

"You simply have no say, Vasily. The effort is being made."

I have touched her, but it is not pity I arouse, and certainly not love.

It is disgust.

Through the window, Elisaveta and I see a portion of the plain. On it, the experiments have congealed into a hundred, a thousand, smooth, slowly pulsing shapes. Above them all looms the shadow of the Coordinator. I feel a bridge being made, links being established. I sense panic in my descendant self, who works without the knowledge of the other tributaries.

Then I am asked: *"Will you become part of the experiment?"*

"I don't understand."

"You are the judgment engine."

"Now I must go," Elisaveta says. "We will all die soon. Neither you nor I are in the final self. No part of the teachers, or the Coordinator, will cross the Between."

"All futile, then," I say.

"Why so, Vasily? When I was young, you told me that change was an evil force, and that you longed for an eternal college, where all learning could be examined at leisure, without pressure. You've found that. Your tributary self has had billions of years to study the unchanging truths. And to infuse them into new tributaries. You've had your heaven, and I've had mine. Away from you, among those who nurture and respect."

I am left with nothing to say. Then, unexpectedly, the figure of Elisaveta reaches out with a nonexistent hand and touches my unreal cheek. For a moment, between us, there is something like the contact of flesh to flesh. I feel her fingers. She feels my cheek. Despite her words, the love has not died completely.

She fades from the cubicle. I rush to the window, to see if I can make out the Coordinator, but the shadow, the mercury–liquid cloud, has already vanished.

"They will fail," the We–ness says. It surrounds me with its mind, its persuasion, greater in scale than a human of my time to an ant. "This shows the origin of their folly. We have justified our existence."

(You can still cross. There is still a connection between you. You can judge the experiment, go with the Endtime Work Coordinator.)

I watch the plain, the joined shapes, extraordinarily beautiful, like condensed cities or civilizations or entire histories.

The sunlight dims, light rays jerk in our sight, in our fading scales of time.

(Will you go?)

"She doesn't need me . . ." I want to go with Elisaveta. I want to reach out to her and shout, "I see! I understand!" But there is still sadness and self–pity. I am, after all, too small for her.

(You may go. Persuade. Carry us with you.)

And billions of years too late—

SHARDS OF SECONDS

We know now that the error lies in the distant past, a tendency of the Coordinator, who has gathered tributaries of like character.

As did the teachers. The past still dominates, and there is satisfaction in knowing We, at least, have not committed any errors, have not fallen into folly.

We observe the end with interest. Soon, there will be no change. In that, there is some cause for exultation. Truly, We are tired.

On the bubbling remains of the School World, the students in their Berkus continue to the last instant with the experiment, and We watch from the cracked and cooling hill.

Something huge and blue and with many strange calm aspects rises from the field of experiments. It does not remind us of anything We have seen before.

It is new.

The Coordinator returns, embraces it, draws it away.

("She does not tell the truth. Parts of the Endtime Coordinator must cross with the final self. This is your last chance. Go to her and reconcile. Carry our thoughts with you.")

I feel a love for her greater than anything I could have felt before. I hate my descendant self, I hate the teachers and their gray spirits, depth upon depth of ashes out of the past. They want to use me to perpetuate all that matters to them.

I ache to reclaim what has been lost, to try to make up for the past.

The Coordinator withdraws from School World, taking with it the results of the student experiment. Do they have what they want—something worthy of being passed on? It would be wonderful to know . . . I could die contented, knowing the Proof has been shattered. I could cross over, ask. . .

But I will not pollute her with me any more.

"No."

The last thousandths of the last second fall like broken crystals.

(The connection is broken. You have failed.)

My tributary self, disappointed, quietly suggests I might be happier if I am deactivated.

* * *

Curiously, to the last, he clings to his imagined cubicle window. He cries his last words where there is no voice, no sound, no one to listen but us:

"Elisaveta! YES! YES!"

The last of the ancient self is packed, mercifully, into oblivion. We will not subject him to the Endtime. We have pity.

We are left to our thoughts. The force that replaces gravity now spasms. The metric is very noisy. Length and duration become so grainy that thinking is difficult.

One tributary works to solve an ancient and obscure problem. Another studies the Proof one last time, savoring its formal beauty. Another considers ancient relations.

Our end, our own oblivion, the Between, will not be so horrible. There are worse things. Much

APPENDIX: EARLIER PREFACES

From the 1983 Arkham House edition of
The Wind from a Burning Woman, my first collection

PREFACE

I have had a passion for science fiction and fantasy ever since I can remember. Science fiction has been a wonderful mother for my mind, showing me that the world is far bigger and stranger than it seems within my province. And in the past few years—after many more years of apprenticeship--it has become a fine, broad landscape on which to test my imagination.

Occasionally I've felt the pressure of limited editors and markets, but I have yet to run up against an artistic boundary. If a thought is expressible in human language, a science fiction story can be written about it. The same cannot be said of any other genre.

Through reading science fiction, I became interested in other forms of literature, in astronomy and the sciences, in history and philosophy. Specifically, discovering James Blish's *Case of Conscience* when I was sixteen led me to read James Joyce; L. Sprague de Camp, Fletcher Pratt, Poul Anderson, and others have given me solid reasons to explore history. Arthur C. Clarke--and through Clarke, Olaf Stapledon—sent me on a wild search through philosophy, looking for similar insights and experiences. (I've usually been disappointed; Stapledon is unique.) In short, my intellect has been nurtured and guided by science fiction.

Some people, reading the above, will sneer the ineradicable sneer. The hell with them. C. P. Snow pinned their little gray moth in *The Two Cultures and The Scientific Revolution;* they are ignorant or afraid of science. They reject the universe in favor of a small human circle, limited in time and place to their own lifetimes. You are not one of them if you have read this far. You are one of the brave ones.

So I will open my heart to you a little bit and talk about the stories that follow.

I have friends who believe the world will come to an end in twenty or thirty years. They foresee complete collapse, perhaps nuclear war. They look on the prospect with either stunned indifference or some relish. Serve everybody right, they seem to say.

What they are actually saying is that within the next few decades—certainly within the next sixty or seventy years—*they* will come to an end. *Their* world will darken. And, solipsists that many of us are, it seems perfectly logical to take everybody and everything with us. The future does not really exist, certainly not the far and unknowable future. Why talk about it?

They are still my friends, but they are as wrong as wrong can be. The future will come, and it will be different, unimaginably so. Then why do I bother to try imagining it?

I could sing you a long number on how science fiction is seldom intended to be prophetic. But I'm willing to bet, in our deepest hearts, that we all hope one of our more optimistic imagined futures, or some aspect of a literary time to come, will closely parallel reality. Then we will be admired for our perspicacity. People in the future, if they still read, might come across an even more fantastic concept and say, "Hey, that crazy Greg Bear stuff!"

Perhaps. But it will be accident, not prophecy.

Like my pessimistic friends, I'm not going to live forever. I may see the first starships; I may not.

But when I write, I not only live to see one future, I experience dozens. I chart their courses, lay out histories, try to create new cultures and extend the range of discovery. When I write—

When I write, I'm immortal.

Sometimes I enter into a kind of trance state and engage so many thoughts and ideas and abilities that I seem to rise onto another plane. And though I seldom think about it while I'm on that plane, I seem to become everyone who has ever thought about the future. I join the greats, past and present, at least for a moment.

I've been writing since I was eight or nine years old. In 1966, when I was fifteen, through something of a fluke I sold my first professional short story. Five years passed before I sold another. The apprenticeship is still not over, and may never be. None of those earlier efforts are represented in this collection; the earliest piece here, "Mandala," was written in 1975 and first appeared in 1978. It also comprises the first third of my novel, *Strength of Stones*, published in 1981.

There isn't much remarkable to record about the writing of these stories. Writing is usually quite dull to an outside observer. It consists of long periods of apparent loafing around, punctuated by hours at a typewriter, highlighted by moments of desk-pounding and fingerchewing puzzlement. (All this, to contrast with the above-mentioned trance state.)

"Mandala" and "Hardfought" were about equally difficult to write, for different reasons. "The White Horse Child" was one of the easiest; like "Scattershot," it emerged while I sat at the typewriter, consciously unaware of what was going to pour out. "Petra" went through several stages, becoming progressively stranger and stranger. (One of the great difficulties with creativity is trying to impose order on the results.)

"The Wind from a Burning Woman" also began as an exercise

in sitting blankly at the typewriter. As in most instances where such stories turn out well, there was a strong emotion lurking behind the apparent blankness-that of repugnance to terrorism. Do the weak have the right to force the strong to do their bidding by terrorist action? To handle the issue honestly, I had to make the "Burning Woman" fight for a cause that I, myself, would cherish. One editor, reading the story for an anthology on space colonies, rejected it because it didn't overtly support the cause. It would have been dishonest to force the story into such a mold; however pleasant or unpleasant the result, my stories must work themselves out within their own framework, not according to some market principle or philosophical bias.

It may be remarkable that, with such views, I've come as far as I have in publishing, where large conglomerates seem to dictate overall marketing of science fiction as if it were some piece-work commodity. ("Take dragon/unicorn/spaceship, add vaguely medieval/ magical setting, mix well with wise old wizard/cute sidekick . . .") Don't get me wrong, I've enjoyed stories with all those elements, but enough is enough. Science fiction is much too restless to accept the same kind of genre regimentation displayed by, for example, Westerns or hard-boiled detective novels, where one Western Town or corrupt Big City can serve as stage settings for an infinity of retold tales.

But enough authorial interference. I will tell you no more about these stories until we meet in person; perhaps not even then, for I'm not certain my interpretations are always correct. "Mandala," for example, has defied my analysis for seven years, and yet I knew what I wanted to say when I wrote it.

That's when I'm happiest with my own work—when the stories say so many things that they become playgrounds for the mind. I hope you feel the same way.

Spring Valley, California

ON LOSING THE TAINT OF BEING A CANNIBAL

From *Bear's Fantasies,* Wildside Press, 1993

I'm reminded of the line delivered by Joseph Bologna in the motion picture comedy, *The Big Bus.* His character, Dan Torrance, once drove a bus through Donner Pass, and of course got snowed in. Desperation quickly set in among the passengers, and some odd recipes were resorted to. Torrance pleads that he did not know what was in the soup, adding, "One lousy foot, and they call you a cannibal for the rest of your life!"

Writing science fiction is one of those odd activities, like being a cannibal, that marks you permanently, even should you later become a vegan.

The odd relationship most people have with science—awed fascination, not infrequently dismay and distrust, and guilty dependence—guarantees a mixed reaction among the reading public: "You actually *enjoy* science? Writing about it, making it up? How *interesting.*"

Their tone of voice tells you that you are now marked forever in their minds.

Science fiction explores the outer limits of the current Western paradigm, science; its playground is all that we know about the universe, and what we imagine we might eventually know.

Many of us, at one time or another, enjoy playing with previous paradigms—mind over matter, magic, dream logic, and so on. Literature does not play favorites; excellent stories have been written in all these areas.

A science fiction writer who writes fantasy, however, is regarded by some as an odd bird indeed. Write science fiction, become well known for it, and—well, your fantasy stories become almost *invisible.* All those times when you *weren't* a cannibal—simply forgotten.

Yet most of the great science fiction writers have written a great deal of fantasy, and I have, as well. But prejudices and snobbery on both sides of the fence have grown in the past ten or fifteen years.

I've never thought of my fantasy stories as dabbling or slumming. They represent an important part of my writing. Some of my very finest work is fantasy. The first novel I ever finished—an early version of what would later be published as *The Infinity Concerto* and *The Serpent Mage*—was fantasy. My second published novel, *Psychlone*, is a ghost story, heavily influenced by Stephen King. In real life I've even gone hunting ghosts in a world-famous hotel, just like Carnacki, though without his spectacular success.

I love fantasy.

Perhaps by gathering some of my fantasy in one volume, I can convince the world that I've had at least a few moments when I was not a cannibal.

But I won't bet on it.

Being a writer of science fiction is just so *odd.*

Thank goodness.

CHARACTERS GREAT AND SMALL IN SF: "SISTERS" BY GREG BEAR

Commentary on the story "Sisters" published in *Paragons*

edited by Reg Bretnor

In "Sisters," the viewpoint character, Letitia Blakely, is familiar enough—an adolescent girl, struggling with painful problems. In outline, "Sisters" reads much like a contemporary story of growing up—with a few words and some set dressing changed to indicate the near future. Yet my intent in this story—as in many of my stories—is to deal with characters within larger characters, to explore how individuals react to change within a larger setting.

If anything has become more and more clear in the past five hundred years, it is that men and women are not the measure of all things, but the *measurers.* A richer, more powerful literature must take into account the nature of larger entities than human individuals.

There's nothing that stops science fiction—often dismissed as merely a literature of ideas—from also being a literature of character, so long as readers understand a larger definition of character. Character is not limited to the nature and actions of a single individual, or even a group of individuals. Character may also describe a nation, a culture, a species, a world—or a universe.

For me, the story of character is not limited to the Jamesian small group of individuals in an unchanging social setting, with all change arising from individually willed action. Yet since James this has been touted as the datum of literature—and not without reason.

Human readers (the only kind I've encountered) enjoy reading about people not greatly unlike themselves. We enjoy watching the lives of others we can relate to. For relaxation, or a historical refresher, we also enjoy reading about the mores and social patterns of the past, in Dickens and Austen and Joyce, or Tolstoy and Hemingway and Dostoevsky. But what involves us most of all is fiction that directly or indirectly models our present situation and stimulates thought about the choices we have and the decisions we make. We enjoy discovering patterns and relationships between strangers and ourselves, and between different societies in different times.

In a sense, science fiction takes its cues from historical fiction, but with no specific arrow of time. The future as well as the past is open. (Alternate times and realities may qualify as well!)

Since there are few if any societies where change from out-side—forced by history, the weather, or other natural phenom-ena—does not have a major impact on individual lives, to focus on change coming about solely through the willed actions of the individual is a very artificial limitation. It produces attractive and moving works, but these works are no more than an aspect, perhaps just a *genre*. At their worst, they give a false sense of comfort. Even at their best, they do not define the range of lit-erature.

Most of my stories draw the lives of characters *within* larger characters, exploring how individuals react to change within a larger setting. Science fiction stories at their most ambitious model changes in nations, in cultures, even in species and worlds.

Writing science fiction puts added burdens on me as a story-teller. I have to do more than just closely observe: I have to extrap-olate. This takes me into dangerous territory, since to extrapolate, I must try to understand the laws and forces that direct the greater characters. I see sociology, psychology, technology, and history as interrelated subsets of biology. This is far from the static and iso-lating world view common in many religions and much philoso-phy; it is also far from the gooey and shapeless "holistic" approach of New Age thinking, where anything goes, and the universe caters to our personal whims.

Just as a sharp observer of individual character strives not to be guided by sentiment and personal animus, an observer of larger characters must adopt a similar objectivity. In my stories, individuals are often shaped by environments that may be only marginally familiar, if at all, to the average reader. Bringing the environment to life is important, and inevitably takes some of the center spotlight away from so-called "pure" exploration of character and motive. But it returns the focus with additional rewards by giving insight into how characters shape and are shaped.

No character great or small lives in splendid isolation. Everything an individual does reflects back, and the mirror is not just society, but nature. Discovering how a larger nature works in a story is as thrilling (and dangerous) to my characters as internal discovery.

Letitia's world has changed in significant ways, and offers her challenges no modern young woman has to face. Facing those challenges reveals her inner self as no contemporary setting can.

Moving between the internal world, the social world, and the external world, breaks down the barriers between. Inside becomes outside. There is no mirror, after all.

ABOUT THE AUTHOR

Greg Bear is the author of over twenty-five books, which have been translated into seventeen languages. He has won science fiction's highest honors and is considered the natural heir to Arthur C. Clarke. The recipient of two Hugo Awards and four Nebula Awards, Bear has been called "the best working writer of hard science fiction" by the *Science Fiction Encyclopedia*. Many of his novels, such as *Darwin's Radio*, are considered to be classics of his generation. Bear is married to Astrid Anderson—who is the daughter of science fiction great Poul Anderson—and they are the parents of two children, Erik and Alexandria. Bear's recent publications include the thriller *Quantico* and its sequel, *Mariposa*; the epic science fiction novel *City at the End of Time*; and the generation starship novel *Hull Zero Three*.

GREG BEAR

FROM OPEN ROAD MEDIA

INTEGRATED MEDIA

Find a full list of our authors and
titles at www.openroadmedia.com

FOLLOW US
@OpenRoadMedia